Enjoy our new two-in-one editions by your favourite authors:

HIRED: GP AND WIFE
by Judy Campbell

THE PLAYBOY DOCTOR'S SURPRISE PROPOSAL
by Anne Fraser

Dear Reader

Welcome to the new look Mills & Boon® Medical™ romances!

Now we're offering you two great value editions with two stories in each, double the medical drama...and twice as many happy endings. All of your favourite authors and all the best stories will still be available—and with **two double** volumes and **two single books** each month, you'll be spoiled for choice!

Look for these great new titles—out now!

HIRED: GP AND WIFE
by Judy Campbell
&
THE PLAYBOY DOCTOR'S PROPOSAL
by Anne Fraser

* * *

PREGNANT MIDWIFE: FATHER NEEDED
by Fiona McArthur

* * *

FOUND: A MOTHER FOR HIS SON
by Dianne Drake

* * *

SECRET SHEIKH, SECRET BABY
by Carol Marinelli
&
HIS BABY BOMBSHELL
by Jessica Matthews

To find out more, visit
www.millsandboon.co.uk/makeover.

Best wishes

Sheila Hodgson
Senior Editor, Medical™ Romance

HIRED: GP AND WIFE

BY

JUDY CAMPBELL

All the characters in this book have no existence outside the imagination of the author, and have no relation whatsoever to anyone bearing the same name or names. They are not even distantly inspired by any individual known or unknown to the author, and all the incidents are pure invention.

First published in Great Britain 2009
Harlequin Mills & Boon Limited,
Eton House, 18-24 Paradise Road, Richmond, Surrey TW9 1SR

ISBN: 978 0 263 86866 1

Set in Times Roman 10½ on 12½ pt
03-0909-51954

Harlequin Mills & Boon policy is to use papers that are natural, renewable and recyclable products and made from wood grown in sustainable forests. The logging and manufacturing process conform to the legal environmental regulations of the country of origin.

Printed and bound in Spain
by Litografia Rosés, S.A., Barcelona

Judy Campbell is from Cheshire. As a teenager she spent a great year at high school in Oregon, USA, as an exchange student. She has worked in a variety of jobs, including teaching young children, being a secretary and running a small family business. Her husband comes from a medical family, and one of their three grown-up children is a GP. Any spare time—when she's not writing romantic fiction—is spent playing golf, especially in the Highlands of Scotland.

To Grace, Megan, Louis, George and Joseph

With Love

CHAPTER ONE

THE little ferry edged towards the dock and the deckhand expertly threw the rope round the bollard and tightened it. The gangway slapped down between the land and the boat and everyone began to disembark. Terry Younger stopped for a second and looked around the little bay with the seagulls mewing above the brightly painted cottages across the road and their backdrop of wooded hills.

She took a deep breath of the tangy fresh air and it hit her throat like champagne, invigorating and bracing. The cool wind whipped her short fair hair across her eyes and she brushed it away impatiently, and stepped ashore. Then, hoisting her rucksack more securely on her back, she tugged her case behind her over the rough terrain, a frisson of excitement mixed with apprehension shivering through her for a second. She stopped and looked across the quayside: steep hills rose quickly behind the little village of shops and cottages fringing the bay and beyond them the vague purple outline of mountains. The Isle of Scuola on the west coast of Scotland couldn't be more different to the leafy suburbs of London that she'd left behind—this was it, then, a fresh start, a future that was hers to make of what she would, and find a measure of the peace she craved after the turmoil of a terrible year.

Dumping her baggage by the wall of the dock, Terry looked around at the small group of people waiting to meet the passengers from the ferry. She'd been informed that her new colleague, Dr Brodie, senior partner in the Scuola medical practice, would be picking her up—according to the woman in the medical agency, he was a large, elderly man with white hair. There didn't seem to be anyone of that description here yet—he must be running late, but, no matter, she would sit on her case until he arrived.

After five minutes the ferry had turned round and begun to chug back to the mainland and there was no one left by the quayside except a man in biking leathers sitting astride a motorbike and talking on a mobile. Terry stood up impatiently—she liked to be punctual herself and the later Dr Brodie was the more nervous she was becoming about her new job.

Another ten minutes went by and the man who'd been on the bike was now pacing irritably up and down the quay and looking at his watch. His leathers gave him a tough streetwise appearance and emphasised his tall muscular figure as he strode impatiently in front of Terry. For a second she was cruelly reminded of Max—damn his memory. Wasn't there a hint in the appearance of this man on the quayside of the bad-boy image Max had liked to project? She shut her eyes as if trying to block out a picture of Max swaggering towards her—sexy, arrogant, sure of her love and supremely selfish. She shuddered—she wanted nothing more to do with that sort of man. She snapped open her eyes again and set her mouth grimly.

She hadn't come to Scuola to remember him or anything that had happened to her because of him…she had to push all that to the back of her mind.

The biker stopped for a moment in front of her to pull off his helmet, revealing ruffled dark hair, and gazed dourly back at the mainland. Terry flicked a closer look at him—he was quite a striking man, and someone with rather a short fuse, she guessed, full of pent-up energy. As he turned to resume his frustrated pacing, a pen dropped out of his pocket and Terry bent down to pick it up.

'We both seem to have been left in the lurch,' she said, handing it to him.

He turned, looking at her with startling blue eyes, as blue as sapphires, Terry thought suddenly—and of course she realised that he was nothing like Max at all. Max's eyes, although sexy, had often been calculating, as if assessing just what he could gain from you. This man's face had an engaging, open look. His eyes swept over her, taking in her petite figure and resting for an intense moment on her face. The hairs on the back of her neck prickled with a sudden flash of self-consciousness under his scrutiny.

'Ah, thank you,' he said, taking the pen from her, then he added brusquely, 'I think the person I'm meeting must be on the next ferry—if he isn't on this one I'll have to go. Damn nuisance but I can't wait.' He had an attractive voice, fairly deep and with a definite Scottish lilt. He leant against a stone wall that jutted out onto the jetty, long legs crossed in front of him. 'You've been stood up too?' he enquired.

His thick dark hair was a little too long at the front and flopped over onto his forehead—it made him look rather boyish, but there was something tough and determined in his demeanour. He wouldn't suffer fools gladly, thought Terry. She smiled to herself. When it came to men, she couldn't trust herself to interpret character through appearances—her track record was pretty poor on that!

'The man meeting me has either forgotten or had an accident,' she said. 'I'd better get a taxi.'

'Maybe he thinks you'll be on the next ferry too and is coming to meet this one—I can see it in the distance now,' suggested the biker. He pushed himself away from the wall and went to the water's edge, staring across the bay at the approaching vessel.

Terry wondered if he was a tourist who'd come to the island for the fishing or walking. She could well imagine him striding over the hill paths, getting rid of some of his angst with exercise, or roaring over the mountain roads on his motorbike.

They both watched the ferry draw up and disgorge its next lot of passengers, but it was soon apparent that the man's friend had not appeared, and there was still no sign of Dr Brodie. The two of them waited as the three cars on the ferry made their way slowly after the foot passengers down the ramp to shore. The last one was a small two-door car, which stalled and then rolled back onto the ship, and the driver, a young woman, looked anxiously out of the window.

'Give it more stick, miss,' advised the deckhand in charge of the vehicles. 'You need to accelerate to get over the humps on the ramp.'

The girl nodded and tried again, revving the engine hard, and this time the car shot forward and skidded over the ramp. It took half a second for Terry to realise with horror that it was arrowing straight across the space between them like a missile fixed on a target. Her feet seemed to be paralysed, be stuck in thick clay—she could see the car careering for them but she couldn't move her body or even cry out. Then, at the last moment when the car seemed almost on top of her, two arms flung themselves tightly round her and she felt herself being lifted away from the danger and dropped not too gently on the ground, underneath her rescuer.

For a second she was winded—unable to breathe or speak—but she was aware that in the background there was the nasty sound of a heavy crash, metal being crushed and breaking glass, then a shocked silence. The body on top of hers scrambled off, allowing her to see the car embedded in the wall of the dock.

'Bloody hell,' said a voice over her head. 'That was a bit too close for comfort!'

She blinked in a dazed way, and found herself gazing into the intensely bright blue eyes she'd just been looking at a few minutes before.

'You OK?' asked the biker. A large graze covered with grit on his chin oozed blood and his thick hair was plastered on his forehead. 'Here, let me help you up.'

'Yes…yes, I'm fine,' she replied, using the strong grip of his hand to get up slowly and shakily to her feet. Her trousers and parka were covered with dirt, but she was alive—thanks to the man.

He looked at her closely then nodded. 'Good. Then I'll see what's happened to the driver.'

Terry watched, stunned, as he sprinted over to the car and peered through the driver's window then tried to pull open the door. She couldn't believe how rapid his reactions had been as the car had hurtled towards them, or how quickly he'd recovered himself to think of the other people involved.

She scrambled up from the ground herself and ran after him to the car, where he was already trying to force the driver's door open. It was a horrific sight, the front stoved in and as crumpled as a piece of crushed foil. The girl in the driving seat turned towards them, looking utterly shocked. An egg-shaped bruise on her forehead was rapidly enlarging and a gash above her eye was pouring blood. She put a shaking hand up to her forehead and started to whimper.

'Wh-what happened there? I…I just touched the accelerator and it took off…'

The biker pushed his hand through the door and turned off the ignition. 'Sometimes these automatic gear changes are quite fierce,' he said gently. He tilted her chin towards the light and examined her forehead as he talked to her. 'What's your name?'

'Maisie…Maisie Lockart,' the girl whispered. Then her eyes widened as she remembered something and she started to scream, trying to turn round in the seat to look at the back. 'Oh, my God…the baby…Amy…she's in the back. Is she all right? Get her out please…get her out!'

Terry looked aghast at the concertinaed front of the car and the way the passenger seat was pushed back right against the rear. There wasn't going to be much room for even a child sitting in the back. She heard the man swear as he gave a desperate tug on the driver's door again and managed to open it another precious half-foot. He peered in the back then gave a little whoop of relief.

'Yes! She's OK. You won't believe this, but she appears to be smiling at me!' He pulled back and said gently to the girl, 'Don't worry—she looks fine, kicking her legs. From here everything looks in working order.'

The girl closed her eyes and put her head back against the back of the seat. 'Thank God,' she whispered. 'Can you get hold of her?'

Terry tapped the man's back. 'Perhaps I could help?' she said. 'I'm a doctor.'

The biker whipped his head round and looked at her with raised brows of surprise. 'Well, well, that's a bit of a coincidence—I'm a doctor too! I must say it's nice to have some support.' He turned back to the girl in the car and commented with gentle humour, 'Funny, isn't it? You can wait all day for a doctor and then two come along at once!'

The girl gave a watery smile. 'We're in good hands, then, aren't we?'

The man turned to Terry and said in a low voice, 'As you can see, she's had a terrific crack to her head and I wouldn't be surprised if she's not got a whiplash injury to her neck. I think you'll agree she needs a check-up and an X-ray. I'll ring for an ambulance if you take over here for a second. Better not to move her at this stage.'

'What about the baby?' said Terry, peering into the back of the vehicle. 'We can't leave her on the back seat. On the other hand, I agree it's risky to move Maisie. We could disturb a fractured vertebrae or a subluxation.'

'Yep. We've got to be cautious if she's displaced a joint,' he agreed.

For a second they looked at each other, trying to weigh up the pros and cons of the problem, then Terry said with decision, 'The little one does seem reasonably happy. I'll watch them and try and stop this bleed above Maisie's eye while you get help.'

'OK. It should only be a matter of minutes…'

Terry scrabbled in her rucksack until she found a packet of tissues, which she pressed firmly against the wound. Maisie had started to shake and tears rolled down her cheeks.

'I'm sorry… I don't mean to make a fuss, but I can't go to hospital—I've got papers to deliver. And what about the baby?'

Terry laid her hand reassuringly over Maisie's, recognising the signs of shock in the girl. 'Don't worry about the papers—they'll get sorted. Just tell me the baby's name.'

'Amy—she's only four months. And…and she'll need a bottle soon.'

'Look, Maisie, you both must go and be checked over and however well Amy looks it's best to make sure she has no hidden injury. They'll want to observe her for a few hours and if she needs feeding, the hospital will make sure she's looked after. And I'll see the papers are delivered if you'll tell me where they're to go to.'

'Thank you,' whispered the girl. 'They go to the newsagent's, Mathesons, just across the road from here.' She sighed bleakly, 'I don't know how I'll tell my boyfriend. It's his car and he'll be furious I've crashed it.'

'He'll just be glad you're both OK,' reassured Terry.

Terry's eyes followed the doctor pacing about the car park as he spoke on his mobile. She might have guessed he'd be a doctor, a policeman or a fireman—someone who was used to dealing with emergencies. He had the confidence of knowing what he was doing, and it showed—he was someone you could trust, she thought wistfully. Then she shrugged irritably, cross with herself for thinking that. Just because he was a doctor, it didn't mean he'd be any more reliable than anyone else. Didn't she know only too well that even the most credible of people could let you down and ruin your life?

The biker doctor came back, stuffing his mobile in his pocket.

'It'll be here very soon…' He halted, his expression suddenly changing to one of alarm as he sniffed the air. 'Hell! We've got to get them out, pronto,' he yelled. 'Can't you smell the petrol? There must be a leak. The damn thing could go up in flames any second. Let me undo that safety belt.'

He turned to the small crowd of onlookers gathered a short distance from them. 'We need a man here to help us,' he shouted.

Two or three men ran forward. 'Tell us what you want us to do,' said one of them.

'Help me slide Maisie out and lift her carefully, supporting her neck, and if two others could take her legs. Then we need to get that baby out of the back.'

For a moment Terry felt herself back in Casualty, forming part of a team in an emergency where split-second decisions had to be taken. This man was right, of course. The risk of fire was imminent, and they had no choice but to get the people out as quickly as possible. She helped to hold Maisie's back as they edged her out, her neck being supported by the doctor, who shouted out instructions to the others, then they laid her on Terry's jacket which she'd put on the ground.

Terry squeezed Maisie's hand comfortingly. It was vital that the girl, already in shock, was kept as calm as possible. 'Now it's Amy's turn,' she said.

The aperture to the back of the car was very small, constrained by the buckling of the car's chassis. No way could a large man get through it.

'I'm doing this,' said Terry firmly. 'I can get through that space.'

'Oh, no, you won't.' The biker tried to push in front of her. 'It's up to me—it's too damn dangerous.'

'And you're too damn big to get through,' retorted Terry angrily. 'I thought you said there's no time to waste. Don't let's argue about it.'

Their eyes sparked across at each other aggressively for a second then reluctantly he gave way, allowing her to push herself into the small opening.

'You win,' he muttered. 'I'll try and force this door a bit more.'

By squeezing herself sideways, she managed to wriggle her body to the squashed rear of the car. Stretching forward with every sinew, she reached the baby and fumbled with the child's safety harness. It seemed terribly difficult to undo but behind her she could hear the distinctive deep voice of the biker.

'You're doing well. Press the button in the middle of the harness firmly and squeeze the two sides together… sometimes they're quite stiff.'

There was something reassuring about that measured voice and when Amy began to scream as this unfamiliar person tried to extricate her from her seat, Terry concentrated on what the biker was telling her and did her best to ignore the smell of petrol that seemed to get stronger every second.

'It's all right, darling—don't cry. You'll soon be with your mummy,' she murmured in her most soothing tones whilst still struggling desperately with the catch on the harness. Suddenly the spring release worked and the belt came apart.

'Ah...gotcha!' she said triumphantly.

She pulled the child towards her, hugging her to her chest and backing out as quickly as she could. Waiting hands took the crying baby to the side of the car park near to where her mother was lying, and Terry toppled back as someone's arms caught her and prevented her falling to the ground.

'Well done,' said the biker's familiar voice gruffly. 'You did a good job there.' His arms held her close to him as he helped her across to the side of the car park. 'Come on, now—let's get you away from this vehicle.'

Her legs felt like jelly but he took her weight easily, almost carrying her to one of the benches by the dock railings. He took off his leather jacket and put it round Terry's shoulders and she gave a shaky laugh. 'You seem to make a habit of helping me.'

He leaned forward and brushed away a piece of mud that was on her cheek. 'Sure you're OK?' he asked, smiling at her, his face so close to hers that she could see the beginnings of evening stubble on his chin and the dark flecks in his extraordinarily blue eyes.

His breath was on her cheek as he looked at her and unexpectedly she felt a funny little shock of attraction ripple through her body. She took a sharp intake of breath and got up hastily from the bench, stepping back from him unsteadily. What the hell was happening? Not so long ago her life had been ruined by a man and she'd vowed it would be a long time before she'd look at the opposite sex again. Here she was only fifteen minutes into her new life and behaving like a schoolgirl who'd just seen a pop star! Her goal when she came to Scuola was to devote her life to medicine and put romance behind her—and that was what she was going to do!

'I…I'm perfectly fine,' she said in a measured tone.

His eyes held hers for a second, his expression contrite. 'I'm afraid I was a bit abrupt with you back then. I just didn't want you putting yourself in danger.'

'We both had cross words—all in the line of duty,' she replied. Quickly she went to kneel beside Maisie and her baby, who was in the arms of one of the men who had been helping, and pushed this hunky guy to the back of her thoughts.

'You'll soon be in good hands,' she comforted the young girl. 'And little Amy looks very lively.'

'Thank you,' whispered Maisie. 'Thank you for getting Amy out. I thought she'd be trapped.'

A few minutes later a police car sped into the car park, followed by an old-fashioned ambulance.

'That car reeks of petrol,' the biker doctor said to the officer who got out of the car. 'I've turned off the ignition, but I'm frightened it might ignite.'

Without a word the officer pulled a fire extinguisher out of his car and started to douse the back of the crashed vehicle with foam, then he shouted to the onlookers, 'Can you clear this area please? This car's not safe to be near and we need room for the ambulance.'

Two paramedics jumped out of the ambulance, one with a medical bag, and the doctor went up to them and explained in his concise and brisk manner the circumstances of the accident. Terry kept up a comforting commentary to Maisie until they came over, noting how she had begun to relax slightly now she was out of the vehicle and her baby was safe.

The paramedics swiftly assessed Maisie's condition, then put a brace round her neck and lifted her onto a board to support her back before placing her on a carrying stretcher. Then she was put in the ambulance with Amy, and Terry and the biker watched as it disappeared up the hill.

Terry sat down on the bench and leaned back, closing her eyes, a mixture of relief and tiredness flooding through her.

The doctor chuckled. 'What you need is a wee dram—that'll put new life in you!'

She opened her eyes to see the doctor bending down beside her, a grin on his mud-bespattered face, blood still oozing from his chin.

Terry shook her head and smiled. 'I'm fine, thanks. In fact, it's quite exhilarating when you get a good result after a bit of drama.' She felt in the front pocket of her knapsack and pulled out a compact, grimacing at her reflection in the mirror. 'What a wreck I look,' she murmured to herself.

'Just a bit mud-spattered,' he said. 'Nothing a good wash won't remove!'

Terry watched as the man picked up his helmet and searched in his pockets for the key to his bike. She realised just what she owed to this stranger, and reflected that her little flicker of attraction to him a few seconds before was probably because of the emotional rebound that often happened after a traumatic event.

'I have such a lot to thank you for. If you hadn't had such lightning reactions I wouldn't be here now,' she said to him. 'I was paralysed when I saw the car coming towards me—I couldn't move. You saved my life, no doubt.'

'Think nothing of it. You didn't do so badly yourself,

getting that baby out. The whole thing could have gone up in flames any second.'

Terry shivered. 'It was the same for you getting Maisie out—a nightmare scenario,' she murmured. She looked at the cut on his chin. 'You know, you ought to have that graze cleaned—it's quite deep and got a lot of dirt in it.'

'Oh, I'll see to it when I get back,' he said carelessly, then looked at her with interest. 'Is this your first visit to Scuola?'

'Yes…not quite the start I wanted,' admitted Terry. She glanced at the smashed car. 'I did promise Maisie that I'd get the papers in her car delivered to that newsagent's over the road.'

'No problem. I'll do that afterwards.'

'Thank you.' She started to take off the leather jacket he'd put over her in the car park. 'You'd better have this back.'

He looked at his watch. 'No, you hang onto it for a while, it's getting very cold. Perhaps I could give you a lift now,' he offered. 'I can't hang around here any longer and it seems as if your chap's forgotten to come and mine must have missed some connection.'

Terry looked nervously at the large machine he was proposing to give her a lift on—not her favourite form of transport. 'Er…that's very kind of you. The trouble is, I've got no helmet.'

Amused eyes twinkled at her as if he guessed her anxiety. 'Don't worry—I bought a spare with me. Where are you going?'

'Not very far. A place called The Sycamores—it's the medical centre on the island, and I believe it's off the main street.'

The man straightened up suddenly from getting out the

spare helmet from the bike's holdall and stared at her in surprise. 'You're going to the medical centre?'

'I'm going to start a new job there,' explained Terry simply.

The man pushed his fingers through his hair so that it stood up in ruffled spikes round his forehead. 'So you're not on holiday, then? I thought you were a tourist.'

Terry shook her head. 'Far from it.'

'Who were you expecting to meet you?' he said slowly.

'Dr Euan Brodie. Do you know him?'

He gave a short laugh. 'I ought to—he's my uncle. I'm Atholl Brodie and I've come to meet a Terry Younger who's taking over from a locum at our practice. Unfortunately my uncle had a major heart attack three days ago and is in hospital on the mainland. I'm sorry I didn't get round to telling the agency that it would be me meeting you and not Uncle Euan. I'm his partner in the practice.'

Terry felt a funny thrill of excitement—could this really be the guy she was going to work with? 'We…we've found each other, then. I'm Terry Younger.' She held out her hand and he shook it rather abstractedly.

'So I gather,' he replied with a wry smile. 'I have to admit this is, er…rather a surprise.'

'Oh? Why is that?'

'Because I thought you'd be a man,' he said simply. 'It didn't occur to me that Terry could be a girl's name as well.'

'Well, I hope it's not too much of a let-down,' Terry said.

'No…no, of course not. But do you know that on top of GP duties to cover the two islands here, we at the practice help a friend of mine doing an outward bound course for four deprived teenagers from Glasgow for a few weeks? I was hoping that the new doctor—'

'Would be six foot four and sixteen stone,' finished Terry impishly. 'As a matter of fact, I did know your requirements,' she added, smiling. 'The agency told me you wanted help with the course.'

Atholl's eyes swept over her slight five-foot-four-inch frame and he shook his head dismissively. 'These lads are large, rough and aggressive. I need someone who's physically tough and can abseil down cliffs, lead hikes on mountain trails, keep discipline—ideally someone who's had a course in Outward Bound activities…'

'And why shouldn't I be able to fulfil all those criteria?' demanded Terry. Suddenly his looks seemed to diminish—he was a more unreasonable man than she'd thought, obviously dismissing females as pathetic creatures who couldn't do anything physically demanding.

She added firmly, 'It so happens I have done a three-day course in hiking and kayaking—the only thing I've not done is abseiling. Anyway, if you think I'm getting back on that ferry today you've got another think coming. I've been offered a job here and I've accepted it, and it's taken since the crack of dawn to get here.'

A cold wind had blown up suddenly and a stinging rain was starting to drive in from the hills. Terry pulled the helmet over her head and stared at him stubbornly. The man may have just saved her life, but she was damned if she'd go meekly trotting back to London just because he'd been expecting a man. Not, she thought wanly, that returning would be an option anyway—she could never return to London.

Atholl shrugged and then picked up Terry's case and rucksack.

'I guess we'll sort it all out later,' he said. 'We'll leave your case at the ferry office and I'll come back for it shortly, after we've talked at the surgery.' He looked down at her with a sudden laugh that made his strong face look younger, softer. 'And I thought Terry was a man's name…is it short for something?'

'No,' said Terry with deliberate emphasis. 'It's just Terry.'

She clambered on the back of his motorbike, and bit her lip. It wasn't just her name—that was who she'd become now, Terry Younger, looking different and feeling different from a few days ago, cut off from the family and friends of her old life, with a whole new persona.

She was on her own, and it was vitally important to her that her job worked out here. She was as far away from London as she could reasonably get and still be in the British Isles—she wasn't about to go anywhere else in a hurry.

CHAPTER TWO

'PUT your arms round me,' shouted Atholl through the wind, 'and lean with the bike!'

He was one powerfully built man—muscles like steel bars, thought Terry as she clung to him nervously, wrapping her arms round him like a vice. She gave a surprised giggle. What girl wouldn't choose to be in her situation? Hugging a man who looked as if he did a daily workout in the gym as close to her body as she could!

Then she closed her eyes in fright as he roared along the winding road out of the little bay and up the hill beyond the colourful cottages on the seafront, the bike leaning frighteningly at an angle when they turned corners. There was probably no need to worry about the job, she decided resignedly. She'd be killed on this bike before she got to the surgery.

They pulled up sharply in the drive of a gracious-looking stone-built house covered with scaffolding. Terry dismounted carefully, wondering if Atholl had deliberately driven the blessed machine at the speed of light to test her nerve or if it just seemed that way.

'You OK?' he asked.

'Of course. I found it exhilarating,' Terry retorted as she removed her helmet. She was damned if she'd let him believe she was a wimp!

She turned to look around at the view—or as much as she could see in the driving rain. It was spectacular, dramatic and gloomy with black clouds looming over the Sound of Scuola. The mainland over the water was just a dark line on the horizon at the moment.

'When the sky's clear and there's sunshine it's a completely different picture—the sea is as blue as a periwinkle. And believe me,' he added with a grin, 'it does stop raining sometimes! Now, come in and get dry and perhaps we can discuss arrangements over coffee and some biscuits.'

It was warm inside—the large hall did duty as a waiting room, and another room with half the wall cut out formed the reception area, with a severe-looking grey-haired woman behind the desk. She looked up as they came in.

'You've taken your time, Atholl,' she remarked sternly. 'You've several calls to do before we finish tonight.' She peered at his face. 'And what have you done to your chin—fallen off your bike? I told you that machine was lethal… and your uncle hates you riding it.'

'Nothing to do with the bike—just a fall, Isobel,' he said lightly.

'And what about this Dr Younger—where is he? You said you were going to meet him.'

He put his hand behind Terry's shoulder and drew her forward, saying drily, 'This is Dr Younger—she just travelled up from London today. Terry, this is Isobel Nash, one of our receptionists.'

Isobel stared back at Terry with surprise, taking in her

bedraggled appearance wearing a leather jacket several sizes too big for her, and said bluntly, 'But she's a woman. We thought from the name that they were sending a man.'

Terry sighed and looked from Atholl to Isobel. There seemed to be a general prejudice against females here!

Atholl saw her expression and explained, 'Apart from having to deal with the teenage lads I told you about, I thought a man might fit more easily into this job for, er, various reasons.'

His glance flicked across to Isobel, who looked grimmer than ever and pursed her lips, saying, 'It's not only that—where's the poor lass to sleep?'

Terry put down her dripping rucksack. 'Look, I'm sorry I'm not who you both thought I was, but do you mind if I get dry while you discuss this?'

'Ah, yes, of course...' Atholl's expression was faintly embarrassed, as if he realised how rude he'd been. 'Isobel, can you rustle up some tea and biscuits for us? We'll go into my room, Terry, and you can dry out a bit. I'll take the leather jacket.'

Terry followed him feeling slightly deflated, her excitement in coming to the island rather dashed by the mixed welcome she'd received. It had been a long day's journey from London and coupled with the drama at the quayside she felt emotionally drained and now worried that she'd come all this way for nothing. How easy would it be to work with someone who had been expecting to engage a man? She gave an inward shrug. She'd just have to show him that she was as good if not better than anyone else would have been.

She took off the damp cardigan she'd been wearing under the borrowed coat, and handed it to Atholl, who draped it over a radiator. She rubbed her hair with the towel he offered and while she was drying herself he walked over to a filing cabinet, took out a file and started to read it. Terry looked at him covertly through the folds of the towel. He really had the rugged good looks and powerful physique of a man used to the outdoors—and she had reason to be grateful that he was pretty strong, she reflected, strong enough to lift her bodily off the ground with seconds to spare when a car was heading towards them.

She suspected that his brisk manner indicated he was the type of person who liked things done his way and was fairly outspoken when put out about something—like getting a woman as a locum when he expected a man! It was such an old-fashioned attitude, she thought irritably. He was probably married to a little mousy woman who wouldn't say boo to a goose.

Atholl glanced up when he'd perused the file and flicked an assessing eye over her as she finished rubbing her hair dry, running her fingers through her short curls so that they formed a crisp halo round her face. He wasn't at all sure that she was the right sort of person to take on this particular job. He would always be worried about her ability to cope with some of the tearaways that he and Pete had taken on—but even more to the point, and most importantly, his experience with the last locum had convinced him that there were too many pitfalls where women colleagues in a small practice were concerned. Especially, he thought with sudden awareness, when the woman was as attractive as Terry Younger! Not, of course, from his point of view—he was damn well finished with women and relationships for a long, long time—more from the aspect of his patients and friends who were all longing to fix him up with the next single woman who came into his orbit.

He sighed and sat down in the chair, leaning forward with his elbows on the desk. If they were going to work together, he ought to find out more about her.

'So you've come up from London today—that's quite a long journey.'

'That's right. I started at the crack of dawn. The agency sent all my particulars a few days ago, except obviously to state that I was a woman,' Terry said drily.

He gave a rather abashed smile. 'I've got the file here. I can't have read it properly,' he admitted. 'It does indeed say you're female—I'm afraid I just looked at your name, Terry Younger, and assumed they'd sent me a man.'

'Well, they haven't pulled the wool over your eyes, have they? Anyway, here I am!'

He blinked at her forthright attitude, and his mouth twitched with amusement. 'You are indeed! Sit down for a moment.' He put the file down on the desk and looked at her curiously. 'You've got some excellent references and it seemed you had a good job in London. What made you want to leave?'

Terry had been expecting that question and even though she'd rehearsed her reply many times, she felt her throat constrict and to her ears her voice sounded rushed and breathless.

She swallowed, trying to let the half-lies she was telling seem light and matter-of-fact. 'I...I felt it was time for a change. I've been living in London since I qualified. I love the outdoor life and it's been a dream of mine to work in Scotland in a rural area for a long time.'

'Can't be easy, leaving friends and family in the

South… they'll surely miss you,' he remarked, his clear eyes flicking over her searchingly. Her heart began to thump. Did he suspect that there'd been something amiss in her past?

She forced a smile. 'Oh, I've not got much family down there now, although of course I shall miss some things,' she said. 'But it's good to have a change, and I like the idea of being in a small community.'

'A small *remote* community. Why choose Scuola—why not the mainland?'

'When the agency mentioned the job and I looked the place up on the internet, it looked so beautiful—such a contrast to London. And remote sounds rather good to me.'

'You didn't want a permanent position?'

'I thought it would be nice to experience a few jobs and get around a bit, having worked in the same place for a some years.' And the fact, she thought bleakly, that she had to resist putting down roots, uneasy that the past might catch up with her some time.

He nodded, seemingly satisfied with this explanation. 'And do you come from a medical family? Are either of your parents doctors?'

She knew the question was casual, a polite enquiry to show that he was interested in her background, but she wasn't prepared for the tight little knot of distress that formed in her throat or the way her cheeks flamed. She'd developed a kind of protective amnesia where her father was concerned but when something jolted her into thinking about him a powerful image of that terrible day when her world had stopped leapt into her mind—and the knowledge that she could never live again in London without the fear of danger always at her shoulder.

'No, my mother was a homemaker until she passed away while I was in my teens. And my father had nothing to do with medicine…nothing at all. He was in the financial world,' she stumbled.

Atholl said very gently, 'Has your father died too?'

Terry nodded and swallowed, pushing back the memories. 'Yes…he had a heart attack a few weeks ago.'

'I'm sorry. It must be a very difficult time for you.'

Difficult enough for her to leave her roots in London, Atholl surmised. He could imagine her background—affluent and comfortable, a girl who probably went to a private school and lived in a pleasant residential area of London. A city girl…just like Zara had been, he reflected bitterly.

He was prevented from asking further questions by the door opening and Isobel coming in bearing a tray with two mugs, a teapot and a plate with some scones, butter and jam on it.

'Here's your tea,' she said brusquely, putting it down on the desk. She looked in her dour way at Terry. 'You're not from these parts, then?'

Terry sighed. It seemed that people wanted to know a lot about her, and she wanted to tell them as little as possible!

'No, I'm not. But it looks a beautiful place—even when it's pouring with rain!'

Isobel's stern face softened slightly and she said, 'Well, I hope you'll be happy.' She looked sternly at Atholl. 'Now, make sure yon lass eats these home-made scones. I've heated them up and she must be starving after coming all that way from London.'

Isobel nodded curtly at them both and then went out to answer the phone that was ringing shrilly in Reception.

'I suspect Isobel's bark is worse than her bite,' remarked Terry.

Atholl chuckled. 'She's as soft as butter inside, but she's bullied and bossed Uncle Euan around for thirty years now—she thinks she runs the practice.'

'And is your uncle very ill?'

'He's making good progress.' Atholl sighed. 'The truth is I think he'll retire now. He was on half-time before, winding down a bit.'

'And that's why you needed someone else to help? Was my predecessor here long?'

A slight tightening of the lips and Atholl's expression changed. 'Not very long,' he replied briefly. He got up from his seat and went over to the table. 'Now, let's have this tea, and perhaps we can sort a few things out.'

He handed her a cup and the plate of scones whose lovely warm smell had been wafting tantalisingly across to Terry. Suddenly she realised how very hungry and thirsty she was—it had been many hours since she'd had anything to eat. She took a huge gulp of the hot strong liquid and its warmth surged comfortingly through her, then she bit into the warm scone covered with melting butter and thickly coated with raspberry jam. No doubt about it, Isobel was a wonderful cook.

He smiled as he watched her face. 'Ready for that, were you?'

'I'm starving,' she admitted. 'I don't care how many calories were in it!'

The blue eyes flicked over her for a second. 'I don't think there's any need for you to worry,' he observed shortly.

She noted his brief comment wryly—it was so different from the flowery response she'd have expected from Max, who had scattered compliments about like confetti—especially when he'd wanted something. How he'd loved to flatter. It made her embarrassed to remember how taken in she'd been by his patronising and glib remarks. But she'd learned her lesson now—she'd never be duped by that kind of gushing sentiment again.

She pushed unwelcome thoughts about Max to the back of her mind and put the plate down. 'Right,' she said crisply. 'You wanted to sort a few things out, so fire away!'

He leaned back and folded his arms. 'Did you mean it when you said you liked the outdoor life? To be frank, you'd be asked to do a lot of things that you wouldn't do in London. To start with there's the mountain rescue team that we are part of. You could be called out day or night, winter or summer—it's not just a hike up the hillside.'

'Tell me what to do and I'll do it.' Terry looked at him challengingly. 'The agency warned me there would be outside duties and I'm prepared for that—it sounds interesting. Anyway, I bet I wouldn't be the only woman on that team. Surely they aren't all men?'

'As a matter of fact they are,' he said. 'And we can't afford to have a weak link in the chain.'

A flash of irritation whipped through her and she sprang up from her chair. 'Look, I wouldn't let you down but, hey, if you can't face working with a woman here please tell me now and I'll take the next ferry back to the mainland and find a job somewhere else. Let's not waste each other's time.'

He looked slightly taken aback at her petite, feisty figure standing rather pugnaciously opposite him, then his face relaxed and he hid a broad grin behind his hand as he stroked his chin reflectively. Terry Younger didn't mind saying what she felt, although he had a gut feeling that there was more to her story about the real reason she'd left London. She'd seemed vaguely uncomfortable when answering some of his questions.

He knew only too well from his own experience that it was often a seismic event in one's life that made one up sticks and move to a another location. But it took guts to come up all this way north without knowing anyone and leaving one's friends behind, and hadn't she just proved she was no slouch in an emergency? Perhaps, he pondered, she wouldn't be such a bad choice after all—and where was he going to get another doctor at short notice, just as the tourist season on Scuola was starting? He couldn't afford to be too choosy, and he'd just have to put up with having a woman to work with, however wary he was after his experience with Zara Grahame, his previous locum.

He twiddled a pencil in his fingers thoughtfully for a second, then, making a sudden decision, stood up abruptly. 'I don't think you'd let anyone down, Terry. After all, I've just had evidence of it half an hour ago at the accident by the dockside. If you think you can hack it here, I'll be pleased to welcome you aboard!'

He held out his hand, his bright blue eyes smiling into hers, and she almost laughed with relief that he sounded quite happy to work with her after all. An extraordinary tremor of excitement and something else she couldn't quite define crackled through her as they shook hands. The thought of working with Atholl Brodie was promising an unknown, perhaps dangerous but exciting flight into the future.

She took a deep breath and grinned at him. 'Thank you, Atholl—and I'll make sure you never have any complaints that I'm not up to the job, even though I'm a woman!'

'I won't ever hold that against you, I promise.' He smiled. 'Have you any questions to ask me?'

'Isobel mentioned something about accommodation difficulties, but the agency said there was a small flat that went with the job?'

'There's a flat in the building,' he admitted. 'But perhaps you noticed the scaffolding on the side of the house? I'm afraid my uncle let the place go a little, to say the least, and there's a lot of damp and mould. Your flat's not fit to live in at the moment.'

'So where do you suggest I sleep?' asked Terry lightly. 'Perhaps a bed and breakfast?'

'Might be difficult over the next few days—there's a folk festival on this weekend and the place is booked solid. My suggestion is that you come to my place…' He hesitated a moment. 'I'm afraid it's a bit ramshackle and rather basic—we're in the process of doing it up. To be frank, I didn't think it would matter if a man was taking the job, but seeing…'

'I'm a woman?' finished off Terry wryly. 'For goodness' sake, if there's a bed and a shower somewhere in the building I'll be perfectly happy.' She frowned slightly. 'You said "we" are doing it up. I don't want to be any bother to your wife…'

'I was referring to the friend who's running this outward bound course for boys,' Atholl said. 'He's helping me with a bit of building work and decorating—and the boys are involved too, which keeps them busy.'

'So do they all live there as well? It must be rather crowded.'

Atholl laughed. 'Certainly not. I share the house with Shona…she's a darling and keeps an eye on the place when I'm not there. I don't know where I'd be without her.'

'Oh…I see. Are you sure there'll be room, then, and that Shona won't mind?'

His eyes danced. 'Plenty of room, and Shona will be ecstatic, I know.'

Was Shona his girlfriend or some dear old housekeeper? wondered Terry, feeling oddly deflated. Perhaps it was the fact that there would be another person living close to her who would want to know all about her, another person to convince that there was nothing untoward about her coming to Scuola. It would have been nice, she thought wistfully, to have had a place to herself so that she could relax after work and not bother about anyone else or their probing questions into her background. Still, perhaps this arrangement would not last too long.

'I suggest I take you there now,' Atholl said. 'You can have a hot bath and help yourself to whatever you want to eat—at least,' he corrected himself with a grin, 'whatever there might be in the fridge. You must be starving.'

'Won't Shona mind me rooting around in the kitchen?'

'Shona will probably join you in whatever you dig out.' He grinned. 'We'll call in at the harbour master's office for your case—and, don't worry, we'll take the Land Rover this time. Even I don't fancy the thought of balancing a case on the bike.

'I'm taking Terry to the cottage,' he told Isobel as they crossed the hall. 'Forward any calls to me on my mobile. I'll do all my visits after that.'

Isobel nodded rather dourly. 'I hope you've got some food in.'

Atholl looked at his receptionist rather defiantly. 'And you'll be pleased to know that Terry's going to be joining us in the practice.'

Even though I'm a girl, thought Terry wryly.

Isobel pursed her lips. 'I hope it works out…'

Terry looked up at him questioningly as they walked out of the house. 'She sounds very dubious about me working here,' she remarked.

He shrugged. 'She a bit of a pessimist where I'm concerned,' he said enigmatically.

The weather had changed in the time they'd been inside. The dark clouds had been blown away and now an eggshell-blue sky was spreading from the west and lighting up the tops of the hills with pale sunshine. Suddenly the place looked far less forbidding and the hedges and trees that arched across the road as they drove along had a fresh green newly washed quality about them. Atholl pointed out various landmarks and told Terry more about the practice on the journey.

'You might think that the practice is only big enough for one doctor,' he remarked. 'But we look after two islands here—there's a little ferry that goes over to the smaller island of Hersa. I do a clinic there once a week but, of course, if there's a real emergency we have a helicopter, which is part of the air sea rescue team.'

'It sounds very varied. How do you get around on Hersa?'

He laughed. 'That's where the motorbike comes in useful. I take it with me on the ferry. There are a lot of patients who live in remote places, not just on Hersa but here as well—it's useful when they can't get to see us. And we're just into the tourist season so the population almost doubles.'

'What do the tourists do?'

He laughed. 'Besides fishing, walking, golf and deer

stalking? There's two distilleries to visit and the big hotel has tennis courts and a swimming pool. And then there's climbing on the mountains you see over there—a very good source of patients,' he said grimly. 'It's amazing the number of naive people who try to get to the top totally without equipment or experience.'

What a contrast to her patch in London, thought Terry. It was almost too much to take in, and she was gradually becoming aware that it wasn't going to be the sort of quiet country practice she'd imagined.

'I'll need to get some transport,' she said. 'And I'd rather not borrow your motorbike!'

'Don't worry about that—you can use Uncle Euan's little car. The main thing is to take a map and your mobile—it's easy to get lost in the hills out there.'

'It's all very beautiful.' Terry peered through the car window at the changing scene in front of them. 'There must be some wonderful walks—I can't wait to explore.'

Atholl smiled. 'There's so many different walks along the shore and back through the woods and the hills I never tire of them.' He glanced at her and said in an offhand way, 'You'd be welcome to come with a small group of us who walk together sometimes if you like.'

Funny how much that suggestion pleased her—she'd been sad for so long that the slightest lifting of her spirits felt almost alien. It was as if a curtain had been drawn apart a little and a small beam of sunlight had filtered through.

'I'd enjoy that very much,' she said. 'Were you born here?'

He shook his head. 'No, I only came here in the school holidays. I was born and raised in Glasgow.'

'I believe it's a lovely city.'

'I lived in a very deprived area,' he explained. 'There's still a lot of poverty in parts of Glasgow, and my family lived—still do really—in a pretty poor way. Not many advantages to life in the area I was brought up in.'

He'd obviously been glad to leave, thought Terry, whereas she had been so very happy with her life in London until…until it had all crumbled around about her ears and she'd been forced to depart. She sighed and leaned back in her seat, trying to blank out that last vision she'd had of her father as he'd lain dying in her arms and her frantic efforts to save him.

She bit her lip, telling herself firmly that she'd just got to put that episode in her life behind her. All that was finished and done with now.

'So you won't go back to live there, then,' she commented.

He shrugged, a wry smile touching his lips. 'My family think I should be back with them. They think I've let them down—sort of leaving the sinking ship kind of thing and coming to a better area when I could be of much more use where they live.' He gave a humourless laugh. 'They imagine I'm hobnobbing with lairds and big landowners—well above my station in life!'

'That's ridiculous!' cried Terry. 'You're helping your uncle out—and you're needed here as well!'

He laughed at her response. 'Nevertheless, perhaps they have a point. The fact is, though, that I needed to get more experience—have a wider take on life. I'd lived and trained there all my life, and I was longing to spread my wings. And once I'd started working here, I fell in love with the place.'

He changed gear and slowed as they turned a corner

and drew up in front of a square stone cottage surrounded by a little copse and protected from the road by a small front garden.

'Here we are—rough and ready perhaps, but it's home to me,' he remarked.

The cottage wasn't very big, but was most attractive, with a Virginia creeper running rampant over the walls and an untidy rose scrambling round the front door. Terry descended from the Land Rover rather wearily and followed Atholl as he went to the front door and opened it.

He whistled as he went into the little hallway, and there was a joyful bark and a large golden retriever came bounding out of the back regions and flung itself at Atholl.

'Allow me to introduce you,' he said. 'This is Shona—she rules the house, I'm afraid!'

Terry looked up at Atholl and laughed, throwing back her head in amusement. 'And I thought Shona was your girlfriend…'

The sun was streaming through the open door and fell on her raised face, catching the gold light in her hair and emphasising her large amber eyes sparkling up at him with amusement, her lips slightly parted. Looking down at her, Atholl felt slightly stunned. He'd realised she was attractive when he'd first seen her. Now he was suddenly conscious that she wasn't just attractive—she was damned beautiful, her eyes like golden sherry set in a sweet heart-shaped face. It unsettled him, made him nervous, thinking again of tattling tongues in the village, trying to matchmake. He'd had enough of that, thank you. He wasn't lonely and he didn't need a relationship with anyone he worked with—not after the last catastrophe.

He flicked a quick look at Terry's bent head as she

ruffled the dog's head—the nape of her neck looked slim and vulnerable, her hair curling softly into it. And for a mad moment he imagined bending down and kissing the soft curve of her cheek. He could almost feel the velvety touch of her skin…

He started suddenly, realising that Terry was smiling at him, waiting for him to say something.

'You'll find your room upstairs on the right,' he said gruffly. 'It's a bit basic, but you can dump your things there, freshen up and then do what you like here while I do my visits.'

'Sure,' Terry said. 'But if you'd like me to come with you I'm very happy to.'

'No, that won't be necessary today. Tomorrow will be soon enough to start work,' he said tersely. 'I'll be off, then. See you later.'

He strode out abruptly and leapt into the Land Rover, revving it up and accelerating out of the little drive with a spurt of pebbles. What the hell was he thinking about, allowing himself to even notice what Terry Younger looked like, let alone visualise himself touching her—and more? How much easier it would have been if the agency had sent a man, or even a much older woman to take the job—anyone but a knockout like Terry Younger.

He pictured her elfin face with those large expressive eyes like liquid gold and the crisp fair hair framing her face. The trouble was, he thought, gripping the steering-wheel tightly, he'd been taken unawares when Terry had come along, imagining that she would be a man. He scowled out at the landscape as he drove along. Just because he'd led a monastic life for the past few months, the last thing he needed was the distraction of sexual attraction with a colleague. Then he smiled grimly to himself. A city girl like her would probably not last long in the remote world of Scuola—after all, it hadn't taken Zara long to find the place was not to her liking.

Terry stood in the doorway, staring after Atholl with a puzzled frown. He seemed to have suddenly become tense, uneasy about something. Was he perhaps regretting offering her the job? She shrugged. It was too late to back out now, and she'd not give up the job without a fight. She bent down to pat Shona, who looked up at her with trusting brown eyes.

'I'll show him, Shona,' she whispered. 'He'll not regret having me in the practice—even if I am a woman.'

CHAPTER THREE

A DOG barking and the sound of horses' hooves on the road woke Terry up with a start from a deep sleep. For a moment she panicked, thinking she was back in London, but there was no sound of traffic and no curtains at the window to cut off the light streaming onto her bed. She relaxed back again. Of course, she was in a little cottage on Scuola—about seven hundred miles away from her old home and quite safe. She searched for her watch on the bedside table and squinted at the face with amazed horror. It was nine-thirty—she must have slept for twelve hours.

Gradually the previous day's events began to unravel through her mind. It had been a day of mixed emotions, leaving her beloved London, meeting Atholl Brodie in the most dramatic of circumstances, then finding out he was the man she was going to be working with.

She lay for a second reflecting on just what kind of a man he was—outspoken, decisive, but probably fair enough in his dealings with people. And, of course, there were his looks… deep blue eyes in a strong good-looking face swam into her mind. She sighed and swung her legs over the bed. Hadn't she learned that drop-dead gorgeous men had too much confidence, things came too easily to them? She was certainly not about to stray into dangerous emotional territory again—especially in a working relationship. But there was a peculiar little flicker of excitement at the thought of seeing him later.

She padded over to the open window and looked out on a brilliant day, catching her breath at the view. The sun was shining on the distant vista of a blue sea she could see over the fields, and just down by the side of the cottage there was a stream that tumbled and sparkled its way under a little bridge and towards a copse. Through the open window drifted the sweet fresh smells of early spring and the sound of the chattering water.

'A far cry from London,' she murmured, peering down to see if Atholl's car had gone from the front of the cottage. There was no sign of it, so he must have gone to work.

There was a scrabbling noise at the door and Shona trotted in, coming over to nuzzle Terry and then lie on her side in a patch of warm sunlight. Terry had a quick wash and threw on some clothes from her case, which Atholl had placed on the small landing. She squinted into the tiny mirror in the darkest corner of the little room as she flicked a brush through her hair. Her image looked back at her—large eyes framed by wayward short curly fair hair. Funny how a slight change in hair colour and cut could make a face look quite different, she thought. She turned to the dog looking up at her with interest.

'Right, Shona, let's see what's for breakfast, shall we?'

The kitchen was a tiny room with just enough space for a sink, fridge and oven. On the working top was a note. 'If you feel rested enough to come to the surgery, please take my uncle's car parked in the layby just down the road. Keys in drawer.'

After a cup of black coffee and a fruitless hunt for anything more sustaining than a stale piece of bread, Terry put on a jacket and made her way to the car.

'Bye, Shona,' she called to the dog, who was watching her through the window. 'If I don't find my way I may be back soon!'

In fact, it was an easy ten-minute drive to The Sycamores. The worst part was parking the car in between a builder's lorry and Atholl's Land Rover in the drive. The house did indeed look rundown, Terry thought, taking a more detailed look at the paintwork on the windows, the battered front door and the small neglected border covered with weeds.

'I could easily make that look better when the flat's ready,' she murmured to herself as she went into the hall.

The waiting room was crowded and there was no one at Reception.

'The doctor's running late—you'll have to wait a wee while,' said an elderly man helpfully, by the door.

'I'm here to work, actually.' Terry smiled, making her way through the room. A battery of eyes watched her go behind the reception counter while she waited for Isobel to materialise. She looked at the disparate crowd of people who gazed curiously back at her. Hopefully soon she would get to know them, and start to feel part of another community.

'Ah, we wondered when you'd make an appearance!' said Isobel, coming into the room with an armful of post.

Terry was getting used to Isobel's forthright manner and pulled a rueful face. 'Sorry I'm late. I had the best sleep I've had in ages, though. Now I'm ready, willing and able…'

Isobel nodded. 'Aye, well, you had reason to be tired, didn't you? Atholl told me about the accident you were involved in yesterday—quite a baptism of fire in your new home!' She pursed her lips. 'And talking of home, did you find anything for breakfast in that fridge of his?'

'Not a lot.' Terry laughed. 'But I'm fine. Fortunately there was plenty of coffee.'

Isobel made a tutting sound. 'I'll get you something soon. No one can work on an empty stomach—any doctor should know that. Now, Atholl says would you use the room at the end of the passage—he'll be through directly to show you how the programme on the computer works and then I'll send your first patient through.'

Terry looked around her new surgery. It was quite a large room with an examining couch at one side, a wash-basin and two enormous cupboards on the other, and a window with a crooked blind over it at the end. A bookcase filled with weighty medical tomes and magazines was squeezed near the door. Probably it was normally Euan's room, she surmised. There were a few yellowing photographs on the wall of groups of students, and surely one of Euan himself, a stern white-haired gentleman glaring into the room, looking very like Atholl might do in years to come. She opened a drawer in the desk and smiled when she saw the contents—a lipstick and eyeliner wasn't anything Uncle Euan would have use for. The last locum must have been a woman!

There was a tap at the door and Atholl entered. He looked much smarter than yesterday in a dark suit and tie, his white shirt emphasising his tanned face. From a purely objective point of view, Terry told herself, he certainly was one eye-catching guy.

Atholl's eyes flicked over her, completed a quick survey of her navy trouser suit and the pink silk shirt she was wearing under the jacket. She looked delectable, he thought wryly. He'd had time to reflect in the last twelve hours on what a fool he'd been yesterday, rushing off rudely like a madman just because he was frightened of a rerun of the situation he'd had with Zara. It wasn't Terry's fault that she was so damned attractive and the poor girl hadn't had a very welcoming reception. If they were going to work well together it was imperative that he maintain a cordial working relationship with her. From now on he'd try and behave sensibly—but keep his distance.

'You slept all right, then?' he asked. 'You'd gone to bed by the time I got back.'

He sounded more relaxed than he had the day before when he'd roared off after depositing her at the cottage, Terry thought with relief.

'Yes, I slept like a log. I'm sorry I was so late. I'd no idea it was halfway through the morning when I woke up.'

He shook his head dismissively. 'It doesn't matter—you were tired.' He gave a rueful grin. 'I'm sorry about the lack of food. Isobel's just been giving me a hard time about that. I'd no time to shop as I was up at the crack of dawn meeting some man from the local health authority who wants us to provide a room for some alternative medicine clinic.'

Terry gathered from his tone that he was totally against that request. She smiled. 'You can buy me a sandwich at lunchtime if you like.'

'I'll do better than that. I've got to take some gear over to the outward bound place before lunch. If you come with me you can meet Pete, his wife and the boys. I'll bring some food and we'll have it on the way back. The quicker you get to know the area the better.'

'Sounds great.'

He bent forward to switch on the computer and said, 'Before I show you the ropes as far as the software we use is concerned, there's a reporter here to speak to you.'

Terry looked surprised. 'Whatever for? What can I have to say to him?'

Atholl smiled. 'It's about your sterling work yesterday in the car accident. It'll make good copy. "New young doctor on Scuola saves baby in car accident."'

'It certainly wasn't just me involved—you were as well. What paper is this?'

'The *Scuola Recorder*—it's just a weekly newssheet about local happenings.'

'I…I don't know if I really want to be featured,' Terry said doubtfully.

He shrugged. 'I know it's a bit of a bore, but they don't have much to talk about here and that's a happy storyline.'

'I suppose…if people are interested.'

'I can assure you that a heart-warming article about a new doctor ensures the patients will be very keen to be seen by you! They're normally a very conservative lot and don't like change.'

Let's hope the story won't spread much further than Scuola, thought Terry. Then shook herself mentally. She'd nothing to fear now, had she? She just had to relax and enjoy her new life.

A few seconds later Atholl ushered in a young gangling lad with red hair and freckles and an eager manner, like a young puppy. He strode towards Terry with his hand held out.

'Hello, there! Ian Brown, *Scuola Recorder.* I just wanted a few moments of your time to get the lowdown on the accident yesterday. I believe you were the heroine of the hour, rescuing a baby from a car?'

Terry flicked a look of embarrassment at Atholl, who was watching the interview leaning against the wall with his long legs crossed. 'There was nothing heroic about it—and, of course, Dr Brodie was very much involved.'

'It was very dangerous, though. The car could have exploded at any second, isn't that right?' persisted Ian.

'Fortunately all was well.' Terry smiled. 'There really isn't much more to tell. The main thing was that Maisie and little Amy weren't hurt despite the car being badly crushed.'

'Of course, of course…but could I just get a little background info? Where you come from, why you're here…you know the sort of thing?'

Terry smiled brightly. 'Well, I'm from the South of England.' She kept it vague. 'I wanted a change of scene away from the city, somewhere more remote, and Scuola is a beautiful place.'

'So you you've never been here before?'

'No, but it sounded just perfect.'

Ian's cheery face raised a sceptical eyebrow. 'Bit of a risk isn't it? Coming to live here without viewing the place first? Jumping into untested waters, as it were…'

'I'm sure it will work out,' said Terry firmly. She didn't want to answer any more probing questions, because they seemed to bring back with startling clarity the reasons that had forced her to come up to Scotland. She sat down behind her desk. 'Look, I'm afraid I really must get on now. I'm already late for my first day and I know Dr Brodie's very busy.'

The young man looked disappointed. 'Well, at least let me take a photo of you both, perhaps with Dr Brodie welcoming his new colleague to the practice…you know the sort of thing.'

Reluctantly Terry allowed Ian to manoeuvre her beside Atholl, and he took several photos of them shaking hands and looking rather self-consciously towards the mobile phone on which he'd taken the pictures.

'Good!' he said with satisfaction. 'You're very photogenic, Dr Younger—they seem to get smashing-looking lady doctors here! That Dr Grahame who was here before was one bonny lass!'

Atholl scowled, not remarking on Ian's observations, and snapped, 'Have you finished, then?'

Terry flicked a glance at Atholl, noting his abrupt change of mood. It had probably been brought on by the cheeky attitude of the young reporter.

'Would you like to see the photo?' enquired Ian, holding up his mobile to her. 'Look, you have to agree, you make a really handsome couple!'

Atholl's expression became even more surly. 'For God's sake, don't start making things up now,' he warned him tersely.

Ian Brown grinned, completely unfazed by Atholl's irritation. 'Don't worry. I'll send you a copy of the article—it'll be a lovely human-interest story! "Doctors to the rescue!" Sounds good, doesn't it?'

Atholl and Terry looked at each other dubiously as Ian gave them a cheery wave and went out of the room.

'Let's hope he doesn't allow his imagination to run away with him,' growled Atholl drily. 'Give the folk round here a little information and they'll have us engaged! It doesn't take much for them to leap to the wrong conclusion.'

'Rumours can fly around on practically no evidence,' agreed Terry. 'It must be hard to keep one's private life to oneself in a small community, I imagine.'

'Too right! My patients can't wait to marry me off, but I've still got my freedom, I'm relieved to say, and I've no plans to change that!'

He sounded quite adamant about it, although Terry couldn't imagine that a man with his looks didn't have a girlfriend somewhere in the background—or, if that wasn't the case, several girls ready to pounce on him if he showed willing! Well, his attitude suited her, because she too was glad that she was fancy-free, free of Max and the way he'd dragged her family down, and ready to concentrate on her work and new life.

She sat down at the desk. 'Now, show me the ins and outs of this system before I see my first patient.'

He sat down beside her and started to explain how things worked.

It had hardly been necessary for young Ian Brown to come and cover the story—every patient Terry had that morning mentioned the accident. News travelled very fast in a small community.

'I'm Maisie's auntie, Doreen Lovatt,' said her first patient, a large, rosy-cheeked woman who limped in slowly with a stick and sat down heavily in the chair opposite Terry. 'Whatever would she have done without you and Dr Brodie?' she began chattily. 'I went to see her last night in the hospital, and she's doing really well, and as for that gorgeous baby... well, it doesn't bear thinking about, does it?'

Terry could see that this consultation could last quite a while if she allowed Mrs Lovatt to discuss her niece's accident and quickly interrupted. 'I'm so glad they're both OK, Mrs Lovatt. Maisie was terribly brave. Now, how can I help you?'

'Well, Doctor, it's my knee. I'm in agony. Years ago I had it, but it's suddenly ballooned up without warning again.'

Mrs Lovatt was equably voluble about her knee, but at least they were on the right subject—the patient's health!

Terry examined the knee and noted how stiff and swollen it was and how painful when moved. She asked Mrs Lovatt if she'd been prescribed any medication for it in the past.

'Oh, no, I don't really like taking tablets, Dr Younger. I'd rather just get by if I can. But it's so bad at the moment I can't look after baby Amy or the other two little ones. That's my job, you see. I'm a childminder and Maisie brings Amy over everyday from the mainland while she works at the newsagent's.'

Terry pondered for a minute, looking at her overweight patient. 'Have you been doing anything out of the ordinary that might have injured the joint?'

Doreen Lovatt blushed. 'Well…you may think it's a bit ridiculous—a woman of my size—but, having not done any exercise for years, my friend persuaded me to join a dance troupe. We call it "Strictly Formation Dancing". We've been rehearsing a lot lately and perhaps I overdid it a bit.'

The vision this presented of Doreen dancing in a revealing dress was a vivid one, but Terry suppressed a smile and said enthusiastically, 'That's marvellous. What a great idea, and such fun. But that sort of high-impact exercise is probably what's aggravated your knee.'

Doreen's plump face fell. 'I thought you'd say it was that. Will I have to give up the dancing?' she asked dolefully.

'I hope not—but you will have to rest it and let the ligaments settle down. I'm not sure if the trauma to your knee has given you a flare-up of arthritis. It could even be a displaced cartilage…'

Doreen looked alarmed. 'How can you tell, then, Doctor?'

'If it's arthritis it should settle down after a few days of rest and some anti-inflammatory tablets. I believe a physiotherapist has a session at the hospital so if we could get you an appointment you could be shown a few gentle exercises to keep the muscles in that area toned. If it's still not right after a week or so, we ought to have an MRI scan done so that we can see exactly what's going on.'

Terry looked kindly at the worried-looking woman. 'One thing I'd like you to do that could help…and I don't think you'll find it too difficult when you're taking all this exercise…'

'What's that, Doctor?'

'If you lost some weight it would help your knee a lot—you might find it settles down completely.' Terry put it as gently as she could. She didn't want to hurt this nice woman's feelings.

To her alarm Doreen's face crumpled and she pulled out a hankie from a large handbag and blew her nose noisily. 'Oh, I have tried, really I have, but it's difficult. I've three sons and a husband who all like huge meals, and I can't stop myself eating with them. I know I look a sight.'

Terry leaned over the desk and patted Doreen's plump hand. Doreen might have a cheery face but it obviously hid the very real worry she had about her weight, and the lack of self-esteem she felt probably affected her whole life. And there were many people who felt like she did, too embarrassed to ask for help.

'You don't look a sight, Doreen, far from it,' she said gently. 'My only concern is for your health. Extra pounds put strain on your body—blood pressure, joints and the risk of diabetes. I don't want you to stop eating with your family, Doreen, just not quite so much.'

'I've got no willpower,' said Doreen mournfully.

'Look, I'm going to suggest I hold a weekly weigh-in at the surgery to try and encourage people who need to lose weight. That and a diet sheet should help your resolve.' She smiled at Doreen. 'You're the first patient I've seen in my new job, so I really want my first patient to do well! Will you come?'

Doreen looked brighter. 'Yes—yes, I'd like that, something to keep me on the straight and narrow. Actually, there's one or two of us in the troupe that are a bit weighty, so they might come along as well!'

She limped out quite happily and when she got to the door she turned and said cryptically, 'It's good to have a sympathetic lady doctor at last—someone who's main interest is in her patients and hasn't got other things on her mind. Well, you know what I mean, Dr Younger.'

What exactly *did* she mean? wondered Terry as she tapped in her notes for Doreen Lovatt. Perhaps when she knew Isobel better she'd make discreet enquiries about this woman that had been the locum before her.

The morning sped by with the usual variety of ills that

presented themselves at a GP's surgery, from chronic backache to glue ear in a small child. And all the patients were keen to talk about Maisie and her accident, which Terry surmised probably added at least half an hour to the morning's work.

Just as she was about to shut down the computer, Isobel put her head round the door.

'Bad news, I'm afraid,' she said grimly.

'Oh, dear...what?' asked Terry, wondering if Isobel ever came in looking happy.

Isobel's voice sank to a conspiratorial whisper. 'Cyril Rathbone—that's the bad news! He haunts this place. I told him surgery was finished but he won't take no for an answer. Always thinks he's at death's door and has to be seen immediately. Mind you,' she acknowledged, 'he and his wife make a wonderful job of running the Caledonian Hotel up the hill and I think that's quite stressful. Shall I send him in?'

'No problem,' said Terry with a grin. 'There's at least one in every practice!' Whatever Isobel said about this patient, this could be the one time he was really ill after all.

Mr Rathbone, short, bald, but nattily dressed, marched into the room. 'Thank you for seeing me, Doctor,' he said briskly. 'I normally see Dr Euan Brodie—we're old friends, sit on the same committees, that sort of thing. He keeps a very good eye on me but, of course, he's not available, which is a nuisance.'

Terry smiled, noting with amusement the way he'd made it clear that he was a special patient of the practice! 'How can I help you, Mr Rathbone?'

'I didn't want to bother you really, but I'm in such pain

that my wife insisted I should come and see *someone,* whoever it was…'

'I see. I hope I can give as much satisfaction as Dr Brodie.'

Her sarcasm was lost on a man like Mr Rathbone, and she wondered, with his brusque manner, how he managed to make such a success of his hotel. Perhaps he was completely different with his guests!

'Well, of course you don't know me like old Dr Brodie,' he said tersely. 'He's a wonderful diagnostician.'

Meaning you don't have any faith in me at all, thought Terry wryly. But she sympathised. The patient-doctor relationship was a very personal thing built over a long time, and seeing someone new could be daunting.

'The thing is, I've got an excruciating blister on my toe,' continued Mr Rathbone. 'I know they can become infected very easily and turn to septicaemia, so I'd like an antibiotic to fight the infection.'

'Let me have a look at it,' said Terry. 'Take off your shoe and sock.'

'There!' exclaimed Mr Rathbone dramatically, revealing his foot with a small red patch on his little toe. 'Can you wonder I can hardly walk?' He took out a folded-up newspaper from his jacket pocket and handed it to Terry, pointing out an underlined headline with a stubby finger. 'Read that! It's all about diabetes and how an injury can be deadly if left untreated if you have that condition.'

Of all the things that could irritate a doctor, reflected Terry, it's when a patient quoted something they've read about a condition and assume they've got it!

She looked through his notes on the computer carefully—there was no history of diabetes or any other existing condition that might make the area on his toe a cause for concern.

'I see you had a blood and urinary test for diabetes a short time ago,' she said. 'They all proved negative, so I don't think we need worry about that.'

'I thought I'd just check that you were aware of the complications should I have had it,' replied Mr Rathbone. 'One can't be too careful.'

Terry bit back the urge to say, *But one can be incredibly irritating!* and said instead, 'It must be rather sore. It's obviously been rubbing on shoes that are too tight. The best thing would be to put surgical spirit on it to harden the skin and a small padded plaster over the affected part. And, of course, wear soft shoes like slippers, if your normal ones hurt, until it's healed.'

'Slippers?' echoed Mr Rathbone incredulously. 'I run a hotel—I can hardly stroll around in front of my guests looking sloppy! What about antibiotics? Surely I ought to have a course of them?'

'I think we'll keep them as a last resort, Mr Rathbone. Hopefully it won't become infected if you do as I suggest. But do come back if it gets worse.'

Terry's voice was pleasant but very firm—she wasn't going to be bullied into giving him medicine he didn't need. Mr Rathbone stared at her in disbelief, then shook his head sadly. 'I only hope you know what you're doing—you young doctors are so inexperienced. You're not from around here, are you?'

He got up and walked with a pronounced limp to the door before turning round and saying dourly, 'I don't know what's happened to this practice—I see a different person every time I come. Where's the other woman that was here?

Not that I had much faith in her, her mind didn't seem to be on the job at all!' He looked scornfully at Terry. 'I suppose you'll be gone soon too—there's just no continuity!'

He went out and Terry blew out her cheeks in amazement, feeling a mixture of irritation and amusement.

'Perhaps he'll see Atholl next time,' she murmured, although she'd be surprised if a man like Atholl would let Mr Rathbone dictate to him. She stretched and yawned, putting the man out of her head. She was ready for that picnic lunch that Atholl had promised after they'd met his friend and the boys.

Atholl had changed out of his smart suit and had on jeans and an old plaid lumber jacket. He looked critically at Terry's outfit.

'It could be cold when we get to the loch, it's right up in the hills.' he said. 'I always keep a spare set of warm and casual clothes here to change into in case I'm called out to a mountain rescue or somewhere that doesn't require that suit I wear for meetings.' He rummaged in the boot of the Land Rover and threw a fleece over to her. 'Wear that when we get there and you should be OK.'

Shona was in the back of the car, leaping about in excitement. 'I just picked her up when I was called out this morning,' Atholl explained. 'I often do that. Some of my elderly patients love seeing her and she enjoys being made a fuss of.'

Terry could imagine what pleasure the lovely dog would give to lonely old people—and a great source of interest to them. 'I've always wanted a dog,' she said, 'but inner-city London wasn't the place to keep one.'

'So did you have a flat or a house in London?' he enquired as they set off towards the hills.

'A flat,' she replied briefly.

'And was it near your work?'

'Fairly—I could walk there.' Her brisk tone didn't encourage further questions.

Terry wasn't very informative about her life in London, Atholl reflected. The way she'd reacted to the young reporter, the guarded way she'd answered his questions…it all added up to someone who wanted to forget her life there. He'd hazard a guess that she'd had an unhappy affair…she wouldn't be the first person to move because of a broken heart. Oddly the thought of Terry in love with an unknown man made him uneasy—though someone as stunning as her must have had hordes of men longing to take her out. He accelerated rather fast up the road that led into the hills, large capable hands on the steering-wheel, intrigued and slightly irritated by this little mystery. He'd find out soon enough, he thought.

'And how did you find your surgery today?' he asked. 'Although I guess ailments are pretty universal.'

'I enjoyed it. Maisie's aunt, Doreen Lovatt, came in to see me with a bad knee but we ended up talking about her worries over her weight.'

'Ah, Doreen—she's a good woman. In fact, all of her family are a bit overweight—you should see her husband and three sons.'

'Poor woman. I tried to persuade her to lose some weight, but I can see it might be difficult for her. I wondered if you'd mind if I had a trial weight clinic for a few weeks? Say, after surgery one evening?'

Atholl flicked an amused glance at her. 'Trying to

improve the lifestyle on Scuola already? But feel free to do that if you wish—in fact, I think it's a good idea. There's quite a few would benefit around here.'

They continued talking in a general way about the practice and Terry mentioned Mr Rathbone.

'There always seems to be someone who's very demanding in every practice,' she commented.

'Absolutely.' He grinned. 'But the day you ignore them, that's the day their severe stomach cramps really do turn out to be appendicitis. Mind you, he and his wife have transformed the hotel they run. It was in a terrible state a few years ago when they bought it, and by sheer hard work they've given it a complete makeover and it's a real asset to the area. However, I don't know how Janet Rathbone stands him.'

'Apparently she insisted he come and see us.'

'To get him out of her hair I should think.' Atholl laughed. 'No doubt we'll see him again next week. By the way, I ought to fill you in a bit about the four lads you're going to meet. They come from the same area that I grew up in, all from broken families. I don't think any of them have had much notice taken of them individually or had the chance to do anything but get into trouble—they've all had run-ins with the police. These few weeks are meant to give them a breath of air, an opportunity to put their energies to good use.'

'That's a great idea. Who started it?'

'Pete and I,' Atholl said drily. 'You see, we were exactly the same at their age—out of control and getting sucked into gangs and dodgy company. We were lucky. We managed to get away from it all just in time, and now we want to give others that chance as well.'

'That's a great thing to do,' she said quietly.

There was more to Atholl Brodie than good looks, then—he was someone who'd made the grade despite a tough start and was prepared to help other youngsters. A flicker of bitterness reminded Terry how different Atholl was from Max, who'd used his good looks and intelligence to such ill effect, hurting so many in his wake.

She flicked a look at Atholl's strong profile and sighed. If only she'd met someone like him two years ago—someone who was kind, generous with his time, concerned for others. Instead, she thought bitterly, she'd been hoodwinked by honeyed words and her own gullibility—as had her father, she reflected. She wondered if she would she ever believe in a man again or trust her own judgement.

Atholl turned off the road up an unmade cart track, bumping over the holes until they came to a barn-like building in front of a small loch surrounded by hills. A washing line hung outside with several pairs of jeans and T-shirts hanging from it.

'This is The Culleens where Pete and his wife have their outward bound venture,' he remarked. 'You'll like Sally—she's a great girl and expecting their first baby in about five weeks. She supervises most of the domestic stuff and Pete's the outward bound expert.'

He opened the car door and jumped out. 'Better put on that fleece—you'll need it here,' he advised.

He opened the rear door and Shona flung herself out and raced madly away towards the back of the building, barking excitedly. Terry followed Atholl as a burly young man wearing a thick sweater came into view from behind the barn. The man lifted his hand and hailed Atholl.

'Hello, there!' he called. 'I was hoping you'd come.'

Atholl turned to Terry. 'Let me introduce you to Pete Brown. Pete, Terry Younger, our new locum at the practice and assistant here.'

Terry smiled, seeing the familiar look of surprise when she was introduced to anyone. 'No,' she said quickly. 'I'm not a man! I know you were expecting one, but I'm afraid you'll have to make do with me!'

Pete grinned and shook her hand in a crushing grip. 'I can tell you're a lass all right!' He turned round and bellowed, 'Sally! Sally! Come here and meet Atholl's new locum! Terry Younger…'

A tall and very pregnant-looking girl wearing jeans and an old coat came out of the barn. 'Hi, there! Lovely to meet you, Terry.' She had a wide, attractive smile and Terry took to her immediately. 'It'll be great to have a woman to talk to sometimes instead of all these men!'

'Talking of which, you'd better come and meet these boys,' Pete said. 'They're doing well on the whole—only Zac's not pulling his weight at the moment, and yet he was very keen to start with.'

He led the way round the side of the building where three large youths were chopping wood whilst one leant against the wall watching them, his jaws working rhythmically as he chewed gum. The other boys stopped what they were doing and watched as Atholl and Terry came up to them.

'Right, lads, meet Terry,' said Pete. 'She's a GP in Atholl's practice and she'll be with us on some of our activities.'

The boy leaning against the wall leered at Terry suggestively. 'Don't mind being overseen by her…'

'Watch it, Zac,' warned Pete sharply. 'Try and be courteous.' He turned to Terry. 'Let me introduce you to Bert, Len, Colin and Zac.'

The boys nodded to her, slightly warily, possibly aware that they were being assessed by this new woman. Terry nodded back. She wasn't going to be effusive about meeting them—it could seem patronising.

'I'm looking forward to seeing you abseiling,' she said. 'I've never done it myself.'

'You coming with us when we do that?' asked one of the boys. 'You could try it then.'

Pete nodded. 'Yes, starting with a trek across the moor and maybe some kayaking as well.'

'Sounds fun,' said Terry.

Zac laughed heartily. 'You wait till you see us—we're bloody hopeless.'

'Why aren't you helping to cut the wood, Zac?' asked Atholl.

Zac shrugged. 'Ask Pete—he says I'm a danger to everyone. I'm quite happy to watch, mind you.' He gave another robust laugh.

'You're just a bit clumsy, Zac,' remarked Pete. 'You nearly lost a finger cutting the bread yesterday—I can't risk you using an axe until that cut's healed.'

Zac giggled. 'I was hungry—did it a bit quickly.'

Pete shook his head in mock despair. 'You're always hungry, Zac, you've an appetite like a horse. I hope you've brought some more basics, Atholl, to keep this lot fed.'

'There's a load of bread, milk and meat in the Land Rover, as well as all the gear I promised you, like ropes and tents. Perhaps the lads could unload the stuff now and take it in,' said Atholl. Terry frowned and looked at Zac closely. He had reddened eyes and his lips were dry and cracked, and something about his slightly manic manner reminded her of some of the kids who'd been patients of hers in London. She watched as the boys carried the gear from Atholl's car to a shed by the barn, Zac's whoops of laughter drifting towards them. She would mention it to Atholl later. They went into the converted barn which was divided simply into various rooms—a large kitchen and sitting area, two dormitory-type bedrooms and a bathroom.

'Are you enjoying yourselves?' Terry asked the three boys who had come in with them. Zac had wandered off to throw sticks in the air for Shona to run after.

'Aye, it's good,' said one of them. 'But we miss the telly. We're only allowed an hour a day.'

'If you behave, that is,' said Pete with a grin. 'Right, lads, you start making the lunch. What is it, Sally?'

'We'll have spaghetti bolognaise with grated cheese on top, bread and fruit,' said Sally, turning to Atholl and Terry. 'Are you going to have some with us?'

'Thanks, but not today, Sally,' said Atholl. 'I'm just giving Terry a mini-tour of the area before we do some visits this afternoon, but we'll be on duty when you do the abseiling.'

'That'll be great.' Sally smiled. 'Better bring your waterproofs! And thanks for delivering the extra provisions—just what was needed!'

Atholl whistled for Shona, who came bounding up happily to them and jumped into the Land Rover. Zac followed and stood watching them stolidly, still chewing gum, his arms folded.

'Go and help your friends make your lunch,' suggested Atholl as he got back into the car and started the engine.

Zac gave that extravagant laugh again, kicked a stone and ambled back towards the barn.

'The boys really seem to have relaxed since they've come here—and they've got stuck into doing things. When they arrived they were sullen and uncooperative,' remarked Atholl as he drove back down the winding road. 'Only Zac seems to have slowed down almost to a full stop.'

'His manner reminded me of some of the patients I used to see in London,' began Terry. 'It makes me wonder if—'

'He's on something?' put in Atholl, turning to her with a wry smile. 'I have to say he seemed a bit hyper.'

Terry looked at Atholl, surprised at his perception. 'Exactly! I've seen it before—the slightly reddened eyes, that excitable laughter. And didn't Pete say he had a huge appetite? All could be indicators of cannabis.'

'It did occur to me as well—I'll speak to Pete about it tonight. The boys all receive post from time to time and although Pete and Sally try to keep a strict eye on the lads, it's something that you could miss in the early stages.' His periwinkle-blue eyes twinkled at her, dark hair flopping over his forehead, and suddenly a flicker of attraction caught her by surprise, flashing through her body like lightning through a conductor. 'Same old problems even in little Scuola, eh?' he said.

'Absolutely,' she agreed, slightly flustered at her reaction to him.

He changed gear as the car started to labour up a steep hill. 'Anyway let's forget about Zac for a while. I want to show you a favourite place of mine—perfect for having a bite to eat. It's good to get away from the surgery for a while.'

It was ridiculous the way her heart began thumping at

the thought of being alone with Atholl, thought Terry. He was a work colleague, for heaven's sake, and the last thing she needed was to fall for another man's charms so easily!

CHAPTER FOUR

THEY had been driving away from the loch and gradually getting higher where the terrain was rougher, and now Atholl turned into a small clearing where a circle of silver birches made a pretty glade overlooking the countryside and the sea between Scuola and the mainland. He shot a look at his watch.

'Just time for lunch and a quick coffee.'

He got out of the car and stretched, his lean strong body looking like an advertisement for some impossibly marvellous health food, and again there was that sudden flutter like captured butterflies trying to escape from Terry's stomach as she watched him.

He held her shoulders and turned her towards the Scuola Sound, and she felt herself tense at his touch. He was much taller than she, dominating her petite form, acting as a windbreak between her and the freezing wind whipping through the trees.

'Look, from here it's a good vantage point to show you where the surgery is in relation to the rest of the island—do you see it?'

'Oh…yes, yes, I can. It's a wonderful view.' Her throat felt a little dry and her voice came out rather breathlessly.

One hand still held her shoulder and with the other he pointed to a small steamer crossing the firth, bending so that his eyeline was the same height as hers, his face very close to her cheek.

'And there goes the *Highland Lady*—a luxury cruise for some lucky people round the islands,' he said. 'They'll probably be sitting down to a fine lunch of lobster and champagne right now.' He grinned down at her. 'Nothing like that here, I'm afraid. It's all rather basic stuff—oat cakes, local baps, cheese, ham and smoked salmon. Take your pick.'

He went over to the car and hauled a basket out of the boot and Terry relaxed slightly. Having him quite so near seemed to be doing devastating things to her mind and body—something she hadn't bargained for at all.

'It all looks delicious,' she said brightly. 'I didn't expect so much. When did you buy it?'

He laughed. 'Isobel did the buying! She doesn't trust me to get the right stuff.' The sound of a ship's siren hooted mournfully over to them and he turned and pointed through the trees. 'Look down there again—you can see where the ferry comes in, and it's clear enough to see where the car rammed into the dock wall when you arrived. And follow the road round and beyond the curve of the hill is the hospital.'

The wind had become even stronger and colder and, despite wearing the fleece, Terry felt chilled as she looked down.

'Lord, this really is Highland weather,' she said, wrapping the fleece more tightly around her slight figure. 'I'm glad of your fleece.'

He laughed and poured some steaming coffee from a Thermos flask into a mug and put it on the ground. 'I told you, you've got to be tough to work here.' He looked at her critically. 'You need to be better clothed for these climes. Let me feel your hands. Good God, they're freezing!' He started to rub them between his warm ones, then took off his scarf and put it round her neck, tying it into a loose knot. He looked down at her with a smile. 'There! That's what's needed!'

What was needed, thought Terry nervously, was for Atholl Brodie to remove his strapping body away from hers. No wonder her pulse had gone into overdrive... Perhaps it was because they were out in the clear fresh air of the outdoors but that treacherous attraction seemed determined to come flickering back, and it was very easy to imagine cuddling up to his chest and out of the biting wind.

What was she like? she thought angrily to herself. Was she so needy that she had to indulge in pipe dreams with a man she had only just met? A man, moreover, who had no time for women—just as she, of course, had no time for men after the way they'd destroyed her life in London.

'Thank you,' she said, stepping back from the danger zone that was Atholl Brodie. 'I'm dying for some coffee, and this food looks delectable. I can't wait to eat it. Everything tastes twice as good in the open air.'

Atholl laughed. 'Hardly cordon bleu!'

As they started to eat, he pointed out the little island of Hersa across Scuola Sound, to the left of the mainland. Far away they could see the ferry, a small craft in the glittering blue sea, making its way back to the dock. Then Atholl pointed up to the sky.

'Look,' he whispered. 'Hovering just to the right of us—a kestrel. Isn't that a wonderful sight?'

She watched as the bird fluttered and then plunged like

an arrow to the ground not far from them, and she smiled at Atholl in delight. 'Do you know, I've never seen that before.'

The wind whipped her hair into a halo round her head and her eyes were sparkling with the pleasure of seeing the beautiful bird. Quite often Terry seemed to have an aura of sadness about her, but in that instant Atholl suddenly saw a beautiful woman filled with a spontaneous enjoyment of life, a joy in the beauty of things—and a shiver of something akin to longing went through him. Terry had the capacity make someone very happy, he reflected. She was good company and, of course, she was damned attractive. It had been a long, long time since he'd met anyone like her.

The expression in his eyes intensified as his gaze swept over her neat figure then rested on her face, and under his scrutiny Terry felt the hairs on the back of her neck stand up. The last thing she'd been thinking of when she'd landed on Scuola was the possibility that there might be drop-dead gorgeous guys on the island like Atholl, and now he seemed to be doing things to her insides that she hadn't felt for a long time—and certainly didn't want to feel!

Atholl wrenched his eyes away from her and moistened his lips. He felt shaken at the total unexpectedness of the attraction he felt for her. Damn it, this was something he hadn't planned. He wanted a quiet life where he could do his work, enjoy his fishing and walking, and he didn't want any distractions from females. That was why he was so bewildered at his reaction because he had the uneasy feeling that if they'd known each other for longer, he'd have taken her in his arms and kissed her soft lips and that little hollow in her neck, and to hell with it being dangerous and getting himself involved in a relationship…

The sound of a bus changing gear noisily as it went up the road brought Atholl back to the present. He took a deep breath and began to pick up the mugs and the Thermos flask. This whole thing was completely crazy. The woman had arrived only yesterday and already he was putting himself in a vulnerable position, allowing himself to be beguiled by a lovely woman. He'd had enough of women to last a lifetime, he thought irritably. It had to be just a spurious attraction, nothing more, a thing of the moment. Keep your distance, Brodie, he growled inwardly to himself.

He put the picnic things in the boot and looked at Terry as she walked towards the car. She was totally different to Zara, yet in one respect they were similar—both had been born to privilege and a world away from the mean streets of the poverty-stricken area he'd come from. They were town girls and he and Terry had very little in common—and he was pretty confident that after a few weeks she would find island life too dull, too isolated and go back to the city, just like Zara.

'It's getting late,' he remarked lightly. 'We'd better get back.'

Terry remained still for a second, wondering if Atholl had felt any spark between them, just as she had. An unfamiliar feeling of excitement that she hadn't felt for so long seemed to glimmer reluctantly into life again like a small bright flame. Then she dismissed the feeling crossly. She was here to give all her attention to work—and through circumstances she'd been given the chance to do just that.

Over the next few days Terry met all the staff at The Sycamores. Bunty was Isobel's part-time assistant, as jolly as Isobel was dour, and Sue was the community nurse, a pleasant woman with three young sons who seemed to be always in trouble at school. The practice shared a manager, Jonathon Murie, with another group of GPs on the mainland and he came over once a week for a practice meeting.

The staff were friendly and relaxed with her, although there had been the familiar double-take when she'd been introduced to them and Bunty had exclaimed in surprise, 'Oh, we didn't think we'd get a female doctor again!' And the others looked at each other meaningfully. When she knew them better, vowed Terry, she would ask them what all these cryptic references to the previous locum meant!

It was the start of another busy day and there had been a quick meeting before work regarding the ongoing building work at The Sycamores. Atholl came into the office behind Reception, looking harassed, and flung some papers on the table in the back office.

'Wouldn't you know it? The damn builders have found some subsidence on that wall with the damp in it, so it's going to take even longer to complete the job. I dare say they'll be here for months…'

Not what she wanted to hear, Terry reflected. That would surely mean the flat at The Sycamores wouldn't be ready for ages and she would have to stay at Atholl's for longer. Despite her vow to make her job her priority, her mind seemed to dwell rather too much on Atholl. Living in such close proximity to him, she couldn't help but be aware of his physical closeness—when she passed him on the narrow little stairs, and when she lay in bed at night, knowing that he was only a few feet away from her in his room. It didn't take much for her lively imagination to picture his muscled, well-toned body lying on the bed. She felt vaguely ashamed of herself.

Luckily, many evenings he had been at meetings or going over to the mainland hospital to see his uncle, so she was able to have some time to herself. There was no doubt about it, however, the time had come for her to get her own place—and fast. She would speak to him about it over the weekend.

'So I've still got to keep all that junk in my room while the builders are here?' asked Sue Calder, the community nurse, with a grimace. 'It's very squashed in there when there's a mother and her children in for vaccinations.'

'I'm sorry, Sue, I do sympathise. If we could make some more room, I would,' said Atholl.

'What about the room I'm using?' suggested Terry. 'It's very big and I don't need all that space, so perhaps we could move some of the stuff near the bookcase where there's a recess—I suppose it was a fireplace once.'

'You sure about that?' asked Atholl. 'We'd tried to keep your room clutter free so as not to frighten off any new locum.'

She smiled. 'No problem. I'm not put off by clutter. In fact, there already are quite a few old files and books in there which perhaps we could get rid of to make more space. Would that help, Sue?'

Sue grinned. 'I'll say. I've practically had patients sitting on my knee to have their BPs taken. Thanks, Terry, it'll certainly help. By the way, have you two seen the local paper? You've got it, haven't you, Bunty?'

Bunty handed Terry a newspaper with an impish smile. 'You'll probably get a film contract out of this! Talk about Superman and his mate!'

Terry stared at an enormous photograph of her and Atholl grinning into the camera, big headlines proclaiming, 'Doctor Duo Defy Danger—Mother and Baby Saved!'

'For heaven's sake!' she said in amusement. 'That's a bit dramatic!'

Atholl peered over her shoulder at it and snorted derisively, 'That young reporter's gone over the top.'

It was actually a very good photo. Atholl looked like someone out of a TV medical drama, Terry reflected, his tall frame looking even bigger beside her dainty figure. She folded the paper and slipped it into her bag—just as a memento, she told herself.

The phones started ringing as soon as Isobel put the lines through at eight-thirty. Sue picked up her bag and some patients' notes.

'I'll be going out to see the Mackie sisters this morning,' she said to Atholl. 'They're both so frail that I feel they're going to need some help very soon—but I know for sure they'll resist any suggestions of that! I wonder if you'd drop by when you've time and give me your assessment of the situation. And don't forget to bring your dog—they've a whole tin of biscuits for her!'

'Will do. Perhaps I can fit it in tomorrow or the day after,' agreed Atholl. He turned to Terry. 'It might be quite a good idea if you were to come with me—I'd like to introduce the sisters to you, and show you where they live.'

He started to leave her room, then hesitated, looking back at her. 'I'm out tonight, seeing my uncle at the mainland hospital again, and I won't be back until later.' He smiled, a warm twinkly smile that did devastating things to her heartbeat. 'And thanks for sacrificing a bit of space in your room—much appreciated.'

Terry walked to her room and pushed the newspaper

cutting into a drawer, then went to the window, flicking aside the crooked Venetian blind for a second and looking out of the window at the spectacular view across the Scuola Sound. How lucky she was to have found such a gem of a place to work in. The unhappiness she'd felt in the last months in London was receding and every day she felt more relaxed and happy here. Of course, she did have bad moments when she missed the friends that she was unlikely to see for a long time, but gradually a general warm kind of happiness had crept in that she hadn't felt for so long, and everyone at work was so nice to her.

Through the window she watched Atholl walk toward his car, stopping to talk to an elderly patient, his tall frame bending forward to listen to her. Terry smiled wryly to herself. She had to admit that part of her happiness was to do with the strange effect Atholl was having on her.

Silly woman, she chided herself. She had to stamp this feeling out quickly. After all, the last thing she wanted was to get involved with a man again, and Atholl seemed very happy to be a bachelor!

She looked up as Bunty knocked at the door and came in with a list of patients for the morning's surgery.

'Here you go. First off you've got Cyril Rathbone,' she said cheerily. 'His weekly appointment, I suppose.'

'I did seem him a week or two ago,' Terry acknowledged. 'I'll just bring up his notes and then call him in.'

On the face of it he seemed to be one of the 'worried well'—someone convinced that they were ill despite constant reassurance. There had to be some deep underlying insecurity there that led to him usir the surgery as a kind of crutch, Terry thought. Perhaps it was the stress of his work. She pressed the button that activated the call screen in the waiting room and after a few seconds Cyril Rathbone appeared.

He cleared his throat and said rather gruffly, 'I…I've not come about myself this time.'

Terry tried not to look too surprised, and he continued, 'It's my wife, she's not well. I know she's not herself, but she won't make an appointment to see anybody—never wants to make a fuss.'

She sounded the complete opposite of her husband, reflected Terry. She leaned forward. 'What makes you think she's not well, Mr Rathbone?'

He looked down at his hands, as if undecided how to describe his wife's symptoms, then said reluctantly, 'It's, well…she seems to get everything wrong. She used to be so efficient. We're in the hotel business and recently the amount of times she's been to the wholesalers and come back with the wrong things on the list is incredible. And she's so clumsy, knocking things over, and then scraping the car going out of the drive innumerable times. The fact is, Doctor…' His voice sank to a conspiratorial whisper, and he looked round as if someone might be listening to them. 'The fact is, I'm beginning to think she drinks—secretly, mind. In our business that would be fatal.'

'Do you smell drink on her breath?'

'No, but it could be vodka—you can't detect that, can you?'

Terry wondered how long ago it had been since Cyril and his wife had had a real heart to heart—it sounded as if they were pretty remote from each other.

'Are you sure you can't get her to come to the surgery? It would be easier. I will come and see her at the hotel if you like but she may refuse to see me if she hasn't requested a visit.'

Cyril shook his head. 'I'm afraid she's not very amenable to my suggestions, and she's always been dead set against anything to do with the medical profession. I can't understand it.'

It would seem inexplicable to him, thought Terry with an inward smile. 'Look, I've got an idea,' she said. 'We're doing a blood-pressure check on all the over-fifties during the next few weeks. Everyone over that age will be invited along, including yourself and your wife. Why don't you suggest you come as a couple as you would prefer someone with you when you have yours done? I could then use the opportunity to ask her in general terms how she feels.'

Mr Rathbone nodded. 'Yes, she might do that. It's a good idea.' He got up from his chair slowly and said with a certain hesitancy, 'The fact is, Doctor, my wife's never been ill in her life—I can't ever remember her complaining about not feeling well. And I suppose it's just come home to me that I'd have to cope if she was laid low.'

And you're frightened, surmised Terry. For the first time perhaps he was beginning to realise how much he relied on her.

'I'm sure you'd be a tower of strength,' said Terry bracingly. 'In the meantime, try not to worry and I'll probably see you in about two weeks.'

It was amazing how comforting the familiar platitudes could be. Cyril even managed a grateful smile as he went out, and the confident and rather arrogant manner he'd had the first time Terry had met him had gone.

At the end of the morning's surgery Terry went into the

office and poured herself a cup of coffee before she tackled the blood test and biopsy results via the e-mails she'd had that day. Isobel was speaking on the phone, looking grimmer than ever. She looked up at Terry.

'Atholl had best get down the glen quickly,' she said, putting the phone down. 'Hamish Stoddard has collapsed in a field there and his dogs won't let anyone near him.'

'What about the ambulance? Anyone called it?'

Isobel pursed her lips. 'Oh, yes, but it's got stuck in the mud and they could do with help anyway, getting it out. It's pouring with rain out there, by the way.'

Atholl had strolled in, also to get a coffee, and raised his eyes to the ceiling when he heard the news. 'Oh, God, poor old Hamish. I bet the man's having a heart attack—he's got a history of angina. I'd better take the Land Rover and get there pronto.' He snatched some biscuits from the plate by the coffee. 'I'll take some of these to distract those bad-tempered dogs of his.' He turned to Terry. 'Fancy having your first taste of rural excitement? If you've got wellies and a mac, put them on and come with me—I may need help.'

Caught up with the potential drama of the situation, Terry rushed out of the room to collect her outdoor clothing, a little buzz of anticipation zipping through her at the thought of working closely with Atholl, and that old familiar rush of nervous adrenaline that a medical drama produced.

The weather had changed yet again and Terry gazed out of the car window at the lashing rain. The trees in the fields bent in the wind, and dark clouds scudded across leaden skies, with the background shapes of black mountains. How snug the inside of the car seemed, cocooned from the weather, and how aware she was of the closeness of Atholl sitting next to her. He peered through the windscreen as the wipers did their best to cope with the deluge. It was like driving underwater.

'Nothing like coping with a heart attack in the middle of a field in the pouring rain,' he commented grimly. 'As I said, Hamish has a history of cardiac trouble and he's a heavy smoker, so it's been a disaster waiting to happen. I've been on at him to retire, but he's a stubborn old fool and won't countenance it. These sheep farmers won't give up easily.'

He swung the vehicle in through the rough track to some farm buildings and a group of men huddled round an ambulance at the far end of the field.

'Here we are,' he said. 'Let's see what we can do for him.'

Atholl grabbed his medical bag and they both leapt out of the car and went as quickly as they could through the muddy field to where the ambulance was. And she'd thought she was coming to a quiet little corner of Britain where nothing much happened, reflected Terry wryly. She was beginning to understand what Atholl had meant when he said she'd probably be dealing with a completely different range of situations from the practice in London!

The elderly man was lying on the ground and two sheepdogs were standing guard by him with a small group of men—farm workers and paramedics—grouped beyond him. The ambulance was heavily bedded into the mud—it looked as if it would need a tractor to pull it out.

'You won't get near Hamish,' said one of the men. 'Those bloody dogs just keep going for us every time we get near him.'

'I know them only too well,' said Atholl grimly.

'They're called Whisky and Brandy, and, believe me, that's what you need when you've dealt with them...but at least they know me. Let's see if we can distract them with these biscuits. Have any of you got belts we can use as leads?'

Two of the men took off belts and Atholl gave the dogs some biscuits to tempt them away from their master, then he edged his way towards the stricken man. Terry swallowed hard, taking in the unpromising situation—a man with an acute myocardial infarction in the middle of a field with rain lashing down, an ambulance stuck up to its axis in thick mud and two mad dogs baring their teeth at them. It couldn't get much more dramatic than this, surely?

'Terry, follow closely behind me and we'll take it slowly towards Hamish. I don't want to upset these dogs more than they already are. Bill, do your best to keep them back from us while I listen to his heart.'

Hamish was lying on his back, his colour a chalky grey as he laboured to take breaths.

'The pain...' he gasped, plucking at the neck of his jumper. 'It...it's crushing me...'

Atholl dropped to his knees beside the stricken man. 'We're here to help you, Hamish,' he said calmly. 'And we'll give you something for the pain.'

Both doctors were doing a quick assessment of the man's situation, noting his pallor and the faint sheen of perspiration on his brow. Terry crouched down and took Hamish's hand in one of hers, putting her other on his forehead and feeling the clamminess of his skin. He had to be reassured and calmed, to feel he was in safe hands even if he could hardly take in what she was saying. The all-consuming pain across his chest would be like steel bars compressing him, impairing his ability to breathe. She bent down close to his ear.

'You'll be OK, Hamish. Don't try and talk.'

Hamish mumbled something, his frightened eyes staring at her, although somewhere in the back of his mind and through the crushing pain was the comforting feeling of Terry's hand holding his. She watched as Atholl pulled up Hamish's shabby jumper to listen to his labouring heart through his stethoscope, and laid two fingers on the side of his neck. Atholl's eyes met hers and he shook his head slightly as he heard the heart giving off the irregular thudding of ventricular fibrillation as the lower chambers of the heart contracted rapidly out of beat.

'Get the oxygen from the ambulance,' he shouted to the paramedics through the heavy rain and the frantic barking of the two dogs trying to get round the men fending them off the patient.

Two men staggered over with an oxygen cylinder, slipping and sliding in the mud, and Terry took the attached mask and placed it over the man's face. She watched Atholl slip the cover from a syringe he'd taken from his bag.

'I'm giving him ten thousand units of heparin split into two doses,' he said. 'I don't want to give it to him all at once and start a massive bleed. We also need some Xylocard. It's in the pack—can you get it into him?'

'Yup,' said Terry. 'Four mils, OK?' She pulled the syringe from the pack, checking it was the right one, then pushed the needle firmly into Hamish's upper arm muscle, giving him the full dose of the local anaesthetic.

'Let's hope that does the trick,' muttered Atholl.

Sounding more confident than she felt, Terry said reassuringly, 'Xylocard's very effective in settling an unstable heart rhythm.'

Although Hamish Stoddard probably didn't realise it at the moment, he was one lucky patient, she thought. Atholl had obviously had great experience with cardiac attacks. She watched his expression as he listened intently to the man's chest after the injection.

'How is it?' she asked, her voice tense.

Atholl closed his eyes to concentrate on the sounds Hamish's heart was making, then after a few seconds he leaned back on his heels and puffed his cheeks out in relief. 'Thank God, it's beginning to get a more normal beat. I think he's settling down now.' He turned round to see what was happening behind him. 'What the hell are we going to do about that ambulance?' he said. 'We've got to get Hamish to hospital pronto—he could still arrest and then we're in deep trouble.'

Terry bit her lip and looked at the men still struggling with the ambulance. 'We've no other option—we'll just have to take him in the Land Rover. If we clear the back, would the stretcher from the ambulance fit in?'

'Could do. Look, I'll go and do that with the lads. You stay with Hamish and monitor him.'

Atholl ran over to the small crowd of men still trying to hold the dogs at bay. They were having a difficult job and suddenly one of the dogs bolted through and tore straight for his stricken master, despite the shouts of the men. Terry sensed that the dog was bearing down on them but she wasn't about to leave Hamish. He needed to see her face and hear her talking to him, someone comforting to hang onto in the sea of pain he must be in.

The dog took no notice of Terry but skidded to a halt

in the mud and licked Hamish's face, then dropped down by his side as if he were guarding him. That's all the animal wanted, thought Terry, to be near the man he loved.

'Leave him here,' she said firmly to a man who had raced over to try and move the dog. 'He's doing no harm, and, who knows, it may be of comfort to Hamish to know that his dog's near him.'

And after that they couldn't get the animal away from Hamish, although he seemed to sense that the people around his master were trying to help him, and didn't actively interfere when Hamish was lifted onto the stretcher and carried to Atholl's Land Rover. He growled ferociously when an attempt was made to shoo him off, but as long as he was allowed to trot by Hamish's side he was quite calm.

'We'll have to let Brandy come with us—the daft animal's not going to let us take Hamish away without him,' said Atholl. He looked up at one of the paramedics. 'Bill, you drive the vehicle and Terry and I will sit by Hamish and try and steady him. More haste, less speed is the byword and, for God's sake, don't go through any potholes.'

Crouched in the back of the Land Rover with a wet dog practically on her lap and the patient and Atholl crushed beside her on the other side was a scenario she couldn't possibly have envisaged when she'd left London a week or two ago, reflected Terry. She held Hamish's hand and squeezed it, trying to communicate to him that he was not alone, there were people caring for him. She smiled grimly to herself. No doubt about it—she'd been thrown in at the deep end!

She looked at Atholl, wet hair plastered like a seal's

over his bent head as he concentrated on monitoring the man's heart, oblivious to everything else but keeping his patient stable. Occasionally he glanced out of the window to see how near the hospital they were, then nodded encouragingly at Terry as she tried her best to hold the stretcher steady over the rougher bits of road.

Hamish's eyes were open now, clouded with pain and fright. He moved his lips behind the oxygen mask, trying desperately to say something to his doctor. Atholl moved the mask slightly and leaned further forward to hear Hamish.

'Get my son to bring the sheep down from the top meadow,' the man whispered.

Atholl patted his hand. 'I will do, Hamish. Don't worry, you're doing fine.'

'Thank you,' whispered the man, closing his eyes, his face looking pinched and grey in the dim light of the vehicle.

After a journey that must have seemed an age to the stricken man, they deposited Hamish at the small hospital outside Scuola village. Atholl had telephoned ahead to warn them of the emergency admission and there was a team waiting to deal with Hamish as they arrived.

Atholl managed to slip a belt through the dog's collar and restrain the animal as his master was transferred to a trolley and pushed at speed to the resuscitation room. Both doctors watched as Hamish was taken away and Brandy whimpered as if aware that it would be some time before he saw Hamish again.

'It's going to be touch and go. Poor old Hamish…he's not out of the woods yet,' said Atholl wearily, bending to stroke the dog.

'You did your best—and at least you got him into sinus rhythm.'

Atholl shook his head and corrected her. 'It was a team effort, Terry. I couldn't have managed without you.'

For a second their eyes locked and a look of relief and triumph flickered between them. They grinned at each other, buoyed up by the adrenaline of success.

Then Atholl said briskly, 'Right, Bill can drive us back to his ambulance and tell Hamish's son to move the sheep. OK, Bill, let's go. I'll hold onto this dog until we've got there. Let's hope they've managed to extricate the ambulance—it's the only one we've got on the island.'

The two of them sat slumped in the steamy back of the vehicle, both feeling the sudden exhaustion that came with the anticlimax of dealing with a dramatic situation. The dog was lying across the edge of the seat, finally quiet as if he too was tired out.

Atholl's gazed drifted over to Terry, lying back with her eyes closed, her lashes sweeping her high cheekbones, wet hair plastered to her head and her mouth slightly open. He smiled to himself. She was as tough as any man—she'd just proved it!

CHAPTER FIVE

THE Land Rover bucked its way along the narrow twisting country road. Now that the patient had been delivered to the hospital, Bill seemed intent on getting back to the farm as quickly as possible, however rough the road was! Stretching his long legs out in front of him, Atholl massaged his shoulders to ease the tension of bending over Hamish for a prolonged time.

'God, that was touch and go,' he remarked. 'If we've saved him, it's been a great day's work.'

'Oh, I do hope so.' Terry brushed wet strands of hair out of her eyes and, despite the adrenaline that had been coursing round her body a few minutes ago, gave a huge yawn and leaned tiredly against the door. She felt depressed despite the fact that they'd helped to save a man's life. She was having one of those black moments when, out of the blue, something would trigger those ghastly memories. In her mind's eye she'd see a vivid picture of her father again, her last vision of him lying in her arms, his lips blue and his breath fading from his body.

The fact was that dealing with Hamish Stoddard had reminded her strongly of her father. He was the same age and the same build as her father had been, with similar thick white hair, and suddenly she felt very alone and far from anyone who cared for her.

She sighed, swallowing a lump in her throat and blinking back tears of self-pity, allowing her body to be jolted as Bill kept his foot on the accelerator as they rounded corners.

Atholl flicked a glance at her sad expression—the look that came over her from time to time. Losing her father had obviously been a terrible blow, but instinctively he felt there was something more to the story that she'd told him, something unresolved in her past, and he hated to see the heartbreak reflected in her eyes and drooping mouth.

'You all right?' he asked. 'Here, lean against me—not on that hard door. You'll be shaken to death. I may be a bit damp, but at least I'm not made of metal!'

He put an arm round Terry to pull her towards him and for a moment she hesitated, as if not quite sure about the offer, looking doubtfully up at his mud-streaked face and the rivulets of water that ran down from his soaked hair and onto his damp jersey that smelt of wet wool. Then the car accelerated over another pothole, jolting her sharply against the door again, and she smiled at him.

'Thanks. It is a bit uncomfortable here.'

She lay back against him, rather self-consciously at first but gradually succumbing to the broad comfort of his chest, and in the small steamy confines of the back of the Land Rover, where it was warm and intimate, the outside world began to recede. Terry forgot about Bill driving the vehicle, or the dog panting by Atholl's side, even the aching sadness of missing her father. All she was aware of was just how close Atholl was to her. She relaxed gratefully against his broad frame with the comforting damp warmth and rough feel of his thick jersey around her, his breath on her cheek.

Did he feel the gradual heightening of the atmosphere too, Terry wondered, or was it just her over-active sensitivity when she was feeling rather down and leaning against a man who oozed sex appeal? She closed her eyes, savouring the comfort of his arm supporting her, feeling her sadness slip away. When she opened them again he was looking down at her intently, then the blue of his eyes darkened and he tightened his grip round her, twisting his body so that she was pulled against his chest.

'You looked rather miserable a minute ago,' he said huskily. 'Is anything wrong?'

To Terry's embarrassment two large tears rolled down her cheeks and she gave an involuntary sob. That was what happened when people were kind to you and you felt very low—your defences came down and your emotions got the better of you. She gulped and swallowed back the large lump that had settled in her throat.

'Sorry, it's nothing really. I don't know what came over me. It was just that I was reminded of something…'

'Yes?' he said gently, bending his head nearer hers so that he could hear her above the noise of the Land Rover. 'Tell me, Terry, what's troubling you?'

She shook her head mutely. Her background had to remain a secret and, however kind Atholl's enquiry, the baggage from her past life was a closed door as far as he—or anyone else—was concerned. It was unlikely that she could ever reveal the whole reason for her flight to Scotland.

'I miss my father very much,' she said at last. 'It comes over me in waves—but I'll be all right. I'm being silly.' She gave a watery smile and brushed the tears roughly away from her eyes.

'You must also be missing your friends and London—your social life,' he suggested.

She pulled away from him abruptly. 'I'll get over it,' she said sharply. 'I've left all that behind.'

Atholl looked quizzically at her. Just what had she left behind? She seemed unwilling to expand on any aspect of her life in London. He stroked away a stray tear on her cheek with his finger and turned her head towards him.

'No pangs, then, for the bright lights?'

The look in his warm blue eyes was compassionate, as if he knew what she was going through, and again she felt those treacherous tears well up in her eyes. Angrily she tried to blink them back. What a mawkish idiot she was being. Atholl squeezed her to him comfortingly, then after a second's pause lowered his head to hers and brushed her forehead with his lips, a feather-light kiss that sent a scorching flood of heat through her body. It was so brief a touch that at first she wondered if he'd actually kissed her. She looked up at him questioningly and then it seemed only natural for her arms to wind round his neck, bringing him nearer, and he kissed her again, this time full on her lips, and his firm mouth felt sweet, salty and demanding.

Oh, how she'd needed this sort of closeness and comfort again, to feel that someone cared for her, was even interested in her… Giddily she wondered at the back of her mind if wasn't rather dangerous to be kissing a colleague like this when she wasn't interested in men—especially a man she hardly knew. Everything seemed to be happening so quickly. A thousand butterflies were fluttering inside her and her heart was doing a mad tattoo against her ribs. Why, only a few months ago she had thought she was madly in love with Max, and only he could ever light her fire. How odd that suddenly every nerve in her body was tingling with anticipation and longing to do more than just kiss a man who was practically a stranger!

As his warm lips sought her cool ones, her lively imagination leapt further ahead. What would it be like to make love to him properly? To feel his hands caressing her, to lose herself in everything but the delight of his touch?

Then all of a sudden she felt Atholl pulling away from her and gently disengaging her arms from around him. Embarrassment made her cheeks redden, and she tried not to look too startled.

He shook his head with a wry smile and said in a joking manner, 'I'm sorry about that…a bit of an overreaction after a tough afternoon. I just hated to see you upset and, well, I…I just wanted to thank you for your help, show you how grateful I am. I didn't mean to overstep the mark!' He grinned at her. 'But we worked so well together, didn't we? It's great to know that we have a good working relationship.'

A good working relationship? It had seemed to Terry for a moment there that it had gone way beyond a 'working relationship', but she'd obviously misinterpreted it—he was making it very clear that that was what he wanted. It had been nothing more than an over-enthusiastic hug to comfort her.

'It was just part of my job—as you said, a team effort,' she said lightly, and chuckled as if being kissed by the most stunning-looking man she'd been near for some time was just a normal occurrence, the usual way one thanked a colleague and of no consequence whatsoever.

But inwardly she felt the acute embarrassment of taking far too much for granted, and it left her slightly deflated. It had obviously been just an honest and kindly gesture on his part to comfort someone who had started blubbing without apparent reason, and she had read more into the situation than Atholl had meant.

She drew back shakily from the warmth of his body. His mouth had felt so sweet on hers, so right, so comforting, and she had responded far too passionately to the light kisses he'd given her. He probably assumed, she thought gloomily, that she wasn't averse to a casual encounter, an easy bit of sex on the side.

She smiled brightly and said briskly, 'So, when we've deposited Bill, it's back to the surgery?'

'Afraid so. It's the mother-and-baby clinic this afternoon—do you think you could take that with Sue? I've got a meeting with that wretched man from the health authority.' Atholl's voice was casual, relaxed, as if kissing her hadn't raised his heartbeat at all. And as if to emphasise that, he shouted out over the noise of the engine to Bill, 'Could you tell Hamish's son about the sheep Bill? Terry and I have to get back.'

Terry had almost forgotten about Bill driving the vehicle, and looked at him with some embarrassment. Had he seen Atholl and her locked in a close embrace in the back? It wouldn't appear so as he and Atholl started up a mundane conversation about the weather and the difficulty of ever getting the ambulance out of the mud, without a hint of self-consciousness. Indeed, Atholl seemed to have forgotten all about her, bending his head to look at the dog and stroking him gently.

Atholl tried to breathe deeply and slowly, endeavouring to calm himself. Why the hell had he just kissed Terry like that—given in to the powerful attraction he suddenly admitted he'd felt ever since he'd first seen her on the quayside less than two weeks ago? She'd looked so uncomfortable and rather vulnerable, sitting squashed in the back of the Land Rover with him, and that was why he'd invited her to lean against him. But once he'd felt that soft body next to his some madness had overcome him and he'd felt an irresistible urge to kiss her, try and comfort her. If he wasn't careful he'd be in too deep with a woman he knew next to nothing about, and who, for all he knew, could cause him as much aggravation as Zara Grahame had.

For a second an image of his forthright mother came into his mind—he could almost hear her scornful words. 'Atholl Brodie, you never learn, do you? I told you to keep away from those high-falutin' girls who've been brought up in gilded cages. You want to stick to your own sort—a girl from your own background and area. You're a fool to try and fit in where you don't belong!'

He flicked a look at Terry. She was looking out of the window, her delectable profile turned slightly away from him, tip-tilted nose, lips slightly parted, and he groaned inwardly. They had had very different upbringings. He guessed from her speech and manner that she had a background of wealth and privilege, but the truth was that now he knew how it felt to kiss Terry, he couldn't wait to do it again—and plunge his life into turmoil once more, he thought savagely to himself.

A day or two later Atholl came into Terry's room to remind her that they were doing a home visit to the Mackie sisters who lived in one of the cottages perched high on the hillside on one of the remote estates on the island.

'It's a good opportunity to show you a bit of the island so that you have some idea of the layout when you come to do your own home visits,' he said.

There was something about his brisk, businesslike manner, with no hint of intimacy, that gave Terry the impression that he wanted to maintain a distance between them after the episode in the Land Rover. He'd also made a point of staying out of the house until she was in bed. And that was absolutely for the best, she thought resolutely, picking up her medical bag and slinging a coat round her shoulders.

Yet again the weather had changed and now the skies were turning blue and the sun was warm on their faces as they got into the car. Shona was sitting in the back, her ears pricked excitedly for the outing, wagging her tail in anticipation of a long walk. But the easy camaraderie of the other day seemed to have vanished and silence hung heavily between them on the journey. Terry very aware that Atholl felt they had become too intimate that day. She tried hard to dredge up some small talk to lighten the atmosphere as they arrived at the sisters' home—one half of a pair of cottages with a pretty little garden to the side and back.

'It's like Hansel and Gretel's cottage,' she remarked brightly. 'A sweet little place.'

'It's part of the Dunsford Estate,' explained Atholl, seeming to relax a little. 'Kate and Sarah's father was the old laird's gamekeeper, or "stalker" as he liked to be called. When he died they continued living here and helping at the big house, cooking and cleaning. Now they're both in their eighties and very independent—it'll be hard to get them to accept help.'

He knocked at the door and they waited for a few moments. He knocked again but there was still no reply, so he tried to turn the doorhandle, but it was locked.

'Funny,' he muttered. 'They aren't very mobile, but they usually sit in the room just behind this door. I would've expected them to answer it more quickly than this—and I've never known them lock the door.' He tried to peer through the lace curtains of the small window by the door, then gave an impatient exclamation. 'I'll go round the back and look in through the windows—you wait here in case they do answer the door.'

Just then a quavery voice sounded behind them. 'Hello, Doctor! We didn't think you'd be here so quickly! We've just been scrubbing up a few early potatoes!'

Two frail figures were making their way towards Atholl and Terry from the garden path that led from a small vegetable patch, both dressed in similar dark coats with felt hats on their heads. One of the old ladies was coughing and wheezing and the other one supported her.

'That's quite a heavy bag you've got there, Kate,' said Atholl, striding forward, taking the potatoes from her and putting one hand under the arm of her sister. 'Have you got the key of the house ready?'

'Aye—it's somewhere in my pocket.' Kate fumbled for it then handed it to Atholl. 'We don't normally lock the door, as you know...but something bad has happened, hasn't it, Sarah?'

The other sister looked up at both the doctors and they noticed she was trembling. 'We've been burgled, Doctor,' she quavered. 'We were down the garden after Sue, your community nurse, had left this morning. When we came back there was a terrible mess…' She stopped and looked helplessly at Kate. 'I…I don't like to think about it…'

It was obvious they'd both had a terrible shock. Atholl looked grim. 'Come in now, Kate, and, Sarah—sit you down, both of you. We'll put the kettle on and you must tell us what happened over a cup of tea.'

His voice was kind and compassionate, but Terry could see the steely anger behind his words. How could anyone steal from these two vulnerable little women who had worked hard all their lives? They all went into the house and the two doctors stared in silent dismay at the overturned chairs, the contents of a small desk thrown over the floor, a cup and saucer that had been knocked off a table and lay smashed on the tiled fireplace.

'We…we couldn't bear to sit in the house,' said Kate. 'That's why we were in the garden.'

'I'm ringing the police,' declared Atholl. 'I want them to come and see this before we tidy it up—there may be fingerprints. But first I want you both to sit on the sofa…'

'And I'll get some nice hot tea,' suggested Terry.

'Ah, I'd better introduce you,' said Atholl, drawing Terry forward. 'This is my new colleague in the practice, Dr Terry Younger. I thought it would be nice if you could meet her and she meet you—I'm sorry it wasn't in happier circumstances.'

Both old ladies smiled tremulously at her. 'It's nice to meet you, Doctor,' quavered Kate. 'It'll be nice for Dr Atholl to have some help, won't it, Sarah, while old Dr Euan recovers?'

While Atholl rang the police on his mobile, Terry served the shocked sisters with sweet tea which they sipped gratefully, the warm liquid and the mere fact of being looked after, helping them to relax.

'Do you know what's been taken?' she asked gently.

'Just a few wee bits of jewellery that belonged to our mother—we don't think it's worth much.' Kate dabbed her eyes and sighed. 'Of course, it meant a lot to us.' Then her expression changed and she drew herself up to her full small height on the sofa and looked belligerently up at Terry. 'If they catch whoever did this I'll give them a piece of my mind—that I will!'

Terry smiled at the feisty little woman. It was good that she was feeling angry and not too broken by the nasty episode. The more she and her sister could talk about it, the better they would feel, and if not come to terms with the situation at least learn to live with it.

'That's right, Kate, you must feel absolutely furious about all of this, but when the police have come we'll tidy it up and make sure everything's secure.'

Atholl came back into the room—his tall figure in the small space seemed a reassuring presence in the wreckage of their little parlour. Something about his stature and calm manner made things seem more normal, safer, despite the abnormality of the situation. The old ladies looked up at him hopefully, as if he could put their broken world back in order.

'The police are on their way now,' he informed them. He sat down by the old ladies and took Sarah's hand. She seemed the more shocked of the two, gazing sadly ahead of her. 'Now, Sarah, don't worry, we'll get to the bottom of this.'

Sarah focussed on him and said in a bewildered way. 'I don't know who could have done it—there's no one around here who would dream of it. Our next-door neighbours and the farmers nearby are friends that we've known for many years and no one else comes up here.'

It was a good point. They were in a remote part of the island and only locals would know that two vulnerable old ladies lived in the cottage. Apart from a few walkers, nobody generally strayed this far up the hill.

She plucked nervously at her collar. 'I…I don't feel safe here any more. Suppose they come back?'

Atholl patted her hand. 'Now, I've had a good idea—how would you like Shona to stay with you for a few nights? She wouldn't let anyone harm you, and perhaps you'd feel safer if she was around?'

For the first time Sarah looked a little brighter. 'Would Shona not mind coming here?'

Atholl laughed. 'She'd love it—doesn't she always get biscuits here which I never allow her at home? She's in the car now—I'll bring her in and she can have tea with us!'

It was obvious that Shona acted as a huge tonic to Kate and Sarah, for they became quite animated and insisted on going into the little kitchen and bringing out a whole box of biscuits.

'Shona was actually born in this cottage,' Atholl explained quietly to Terry as Shona bounded in, wagging her tail delightedly at the prospect of being spoilt, going over to the old ladies and pushing her nose onto their laps. 'She was one of a litter that Kate and Sarah's old dog had four years ago. Sadly Polly died not long after that, but Shona looks remarkably like her.'

'It's a wonderful idea.' Terry smiled. 'They've really cheered up and it's given them something else to think about.'

Both doctors watched in amusement as the sisters fussed over Shona and found Polly's old basket for her to sleep in. But Terry noted how badly the old ladies walked and the difficulty they had getting up from their chairs.

'They look very unsteady,' she murmured to Atholl. 'What are the chances of them slipping in the bathroom—or anywhere else, for that matter?'

Atholl nodded, and while they waited for the police to arrive he broached the subject gently of someone coming in daily to give them a hand. They both shook their heads vehemently, protesting that they could look after each other.

'We don't need or want anyone fussing over us every day—we're fine as we are,' said Kate stoutly.

'Why don't you at least consider wearing an alarm disc round your neck?' suggested Terry. 'You are very isolated here and if you're in trouble of any kind—from falling to being worried about prowlers—you press the disc and that goes through to a central monitoring system that will send help if they can't get hold of you over the monitor in the house.'

'Ah, but we could easily press it by mistake, and we'd be very embarrassed,' protested Kate.

'No problem. You just tell the person who contacts you a few moments after the disc has been pressed that it was done in error, and no one will come. Several of my patients in London had it, and on at least two occasions it saved their lives. No one disturbs you unless you need help.'

Both sisters looked at each other questioningly, seeking the other's approval before agreeing to anything.

'It really would be a good idea, you know,' persuaded Atholl gently. 'It would stop all of us worrying—and, of course, Sue would still come and see you on a regular basis to check your general health.'

'Well, perhaps,' said Sarah slowly. 'Now we've had this nasty business it could be reassuring to know that we can call on someone easily—if we weren't near the phone and we needed help urgently, that is. Would you be able to organise that?'

'Of course,' said Atholl, shooting a relieved glance at Terry. 'I think it would be a wise move.'

After the police had been and gone, Atholl and Terry quickly put the scattered things back into place. Kate showed them an old photograph she had of her mother wearing a piece of the jewellery that had been stolen—a pretty little Victorian necklace.

'I don't suppose we'll ever see it again—but at least we're both OK, and that's all that matters,' she said. 'And we'd like to thank you doctors for all your help, wouldn't we, Sarah?'

'No trouble at all,' said Atholl. 'Now, I'll go and get Shona's lead from the car, and an old bone she likes to play with.'

He went out and Sarah put a restraining hand on Terry's arm, holding her back for a second. 'It's good to see young Dr Atholl has some reliable help now—he's been through such a bad time with that Dr Grahame.' She put a hand to her mouth guiltily. 'Oh, dear, perhaps I shouldn't be saying that—but maybe you'll be just the girl to cheer him up!' Her eyes twinkled and she turned to her sister. 'He needs a bit of fun in his life, doesn't he, Kate?'

Kate nodded gravely. 'Aye, he's a good man who's had a rough time. We'd all love to see him settled happily. We've known him since he was a little boy and used to come for the holidays with his uncle.'

'I suppose he feels almost like one of your family,' remarked Terry, longing to know just what the story was about this Dr Grahame and how she'd affected Atholl's life so much. To ask him outright would seem too intrusive, she reflected, but surely she could find out from Bunty? She determined to do that when the moment seemed right.

'It's a very odd thing about that burglary,' Atholl said as they drove back to The Sycamores. 'There really aren't many people walking or even living near the Mackie sisters. A few campers in the middle of summer perhaps, but I know there's no one at the site at the moment.' His jaw tightened. 'I just hope they pick up whoever's burgled those old ladies.'

'They're very fond of you,' said Terry. 'They said they'd known you for many years.'

'That's true—I remember them plying me with sweeties when I went with my uncle on a visit sometimes. In a place like this there's often a long-standing relationship with your GP.'

They were back at The Sycamores and Terry got out of the car. 'I'll see you tomorrow, then. I know you're off to see your uncle again now and I'll be in bed by the time you get back. I hope he's doing well.'

He smiled at her and said quietly, 'Thanks...and thank you again for your help today.'

There was sudden self-consciousness between them, as if they had both remembered at the same second that intimate interlude a day or two ago in the back of the Land Rover. Their eyes locked and in Terry's mind she felt again the soft touch of his lips on hers, the thudding of his heart when she'd leant against him, the scratch of late-day stubble on his chin. It might have meant nothing to him, she thought wryly as she ran up the steps of the surgery, but it had been a moment of bliss that she wouldn't forget in a hurry.

She bit her lip and looked back at him for a second before she opened the surgery door. How stupid she was being—surely the last few months had taught her that men were not to be trusted. Max had destroyed her happy life, and it would surely never be the same again.

Atholl watched as she disappeared, looking deliciously feminine in her neat skirt and pale blue silk blouse. She probably thought he'd been a chancy character trying it on with her the other day, although she'd been decent enough to make light of it. He sighed. The moment that he'd kissed her should never have happened, but a sudden impulse that had driven him on to throw caution to the winds—and now he couldn't stop thinking about her.

Atholl revved up the engine, turning the car round in a tight circle in the drive, and started out towards the ferry, trying to make sense of his mixed emotions. He parked the car in the car park, and sat for a minute staring out at the sparkling sea. For some time now he'd been treading on eggshells where women had been concerned—he'd been bruised and humiliated by one woman and he was damned if he was going to take the chance of any other female doing the same to him.

An image of Terry's sweet face came into his mind and he sighed. She had lit more than a little spark of attraction in him—but she was essentially a city girl like Zara and she was only going to be here for a short time. No good thinking they could form any permanent relationship—it would just be a rerun of the scenario with Zara.

He got out of the car and looked towards the little ferry

sailing across the sound and shrugged. He would look forward to spending a whole day with Terry when they went to help at the outward bound course. She would be a pleasant companion and it would be fun to show her the beautiful countryside, without getting too involved. And perhaps he'd find out more about this beautiful woman with the background she kept so close to her chest.

CHAPTER SIX

THE Sunday they were scheduled to go to the outward bound centre dawned bright and clear. Atholl banged loudly on Terry's bedroom door.

'Time to get up,' he called. He got a muffled grunt in response, so he banged again. 'Come on, Terry, no time to lose!'

Still no response, so he opened the door and peered round. 'Wake up!' he bellowed. 'The weather forecast's good for this morning but dicey later on, so we need to get a move on or the abseiling might be off.'

Terry stirred slightly then relaxed again, lying curled up on her side with one hand supporting her head, long lashes sweeping the curve of her flushed cheek. There was something so vulnerable about her, her lips slightly parted as if just waiting to be kissed. Atholl felt a moment's shame as he looked at her. He shouldn't be here in this room without her knowledge—it was as if he were taking advantage of her somehow—but he did have to wake her, didn't he? He was holding a mug of tea in one hand and with the other he reached down and tickled her nose.

She stirred again and brushed his hand away. She'd

just been enjoying a wonderful dream where she and Atholl had been swimming in one of the little coves on the island. The sea was rather rough and the waves kept tossing her into his arms as they were swept towards the shore. His body was wet and slippery against hers and he held her tight to him so that she wouldn't be submerged by the next wave. She could feel every muscle in his taut body, his legs firm against hers, bracing her against the swell of the sea. He was laughing down at her, white teeth in a tanned face…then suddenly a little feather landed on her nose and started to tickle it. Impatiently she tried to brush it away, longing to get to the next stage of her dream, but it continued to irritate her.

She opened her eyes in exasperation and sat up suddenly in bed, looking slightly bewildered when Atholl's familiar face only a foot away from her swam into view. She clutched the sheets against her when she realised that she was no longer dreaming but the subject of her dream was looking down at her!

'What the…? What's happened? What are you doing here?'

Atholl's gaze took in her flushed cheeks, dishevelled hair and a flash of soft creamy breasts as she tried to maintain her modesty, and felt his heartbeat accelerate as if a button had been pressed. What wouldn't he give to tear off his clothes and leap into the warm bed with her and to hell with going over for the day with the outward bound group! He was beginning to realise that having Terry living in the same house as him could be one big temptation.

'Wake up, sleepyhead,' he said huskily. 'Sorry to disturb you, but we ought to get going if we're to get to the outward bound group before they set off.'

Terry's eyes widened. 'Oh, I'd forgotten all about that. I was so exhausted after the past few days…'

He grinned. 'Exhausted? It's just a normal everyday story of country doctors, reviving someone with a heart attack in a rainstorm, helping two old ladies who'd been burgled….'

She laughed. 'So I'm beginning to realise! But I'd been dreaming, you see.'

'Not a nightmare, I hope?'

A warm flush suffused Terry's cheeks as she recalled just what the subject of her dream had been. 'No,' she murmured. 'Definitely not a nightmare.'

He stood looking at her with twinkling eyes as if he could read her mind and was amused by it. She waited for a moment, slightly embarrassed, expecting him to leave.

'I'll be down soon,' she hinted. 'It won't take me long.'

'Sorry—didn't mean to intrude. I thought you'd like a cup of tea, or rather a mug,' he added with a grin. 'I don't do cups!'

He held out a mug and she leant forward to take it, but in trying not to let the sheet fall down and expose the skimpy baby doll she wore in bed, she fumbled it and the mug clattered to the floor, spilling the tea over the sheets.

'Oh, no! What am I like?'

She bent over the bed to retrieve the mug at the same time as Atholl bent down to pick it up. Their heads almost collided and they both froze in mid-action, their faces inches apart.

'Sorry!' they exclaimed in unison, then stopped and gazed at each other, a crackle of attraction between them springing into life like a current between magnets.

How close they were. Terry could see the black flecks

in his blue sexy eyes, the black lashes fringing them, and smell the just-washed soapy clean, male smell of him. It was almost as if her dream was continuing. All her senses screamed out to lean towards him and feel once more those firm sexy lips on hers, his hand caressing her body. Somewhere in the back of her mind a hundred warning thoughts whirred round. Was she going to embarrass them both as she had done last time? He'd no doubt think she was up for sex at any opportunity! Even more to the point, once they'd started kissing in such a setting as this bedroom, for God's sake, where would it end?

'There's still some tea left in the mug,' Atholl said gruffly. 'Why don't you drink it now?'

Terry pushed herself back properly into the bed and pulled the sheet up to her chin. 'Er…I'll have it in a minute, thank you,' she said breathlessly, aware that he was looking down at her, an unreadable expression in his blue eyes.

He put the mug on the bedside table carefully and sat down on the bed, taking out a handkerchief to mop up some of the spilt liquid on the sheets and over her arms.

'The tea didn't scald you, did it?' he asked.

'No…not at all.'

Terry's voice came out in a husky little croak, her pulse speeding up slightly at his proximity and the thought that if she wanted to she could throw off her sheet and pull him alongside her with no trouble at all! She couldn't help but give a nervous giggle at the thought, turning it unsuccessfully into a cough.

He smiled at her. 'Right. Well, I'd better go and get breakfast started,' he said, not moving, his gaze travelling slowly over her face.

Terry licked her lips nervously, aware of his close proximity to her, half hoping he'd move and yet longing for him not to.

'You…you've still got quite a scar from the accident,' she said at last, to break the tension between them. Her hand went out to touch the cut he'd sustained on his chin trying to get Maisie out of the car on the day Terry had arrived.

'And you've got a piece of hair across your eye,' he murmured, leaning over her and removing a wisp of hair from her forehead. His hand stayed on her cheek for a moment, then strayed across to her ear before he took it back. She froze for a second, a mixture of excited anticipation and apprehension flickering through her body.

'Funny how long we seem to have known each other,' he murmured.

Terry's voice caught in her throat. 'Only a few weeks actually…'

He smiled. 'True, but I want to know more about you. Was losing your father the only thing that brought you to Scuola? You've only given me sketchy details…'

His piercing blue eyes looked intently into hers as if he could decipher just what had happened to make her leave London. He watched her eyes slide away from his and he was sure that she was withholding something. Suddenly he was determined to find out more, to crack the mysterious code that was Terry's past.

She answered pugnaciously, 'I told you before—I wanted a change. My father's death precipitated that. I don't need to elaborate. Anyway, is it relevant to our situation?'

Terry turned her face away from that searching look, determined not to divulge any more, but he took her chin in his hand and gently turned it back so that she had to face him.

'I've got to know what makes you tick,' he said gently. 'Don't you see that if we're to work well together we have to be friends? Friends usually know each other's backgrounds, don't they? I'm making a shrewd guess here, Terry. I've a feeling that it was a broken love affair that first made you think of leaving London, before your father died.'

He watched the stricken look in her eyes and felt he'd hit on something like the truth. Terry was silent. She couldn't tell him everything, but she felt that perhaps he did deserve to know a little about her background.

'That was part of it,' she admitted at last. 'The truth is, I fell for my ex, Max, because I thought he was everything I wanted—charming, charismatic, good fun, good looks…' She gave a mirthless laugh. 'And he could give a girl a good time!'

'Sounds as if he ticked a lot of boxes,' remarked Atholl drily, his clear eyes never leaving her.

'Oh, yes, on the surface it looked good.' A bitter tone entered her voice. 'Underneath he was a devious and selfish opportunist, and he did things that had, well, wide-ranging consequences. It taught me the lesson never to let my heart rule my head. That's basically it, Atholl. It was enough to make me want to leave the area.'

There was no need for her to go into any more details. The rest of her story was one she couldn't divulge—that had to remain a secret. Then, as if pushing that thought to the back of her mind, she said lightly, 'Let's stop talking about me—what about you? What happened between you and my attractive predecessor, Dr Grahame, I keep hearing about?'

A startled expression crossed Atholl's face, as if he hadn't anticipated Terry asking him such a blunt question. He stood up and walked over to the window, looking out at the fields beyond and bunching his fists tensely in his pockets, before turning back to her with a wry grin.

'Tit for tat, eh? It seems we've had similar experiences—although in my case much of the blame was mine. But it's a long story, rather boring really.'

Boring? Not to Terry, fascinated and intrigued to know more about the background of this sexy, good-looking man.

'Please go on,' she said. 'I…I'd be really interested to know what happened.'

He shrugged. 'To put it briefly, Zara was a liar—she strung me along. She deceived me, and deception is an act of betrayal in my eyes.' His eyes became flint hard. 'And God help anyone who tries to deceive me again.'

Terry felt a shiver of worry go through her. How would he react if he knew that she wasn't the person he thought she was? That she was a sham, someone built on a tissue of lies, a woman whose background had had to be obliterated?

'Wh-what did she lie about?'

He gave a mirthless laugh. 'I don't think you'd believe me if I told you. I was so incredibly naive—idiotic actually.'

Terry sat up, hugging her arms around her. 'Why shouldn't I believe you? Come on—tell me what she did.'

Atholl sighed and suddenly looked a little older and tireder. 'We met at medical school. She was very attractive, one of those girls who seemed to have everything—good looks, good fun, full of confidence.'

Terry felt a sudden surge of jealousy over this paragon of attraction. 'You fell for each other, then?'

'I should've known better. She and I came from completely different backgrounds. Her family were wealthy, rubbed shoulders with privileged people. I was from the Glasgow Gorbals and that was a very different world.'

'But you were just as good as she was—why should that make any difference?'

'Because we saw things differently. I was used to scraping together every penny I could—Zara didn't have those worries. But then when we started working as junior doctors there wasn't much time to spend money anyway, and the differences between us weren't so noticeable.'

'And so…what happened then?'

Atholl sat on the windowsill, leaning back against the window, a remote expression on his face. 'We became engaged.'

'So you loved her,' stated Terry rather flatly. Somehow it seemed that there was a lot hanging on this question.

There was a short silence and Terry watched his face turn to one of bitterness. 'I thought I did,' he said at last. 'She was attractive, the centre of attention. I suppose I was flattered when she made it plain she fancied me.'

'And were you happy?'

He shrugged. 'Life was fun when we could manage time off together. Zara loved nightclubs, partying, shopping…it was a hectic social whirl and I didn't realise that actually deep down I didn't terribly like doing those things. But she was a city girl through and through. I know now that we were totally incompatible.'

'But you had come from a city too,' pointed out Terry. 'Surely there must have been some understanding between you?'

He nodded. 'Possibly—but then my uncle began having

health problems and offered me a job on Scuola, a place I loved from coming here as a child. It was going to be a temporary arrangement so Zara was happy to come here and join the practice for a while. But Uncle Euan decided to cut back on his hours even more and it became plain that he would never come back full time.'

'So you wanted to stay and Zara didn't?' suggested Terry.

'She began to hate it here. We'd set a date for the wedding—just a small affair, although, of course, it was of great interest to everyone on Scuola—local GP in love match sort of thing,' he said drily. 'Zara was quite pleased to be married here in the pretty little church down the road. A television company was doing a film about the area and our wedding was going to be featured in it—that appealed to her.'

'So…so you got married then?'

Atholl shook his head and his voice was unemotional, detached. 'Two days before the wedding I came back to the flat we were sharing rather earlier than usual. I found Zara in bed with one of her brother's friends—a guest at the wedding.'

Terry stared at him in horror. 'You found her…just before the wedding day?'

'Thank God it wasn't after the wedding,' Atholl remarked lightly. 'She made a fool of me, deceived me, and it hurt. I won't pretend it didn't, even if I'd realised deep down that we weren't meant for each other. I won't make that mistake again.'

Terry was silent for a moment, then she said softly, 'Wow, what an awful story, Atholl. I reckon you had a lucky escape, then.'

No wonder Atholl was so happy to be single! She looked at his dark, sexy eyes and the hard-boned structure of his good-looking face. It was no surprise that Isobel was nervous that he was prey to any female who joined the practice—she didn't want him to run the risk of being hurt again.

Terry looked away, a little chill of worry flickering through her mind. What he would say if he knew her whole story? Then she reasoned that she hadn't deceived him all that much about herself—just a few little white lies. And at least she'd told him about Max—or at least some of the story about Max.

'So now we have no secrets between us,' said Atholl with a grin. 'We're open books to each other!'

'You only know a little about me,' she parried nervously.

He laughed. 'Don't be so mysterious. I know enough about you to see how uncomplicated you are. You're a great doctor, I like and trust you,' he said with emphasis. 'And something else,' he murmured slowly, touching her face and looking down at her intently, 'You're very, very...'

Then an unreadable expression crossed his face and he checked himself, his voice trailing away as if he was about to say too much, reveal more of his thoughts than he should. He stood up abruptly, shooting a look at his watch.

'Hell—it's nine o'clock!' he exclaimed, raking a hand through his hair and striding to the door. 'I forgot our date with Pete and the boys at The Culleens. Let's get going!'

Terry stared after him as he thundered down the little stairs, and sighed, a mixture of thoughts racing through her mind. She'd been certain for a second that Atholl had been going to say something rather complimentary to her then—but it was clear that after his experience he was loath to speak those thoughts aloud. At least he'd said he liked her, even if Zara Grahame had made him as wary of commitment as putting his hand in a fire.

The little party of people strode away from The Culleens towards the outcrop of rocks at the base of the hills, leaving behind the loch and a buzzard lazily circling above it. The sun was shining brightly and it was quite warm. All around them was the low murmur of bees and somewhere high above a lark was singing its heart out over the sweep of moorland before them.

Terry glanced across at Atholl, his rangy figure dressed in old shorts revealing strong muscular legs, his powerful body carrying a huge rucksack as if it were no more than a bag of cotton wool. A mixture of happiness and apprehension flickered through her. This was the guy who'd made it fairly clear only an hour ago that he thought quite well of her—but he'd also made it clear that he regarded anything less than the truth as an act of betrayal. How would he react if he ever learned that she was not the person she claimed to be?

She shifted her rucksack to a more comfortable position on her back and shook herself mentally, forcing her worries to the back of her mind. Whatever happened, today she was going to live for the moment and enjoy this lovely day as much as she could!

She, Atholl and Pete walked briskly together behind the four strapping young men.

'This is all so beautiful,' she breathed. 'I can hardly believe it's real!'

Atholl turned his face and winked at her, then held her eyes in his for a second too long for comfort. 'It's certainly a place of natural beauty—don't you agree, Pete?' he said teasingly.

Terry made a face back at him then quickly changed the subject, saying brightly, 'Is Sally OK? It's only a week or so to go now before the baby comes, isn't it?'

Pete patted his mobile. 'She promised she'd let me know when she feels the first twinge—in fact, she's gone into Scuola village today to see a friend, so I do feel a little more relaxed about things. At least she's near the hospital and I can concentrate on the boys here.'

'Did you tackle Zac about taking cannabis?' asked Atholl.

An expression of exasperation passed Pete's face. 'Yup, he did actually admit to having a few spliffs, almost as if he wanted to see how far he could go. Sally and I were mortified that he'd managed to hide the stuff and I threw the book at him. One more strike and he's out.'

'And how did he take that?'

'He looked relieved, as if he'd expected to be sent back to Glasgow. He promised he'd tread the straight and narrow.' Pete smiled wryly. 'I just hope he can stick to it.'

Atholl turned to Terry. 'He's the one with the most troubled background. He has a disabled mother who was virtually abandoned by Zac's father, although the man keeps coming back and abusing them both when he wants a roof over his head. But I know Zac does like it here—enough to make him try and keep clean.'

'What about the others?' enquired Terry. 'They've settled OK?'

'Oh, sure,' said Pete. 'They've even become part of the community in a small way. They were all helping to dig and tidy up some of the older people's gardens the other day!'

Pete stopped walking and pointed to a high outcrop of rock on the other side of the river running beside them.

'Here we are. We can go over the bridge here and walk up the hill to the side of the rock to the top and then do some abseiling before we have lunch.'

Terry swallowed and looked up at the steep drop. It looked horribly high and suddenly she didn't seem quite as hungry as she had been earlier! She felt Atholl's amused, perceptive eyes on her and stuck her chin out in determination. She wasn't going to give anyone the chance to say she'd wimped out!

'I can't wait.' She smiled.

From the top it looked even more of a sheer drop. The sheep grazing on the moors below seemed like toys. Atholl put on a helmet and began to buckle on his harness and Pete clipped the safety rope to it before Atholl began to descend.

Terry's eyes flicked over his athletic body as he leant back against the rope, confident and relaxed, and her heart did a quick flip when she thought of that same body pressed against hers in his vehicle the other day. She bit her lip. Delightful though it was to let her thoughts stray to Atholl, she had to stop thinking of the man so much. She was here to assist, not moon about like a lovesick teenager! She made herself concentrate on what Pete was saying, hoping some of the information would rub off on her.

'Now, boys,' instructed Pete, 'watch what Atholl does—how he braces himself against the rock with his feet, keeping his legs straight. He's leaning back and feeding the rope through his hands in a controlled manner. The braking device on his harness won't let him slip.'

It seemed to Terry that Atholl took about two minutes to almost float down, although she was sure it would seem a lot longer than that when she did it!

Zac was chosen to go next, and he seemed very enthusiastic, stuffing his shaven head into a helmet and eagerly scrambling over the drop.

'Not too fast,' warned Pete. 'Take it slowly. Once you've got experience you can go more quickly.'

Zac grinned around at the others. 'Knowing how to do this could come in handy if I have to make a quick getaway,' he remarked cheekily, and winked at Terry.

She laughed. There was something of the lovable rogue about Zac. 'Be careful what you say, Zac...' she smilingly remarked.

Pete murmured wryly to her, 'Unfortunately, what he says has a kernel of truth in it—some people say this sort of activity holiday just makes these lads fitter to do more crime!'

At last it was Terry's turn and she forced herself to look excited and enthusiastic as she peered over the edge to the small figures below, looking up at her.

'You'll be fine,' said Pete encouragingly, as if he could read the panic raging through her.

She swallowed hard and somehow managed to lower herself gingerly from the top, her face perilously near the rock face as she started to descend inch by cautious inch.

'Keep moving,' called Pete. 'You're doing really well! Don't look down!'

Terry imagined several pairs of eyes, including Atholl's, glued to her as she descended, and gritted her teeth, forcing herself to keep calm and not freeze. Fleetingly she thought of the predictable working life she'd led in London when the most nerve-racking thing that had happened had been a man appearing with a knife at the health centre one evening. Somehow this seemed much more daunting. Then gradually she began to get the hang of it, finding a kind of rhythm as she paid out the rope, and a feeling of exhilaration swept through her as she relaxed against the harness and allowed her legs to guide her down the cliff face.

'This is fun!' she yelled as she swung down, and in no time at all her feet touched the ground. There was a feeling of achievement and satisfaction, and from doing it herself she realised just how much these under-privileged boys would get out of it—how good it would be for them to pit their energies against something challenging and exciting. She understood the value of bringing them away from their old environment and encouraging them to put themselves to the test.

She grinned happily round at Atholl and the boys. 'Nothing to it, is there?' she remarked.

'Well done, there,' said Atholl, looking genuinely impressed. 'We'll have to try a steeper one next time!'

His eyes danced at her, his gaze lingering appreciatively for a second on her petite figure. She was one feisty girl—he knew that it had taken all her courage to do the descent for the first time, and he admired the way she'd kept her fear under control. Someone like her would command the respect of the young lads watching her and he smiled at his own reaction. Why on earth had he imagined that a man would be so much better to be involved on this outward bound course?

Pete had begun his descent, having secured the rope at the top. He was efficient and able, swinging down quickly, but just as he was reaching the ground there was an odd rumbling noise above them. Instinctively they all looked up and watched incredulously as a mini-avalanche of small boulders broke away from an overhang above Pete and started to rain down around him.

Before anyone could move, Zac had raced forward and pushed Pete away from the worst of the fall. Both men fell heavily to the ground, then instinctively coiled their bodies and rolled away from the danger.

Everyone froze for a second then, as if a button had been pressed, they all raced together towards Pete and Zac. Pete was already getting to his feet. His helmet had saved him from the worst of the avalanche, but Zac still lay on the ground. He turned over slowly, his face screwed up in agony.

'Aagh...bloody shoulder,' he groaned. 'I've done something to it. It's agony...'

It seemed to Terry, racing towards the stricken man, that she and Atholl seemed to attract more than their fair share of accidents!

CHAPTER SEVEN

'I DON'T believe this,' muttered Atholl, exchanging a quick look of concern with Terry.

'Let's getting him sitting up,' said Terry. 'We can't see what he's done otherwise.'

Atholl crouched down behind Zac and pointed to Len, the biggest lad there. 'Len, you take the good side and I'll support his back and try to keep his shoulder still while we lift him together. Gently now…'

It was obvious that Zac was in acute pain, and when they'd managed to sit him up, he looked white and shaky, shock kicking in.

'What's happened? Have I broken my arm? You won't touch it, will you?'

'Don't worry, Zac, we just need to look at it carefully. We're not going to do anything to it,' reassured Atholl.

Both doctors looked critically at the injured area, and Terry said after a few seconds of deliberation, 'From the way he's holding his shoulder, I would say he's displaced the head of the humerus—what do you think?'

'What the hell does that mean?' growled Zac, grimacing as he held his arm to his side.

'I'm afraid it means you've probably dislocated your shoulder,' explained Terry. 'Let me cut this T-shirt off so that we can get a proper look. Sorry, it's going to be a bit uncomfortable.'

'It looks like a typical forward dislocation injury,' said Atholl. 'You see, the top of the upper arm bone is like a ball, and it's been forced out of its socket just beneath the acronium. Poor lad.'

'And all because he was helping me,' said Pete, also crouching by Zac. 'You were a star there, Zac. I'm so sorry you're the one that's copped it and not me.' He looked at the two doctors. 'Can we do anything about it?'

'The thing is,' said Terry, 'we really need an X-ray to make sure there isn't an accompanying fracture. Then the treatment is to manoeuvre the head of the humerus back into the socket. I don't think we should attempt to do that without knowing if there's further injury, do you, Atholl?'

He nodded. 'We'd be better to put a sling on and possibly strapping the upper arm to the chest so that it's kept immobilised to minimise pain when he moves.'

Terry looked at the young man assessingly. 'There's no way he can walk back—he's in shock,' she said decisively. 'The sooner we get Zac to hospital, the better.'

'Then we'd better get the mountain rescue people out here. They've got a four-by-four that can get over this moorland without much difficulty…I'll call them now.'

Pete pulled out his mobile phone and stabbed out some numbers. The others all looked rather mournfully at each other—in the twinkling of an eye the day had changed to disaster. Under Terry's supervision they all started putting one or two rucksacks in a supporting wedge round Zac so that he could relax back slightly, although any pressure on the injured side made him wince.

Then Atholl undid his medical pack, taking out the sling he would use to hold Zac's upper arm steady and a big sheet of metallic insulating material to cover the boy and keep him warm. Despite the heat, Zac was shivering with shock.

'Good job we've got the medics with us,' said Len cheerily. 'Otherwise you'd be in a right pickle, mate.'

Zac managed a weak grin. 'I thought coming down the rock would be the most dangerous bit—I didn't realise it was worse on the ground!'

Terry walked back to where her rucksack was and something glinting on the ground by Zac's jacket and spilling half out of a pocket caught her eye. She stopped and looked at it curiously, then bent down and picked it up—it was a pretty Victorian necklace and two little pearl earrings.

Her heart sank and she looked over at Atholl, who had just finished attending to Zac. She walked over to him and said in a low voice, 'Can you just come over here for a moment?'

He looked up, surprised at the urgency in her tone. 'OK. What's the matter?'

She opened her hand and he looked down at the bits of jewellery she was holding.

'Hell,' he muttered slowly. 'These belong to the Mackie sisters, don't they? Where did you find them?'

'Near Zac's jacket by his rucksack,' she replied. 'What do we do now?'

Atholl looked furious, his blue eyes as cold as chips of ice. 'I did hope that these boys would grab this chance to keep on the straight and narrow. What the hell does the boy think he's doing? First smoking dope and now stealing from two old ladies.'

'We're not absolutely sure it's Zac,' pointed out Terry, putting a calming hand on his arm. 'And if he did, he's not all bad. Look at the way he leapt to save Pete.'

'I know, I know,' said Atholl. 'I'm just exasperated that he can be so damned foolish when he's got the potential to do better things in his life. I'll speak to Pete.'

'Meantime, I'll get the boys to make some tea and they can have something to eat by the river while we wait for this rescue vehicle,' suggested Terry. 'I'll join you in a moment.'

When Pete was shown the evidence of the theft he swore angrily. 'I guess it happened when the boys were doing the sisters' next-door neighbour's garden. There was plenty of time for one of the boys to get into their house.' He looked across at Zac lying uncomfortably against the makeshift support. 'Damn it, I don't want to give up on the lad—he's not all bad. He admitted taking cannabis and he saved me from serious injury. Why the hell did he filch this jewellery?'

'More drugs?' suggested Atholl.

Pete shook his head. 'I don't know about that. Who's he going to sell that necklace to out here? Look, while the others are having lunch we'll just tackle him about this.'

It was almost too easy. Confronted by the evidence of the necklace and earrings, Zac looked almost comically dismayed.

'Why in kingdom come did you take the stuff?' demanded Pete angrily. 'Were you going to buy more drugs?'

'No,' muttered Zac. 'It wasn't like that.'

'What was it like, then?' asked Atholl, frowning at him.

The boy looked mulishly at the ground and was silent. Atholl crouched down opposite him.

'You've let us down, Zac,' he rasped. 'We give you this chance to do something for yourself, use your body and mind in a lovely place, and you throw it back in our faces. Just why the hell did you have to steal from two harmless old ladies, let alone leave a hell of a mess in the room?'

To their amazement a tear rolled slowly down the boy's cheek and he brushed it away impatiently with his good arm. 'I fell over the chair as I was leaving—I didn't have time to clear it up. The jewellery was for my mam. I…I thought it would cheer her up. She never goes out or nothin' like that, and she's not been well. She's stuck inside in that wheelchair all the time. I wanted to take her something back she'd like—she's got nothing pretty.'

'For God's sake, lad, can't you see that, whatever the reason, you're not to steal from anyone?'

Zac looked at the three adults staring at him and said aggressively, 'You don't know what it's like living in that street…there's nothing for anyone there.'

'Yes, we do know, Zac,' said Atholl sharply. 'We came from where you live. We know about the poverty, the broken families—and the parents who do their best in awful circumstances to keep things going. I guess your mother is one of those. She wouldn't want you to mess this up. She knew it was a chance for you to get away from your life in the Gorbals for a little while—prove yourself in a challenge.'

Zac shook his head and muttered, 'I didn't mean to hurt no one…'

There was something pitiful about the boy and Terry felt the fact he wanted to give his mother something she could never have had showed a loving side to his character—if what he said was true.

'Look, Zac, I said after the cannabis incident that you'd go home if you mucked up again,' said Pete grimly.

Zac continued to look sullenly down at the ground. 'So have I got to go?'

Pete sighed. 'You've just saved me from being injured with no thought of your own safety—I think that speaks a lot about you.' He looked at Atholl and Terry. 'If they can manipulate his arm back into place, shall we give him another chance? There's only a short time to go anyway.'

Zac remained gazing down rather like a condemned prisoner. When Atholl and Terry nodded their heads and said in unison, 'One more chance, then,' he looked up, quite startled, as if he hadn't believed he'd ever be given another opportunity.

'It's up to you, Zac,' said Atholl quietly. 'You either go back in disgrace to your mother or stay on the straight and narrow. We've already reported it to the police so I'm afraid you'll have to wait and see if they prosecute you. Perhaps when they hear that you've returned the jewellery and apologised to the Mackies they'll let it pass this time.'

The boy nodded miserably. 'I have let you down, haven't I?' he muttered. 'I like it here—I don't want to mess this up.'

'Well, see you don't, then.' Then Pete's face softened and he patted Zac's good shoulder. 'I'm still very grateful to you for your quick actions, Zac. I know you're a good lad at heart.' He turned round to Atholl and Terry. 'What about some hot, sweet tea for him?'

Terry looked at her watch and said dubiously, 'He may have to be anaesthetised to put his shoulder back—I wouldn't like to jeopardise the timing of that, so perhaps not.'

Pete's mobile started ringing and he pulled it out of his pocket. They saw the expression on his face change to a mixture of amazement and concern as he answered it, then he turned to Atholl and Terry.

'I—I don't believe this,' he stuttered. 'Sal's gone into labour—she's in the hospital now!'

Atholl laughed. 'That's great news, and every cloud has a silver lining, Pete! It's a good job you've got the mountain rescue team coming for Zac—they can take you back with them to the hospital! Terry and I and the lads will go back to The Culleens on foot.'

Pete looked worriedly up the glen where the mountain rescue team would appear from. 'God, I hope they hurry—she could have had it by the time we get there!'

'Calm down, Pete.' Terry smiled. 'It's her first baby—it's going to take a few hours yet!'

'My Sal's never late for anything,' said Pete gloomily. 'I bet it comes quickly!'

It was late at night and the boys had built a campfire when they'd got back to The Culleens down by the loch. The smell of cooking sausages and steak drifted over to Atholl and Terry sitting on the steps of the building away from the others. Len was softly strumming a guitar and Atholl slung his arm carelessly around Terry's shoulders.

'Will you look at those stars? It's a brilliant night,' he murmured. 'It's been a good day, despite poor old Zac's accident—even if we did find out what a fool he's been.'

Two months ago she had been at her lowest ebb, reflected Terry, and now here she was, close up and dangerously near to one of the dishiest and kindest men she'd ever met, in the most romantic setting! She could tell that Atholl was just being casually affectionate. He didn't pull her against him, although every nerve in her body was telling her to put her head on his shoulder. How could she ever have believed that she was in love with Max, concerned only with himself and what he could get out of people? Of course he'd been a conman and duped everyone—including her father.

She looked up at Atholl's firm profile, outlined in the dark, a quiff of dark hair falling over his eyes. What a contrast! Atholl was genuine, she could trust him, she was sure of that. Perhaps that was why she felt so guilty about not being entirely honest with him and what had really brought her up to Scuola. But she couldn't tell him—not just yet, not until she was sure that there would be no repercussions because she'd given her word that she wouldn't divulge a thing.

'You know, I don't think Zac's a bad lad at heart,' she remarked. 'No one who puts his own skin at risk to save someone else's life can be all bad. And perhaps it's almost a reflex action to steal something he thinks will be nice for his mother…'

Atholl looked down at her and smiled. 'I don't think you can imagine the world that Zac and I come from. Sometimes stealing is a way of life when you've nothing—can you understand that?'

Stealing a way of life? Terry pulled away from him suddenly, her expression hidden in the shadow of the wall. She understood only too well what he meant.

'Dishonesty isn't confined to the under-privileged,' she said in a strange little voice. 'Surely you know that, Atholl? Just read the newspapers if you want to know about everyone from politicians to solicitors who've strayed from the straight and narrow.'

She stood up and stretched, suddenly wanting to change the subject, to forget about crime and the reasons why people committed it. Atholl looked at her in surprise, sensing the change in her attitude, the raw nerve he seemed to have touched, and that fleeting sadness she sometimes showed. He was sure it was something to do with this Max who'd let her down—badly hurt her.

Then the sound of a vehicle drawing up by The Culleens made them both turn round and they could see Zac getting out of a taxi.

Terry welcomed the distraction—she didn't want to get drawn into a conversation about criminals.

'Zac! How's the shoulder?' she asked, walking towards him.

Zac grimaced. 'Not so bad, I guess. They've put it in a sling and given me a note to go to my local hospital.'

Atholl joined them and Zac looked at the two doctors rather miserably.

'I…I've something to say,' he muttered. 'I…I'm sorry about the necklace. I'll go and see the old biddies tomorrow. I didn't think about them when I did it. I just thought saw those things on a table when I looked through the window and thought they were pretty wee trinkets.'

'Perhaps you will think now, Zac, before you do something so damn stupid again,' growled Atholl. 'You gave those old sisters a terrible shock. However I know they'll feel better when you've apologised to them—and taken back the jewellery.'

'Will the police bring charges?' The boy's young face looked stricken. 'It'll do me mam's head in if she knows I've been in trouble again. I'll be for the high jump.'

'I don't know. Perhaps if the Mackies speak up for you, you may just get a caution.' Atholl's voice was rough. 'You'll just have to pick yourself up again, Zac. I got into trouble but I managed to turn my life around. You can do the same.'

'I think you've realised what a silly thing it was to do, haven't you, Zac?' said Terry. She was sure the boy was genuinely contrite about what he'd done. 'Now, go and have some of that food the others are barbecuing—you must be very hungry.'

Zac nodded and slouched off, and Atholl sighed as they watched him. 'Who knows? It may possibly have taught him something about being responsible for his own actions. If he'd done this in Glasgow he might never have been caught—perhaps told his mother he'd just found the jewellery or something.'

'I think you're right. He's been caught twice here and he feels a fool.'

There was the sound of another vehicle drawing up, a slamming door and a hearty shout. Everyone turned round and a figure that turned out to be Pete came running towards them in the dark, waving his arms and yelling excitedly.

'Hi, everyone. It's a wee girl! Sally's just given me a beautiful daughter! And they're both absolutely fine!'

After the celebrations, toasting the new baby in beer and wine that Pete had brought back with him, Atholl, Terry and Pete strolled back from the barbecue to the barn. The boys had all turned in and the fire had been damped down. The air was warm, not a breeze stirring the trees by the loch.

'What a day! I'm absolutely shattered. Becoming a father is extremely tiring,' yawned Pete. 'I'm off for some shut-eye. There's spare sleeping bags in the cupboard, so make yourselves at home. You can have my office to sleep in, Terry—there's a camp bed in there, and Atholl can kip with me.'

'Thanks. I'll be along soon,' said Atholl.

Pete disappeared to his room and Terry lingered for a minute, smelling the balmy air of the warm night and listening to the rustlings and little sounds that were part of the surroundings. It seemed so peaceful after the excitement of the day, a time to reflect and wind down. Rather woozily she reflected that perhaps they'd all been a bit too enthusiastic in their celebration of the new baby's birth. The result of drinking a glass or two on a relatively empty stomach had made her feel delightfully relaxed.

She was vaguely aware that Atholl had come to stand by her, looking at her profile as she dreamily watched the night sky.

'What a lovely ending to the day—a new baby arriving!' she murmured.

'Yes—a lovely ending.' His voice was very quiet.

In the silvery light her hair looked fairer, her dark eyes larger. God, she was beautiful. Atholl felt his throat catch at the sweetness of her face, the tip-tilted nose, soft lips and high cheekbones that gave a heart-shaped definition to her face. Since the morning when he'd gone to wake her up in her bedroom, he had become more and more aware as the day had gone on that Terry was everything he wanted—

the kind of woman he'd dreamt about but had thought he'd never have a hope in hell of meeting.

When Zara and he had split up, yes, he'd been bruised and mortified—but mostly he'd been furious that she had duped him. If this was what happened when you thought you'd met the right person, he'd vowed he'd be very, very wary before getting involved again. And now Terry had come into his life and the picture was changing rather rapidly.

Atholl bent down, picked a stone up from the shore and skimmed it across the loch, so that it bounced three times and the circles of water rippled out, gleaming in the moonshine. He wondered how long he could go on working and living so close to Terry in a kind of teasing no-man's land where they flirted with each other, then backed off in a tantalising dance. He had to tell her honestly what he felt—and he wanted to know how she felt about him.

'I think I'll turn in now,' Terry said, starting to walk back across the shingly shore.

Atholl put out his hand and took hers, pulling her back slightly. 'Terry…wait a moment. Don't go yet.'

She turned round to him, slightly startled, and then the moon went behind a cloud and for a second they were plunged into almost total darkness. Terry's foot slipped on a smooth rock as she stepped back and she stumbled, almost falling to the ground before Atholl grabbed her, slipping his arm round her waist.

'Careful, we don't want any more accidents today,' he murmured.

Terry giggled, the effect of the wine beginning to kick in rather forcefully.

'You're making a habit of this, catching me when I fall.'

'That's fine by me. I want to be there for you whenever I'm needed.'

'That sounds rather serious,' she said flippantly.

She leant against him for a second, thinking how heavenly it was to relax against the hard wall of his chest, feel the thud of his heart against hers.

'You're very strong,' she teased, the inhibitions she'd had about getting too intimate with Atholl floating away rapidly.

He grinned, his teeth white in the dark. 'I need to be strong, with you falling about all over the place…'

His arms tightened about her and he bent his head to hers, and she felt the evening stubble of his chin prickly against her skin. His lips touched hers gently and it felt like a thousand butterflies were fluttering inside her—then that puritanical voice at the back of her mind whispered that she should march away quickly at this point. With a great effort she pulled away from him, putting a few paces between them.

'We shouldn't do this, Atholl,' she said, rather fuzzily, trying to enunciate carefully. 'Let's keep things strictly platonic, then neither of us will get hurt, like I was with Max and you with Zara.'

A moment's silence and then he said harshly, striding forward and catching her arm, 'That's laughable, Terry. You're nothing like that woman. You and she… Why, there's no comparison. She cheated on me, told me so many lies.'

'But everyone has baggage from the past that they might not want to reveal. Atholl, there are things about my background—' she started to say.

Atholl put his finger on her mouth. 'Hush. You're perfect as you are.' His arms tightened around her and he gazed down at her silently for a moment, then murmured, 'There! I've said it! God, Terry, I know you feel something for me too. When we're in the same room it's like there's no one else there—just the two of us. Sparks fly when we're together, honey, admit it!'

He started to kiss her face, covering her brows, her mouth and neck with soft kisses, making her dizzy with delight. She put her arms round his neck and looked into his eyes.

'Yes,' she whispered. 'I admit it.' Had they reached a watershed of some kind on this soft, balmy night? She stroked his thick dark hair back from his forehead and smiled. 'I want to forget about Max and…everything,' she said simply. 'I want to enjoy myself.'

He grinned. 'I'll try and ensure that you will, darling.'

And Terry didn't draw back when he pulled her gently onto the soft mossy ground under the trees by the loch, where the smell was earthy and sweet. He ran his finger down her jaw and her neck, smiling as she responded with a delighted wriggle of her body.

Then he started kissing her face, her lips, trailing his warm mouth down her neck, murmuring her name. Terry felt as if she was back in her dream—Atholl holding her against his chest, his hands stroking her body gently but insistently until every erogenous zone in her body screamed for more.

She lay back on the soft earth and stretched languorously, loving the feel of Atholl's hard muscled body, and the certain knowledge that he was as aroused as she was! Then he knelt up for a second, his legs on either side of her, looking down at her with twinkling eyes.

'What a way to end the evening!'

And Terry laughed because it was exciting and wonderful to undress him as he did her, forget any qualms and enjoy the moment. Funny how quickly it had come to this, she thought dizzily, both of them naked against each other, warm skin against warm skin, his hands doing wonderful things to her body—just as she had dreamt.

Atholl's lips nibbled her ear, and he said throatily, 'You know something—I'm glad I didn't get a man to join the practice.'

She smiled. 'So am I, Atholl, so am I.'

Then they lost themselves in each other, both seizing their moment of happiness, limbs entwined, revelling in the waves of sweetness that swept through them. And afterwards they lay for a long time side by side, under the velvety sky, looking at each other as if almost surprised by the wonder of what they'd just done.

At last Atholl rolled over on his stomach and looked down into Terry's eyes. 'We've been and gone and done it now!' he sighed. 'And just how wonderful it was, my sweet princess!'

Terry looked up at him, seeing his eyes dark and intense in the moonlight, his warm breath on her cheek, and felt a flood of happiness engulf her. It was time to look forward, and she didn't care that she still hadn't told him her full story. She wouldn't worry about that now!

He took her arm as they strolled back together to The Culleens in companionable silence, then he kissed her gently on the steps before she went in.

Atholl stayed outside for a minute, leaning against the wall, gazing across the dark loch with a silver path across it where the moon's light fell. For the first time for many months he felt genuinely at peace with himself and filled with the contentment that came after making love to the most wonderful woman in the world.

He chuckled to himself. He realised that he was in love with Terry, and perhaps he had been since the moment he'd offered her a job the first day she'd come!

CHAPTER EIGHT

TERRY hummed happily as she poured herself a mug of coffee and peered at the computer to see what her list was like for the morning.

Isobel was just finishing a phone call and she turned round to Terry with the slight smile that was the most levity she usually allowed herself.

'Someone's happy,' she remarked. 'So did you have a good weekend, then?'

Only the most wonderful, fantastic day she'd had in her life, thought Terry, a vivid picture of Atholl and her by the loch in the moonlight and the realisation that they both liked each other a lot. Maybe it wouldn't lead to a lifetime's commitment—after all, they'd both had fractured relationships—but suddenly the future looked very bright indeed. She was surprised how calm her voice sounded when she replied.

'Mostly good, thank you, Isobel. On the downside, one of the boys dislocated his shoulder, but Pete's wife gave birth to a little girl at the hospital, which was very exciting. Atholl and I took over for a while when he went to visit Sally.'

Isobel started to pin a notice on the board and didn't

speak for a moment. Then she said casually, 'I'm glad you and Atholl get on well—it makes it easier when you work together.'

Was there the slightest emphasis on the words 'work together'? Terry wondered if there was a hidden agenda to Isobel's remarks.

'Yes,' she replied lightly, 'I think we're on the same wavelength when it comes to work.'

Isobel nodded. 'Aye, it's good to see him concentrate on the practice. As you probably know, he had a distressing time with Dr Grahame. It wasn't a good thing for him to mix work with socialising—if you know what I mean. It can lead to all sorts of...shall we say complications? He was most unhappy.'

Was this the gypsy's warning? A caution for her not to get too close to Isobel's darling Atholl? Isobel might be right—work and social pleasure didn't always work out, but if one was careful, surely it needn't be disaster?

'He did tell me about her,' she admitted. 'It was obviously horrible for him.'

Isobel gave a grunt of disgust and started to type something furiously on the computer.

'You could say that. Aye, there were a lot of things Atholl didn't know about that one, and when he did, it was almost too late. Thank God he found out the truth about her.'

Terry bit her lip. What on earth would Isobel say if she really knew what had happened the night before? But a little wave of happiness rippled through her. She really didn't care what Isobel thought!

Sue and Bunty came in, taking off their jackets, and Sue sank into a chair looking her usual harassed self after a weekend looking after her family.

'What a morning! Just try getting three quarrelling boys off to school on time with all their homework and lunch boxes—and then, just as I think I've got them through the gates, Jake says he's forgotten his sports kit!'

'Have some coffee.' Terry grinned, handing her a cup. 'You can relax now you've come in to work!'

Sue gave a mirthless laugh. 'Relax, did you say? Baby clinic first and then all the check-ups later this morning for the over-fifties. Then this afternoon—'

She was interrupted by a small commotion in the waiting room, a child wailing and an adult's soothing voice saying, 'You'll be all right now.'

'I want my mum. I want her to make it better!' screamed the child over the top of the adult's voice. 'Go and get her *now!*'

'What on earth's happening?' said Isobel sternly, getting up from her chair and marching through to the waiting room. A few seconds later she appeared again, holding a small sobbing boy by the hand.

'Look what I've got, Sue. I think he belongs to you!'

'Jake!' cried Sue in astonishment. She put down her coffee and ran towards the child, cuddling him. 'What's the matter? I've only just dropped you off at school!'

A rather flustered-looking woman appeared at the door. 'I'm afraid Jake's trapped his finger in a door and his nail's gone very black—it looks most painful. I thought it best to bring him straight here, knowing you worked at the medical centre.'

'Mrs Milnthorpe!' Sue turned to the others. 'This is Jake's headmistress. Oh, thank you so much for bringing him here.' She knelt down by her sobbing little boy, who was guarding one hand within the other one. She tried to prise it open. 'Let's have a look, Jake. It's alright, darling, we'll do something about it.' Sue looked up at Terry. 'What do you think? The nail's gone black and it's very swollen.'

Terry looked at the small finger with a purple nail on it proffered very reluctantly for their gaze by the tearful child, and grimaced.

'Poor old Jake! It's obviously bleeding behind the nail and there isn't much space to bleed into, so no wonder it's painful. But don't worry—I've got a great way to make it feel a lot, lot better!'

Jake began to scream. 'I don't want you to touch it. Keep away!' He pulled his hand away from Terry and protected it with his other hand again, looking at them defiantly with tear-filled eyes, then buried his head in his mother's shoulder, squirming when she tried to extricate his arm. Sue looked back at the other women rather helplessly.

'It's not easy when you're related to the patient,' she said wryly.

'Normally the patient isn't using you as a shield!' remarked Terry, squatting down by the little boy and attempting to pull him round to face her. 'Just let me see your poorly finger for a minute, sweetheart. I promise it won't hurt,' she said.

A muffled bellow was all she got in reply.

'Well, well, now—is somebody in trouble here?' said a familiar deep voice.

Atholl's tall figure was looming at the door. He looked around at everyone clustered round the little boy, his eyes holding Terry's for a second of intimate scrutiny so that her pulse bounded into overdrive. Then, quickly assessing the situation, he strode over to the little boy and bent down beside him. He prised the child away from his mother gently but firmly, taking no notice of the child's resistance or the increasing volume of his screams.

'Come on, wee lad,' he said coaxingly, a mixture of understanding and rallying in his voice. 'You're a brave boy, I know.'

He held the frightened child close to him, patting his back, letting the little boy calm down as naturally as if it had been his own son, thought Terry. She sighed, remembering how tender her father had been to her when she had been little, always on her side, always there for her when she'd needed him.

Atholl was still speaking to the little boy. 'Let Dr Terry and I get rid of that pain for you.' He looked up at Terry with a wink. 'We make a magical team, you know!'

Terry leapt back into the present, pushing the flashback away. Atholl delved into his jacket pocket and brought out a tiny model car, waving it in front of Jake.

'See this, Jake. Look, when I push it along the floor the headlamps light up—can you see them?'

There was a moment's silence as the little boy's interest was caught, following the toy with his eyes as it raced along until stopped by a chair leg.

'Would you like that, Jake?' The child nodded silently. 'Well, just let Dr Terry look at that finger for a minute, then it's all yours.'

'Right—has anyone got a match?' asked Terry. 'I've got the rest of the equipment in my bag. Here it is…a pin and a pair of tweezers!'

Isobel came forward with a box of matches and everyone watched goggled-eyed as Terry gripped the pin in the tweezers and then held the tip in the flame of the match. Atholl had a firm arm round Jake and he swivelled the child round so that he was pointing towards the window, and at the same time held the little boy's hand out towards Terry.

'Look, Jake,' he said urgently. 'Can you see that squirrel running up the tree outside? He's just stolen some nuts from the bird table out there…'

During the time that Jake's attention was diverted, Terry took his finger and pressed the glowing pin tip firmly into the injured nail. There was a faint hiss as the hot metal burnt a hole in the nail and blood started to ooze out through the freshly made aperture.

'Oh,' breathed Bunty, impressed. 'That was neatly done! How amazing!'

Terry laughed. 'Not to be done at home, but it worked because Mrs Milnthorpe got Jake here before the blood began to clot.'

Jake twisted round and looked at his finger doubtfully, then back at the adults round him. 'It's not hurting now!' he said wonderingly.

'I told you that Dr Terry and I are good when we get together!' Atholl's mischievous eyes met Terry's, and she looked away hastily. Did he want the whole room to know about them?

'I think brave boys deserve a chocolate biscuit and some milk,' she said quickly. 'And then you can go back to school—that finger won't give you any trouble now!'

'I'll take you back,' said Mrs Milnthorpe. 'You will have a lot to tell your friends, won't you? Quite a hero!'

After a farewell hug from his mother, Jake trotted off quite happily, clutching the little car, and Sue sank back into a chair, blowing out her cheeks.

'That child—he's always getting into scrapes,' she sighed. 'Thank you so much, both of you, for that procedure! By the way, Atholl, do you carry a stock of those little cars?'

'It's like a toy shop in my pockets.' He grinned. 'Anything else we can do for you?'

Sue's eyes twinkled. 'Well, I hate to mention it…but as a matter of fact I thought one of you was going to clear some rubbish from your room this weekend so that I could transfer some of *my* rubbish in the space you'd made! There's still only just enough space in my room for one thin patient and me at the moment!'

Terry clapped her hand to her forehead. 'Oh, God—so sorry, Sue! Er…I'm afraid it just went out of my head completely. You know we had The Culleens outward bound course yesterday and then Pete's baby arrived…and one thing and another…'

'I know, I know.' Sue smiled good-naturedly. 'I'm sure your mind was on plenty of things other than The Sycamores!'

How right she was, thought Terry wryly, almost able to feel the mischievous grin that played across Atholl's face! She averted her gaze quickly—all these double entendres were getting embarrassing!

'I promise I'll do it this evening—honest,' she said.

'Would you like me to help you sort things out?' asked Sue.

'No, I'll be fine. I've got to be really ruthless—there seem to be loads of ancient files stacked in a corner which I'm sure are completely out of date. Atholl's uncle obviously doesn't like throwing things out!' She turned to go to her room. 'Right, I'll get on with some of the BP checks now—would you bring the blood test results and post when you've got them, Bunty?'

Janet Rathbone was her first patient that day, small, slight and softly spoken, in complete contrast to her husband, thought Terry with amusement. He had obviously managed to persuade her to come in for a blood-pressure check. She had a large bruise on her cheek below her eye, and resembled a little bird, looking at Terry with her head cocked on one side.

'That bruise looks painful,' Terry observed, as she prepared to take the woman's blood pressure.

'I walked into the glass door of the hotel dining room,' explained Mrs Rathbone. 'Very clumsy of me—I was deep in thought.' She smiled pleasantly at Terry. 'I hope you're enjoying life here, Dr Younger. I believe you've taken over from Dr Brodie's uncle?'

'That's right. And, yes, I love it here on Scuola. Now, if I could just ask you a few questions about your general health to update our records?'

'If you wish—but I'm very lucky,' replied Janet. 'Some people, like my poor husband, seem to have to visit the doctor a lot. I've been blessed with a very strong constitution.'

Was there a twinkle in her eyes as she said this? wondered Terry. She knew her husband better than anyone and was well aware of his worries over his health. Janet herself did indeed look healthy—no tremors, a good colour, strong nails and, listening to her heart through her stethoscope, a good, regular beat.

'That's great. I suppose you keep up with dental checks, eye examinations, and so?'

The slightest hesitation made Terry look up at the woman questioningly.

'I will make sure I do,' Mrs Rathbone assured her quickly. 'I have been meaning to have my eyes checked.'

A glimmer of an idea occurred to Terry and she opened a drawer and pulled out an eye chart. She hooked it up on the wall behind the desk.

'Can you read me those lines as far down as you can go?' she asked.

There was a silence, and then very slowly the woman began to read the first line, petering out after a few letters. 'I…I'm sorry. It does seem a little blurred.'

'Do you wear glasses for distance, Mrs Rathbone?'

'No, no, my sight's always been fine.'

'What about reading glasses?'

'Oh, I've never needed them…'

Terry reached into a drawer and pulled out the *Scuola Recorder* that Bunty had given her a few days ago, showing Mrs Rathbone the large photo on the front page.

'By the way, have you seen this?' she asked. 'See anyone you know?'

The woman peered at it, screwing her eyes up, then said at last. 'It's not a very clear photograph… Is it Dr Atholl? It's a bit like him…'

Terry leant back in her chair and smiled across at Mrs Rathbone, pretty sure that she knew what was causing Mrs Rathbone's clumsiness.

'I'm sure there's nothing to worry about, but I have to say I think you really do need glasses. Your sight has probably deteriorated since you last had an eye test—quite normal for everyone to get changes in their sight as they get older.'

'To be honest, I've never actually *had* an eye test, although I did begin to wonder why things didn't seem to be as clear as they were. In fact,' Janet admitted, 'I really don't do any reading now—no time, I suppose. Frankly, I don't really hold with all this worrying about health and testing all the time.'

'Well, while you're here, let me just have a quick look at your eyes,' said Terry, taking her ophthalmoscope out of a drawer. 'I'm by no means an expert on eyes, of course, but I can get a general idea of their health.'

Through the instrument Terry could see the entire area of the retina, the head of the optic nerve and the retinal arteries, all being illuminated by a perforated angled mirror.

'It all seems to be fine,' she said reassuringly, putting the instrument down. 'But please do make an appointment to see an optician pretty soon. Don't think that somehow you're "giving in" by having glasses. To be honest, on the basis of reading that chart, you shouldn't drive without them.'

Janet looked with slight embarrassment at Terry. 'Oh dear—how very remiss of me... I should have realised that—both my parents had very poor sight.' Then with a burst of candour she said, 'The thing is, Doctor, Cyril is a great one for his health and the more he goes on about what he might have wrong with him, the more I seem to want to prove that I'm in the peak of condition!'

Terry laughed. 'And I'm sure you are! You're very slim—no weight worries. I'll take your BP now, but I bet it's normal.'

'I promise to make an eye appointment. I have put things like that off because this is our busiest time of year at the hotel, of course, but I realise how important it is to have my eyes checked,' said Janet when Terry had finished.

She picked up her handbag and got up from the chair. 'One thing, though, Doctor. Please don't say anything to Cyril—he'll only say he told me so and never let me forget it! I shall pretend I'm going to the optician off my own bat!'

'Whatever goes on between us is strictly confidential,' assured Terry. 'But please come to see us if you don't feel well, even if you do feel you've got to prove something to your husband!'

So that was that, thought Terry wryly as the woman went out. In fact, it was a very good thing that Cyril had persuaded his wife to come in for a check-up before she had a major accident—there were definitely times when it paid to be fussy!

It was a busy morning and Terry made one or two house calls during her lunch-hour before dashing back to a mother and baby clinic at two o'clock. By three-thirty she was back in her room, stretching her stiff back and yawning as Bunty came in with a pile of papers in one hand and a cup of tea in the other.

'Here's the blood tests,' she said cheerily. 'And lots of mail to keep you occupied. And a cup of tea to wake you up—I saw that yawn!'

Terry laughed. 'I could just flake out now,' she admitted. 'That tea's really welcome. I'll make a start on the paperwork now.'

Then Terry's intercom buzzed and Bunty put the papers down on the desk and went out.

'When you're free, can I have a word?' asked Atholl.

'Yes. I'm just going to get to grips with some paper-work.'

She looked up as Atholl came into the room, a familiar

rush of desire and happiness mingling when she saw him. He stood for a second looking at her from the doorway, dark hair standing up in little peaks over his forehead, his blue eyes smiling at her. Then he strode over to her, looking down with a tender smile.

'Was last night wonderful or what, sweetheart?'

Then, before she could answer, he held her face in his hands and kissed her full and passionately on her lips.

'For God's sake, Atholl—we're at work!' she protested, half laughing and putting her hands on his shoulders to push him away.

'I know,' he said imperturbably. 'So what? Just a friendly greeting! You left pretty promptly this morning. I thought you might have been tired and had a lie-in after last night…' He looked mischievously into her eyes.

'I certainly had a good night's sleep,' she said rather primly.

'I wonder why that should be?' he teased.

And Terry smiled up at him radiantly. 'It was wonderful Atholl, but we must cool it in the office.'

'I'm just being friendly,' he murmured, pulling her up from her chair, and kissing her neck and cleavage with soft butterfly kisses that sent little electric shocks of pleasure through her body. And, of course, her good resolutions were forgotten, and she responded ardently, allowing him to tease her lips open, arching her body against his, feeling his hands caressing her curves, until she knew that unless he stopped fairly soon she might throw caution to the winds and allow him to make love to her on the floor of her surgery! He drew away with a chuckle and held her at arm's length for a second, his eyes dancing with amusement.

'I'd love to finish this off properly, my sweet, but

perhaps, as you said, this room isn't quite the right place during surgery hours…'

Terry laughed. 'Saved by the bell! I had visions of Isobel coming in and finding us—and I don't think she's too keen on you having female followers!'

Atholl grinned. 'She regards me as a surrogate son and after my experience with Zara she's like a Rottweiler where my welfare is concerned! However, back to work, I'm afraid. We've got a potential worry at the Caledonian Hotel.'

Terry frowned. 'Isn't that the place that belongs to the Rathbones? Janet was my first patient this morning.'

'Poor woman—she'll be very worried at the moment. They had a small wedding party there at lunchtime and one or two of the guests collapsed shortly after eating the lunch.'

'Oh, no! Food poisoning, I suppose?'

'It's all rather mysterious—not the usual symptoms, from what I can gather. The victims have been taken to hospital but the public health people will be some time getting across from the mainland, so I'm afraid it's up to you and I to go and take samples of everything in the kitchen to get them analysed as quickly as possible. I've telephoned through to say that the kitchen must be sealed off until we get there.'

Terry grabbed her medical bag, and put the e-mails and post to one side of the computer—she would look at them later.

'What are the symptoms?' asked Terry as they drove over to the hotel.

'Pretty grim—numbness, a weak pulse, thirst, and two of the victims have had convulsions and paralysis of the limbs,' said Atholl. 'The last thing a place like Scuola needed with the start of the vital tourist season is an outbreak of illness in a hotel—the sooner we can trace its cause, the better.'

The Caledonian Hotel looked out over the Scuola Sound and had pretty gardens surrounding it. As they drove up, Terry could see a young couple playing tennis on a court at the side of the hotel and at the front was a beautifully mown lawn with croquet hoops on it. Everything looked immaculate and cared for.

'It's very popular with holidaymakers and the locals,' explained Atholl as they got out of the car. 'Whatever one can say about Cyril as a patient, he and Janet work like the devil—it must be quite stressful. They have an excellent chef and the food's terrific. I just hope to goodness they haven't got salmonella or the like on their hands—it could ruin their reputation.'

Janet met them at the door, her face showing the strain of the past few hours. 'Thank you for coming so quickly,' she said. 'I'm so worried, we seem to have an outbreak of some kind on our hands. I can't believe it's food poisoning—we're absolutely meticulous about everything that's produced here.'

Atholl patted her shoulder kindly. 'I know how careful you are, Janet. Try not to worry. We'll go straight to the kitchen and start taking samples straight away—it could be something that's been brought in from outside. Nobody's disturbed anything, have they?'

Janet trotted along beside them, her words tumbling over each other. 'It was awful. They simply started shaking and collapsed about half an hour after eating. At first we thought one of them was having a heart attack as he suffers from angina, but it was soon obvious that it was affecting quite a few of them. Oh, what can it be?'

'What had they been eating?' asked Terry.

Janet looked a little tearful. 'The wedding party had roast beef, and Cyril and I had a roast beef sandwich for an early lunch—but we haven't been affected.'

'We'll get the samples for analysis now, and then go over to the lab at the hospital to get them done as soon as possible and look at the victims while we're there.'

It took a good hour to go through everything in the kitchen, collect all the samples and then rush them to the hospital laboratory.

'We'll try and get them done today,' said the technician. 'Everyone's going to work flat out.'

'Then let's sit down and make a definitive list of absolutely everything these people ate this lunchtime—to the smallest thing,' suggested Atholl, pulling a pen from his pocket. 'One good thing—no one seems in immediate danger although it would be very helpful if we knew the cause.'

It seemed to be a fairly random attack—a husband would be affected, but not the wife, a parent, but not a child. They interviewed everyone they were able to at the hospital, and Terry observed in a puzzled way when they were back in the hotel office with the Rathbones, 'Everyone seems to have had the same—roast beef.' She looked at the list they'd made, tracing the ticks against each name. 'There's only one thing I can see that differs from one group to the other, and that's the fact that some had the horseradish sauce and others didn't.'

Atholl stared at her for a moment, then said slowly, 'You know, you may be on to something there. It's a long shot, but at the back of my mind a bell's ringing. I think it's time we interviewed the chef!'

'What do you think it is?' asked Terry curiously.

'I can't be sure—it seems almost too far fetched, but I have come across it once before,' replied Atholl cryptically, striding through to the kitchens with Terry and the Rathbones behind him.

Bernie, the chef, was defensive when questioned. 'Everything I serve is home prepared—the meats from local suppliers, the vegetables are from the kitchen garden—'

'Ah, yes, the vegetables,' interrupted Atholl. 'Where do you get your horseradish sauce from?'

'As I told you,' said Bernie proudly, 'it's all home made. The horseradish grows in the garden.'

'Then let's go into the kitchen garden and see the exact spot you got the roots from,' said Atholl. He paused and asked Cyril and Janet, 'Tell me, when you had your roast beef sandwiches, did you have horseradish sauce with them?'

Cyril and Janet Rathbone looked at each other in puzzlement. 'No, we don't like spicy hot stuff,' said Cyril. 'Don't tell me it's something to do with that?'

Atholl didn't reply but went with Bernie into the walled garden where the vegetables were grown. At the far end there had been some excavation work to demolish a shed and the ground was fairly churned up.

'Show me the roots you used,' said Atholl.

Bernie bent down and pulled up the familiar horseradish roots from the disturbed soil and handed them to Atholl, who scratched their surface and sniffed them, then smiled rather grimly.

'I think we've found the culprit,' he said looking up at them. 'These tubers look like horseradish roots but, in fact, I'd bet my life they're aconite or monksbane, which is highly toxic. It's very easy to confuse the two roots, especially when the earth is churned about and the familiar leaves have been trampled on.'

There were quick indrawn breaths of amazement from the others.

'What made you think of it?' asked Terry.

'When I was working in A and E we had a similar case. It's a few years back now, but when I heard that word "horseradish" it brought it back to me. A farmer's wife supplemented her income by making sauces and chutneys and had made the same mistake.'

'Oh, my God!' said Bernie in a broken voice. He turned ashen and sat down suddenly on a bench. 'I'd no idea… I…I can't believe I nearly killed all those people…'

'It wasn't you who picked the roots,' cut in Janet suddenly. 'It was me. I just handed them to you.' She turned to Terry, her face a white mask of horror. 'Perhaps it was because of my bad vision. I didn't notice the difference in the leaves…'

Atholl shook his head. 'As you saw, the ground had been so churned up, there were no leaves, and the tubers of both plants are very similar.'

The Rathbones and Bernie looked completely shocked. Terry said briskly, 'Look, no one's in danger. I've just rung A and E and I think we can breathe a sigh of relief. If it's confirmed that Atholl's right, they'll know what they're dealing with. I imagine that people only had a tiny bit of the sauce because it would have tasted rather peculiar.'

'I…I'd no idea that we had monksbane,' said Janet miserably. 'I hope it won't ruin our reputation…we've worked so hard to get this place on its feet. I couldn't bear it if the whole thing went down again.'

'I don't think so,' said Atholl gently. 'It's a harsh lesson but now you know all in the garden isn't necessarily roses, I'm sure you'll never make that mistake again. Look,' he added cheerfully, 'I'm not in the least worried—in fact, I'd like to book Dr Younger and I in for a meal tomorrow night!'

Janet looked at him in grateful surprise. 'Of course—and it'll be on the house!'

Atholl shook his head firmly. 'Oh, no, we'll pay our way. What do you say, Terry?'

'Sounds a great idea to me.' Terry grinned. 'And I can't wait to taste your roast beef!'

The next day Terry came into the surgery early to deal with the paperwork she'd been unable to look at the day before because of the incident at the Caledonian Hotel. There was a message from Atholl to say that the laboratory had confirmed that aconite had been found in the horseradish sauce sample and that the patients were all doing well—and that he was looking forward to their dinner together that evening!

Terry sat down in front of the usual pile of circulars from drug companies, medical magazines and letters that came in on a daily basis, sorting them out with a light heart. She mused rather distractedly on what she would wear that evening. Her wardrobe was decidedly meagre, and she decided to nip out during the lunch-hour on the off chance that the small dress shop in Scuola had anything remotely glamorous she could buy.

One of the letters was a private one, with a handwritten envelope. Odd, that—she never received personal mail nowadays. After all, no one knew where she lived, except her father's solicitor, and that would surely be typewritten.

She turned the envelope over in her hand. There was just the barest address there. 'Dr T. Younger, GP on Scuola.' There was something familiar about the handwriting.

Curiously she slit open the envelope and pulled out a note together with a newspaper clipping—it was the article and photograph about her and Atholl rescuing the baby from the quayside the first day she'd arrived in Scuola. It had obviously been taken up by a national newspaper.

She read the note slowly, hardly comprehending it at first, then reread it with mounting horror. Her mouth suddenly went very dry and her heart started to thump uncomfortably, the light-hearted happiness she'd felt a moment ago draining away from her. She put the note down and stared at it, huddled back against her chair.

'My God,' she whispered. 'What on earth can I do?'

She got up and walked unsteadily over to the window, drawing aside the blind and looking out at the view of the hills and the sea beyond. She was so happy here—happier than she could ever have imagined, coming to a place that was new to her and leaving all she'd known behind. Life was interesting, the people were friendly, and, of course, above all there was Atholl, a man that she knew now that she'd fallen for, hook, line and sinker, in the few weeks she'd been here.

Was all that going to be put in jeopardy because her past had suddenly and horribly caught up with her?

CHAPTER NINE

SHE let the blind go with a snap and went back to the desk, sitting down with her head in her hands, trying to remain calm, to think about what she ought to do. She took up the piece of paper again and reread it, as if by so doing it would be different this time.

Hi, darling,
Bet you didn't think that I'd be in touch with you! No wonder this photo caught my eye immediately—you can change your name but not your looks, even if your hair is shorter! It's amazing how news travels fast, even when it's from a little place like Scuola, isn't it? Now I know where you live, I've come up to the area to have a little chat with you, but mostly to warn you I need some ready cash—a few thousand would help. I'd like you to get this a.s.a.p. I'll give you four days to organise cash in used notes. Better if you keep your mouth shut about this, sweetheart. If you don't, your nice Dr Brodie might get hurt (accidentally of course).
Be seeing you, Max.

Terry shuddered. That damn newspaper! Even though she thought she'd disguised her looks well, had convinced herself that nobody would guess where she was, and had begun to feel relaxed in her life here, Max had found her! The man she'd once thought she'd loved so much had found out where she was and was blackmailing her.

She put her head in her hands, the whole dismal scenario of what had happened to her father reeling through her mind. She'd thought she was so safe up here in Scuola—but it seemed there was to be no hiding place from the implied threats in that horrible little note. And Atholl was in as much danger as she was—she was under no illusion about what Max was capable of. Her father had paid a high price for her involvement with Max because Max didn't care who he hurt.

What the hell could she do? She leaped up from her chair and started pacing about the room, trying to control her panic.

One thing was certain—she couldn't put Atholl at risk by staying at his cottage any longer. In fact, it would be better altogether if they ended their relationship, she thought miserably. He mustn't in any way be sucked into the vile and corrupt world that Max represented. She could imagine Max demanding money from Atholl, and threatening to harm her if Atholl didn't agree.

She would have to inform the police, although it was hard to see how letting them know about this grubby little note would do any good. There weren't many policemen on the island and they could hardly give her twenty-four-hour protection. She would have to move on.

She took the note and put it in her handbag, snapping it shut viciously. She had been naive to think that she wouldn't be discovered—letting herself be photographed for the paper had been a careless mistake. With cold logic she realised that realistically her only option was to leave Scuola and get as far away from Atholl as she could. She could face Max herself but she was damned if Atholl was going to be mixed up in this sordid scenario.

A lump of sadness lodged somewhere in her throat. How could she leave her lovely life here? But Max was her problem, not Atholl's, and she must make her own decisions. It had been too good to be true anyway, she mused sadly. Happiness such as she had started to experience lately could never last—the past had been bound to catch up with her. Somehow she had to be strong and tell Atholl that it was over between them and that she was leaving Scuola.

Atholl was already home when she returned to the cottage.

'Hi, sweetheart.' He smiled, his whole face lighting up as his eyes wandered over her. 'Let's get going—I'm starving! Go and put on your glad rags. Oh, by the way, we're needed in Hersa tomorrow morning—that's the little island I pointed out to you. There's been a case of meningitis affecting a child who was visiting her grandparents on the mainland, and all the children who may have come into contact with her need to be given antibiotics pronto. It needs two of us again, so I'd be much obliged if you'd come with me. Sue's already involved with doing MMR vaccinations here at the baby clinic.'

He waited expectantly for her reply. What could she say? It was an emergency after all.

'Yes...yes, of course I'll come,' she said distractedly.

She closed her eyes briefly, trying to compose herself, psych herself up to tell him that their affair was over and an intimate and romantic dinner with him was not on that evening.

'Atholl, I, er…' She paused for a second, gathering her courage, then swallowed hard and said in a rapid voice, 'Atholl, I can't go out with you tonight.'

He looked at her in surprise. 'Why not?'

She sat down at the little kitchen table and gripped her hands together. 'Because…because I've something I've got to tell you as soon as possible. It's very hard to say this. It…it's about us…'

Atholl looked at her with twinkling eyes. 'Oh, dear, you sound very serious, sweetheart. What is it about us?'

God, this was difficult! Terry twisted her hands together wretchedly. How could she put it to him that although they'd made wonderful love only the evening before, now she wanted to finish their liaison, leave her job?

'The thing is…' she started haltingly. 'The thing is, I think we've been too hasty, Atholl. I…I've been thinking it over and I don't feel I can get involved in a relationship at the moment. It's too soon after Max…I've been too impetuous.'

Atholl sat down on the chair opposite her, his expression changing slowly from humour to incredulity. 'What the hell are you talking about?'

'I…I mean I've just had one intense relationship. I can't leap into another one so quickly.'

'You mean you think you're on the rebound?' He laughed and said in amusement, 'Are you trying to say it's over between us? Good God, we've only just started.'

'I know, I know! That's why I think it's best to stop things before we get too…committed.'

Those amazing eyes bored into hers and she looked

away hastily. 'This seems to have come on very quickly. I didn't notice you holding back yesterday when I kissed you in the surgery,' he commented quietly.

'I had time to think about it when I was clearing things out in my room for Sue. It suddenly came over me,' Terry replied helplessly.

'Come on, sweetheart,' he said gently. He reached across the desk and took her hand. 'We don't have to break up. We can just take things a little more slowly if you feel a bit overwhelmed by it all. As a matter of fact, I also feel as if a steamroller's gone over me—it's been an incredible experience!' He grinned at her. 'Perhaps you feel that, like fine wine, we should savour what we feel, not gulp it down too greedily!'

Terry drew her hand from his and said dully. 'No…half-measures are no good, Atholl.'

He frowned, then said flatly, 'I don't believe you. What's brought this on?'

'I told you—it's too soon after my involvement with Max. I'm in a muddle about my feelings.'

'For God's sake…' Atholl got up from the chair and paced up and down, looking across at her in bewilderment. 'You said Max was a bastard, only wanting what he could get. I'd have thought he was easy enough to get out of your system.' He stood still for a moment, gazing down at her, his eyes like two blue chips of steel lasering their way into her.

'I…I can't switch on and off like that,' said Terry wretchedly. 'I need space, Atholl. I want to move from the cottage and lead a completely separate life. In fact…' Her voice trembled slightly. 'I think it's better if I leave the practice. It would be incredibly hard to work so closely with you after what's gone on between us and then to go on as…as mere colleagues.'

He shook his head, then came round the table and put his hand under her chin and tilted her face to his. 'What's gone wrong, darling?' he asked softly. 'Only a couple of days ago you and I were in each other's arms, making wonderful love. We had the most magical night together. I shall never forget it…'

He pulled her towards him and took her face in his hands, kissing her with tender gentleness, then putting his arms around her and holding her so close to him that she could feel his hip bones next to hers, his heart thumping against her breast. God, what she would have given to have told him everything, to have made love to him then and there!

Terry gritted her teeth. She had to be tough, no good being half-hearted about this, although it was like cutting off her right arm. She tried to pull herself away from him, but he held onto her with a grip of steel, looking down at her with his incredible eyes.

'Don't tell me Sunday night meant nothing to you, Terry,' he said huskily.

'Of course not. I enjoyed it very much Atholl.'

Atholl's hands dropped to his sides abruptly, and he stepped back a pace.

'Enjoyed it?' he exploded, staring at her incredulously for a second, then he sank back into the chair, shaking his head. 'I thought it would mean more to you than eating an ice cream.'

'As I said, once I realised I didn't want total commitment, I decided it was better to finish things promptly. You once mentioned that relationships between doctors didn't work, and perhaps you're right—better not to risk it.'

Atholl laughed shortly. 'For God's sake, that was a throw-away remark, a joke, sweetheart.'

'I...I feel I'm not sure about anything at the moment. It wouldn't be fair to lead you on like Zara did and then let you down.' Terry's voice was stony, unemotional. It was the only way she could do it.

'Don't bring Zara Grahame into this,' he said roughly. 'I thought you loved it here, even before we got together. You told me you loved the people, the countryside,' he added. 'And I thought you loved me a little too.'

Terry licked her dry lips, and said nothing. It was too dreadful: she was telling lie after lie. Of course she loved him, more than ever now, and that was why she had to cut herself off from Atholl and any danger she might put him in.

There was a long silence, then Atholl stood up again abruptly, his expression becoming cold and his mouth a grim line. 'I see. I didn't realise it was just to be a one-night stand...'

'No! It wasn't—it wasn't anything like that!' Terry cried. The words dragged out of her. 'I just need time to think... without being too near you.'

'You've made your mind up pretty quickly.' His voice was grating. 'And where do you propose to stay in the meantime before you leave the area? The flat here isn't ready yet.'

'I'll go to a B and B I've seen down the road for the time being.'

'Got it all planned, haven't you?'

She looked down at the table, trying to control the tell-tale tears that threatened to engulf her. 'I think it's best, Atholl. You wouldn't want me to be with you unless I was sure, would you?'

'Of course not,' he said with cold politeness. 'You must do what you think fit. I presume you'll take your things fairly soon, then.'

Atholl walked towards the door, turning round just before he opened it. 'I take it you're still working with me here for a little while to give me time to get someone else?'

'Yes,' she whispered. 'But the sooner the better—for both our sakes.'

There was bafflement and grief in the look he gave her, and Terry had a sudden urge to run towards him and fling herself in his arms and tell him that she loved him more than anything else in the world, but she nodded wordlessly, aware that if she said anything she would burst into tears. She heard him bang out of the house, shutting the front door with a crash and then driving down the road with a roar of acceleration.

She shook her head helplessly. She'd gone about this all the wrong way. She should have left as soon as she'd got the note, disappeared out of Atholl's life completely and just written to him later. But she was too selfish, wasn't she? She needed to try and give him some explanation so that he wouldn't think too badly of her, so that he would have time to get help with the practice. As it was, he probably despised her for leading him on and then abandoning him.

She ran upstairs to the little bedroom where she'd been so happy and started stuffing her clothes into her suitcase, sobbing her heart out.

What the hell had gone wrong? Atholl changed gear savagely as he accelerated up the road and into the hills, trying to make sense of the conversation he'd just had with Terry. His thoughts flickered back to their love-making on the shore of the lake by The Culleens. He could swear that the passion and happiness she'd shown then with him hadn't been made up. He could, perhaps, understand that she might want to take things slower—their attraction to each other had been like a thunderbolt, unable to keep their hands off each other. But to finish completely? To leave the practice? It just didn't add up, he thought.

He parked the car at the top of the hill in the little glade he'd taken Terry to on her first day of work, and got out, trying to clear his head in the fresh air. Perhaps, he mused bitterly, he was just a bad judge of women, and he'd learned nothing from his experience with Zara. But deep down he was sure there was something more to this than Terry wanting to take things more slowly. How could she finish a relationship so abruptly when he just knew that what they felt for each other was so strong? His face hardened as he stared unseeingly down at the blue waters of the Scuola Sound. He wouldn't give up on her yet, not while she still remained on the island. He had to find out what was behind this devastating change of mind.

It was such a beautiful morning as the little ferry made its way to Hersa over the calm Scuola Sound. The sea shimmered in the golden sunlight and a flock of terns skimmed over the water to the side of the boat. Terry leaned miserably against the rail and watched the island come closer, unaware of the beauty all around her, her thoughts completely taken up with the horrible situation she found herself in. It was bad enough that that bastard Max was out there somewhere, hunting her, trying to silence her. Almost worse than that was the fact that she had finished things between her and Atholl and she couldn't explain to him the true reason why she'd done it.

Atholl was standing at the other side of the deck, his back to her, ramrod straight. He had merely nodded briefly to her when she'd arrived on the quayside. Now he was on his mobile phone and had started pacing up and down, and Terry could sense his restless energy and the anger he felt sparking off towards her.

He put the phone back in his pocket and folded his arms, looking at the wake creaming behind them and smiling grimly to himself. His mother had just informed him she was coming to stay for a few days soon and he could well imagine what she would say if she knew what had happened between him and Terry. 'She's out of your league, son. She doesn't want to be involved with a boy from the Gorbals. I could have told you this would happen!'

Perhaps that was it. His mother would see what he could not, blinded as he was by attraction for Terry. Terry must suddenly have realised that she was hitching herself to someone from a completely different world from his. He gazed stonily over the water, his lips set in a firm line. He wouldn't have thought it of Terry—she had seemed so fresh, so straightforward—but, then, what did he know about women? He'd made one bad mistake so the odds were that he could easily make another.

And yet…he turned round and looked at Terry standing by the rail, her slender figure looking vulnerable, her short fair hair whipping across her elfin face. He'd thought he'd known her so well—she seemed to be the last person in the world who would be concerned with something as trivial as the background one would come from, and he couldn't really believe that she felt that about him.

At that moment she turned round and looked at him, and her expression had such pain and sadness in it that he could swear that she still felt something for him. She had been so intransigent about them parting and yet he couldn't believe that that was what she really wanted.

What was he to do? He couldn't force Terry to change her mind, but he was damned if he'd just sit back and let her go away without a fight. And he'd find out the cause of this sudden change of heart if it was the last thing he did.

Terry went over to a bench and sat down. It was no good regretting what she'd done—it was the only option that she could see. She had contacted the police and they were aware of the situation, giving her a special number to ring if she felt threatened. It hadn't made her feel any safer.

They were drawing up to the little dockside now and the ropes had been thrown over the bollards to hold the ferry steady. Atholl was pushing his motorbike down the ramp and Terry followed him, horribly aware that she would have to get on the back of it and cling to him when they rode to the clinic. The last thing she needed was to be as close to him as that, holding onto his muscled body, awakening all kinds of feelings she was trying to suppress.

'Put this on,' he said unsmilingly as he handed her a crash helmet.

She took it wordlessly and then climbed onto the pillion seat behind him. He stamped on the accelerator and they whirled off. Terry closed her eyes and gritted her teeth as she pressed against him—so close to him physically and yet already so far from him emotionally. She had hurt him desperately, she knew, and he was angry and frustrated at her inexplicable change of heart. His manner had become cold and distant even now as if to cut himself off from her—and who could blame him? He must feel he hadn't had much luck with women, reflected Terry miserably.

They stopped outside a small building with the words 'Hersa Community Hall' across the front, where a queue of children with parents were going in. Atholl and Terry got off the bike and he propped it up against the wall and took out a bag from underneath the pillion seat.

'Come on,' he said brusquely. 'Let's get this done.'

There were plenty of children there, some from one of the other tiny inhabited islands near Hersa but who attended the local school. Their parents were all extremely worried and a lot of reassurance had to be given that their offspring were highly unlikely to contract meningitis and that the antibiotics were merely a precaution.

Sitting so close to Atholl and working steadily through their young patients, it would seem to the outsider that there was nothing amiss between them, reflected Terry. Atholl was courteous to her when he spoke, but had introduced her to the parents as 'Dr Younger, who is just filling in for my uncle for a short time'. When he said that, his eyes caught hers for a second and there was mutual misery in their locked gazes. Terry turned away abruptly to deal with her next small patient, a little boy with a snub nose and freckles.

'And your name is…?' she asked him.

'Jimmy Scott, miss.' He grinned at her as she gave him the injection, seemingly unaffected by the thought of a needle in his arm. 'So are you and Dr Brodie sweethearts?'

he asked cheekily. 'My auntie on Scuola says you make a lovely couple—I've heard her tell my mam!'

A posse of children around him burst into a fit of giggles and some of the parents remonstrated with them.

'Will you hush up, Jimmy?' scolded his mother. 'You're so rude. Do forgive him,' she pleaded. 'I'm afraid rumours get round this area very quickly…'

'It's quite all right, I'm immune to rumours,' said Terry, stretching her mouth into a false smile. 'There you are, Jimmy, you're all done now.' Beside her she was intensely aware that Atholl couldn't have helped but hear the exchange.

'I hope you've enjoyed your time in this area,' continued the woman politely.

'Yes,' sighed Terry. 'I have—very much.'

The last of the children had been seen and the hall was empty. Atholl started to push the chairs that had been used back against the wall and Terry wandered outside, unable to stand the atmosphere between the two of them in the empty room.

He came out into the sunshine and stopped for a second, taking in her woeful expression and the sad droop of her shoulders. Finishing their relationship evidently hadn't made her any happier, he thought.

'Right,' he remarked. 'Back to Scuola—and do I take it you're staying at the B and B tonight?'

'Yes. You can drop me off there.'

He nodded and got on the bike, and again there was the exquisite torture for her of being so close to Atholl as they flew along the road as she had been on the shores of the lake. Terry gave up trying to lean away from him as they drove along a winding road and allowed herself to squeeze up to his solid body, burying her head in the back of his leather jacket and savouring the warm, masculine smell of him. This would be the last time she would ever be this close to him, she cried inwardly to herself.

When they got off the boat the attractive house that did bed and breakfast was only a few minutes away. Atholl drew to a halt outside it and sat for a minute, waiting for Terry to dismount, then he got off the bike and took off his helmet, his dark hair ruffling in the breeze.

'I'll be ringing the agency for an emergency locum this afternoon,' he said tersely. 'Hopefully I can get one short term, starting in the next day or two.'

'Very well. I think it's for the best, Atholl.' Terry tried to sound calm and measured, to disguise the little catch in her voice. 'You'll let me know when one becomes available.'

She turned and went into the house and Atholl went back to The Sycamores and parked his bike against the wall as he was just going in to catch up on his e-mails. A young man smoking a cigarette and smartly dressed in a casual suede coat and cream cords was standing near the entrance, looking at the brass plaque on the wall that listed the doctors who worked there. Terry's name had not yet been added, so there were only Atholl and his uncle's names on it.

'Can I help you?' asked Atholl.

The man turned round and smiled. He was good looking in a tough kind of way, but with a hardness about him that reminded Atholl of the kind of youths he used to hang around with in Glasgow, although this man had a veneer of sophistication and polish about him.

'Thanks. I believe that Dr Younger works here—but I

don't see her name on the plaque. I was hoping to meet up with her.'

'She has been working here,' answered Atholl brusquely. 'But she's leaving.'

'Ah...I see.' The man frowned slightly. 'And you are her colleague, I take it?'

'Yes, I am.' Atholl didn't elaborate—he felt tired and irritable and not willing to enter into a conversation with a stranger.

'You don't happen to know her address, do you? I seem to have mislaid it.'

Some instinct made Atholl wary of giving the man that information. 'I only know she's moved from the place she was living in very recently,' he said evasively. 'Are you a close friend?'

The young man smiled. 'Oh, yes, we were very close—and I knew her father very well.' He flicked his cigarette into the grass verge. 'Never mind, I'll catch up with her. As I said, she'll be expecting me.'

He walked off down the road and Atholl's gaze followed him. The first hint of anyone from Terry's background to have surfaced, he reflected as he went into the building, then his mobile phone rang and he answered it, putting the man out of his mind.

CHAPTER TEN

'I've got an emergency locum,' said Atholl tersely the next day, standing in front of the desk and looking down at Terry. 'He's starting tomorrow.'

So this is my last day here, and my successor is a man, Terry thought wryly. Not that she could blame Atholl—he'd surely never employ a woman again! She nodded wordlessly and sighed. The happiness she'd found in Scuola had been so short-lived. If only she could tell Atholl why she was leaving, what the whole background was. Impossible now. His safety depended on her cutting off any connection with him.

She bit her lip and said in a choked voice, 'Thanks for telling me, Atholl. I…I'm sorry it worked out like this.'

A moment's silence, then he said softly and unexpectedly, putting his hands on the desk and leaning towards her, deep blue eyes holding hers, 'So am I, Terry, so am I. You know it doesn't have to be like this. Are you quite, quite sure you want us to end things?' He looked at her searchingly. 'Is there something you're not telling me?'

She turned her face away from his, unable to meet his

eyes, biting her lip. 'How do you mean?' Her voice was edgy, cautious.

Atholl shrugged and said simply, 'Because everything seemed so right—you, me, the way we worked together. Sweetheart, I'm adding two and two together here and it's making five—there's no sense to it.'

His tender voice hung in the room so tantalisingly, just as he had sounded when he had made love to her that wonderful evening by the loch, and it was heart-breaking. Terry took a deep breath and got up from the desk, walking towards the window to get away from his scrutiny.

'It's for the best, believe me…'

He frowned and looked at her assessingly. She hadn't really answered his question. He stepped towards her and put out his hand to pull away a stray tendril of hair that covered her forehead, and she stiffened, willing him to move away again, to be anywhere but in that danger zone of closeness that made her stomach turn over. His hand strayed down her cheek and traced the line of her jaw down to her neck, and involuntarily she turned towards him, her face a picture of misery.

'Please, Atholl…don't…'

His hands were on the wall either side of her head, imprisoning her against it so that she couldn't escape, and his body was nearly against hers as he gazed at her with those clear blue eyes. He was too close—far too close for comfort!

'Tell me you don't love me, Terry,' he said roughly. 'Tell me now that we aren't meant to be together. It's not too late.'

His mouth came down and kissed her full on her lips, gently but possessively, his hands running lightly over the curving fullness of her breasts, turning her insides to liquid and reminding her of just what she would lose when they parted. And he was right—they should have been together, she thought in anguish. His touch became more demanding, his lips plundering hers, teasing them open, his body pressing urgently against her, and she felt her resolve sliding away, starting to respond helplessly to his passion.

Then Max's horrible note seemed to dance in front of her eyes and she forced herself to think of the danger she was putting Atholl in the longer she was near him. With every ounce of energy and resolve that she had, she twisted away from him and stood by the window, touching her lips where he had kissed them, still feeling them tingle.

'I can't get back with you, Atholl…I just can't,' she said desperately.

He straightened up and ran a hand roughly through his hair. 'I'm sorry, Terry.' He walked back to the desk, his back view slightly hunched as if gathering himself together, and after a few seconds turned round and said slowly, 'Very well, I shall have to accept it.' Then after a few seconds he added more briskly, 'By the way, some man was asking about you last night—said he was an old friend of yours and knew your father.'

A sudden chill of foreboding laid its fingers on Terry's heart. It had to be Max. There was no one else it could possibly be. So he'd got here already. Thank God she'd moved out of Atholl's cottage.

She swallowed and forced herself to say lightly, 'Really? Did you tell him my new address?'

'I'm not in the habit of giving private information to people I don't know.'

It was hard to hide the relief in her voice. 'No, of course not. Did he give his name?'

'No…I didn't have a chance to ask him. He was quite tall, fair haired—ring any bells?'

Terry shook her head. 'Can't think who it might be. Anyway, he'll probably find me if he needs to.' Her heart thumped uncomfortably, a picture of Max and those lazy hooded grey eyes smiling at her flashing into her imagination, and she shuddered. She forced herself to calm down and speak normally. 'I'll tidy up my desk, then, and update the notes for the new locum. I'll, er…see you before I go after tonight's surgery.'

'If you want to. I'll be here until I go to visit my uncle tonight.' Atholl turned round and went out of the room.

He walked slowly down the corridor to his surgery. Funny how she hadn't seemed excited that someone from London had come up to see her—someone who had known her father. But, then, Atholl mused, she never talked about her life in London or reminisced about her family. It was as if she had obliterated everything that had gone before her arrival in Scuola.

In the end Terry couldn't bear to say good bye to anyone. She knew how incredulous they would be that she was leaving when she had seemed to be so happy in her work. Instead, she left a note saying how much she had enjoyed her time with them, but unavoidable circumstances had meant she had to move on urgently, and that she would always remember Scuola and think of it fondly. She also left a short letter to Atholl.

The girls had all gone home, although she knew Atholl was still at the surgery because his bike was outside. She put the notes on the desk in the office and then after a wistful final look around the room she let herself out of the building and walked down to the bed and breakfast, looking around carefully to see no one was following her.

Atholl watched Terry walk down the street from his surgery window, until her slight figure neared the corner. Perhaps it was for the best that she hadn't come back to say goodbye personally. He sighed and was about to turn away when he noticed a man appearing from a side street and start to walk in the same direction. Nothing unusual in that, except that he recognised him as the man he'd spoken to last night who said he'd known Terry's father.

He watched as the man caught up with Terry. He must have said something to her because she stopped and turned round, then took a step back before the man took her arm. She seemed to be having a conversation with him and then, with the man still holding her arm firmly, they disappeared round the corner. She didn't look particularly surprised to see him.

Atholl wandered into the office, his mind preoccupied, slightly edgy. He saw two notes on the desk, one in Terry's writing addressed to him. He smiled bitterly as he picked it up and tore it open. It wouldn't be a love letter…

Atholl, please don't think badly of me. Believe me when I say I've never felt so happy as I did here with you. Meeting you was like coming alive again—a complete knockout to the heart. Perhaps I haven't put my reasons for leaving very clearly. I only know it's best that we part. I shall never ever forget you,
Terry.

He frowned, fingering the note thoughtfully. She was saying that she hadn't been entirely clear about why she wanted to leave—was that a hint that there was more behind all this than she had told him? The uneasiness he had felt before flickered like a gathering fire through his mind. Something was not quite right about the whole thing. Intuitively he felt she was keeping something back from him.

A sudden wave of determination swept through him. Damn it, he would go and see her at the bed and breakfast, whether that man was there or not, try and question her once and for all about this extraordinary decision of hers. He deserved a fuller explanation than she'd given him.

Mrs Bedowes, the woman who ran the bed and breakfast, answered the door.

'Dr Brodie!' she said in surprise. 'Can I help you?'

'I wondered if Dr Younger was here. I believe she's staying with you for a night or two?'

Mrs Bedowes shook her head. 'Well, no. She's just checked out, actually. She and her young man just came to collect her things—she's decided to leave tonight.'

Atholl raised an eyebrow. 'Her young man?'

'Oh, quite a charmer he was too. So much in love with her—he wouldn't let her out of his sight. He said he wished they'd had time to stay longer in such a lovely place as Scuola. Apparently Dr Younger has to do a quick home visit before they go off for a break, so she picked up her medical bag and case.'

'A home visit?' repeated Atholl, puzzled. As far as he knew, Terry had finished work and had no home visits planned.

'That's right,' said Mrs Bedowes with an indulgent smile. 'Her boyfriend wants to take her on a little holiday—they're such a sweet young couple. They were clinging to each other as if one of them might disappear!'

Terry's boyfriend? Atholl stared at the woman as a sudden extraordinary thought struck him. Was it possible that Max had come back into the picture? Was that why she'd finished things between them, because she'd realised she still loved the man, and knew he was coming to see her?

'Did...did you happen to catch this man's name?' he asked diffidently.

Mrs Bedowes smiled. 'Oh, yes, but only his first name. He answered his mobile in the middle of talking to me. I heard him say, "Max here."'

So that was it! Suddenly things were becoming clearer. Atholl stared at her wordlessly for a second, feeling as if someone had punched him in the solar plexus. Why the hell hadn't Terry told him the truth? Why keep it a secret that she was going back to Max, instead of reeling off all this garbage about not wanting to commit herself so soon after her affair with Max, and that things between himself and her had been going too fast?

She'd pretended that she hadn't a clue who Max was when Atholl had told her that a man had come to see her. But it had been a lie. She must have known damn well it had been Max but hadn't wanted Atholl to know.

A mixture of betrayal, rage and deep hurt flooded through him, but with a great effort he managed to control his voice, and said pleasantly enough, 'How long ago did they leave? I saw them going towards your place ten minutes ago.'

'Oh, they've only just gone.' The woman pointed up the road. 'They're in a blue car—they went up the main road towards the hills.'

'Thanks!' shouted Atholl over his shoulder, as he ran towards his motorbike and tried to kick-start it. It sputtered reluctantly into life and he roared off in the direction the woman had indicated. Again he felt slightly puzzled about Mrs Bedowes's reference to Terry going on a home visit. He tried to think of the patient she might be seeing on this route, thinking that at least it would give him a chance to catch up with her before she disappeared on this jaunt with a man she'd said had caused her great unhappiness.

What a fool he'd been! He should have realised that she was still hankering after that damn Max, but he had to confront her and hear from her own lips the whole truth this time. He was damned if he'd be fobbed off with a load of lies and half-truths.

If she was leaving because Max had come back into the picture, why hadn't she had the guts to tell him? Atholl felt a knot of anguish in his stomach—he'd thought more of Terry's honesty than that.

The bike was not performing well—he'd been meaning to strip it down and clean the plugs for some time. Every few minutes it seemed to die on him before surging back into life, and he decided that as he was passing his cottage, he'd stop there and take his car instead.

He was surprised to see that Shona was in the little garden when he arrived, barking her head off. He was sure he'd left the door closed when he'd gone to work. He got off his bike, propped it against the wall and bent down to ruffle Shona's fur.

'Have you seen Terry, old girl? And why are you outside?'

Shona wagged her tail furiously, then ran up and down the path, whining and looking back at Atholl. He looked around. No sign of anyone. It all looked very quiet, but Shona was obviously agitated. He followed the dog up the path and went up the step to open the door.

As soon as she felt that hand on her shoulder, Terry knew it was him—Max had caught up with her. She turned round slowly and looked into the distinctive pale grey eyes of the man she'd once thought she loved so much, and whom she'd last seen jumping into a car outside the bank on the day of the robbery. That was the day her father had been found bound and gagged in the office, the day he'd died of a heart attack.

Max had been wearing a balaclava and a tracksuit, but she'd known it was him all right—there was no disguising those unusual eyes of his and the old scar that cut across his eyebrow. She had recognised his accomplice in the get-away car—Max's brother, Harry, and he hadn't been wearing anything over his face. They'd screeched off round a corner and she had stood rooted to the spot, immobile with shock, shattered by the realisation that Max Carter was a criminal.

No one else had been in the road—it had been an early summer's evening and people had finished work and gone home. Terry had managed, with trembling fingers, to call for the police and, by some inner instinct, for an ambulance, then she'd gone and found her father tied up in his own office, obviously gravely ill. She'd tried desperately to massage her father's heart back to life, although she'd known that it had been too late—her beloved father had died.

In the months that had elapsed since that day, Max and Harry had gone to ground—completely vanished—and the police had said it was most likely they'd managed to flee the country, but they couldn't be sure. And now here was Max standing two feet away from her and looking at her with a familiar grin—good looking, charming even, but, as she now knew, an evil bastard.

'Hello, Theresa, surprised to see me?' he said. 'You didn't think I'd catch up with you so soon, did you? Thought changing your name and getting a new hairdo would be enough to keep you hidden?' He laughed softly. 'I'm not put off the scent that easily, you know.'

Cold terror gripped Terry's chest like a band forcing the air out of her lungs, but she looked back at him steadily, her voice coming out strongly, scornfully, belying the fear she felt.

'I've nothing to say to you, Max, except this—you as good as murdered my father and you deserve to be in jail. I've informed the police about your horrible note.'

Max frowned, narrowing his eyes. 'You shouldn't have contacted the police, darling, not a clever thing to do. That note was between me and you, just to warn you that I need the money—when we've had our little talk.'

He took her arm and pulled her with him. 'I know where you're staying. I watched you take your cases to that B and B yesterday. Now you're going to come on a little holiday with me.'

Terry hung back, looking at him defiantly and telling herself what an insignificant-looking man he was. 'You can't make me. Anything you've got to say to me you can say it here and now!'

He came closer to her his lips a thin line. 'You know what I want. I need money to get away from here, start a new life.'

'I've no money on me…I can't arrange it so quickly,' Terry started to say.

He scowled. 'I told you to get some. I'll take you to a bank on the mainland and you can get some out—you doctors are well paid.'

By this time Max had pulled her round the corner and towards an old blue car just past the bed and breakfast place.

'And how will you make me do what you want, Max?' asked Terry coldly.

Max put his hand in his pocket and pulled out a handgun, at the same time pulling her towards him in what looked like an embrace to any passer-by. 'Perhaps this will persuade you, darling. Any nonsense and I won't hesitate to use it on you…or on anyone in our way.'

He meant it, thought Terry, her body shaking as she felt the muzzle of the gun press into her ribs. Max continued to hold her close to him.

'Before we do anything else I need some of your professional expertise, sweetheart. Harry's met with a little accident and I want your help in getting him right.'

'What's happened to him?'

'He got a bullet wound through his leg from an…acquaintance. The wound looks a bit black.'

Terry's mind raced—anything to buy time that might allow her to ring the police. 'I'll need to get my medical bag—it's at the B and B. We'll have to pick it up—I can't do anything without that.'

Max frowned. 'I thought you were a doctor—why do you need equipment?'

'If he's got any infection, he'll need antibiotics. There's penicillin in the bag…I may need tweezers to get the bullet out.'

Max pondered, biting his lip. 'OK,' he said at last. 'But

you do what I say—we're lovers, understand?' Then with a cruel smile. 'Quite like old times, eh? Keep close to me and don't say anything you shouldn't.'

It took only a few minutes to get the medical bag and Terry's case. Mrs Bedowes, the owner of the B and B seemed unconcerned that Terry was checking out, and soon Max was pulling her back to his car, hugging her close to him. Harry was sitting in the back seat, lolling back and looking ashen, and a stain of blood had spread across his trouser leg. Terry was shoved in beside him and Max gave the gun to Harry.

'Keep that pointing towards her,' Max said. 'Don't worry, Harry, it's plain sailing so far. She'll fix up that leg of yours when we've got out of here.'

'It looks as if he's lost a lot of blood,' said Terry. 'I'll have to look at the wound pretty soon before he passes out.'

'Well, you're not looking at it in the village. We'll go into the hills first.'

Terry lay back in the car seat, her eyes closed. She knew it wasn't just money they wanted, or for her to look at Harry's wound—they needed to silence her for ever. She was, after all, the only witness who had seen the robbery, who knew for sure it was Max and Harry that had robbed the bank and caused her father's death.

The car stopped and she opened her eyes and saw that they'd parked the vehicle in a little copse before Atholl's cottage: it couldn't be seen from the road.

'Come on, darling, out you get.'

Terry was bewildered. 'Why have you stopped here?'

'For you to attend to Harry, of course. We know it's Dr Brodie's place, but I've been monitoring him. Tonight he's going to the mainland to see his uncle, and he won't be back for hours. Plenty of time for you to do the doctor bit for Harry and for us to have a coffee before we get going again.'

'I can't think why you're bothering with Harry—you didn't show such compassion for my father when you left him dying at the bank.'

Max grinned. 'Harry's my brother—the only person in the world I can trust.'

There were sounds of a car coming up the road behind them. Terry couldn't move her arms as they marched her along, but she threw back her head and screamed as loudly as she could. The car swept past, ignoring them.

Max pulled to a halt and turned Terry round towards him, drew back his hand and slapped her hard across the face, the signet ring he had on his little finger catching her cheek and slitting it open.

'Don't try that again. The next time it'll be more painful,' he snarled.

Terry sucked in her breath, her eyes stinging with tears at the pain, feeling blood oozing down her cheek. They pulled her up the path. Easy enough to kick the door open, and then throw her inside. Shona bounded towards her, barking delightedly and jumping up at her.

'Get that animal out of here,' growled Max to Harry. 'I don't like dogs.'

Harry gave Shona a casual kick out of the door and the dog yelped loudly, then turned round and snapped at the man's shoes. Another kick and poor Shona was out on the path and the door was slammed shut.

'How could you?' Terry screamed at Harry. 'What's the poor dog ever done to you?'

'Be quiet!' snapped Max. 'Sit down on that sofa.'

Terry sat down, trying to stop her limbs from trembling. She was damned if she'd show these men how terrified she was. At least they'd be gone by the time Atholl returned from seeing his uncle and he wouldn't be involved.

Then suddenly they heard the uneven sound of a motorbike coming up the road and stuttering to a halt in front of the cottage.

'Who the hell's that?' Harry turned a white, frightened face towards the door.

Max pulled Terry in front of him and held the gun against her head. 'Whoever it is, I won't give them the chance to get away.'

Terry looked in terror towards the door. She could hear Shona barking joyfully—it had to be Atholl returning early. Any minute he'd come in—and then what? They all waited, frozen, hardly breathing. A few minutes passed—still no sound except distant traffic coming up the road towards them.

'Where the hell is he?' muttered Harry uneasily. 'Perhaps he's taken the dog for a bleedin' walk.'

'Shut up!' snarled Max, tiptoeing to the window and peering out of the corner. 'He's not there. I think you're right, Harry, he's taken—'

There was a crash and the door from the kitchen burst open behind them. The men spun round and Atholl said, 'What the hell's going on?'

His gaze took in the scene of Terry with Max holding a gun to her head, and the prone body of Harry lying across the sofa with a large wound on his leg.

He sucked in his breath. 'Good God, Terry…' He turned to the two men and said in a low, harsh voice, 'What the hell have you done to Dr Younger?'

Max laughed unpleasantly. 'Dr Younger? You've been misinformed, my friend. Allow me to introduce Dr Theresa Masterson.'

Atholl frowned and made to come towards Terry. 'I don't know what you're talking about, but put that bloody gun down.'

Max pressed his gun more firmly against Terry's head and said unsmilingly, 'Don't come any nearer, or else your colleague will get hurt. If you co-operate, we'll let her go, eventually.'

Atholl stood stock still, his blue eyes bright with fury, a muscle working in his cheek. 'You bastards…'

Max laughed, a coarse, cruel laugh. 'She knows a little too much about us, don't you, darling? We need to make a new life and we don't want her putting a spoke in our plans. A little money to help us get away would be a good start.'

'I see.' Atholl stepped back, looking at the men assessingly. Then he said in a voice that was dangerously cool and unflurried, 'And how much were you thinking of?'

'We were thinking of ten thousand, but now you've appeared on the scene we might be tempted to take more…'

Terry watched Atholl with anguished eyes. He had been dragged into this and it had been her fault for not leaving the moment she'd known she'd been discovered. He looked so cool, so relaxed, as if there was nothing unusual about a gangster waving a gun in front of him.

Then several things happened at once. An explosion of sound. Both doors suddenly crashed open and several uniformed, shouting policemen burst into the room. Almost before they'd come in Atholl leapt at Max in the split second the man's attention had been diverted and punched him to the floor, forcing the gun out of his grip. Max lay there stunned for a minute, having hit his head hard on the fireplace surround, and was leapt on by one of the policemen. Harry was being held down on the floor between two policemen, his wrists handcuffed.

A large policeman helped to haul Atholl up from the floor where the force of the punch he'd given Max had landed him.

'We told you not to go in, Dr Brodie. You could have ruined the whole operation,' he growled. 'It was a risky thing to do…both of you could have been killed.'

Atholl looked slightly abashed. 'I couldn't wait,' he said simply. 'You weren't going to go in for ten minutes. God knows what could have happened in that time.'

'I'll be putting a report in,' grumbled the officer.

Atholl ignored the man and strode over to Terry, who was watching the scene with a mixture of bewilderment and relief. He sat on the sofa and put his arms round her. 'My darling, what's been going on?' he asked gently, touching her bruised and bleeding face delicately. 'Why didn't you tell me you were being threatened before? I was actually on my way to try and find you, and stopped off here to pick up my car. I was just about to open the door when a pack of policeman burst out of the bushes—apparently they've been shadowing you, hoping you'd lead them to these two brutes.'

Terry closed her eyes and big tears squeezed themselves out and rolled down her cheeks. 'I couldn't,' she whispered. 'I was told not to say anything about what happened in London. I'm so sorry, Atholl. I didn't think they'd find me here. I thought I was safe…and I didn't want you involved when—'

'It doesn't matter, it doesn't matter, sweetheart,' he murmured, cradling her head on his shoulder and rocking her backwards and forwards as one would a frightened child. 'All that matters is your safety. It's all behind you now.'

One of the policemen gave a polite cough. 'Excuse me, sir, we're taking these men away now. Er…perhaps when Dr Younger's had time to recover a little, you'd both come down to the station. I believe the Met will be sending up an officer to complete all the enquiries.'

As Max was led out he turned round to look at Terry. 'Didn't take long to find yourself someone new, did it, sweetheart?' he said bitterly.

The house seemed very quiet when all the policemen had gone, escorting Max and Harry to a police van. For several minutes Atholl remained holding Terry, neither of them speaking, then he turned her face toward him, bending his forehead to hers.

'And I thought you and that bloody man had got together again, and that was the reason you'd finished things between us,' he said softly. 'That was why I came roaring after you, to make you tell me the truth, force you to admit that you still loved him.'

'How wrong you were,' said Terry wanly. She looked at Atholl with tears in her eyes. 'I couldn't tell you the truth because I loved you so much. I didn't want you to be involved. I'd been told it would be complete folly to reveal my background.'

Atholl took her hands in his. 'I can make an educated guess that you've been given a new identity—some sort of police witness protection?'

Terry nodded. 'It was all taken out of my hands really.

Even the BMA was informed about my new name and the records changed. I was to get another job far from London through the agency you used. You see,' she added sadly, 'I thought Max really loved me. I was wrong. He wanted to get in with my father, gather information discreetly about the bank my father worked for, the times of cash deliveries—things like that.'

'Max seemed quite well spoken and educated—not the kind to want to rob a bank,' observed Atholl.

'He and his brother were gamblers—they needed plenty of money to pay their debts and fund their lifestyle.'

'But surely your father was very discreet about anything to do with the bank?'

'My father was quite a lonely man after Mum died. Over a few months he came to adore Max. They played golf together, Max took him racing, we all went to the theatre. Dad regarded him as the son he'd never had. Dad was thrilled I was going out with such a seemingly charismatic and successful man.'

Atholl nodded. 'He built up a rapport with your father, I'm sure, and your father would trust him.'

'Exactly. Max had led us to believe that he was a producer and a writer for a television company and my father was fascinated by the media world. After a while Max told him he had an idea for a play about—would you believe?—a gang of bank robbers. He asked my gullible father to help him write it. Of course, Dad was intensely flattered and excited—it gave him a new lease on life.'

'And after that I guess it was easy to extract information about bank practices regarding security, times of cash deliveries, and so,' said Atholl grimly.

Terry sighed. 'Dad was an innocent—and so was I, of

course. Max manipulated my father so that he never realised he was being indiscreet.'

'But why were you on witness protection?' asked Atholl.

Terry took another long sip of her whisky, draining the glass, then said grimly, 'I was at the bank when the raid took place. I'd gone after work to meet my father, which I often did. We were going to have a meal out together. I waited by the side door I knew my father would use. I…I remember there was no one around, but a car with its engine running was parked at the other side of the street…'

Terry's voice faded a bit as the scene replayed itself in her mind.

'Go on,' prompted Atholl gently. 'Tell me everything.'

'Suddenly a man burst out of the door, almost knocking me over, and ran across the road to leap into the car. I knew instinctively it was a raid and rang the police on my mobile—and for some reason the ambulance as well.'

'And you knew who the man was?'

'Oh, yes.' Terry's voice was bitter. 'I could tell it was Max. His face was hidden, but he looked me right in the eyes—there's no mistaking his eyes, they're a most unusual colour. I could easily see it was Harry, his brother, in the car—he wasn't covered up at all. Until that moment I had no idea that I'd been going out with a criminal—the man who caused my father's death.'

Atholl said quietly, 'Your father died—did they shoot him?'

'No,' said Terry in a small, sad voice. 'He'd been bound and gagged and he had a heart attack. I…I couldn't save him. I knew as soon as I saw him when I ran to his office that it was too late.'

Atholl hugged her to him, stroking her back comfortingly. 'A terrible, terrible thing…' he whispered. 'And I guess the police wanted you as a witness?'

'Without me, the police felt they didn't have enough evidence to secure a conviction even if they caught Max and Harry. I was told my life would be in danger if I stayed around while they were still at large.'

Atholl grinned. 'That's one thing you won't have to worry about now—those two won't be going anywhere in a hurry.'

Terry got up and wandered to the window, looking out at the beautiful view. She turned round and smiled brilliantly at Atholl. 'Yes, thank God. No more deception, no hiding the real story. At last I can be me again…Theresa Masterson. I'm a free woman!'

'I don't care what name you go under,' growled Atholl. 'When we made love underneath the stars that night on the shores of the loch, I knew that I'd found the woman I wanted to spend the rest of my life with. We've both had lucky escapes.'

Terry shook her head. 'I thought I'd never see you again,' she said. 'I thought you'd hate me for ending things so abruptly.'

'No, don't interrupt.' Atholl put his finger to Terry's lips for a second, gazing down into her eyes. 'When you said you wanted to end it between us it was the saddest day I can remember—but you know something? I didn't really believe you wanted to go—and I was right, wasn't I?'

He stroked a tendril of hair from her forehead, and Terry's heart began to do a little tattoo of happiness against her chest. She looked up at this man that she'd learned to love and thought she'd lost, and began to laugh.

'"Oh, what a tangled web we weave, when first we practise to deceive,"' she murmured, and looked up into his kind, wonderful face. 'If you really want me back, Atholl Brodie, that's all right with me!'

'I want more than that, Terry,' Atholl said with dancing eyes. 'I want you to change your name again—but for keeps this time. Don't you think Theresa Brodie sounds pretty good?'

EPILOGUE

SUNSHINE bathed the gardens of the Caledonian Hotel, and the little crowd of people on the terrace spilled down the steps and onto the lawn. Their happy chatter and clink of glasses drifted across the air and down to the shore of the sound, where the hotel had a little private dock with a small boat moored to it.

Atholl looked down at his dainty bride, sparkling in her long, fitted cream dress with its low-cut neckline and bodice covered with tiny seed pearls.

'You look so beautiful, Mrs Brodie,' he said huskily. 'I don't think I can wait to get this reception over and board the boat to go over the sea to our little bit of heaven on Skye…'

Terry looked up at impishly. 'You'll just have to contain yourself, darling. There's sixty people waiting to hang on your every word before we set off!'

Atholl groaned. 'Then I'll make the speech short for all our sakes!'

There can't be many moments in life that as are magical as this, thought Terry, looking across at the sun-kissed, sparkling sea and back to the guests surrounding her and Atholl. When she'd come on that first apprehensive day to Scuola she could never have imagined that a few months later she would be feeling this happy, her whole being bubbling with the euphoria of being loved by a man she adored. After the horror of Max, she'd given up on men, distrusting her own judgement, frightened of being betrayed again. And yet, against all the odds, she'd found just the man she needed.

'Are you not going to cut the cake yet, Atholl?' A tall woman with Atholl's blue eyes came up to them. 'Come on, son, we want to hear what you've got to say and then you can get off on that boat!'

'Don't worry, Mother. I'm as anxious to get off as you are to get rid of me!' Atholl grinned.

Mrs Brodie turned to her new daughter-in-law. 'And I'm very pleased that he chose the right lass—it took him long enough to find you,' she said softly, and her eyes twinkled. 'And it's about time I had some grandchildren!'

Cyril banged a gavel on the table holding the cake and said importantly, 'Ladies and gentlemen, pray silence for the groom, please!'

Atholl stood before the guests and pulled his bride towards him, looking down at her tenderly. 'Today, everyone, you see a man who couldn't be happier,' he said simply. 'I've met the love of my life, the most beautiful and marvellous woman in the world. I think I must have fallen in love with her the moment I first saw her on the quayside by the harbour the day she arrived. I know her parents would have been so proud of her, and I wish I could have met them to tell them that I will look after their darling daughter most carefully for the rest of my life!'

He raised his glass and smiled. 'To happiness,' he said. 'And to my precious Terry.' Then he kissed her gently.

Terry looked round at the assembled crowd and all the friends she'd made during her short time on Scuola—at Isobel, outspoken, unsentimental, but still dabbing furiously at her eyes with a little hanky. Bunty and Sue were cheering loudly and Shona lay on the lawn, panting happily with a huge pink bow round her neck that Isobel had tied on. Even the two old Mackie sisters were there, sitting primly on chairs to listen to the speeches and sipping champagne rather cautiously.

'Help me step up onto the chair,' she whispered to Atholl, and then, once she was up, she smiled brilliantly at the guests, who fell quiet as they watched her.

'No need to tell you how happy I am,' she said. 'You on Scuola have become my family now, and I look forward to being part of your lives. I was very unhappy before I came here, but now…' She looked down at Atholl and smiled at him. 'Now I've found Atholl, everything's changed. It…it's like a dream come true!'

Then amidst the clapping there was the sudden skirl of pipes and a piper walked down the garden, playing a lilting tune. Atholl swung Terry down from the chair, and as people organised themselves to do an eightsome reel, he grabbed her hand.

'Come on, sweetheart, let's make a dash for it. Your case is on the boat so you can change later when we're out of sight!'

A few minutes later they were drawing away from Scuola across the sound, with the sun still dancing on the waves and the sky a rosy evening pink behind the hills. Atholl put his arm round Terry and pointed out to the water behind them.

'Looks like some other residents have come to wish us happiness,' he murmured.

A school of dolphins was leaping rhythmically out of the water, starting to follow the wake of the boat, their curving bodies silver in the sun.

'How perfect,' breathed Terry.

Her eyes filled with happy tears. How unexpectedly her life had turned around—from deep sadness to unbelievable happiness. A sudden cheer floated across the water from the guests as they realised that Terry and Atholl had left the party, and they both laughed and waved back to them.

'Dr and Mrs Brodie sail off on their new life,' whispered Atholl in her ear, hugging her to him.

A new life…the past forgotten, the future tantalising and exciting. And Terry knew that, whatever storms lay ahead, they could weather them together.

THE PLAYBOY DOCTOR'S SURPRISE PROPOSAL

BY

ANNE FRASER

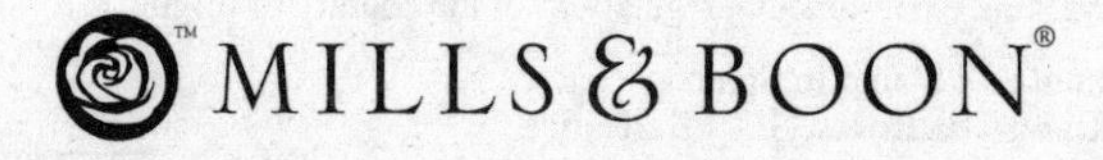

All the characters in this book have no existence outside the imagination of the author, and have no relation whatsoever to anyone bearing the same name or names. They are not even distantly inspired by any individual known or unknown to the author, and all the incidents are pure invention.

First published in Great Britain 2009
Harlequin Mills & Boon Limited,
Eton House, 18-24 Paradise Road, Richmond, Surrey TW9 1SR

ISBN: 978 0 263 86866 1

Set in Times Roman 10½ on 12½ pt
03-0909-52257

Harlequin Mills & Boon policy is to use papers that are natural, renewable and recyclable products and made from wood grown in sustainable forests. The logging and manufacturing process conform to the legal environmental regulations of the country of origin.

Printed and bound in Spain
by Litografia Rosés, S.A., Barcelona

Anne Fraser was born in Scotland, but brought up in South Africa. After she left school she returned to the birthplace of her parents, the remote Western Islands of Scotland. She left there to train as a nurse, before going on to university to study English Literature. After the birth of her first child, she and her doctor husband travelled the world, working in rural Africa, Australia and Northern Canada. Anne still works in the health sector. To relax, she enjoys spending time with her family, reading, walking and travelling.

Recent titles by the same author:

FALLING FOR HER MEDITERRANEAN BOSS
POSH DOC CLAIMS HIS BRIDE
HER VERY SPECIAL BOSS
DR CAMPBELL'S SECRET SON

CHAPTER ONE

HE PLUCKED her out of the sea. One minute she was floundering in the water, the next she was being manhandled to shore by a stranger with bronzed muscles and nutmeg-coloured eyes. It was by far the most embarrassing thing that had happened to her for as long as she could remember.

Ten minutes earlier, Caitlin had plunged into the Pacific, gasping as the cold water chased the heat of the Australian sun from her skin. She had ploughed through the water for a few moments until life had returned to her frozen limbs, then turned on her back and floated.

Her sister, Brianna, and the rest of the group were on the beach. Niall was fussing around lighting the barbecue, while Brianna relaxed with a book. The children were making sandcastles on the startingly white sand, and the sounds of their laughter drifted over to Caitlin on the perfectly still air. She could still scarcely believe that she was here in Brisbane. Months of planning followed by a forty-eight-hour journey from Dublin and finally here she was. She only wished her trip could have been made under happier circumstances. Flipping over onto her stomach, she swam for a few more minutes, then trod water. Brianna's husband, Niall, had promised her that she was safe from sharks this close to shore, but Caitlin wasn't going to take any chances. She'd keep the beach within easy distance.

Looking towards the shore, she could see Niall and Brianna waving to her. Without her glasses, they were slightly fuzzy shapes against the glaring white of the sand. Caitlin waved back. Just a few more minutes then she'd return to shore and help her sister with lunch.

Her stomach gave the familiar flutter of anxiety that she always experienced these days when she thought about her older sister. Although Brianna was recovering well from her treatment, the sight of her nearly bald head with the wispy tendrils of hair had brought tears to Caitlin's eyes when she had first seen her at the airport. It had taken all her resolve not to show how shocked she was when she had hugged her sister and felt the fragile bones. Still she was here now. When she wasn't working, she'd be around to help, at the very least offer moral support.

The next time she looked up the beach had receded. She became aware that Brianna and Niall were still waving and Caitlin waved back again. They probably wanted her back on shore.

Flipping over on her stomach once more, she struck off towards the beach. She was a good swimmer, managing twenty lengths most mornings at her local pool before she left for work. Caitlin believed that routine and discipline were essential parts of life.

Stopping for a moment, she lifted her head out of the water to check the distance to the beach. To her dismay, she didn't seem to have made any progress. In fact, if it was possible, she appeared to have moved away from the shore and further out to sea. For the first time, Caitlin felt a flutter of anxiety. Niall had warned her about the currents but she hadn't paid too much attention, putting his concerns down to him being an anxious brother-in-law. Now, she realised grimly that he hadn't exaggerated. Clearly she was caught in a current that was dragging her out to sea. She felt the first flicker of real alarm.

She had read somewhere that the best thing to do was to swim across the current rather than against it. That way you'd eventually reach a point where the current would disappear. From there it should be easy to swim back.

By this time Niall had waded in up to his thighs and was gesticulating wildly. He had been joined by another figure, and although it was too far for Caitlin to see more than blurry outlines, she could see enough to know that the figure was tall, topping Niall by a good couple of inches, although her brother-in-law was no slouch in the height stakes. Caitlin had just enough time to wonder if the new figure was Andrew, her new colleague, who she'd been told was to join them for lunch, before she started swimming again.

Don't panic, she told herself as she cut through the water. *You've been in difficult situations before, and panicking never did anyone any good. Just swim parallel to the beach and everything will be fine. Eventually.*

She had only been swimming for another couple of minutes, but already she could feel the energy sapping out of her limbs. Swimming in the safe confines of her local pool was not the same thing as swimming in the sea. If she were to make it back safely she would need to conserve her energy. She would tread water for a few moments, just long enough to get her breath back, then start swimming again. She shuddered as she saw a mass of translucent blobs float past her. That was all she needed—jellyfish. She'd been told that Australian jellyfish could be lethal, along with hundreds of other snakes, sharks, spiders and goodness knew what else that seemed to favour the continent. And Caitlin didn't do dangerous animals. But typical of the way her luck had being going lately, she felt a sudden pain in her calf, as if she'd been stung by a thousand wasps. She cried out in pain and shock, swallowing water, and as she grabbed her leg, she felt herself go under.

She popped up again, gasping and choking. Now she was really worried. What if she had only a few minutes to live? One way or another right now her chances of survival seemed grim. At that moment she felt something touch her shoulder. What now? She twisted her body round to face this new threat and found herself looking into a pair of unfamiliar brown eyes. She guessed immediately it was the man she had seen standing with Niall.

'I've always wanted to rescue a damsel in distress,' he drawled. His wide grin made Caitlin furious. What on earth did he find amusing about her situation? Couldn't he see she was in trouble?

'I need to get ashore,' she panted. 'I've been stung.' She spluttered as a wave rolled over her, forcing more salt water down her already choked-up throat.

Hands reached for her. All trace of amusement vanished. 'Just do as I tell you and don't fight me,' he said, his deep voice calm. 'Just roll over onto your back and relax. I'll take you in.'

Caitlin hesitated. Despite her terror there was no way she was going to be dragged ashore like so much flotsam.

'Or, so help me, I'll knock you out if I have to,' he threatened as if he read her mind.

The hardness in his tone made Caitlin realise he was deadly serious. He would knock her out—she didn't doubt him for a second! The last thing she had the strength for was a brawl. And she did need help. Her leg was agonising and she was finding it difficult to breathe. Giving up all pretence of being able to get herself out of her predicament, she rolled over on her back and let herself float. She felt firm hands grasp either side of her head, and then she was being tugged towards the shore.

It could have only taken a few minutes but, exhausted and mortified, it felt like hours to Caitlin before she was being helped up the beach and onto a blanket. She dropped to her knees while Brianna dropped a towel around her shoulders.

'My God, Cat. Are you all right?' Brianna pressed a tumbler of water to her lips and Caitlin drank the liquid gratefully, washing away the taste of sea water. Over her sister's shoulder, Caitlin was conscious of the curious gazes of her niece and nephew. She shivered, trying to catch her breath, acutely aware how close she had come to being swept out to sea. Her rescuer knelt beside her and to her consternation gently lifted her calf and examined the place where she had been stung. Caitlin had the briefest impression of broad shoulders the colour of toffee and thick black hair.

'How's her leg, Andrew?' Niall asked, sounding concerned.

'It'll be okay. As soon as I get some vinegar on it.'

Caitlin's embarrassment deepened. So she'd been right. The man who had been forced to come after her to bring her ashore as if she were some helpless female was her new colleague. Dr Andrew Bedi. What a way to make a good first impression, she berated herself. He must think her all kinds of an idiot.

'I've got some vinegar in the boot of my car. If you could fetch it, Niall?' Andrew continued. He turned to Caitlin and smiled sympathetically. 'They're always getting me. It will sting like crazy for a while, but I don't think there's any lasting damage. You're lucky that you got stung by these babies. Now, if it had been the ones up north, you'd really be in trouble.' He raised his eyes to Caitlin's and once again she was aware of the intensity of his gaze. She felt a tingle in her leg, but whether it was from the feel of his hands or the shock of her recent experience, she didn't want to know. He was tall, at least six feet four, with short black hair. He was only wearing Bermuda shorts and Caitlin was acutely aware of his bronzed, muscular chest. Deep brown eyes, framed by impossibly thick lashes, glinted as if he found the whole world amusing. His features were perfectly sculpted, high cheekbones and a full, generous mouth. People might have called him beautiful, if it weren't for his nose, which looked as if it had been broken and badly set. He was simply by far the sexiest man Brianna had ever seen—and she was to be working with him!

'Did no one warn you not to go too far out?' he said, frowning at her. Although he looked as if he was of Indian descent, his accent was Australian.

Caitlin prickled at the disapproval in his voice. She wasn't used to people telling her off. 'Yes. But I didn't notice how far the current had taken me until it was too late.' Caitlin pulled her leg out of his grasp, annoyed. Okay, so he'd had to rescue her, that was embarrassing and she owed him, but there was no need for him to talk to her as if she were a naughty child. 'Thank you for helping me out. I am very grateful…' She was aware that she sounded less than appreciative, but she desperately wanted to regain some dignity as quickly as possible. She wasn't used to feeling at a disadvantage, as if she was in the wrong. 'And I can promise you, I will never ever put myself, or any one else, in that position again. Okay?' She tried a smile and tugged her leg from his grasp. It was still stinging like hell, but she would just have to grit her teeth until the pain subsided.

'Oh, Caitlin,' Brianna was saying as Niall returned carrying a large brown leather bag. 'You gave us all such a fright.'

Caitlin hugged her sister. 'I'm sorry, sis. Particularly seeing as it's me that's supposed to be watching out for you.'

'Anyway, all's well that ends well,' Andrew said, taking the bag from Niall. After hunting around for a few moments, he pulled out a bottle and a dressing. He reached for Caitlin's leg once more and propped it on his knees. Caitlin was deeply aware of the heat of his skin on hers. Once again there was that tingle. Dismayed, she tried to pull her leg away again. Equally determined, he pulled it back and held it there with a steel-like grip. Caitlin gave up, knowing that if she entered into a tug of war with this man she was likely to come out the loser, and would look even sillier than she felt right now.

He glanced up at her and Caitlin could see laughter in his deep brown eyes. 'Just do as you're told for a few minutes,' he drawled. 'Brianna did warn me that you were a stubborn woman. Goes with the red hair, I guess.' He looked from Brianna to Caitlin. They both had auburn hair—or at least until Brianna's had fallen out as a side effect of her treatment. But where Brianna's hair had been a mass of curls, Caitlin wore hers longer, tamed into a silky curtain of thick waves. But adding to her discomfort, Caitlin was conscious that as her hair dried in the heat of the sun it was beginning to frizz. At the moment she was as far away from the sleek professional she liked to present to the world as was possible.

'I did not!' Brianna protested. 'I said she was determined—not stubborn.'

'Well I guess we both know who the other is, then,' Caitlin said, feeling ridiculous as she held out her hand. She in her bikini, frizzing hair plastered to her scalp, her leg in the lap of her colleague and now here she was holding out her hand as if they had just met at some cocktail party. It was so ludicrous she had to smile.

'Dr Caitlin O'Neill,' she said with a grin.

He stopped what he was doing for a moment and engulfed her hand in his. 'Dr Andrew Bedi. At your service.' Then he too smiled. The effect was devastating. His teeth were a flash of white against the darkness of his skin, his dancing eyes crinkled at the corners. He really was the most incredible-looking man. Caitlin's pulse, which had been beginning to resume its normal rhythm, uncomfortably started pounding again.

Eventually, having dressed her leg, he placed it back on the blanket. 'It'll feel a little bruised,' he said, 'and might be sore for a day or two, but that's all. You've been lucky. If it had been one of the brutes up the coast a bit that had stung you, you'd have been a goner for sure.'

Caitlin shuddered, her gaze shifting to the clear blue Pacific. There was no way she was going back in there unless she was sure it was perfectly safe. Once stung twice shy.

'I think we should go back to the house,' Niall said. 'And have our barbie there. Andrew, if you could take the girls, I'll follow with the kids once I've packed up here.'

'Please don't,' Caitlin said. 'I don't want to spoil everyone's day. If Andrew thinks my leg is okay, we should just carry on as if nothing has happened. C'mon, Niall. Please. I don't want to spoil it for everyone.'

'Yes, Daddy. Let's stay,' Caitlin's nephew, Ciaran, begged. 'We haven't been down to the beach since Mummy got sick. And Siobhan and I have only half finished our castle.'

Caitlin was stricken with remorse. She was supposed to be here to help make things easier for the family. Now it looked as if she had ruined their first proper day out.

'I insist we stay,' she said firmly. 'Brianna and I will lie on the blanket here and chat. We still need to catch up properly. And as Andrew said, my leg will be perfectly fine.'

'Yippee,' Siobhan yelled in delight. 'Uncle Andrew was going to show us his tricks on his board. Now he can.' Now the drama was over, the little girl flung herself at Andrew, who pretended to be knocked over. He fell back in the sand, taking Siobhan with him. Seconds later, Ciaran had jumped on top of him too. Andrew seemed used to this behaviour. After a few minutes of horseplay he picked up Siobhan and threw her over his shoulder.

'C'mon, then. You kids can help me get my board set up. Your dad has to help too.'

As the two men walked away, two excited children off their shoulders, Brianna turned to Caitlin.

'Well, what do you think?' she said, her green-grey eyes twinkling.

'About what?' Caitlin replied, although she knew full well what her sister meant.

Brianna smacked Caitlin playfully on the shoulder. 'About Andrew, of course.'

'What about him? He seems very nice. Rescuing me and all that. Very civil of him,' Caitlin said dryly.

'C'mon, Cat,' Brianna said warningly. 'Don't you think he's gorgeous?'

'I suppose some people would think he's good looking,' Caitlin replied slowly, studiously ignoring her sister's look of incredulity. 'But he's a bit Crocodile Dundee for my liking.'

'I don't believe you don't find him sexy as hell,' Brianna retorted. 'Every single woman I have ever seen meet him gets that same ga-ga look as you have. It's written all over your face.'

'Okay.' Caitlin laughed. 'He's a hunk. But he's so not my type.'

Her sister sighed. 'Just as well, I suppose, because I hate to tell you, sis, you haven't a hope as far as Dr Andrew Bedi is concerned.'

Caitlin popped a sun hat on her head and scrabbled around for her glasses. The world swam back into focus. Andrew, Niall and the two children had returned to the beach carrying a board and a sail. It looked like a windsurfing board to Caitlin, although she wasn't an expert. Andrew had pulled on a wetsuit over his Bermuda shorts and the fabric clung to his body, emphasising his height and muscular build.

'Why do you say that?' Caitlin asked. 'Not that I'm remotely interested, of course.' The two sisters shared a smile. 'You know me, Bri, I'm much too happy with my life as it is to want to get involved. Men and kids aren't part of the plan. Not for a few years anyway. But I'm a bit offended that you think I haven't a chance. What makes you think he's so out of my league?'

Caitlin had never really thought about whether men found her attractive. She had been happy with David for the last few years and, until a few weeks ago, had thought that one day they would marry. Undemanding and not the least bit resentful of the time she spent at work, they had rubbed along well enough. And if it hadn't been the most exciting relationship, at least it had been comfortable. However, Caitlin had been surprised at how easily they had parted when she'd told him she was coming to Brisbane for six months. David had told her that she was mad to jeopardise her career just when it was really taking off. But to Caitlin there was no competition. Her sister needed her and that was that. They had split up with surprisingly little regret on either side.

'Oh, you'll find out about Andrew in good time. But let's just say he's a man who likes women and seems determined to have as much fun with as many as possible before settling down—if he ever does. And you, my darling sister, are far too serious for a fun-loving guy like him.'

Caitlin let out a low whistle, then wrinkled her nose disapprovingly. She looked over to the water's edge. Niall and Andrew had rigged the sail on the board and were pointing it towards the sea. Then with a push of his foot, Andrew was on the water and heading out away from the shore. Within seconds he was racing across the sea. With her glasses back in place, Caitlin could see him attach something that looked like a rope to the sail and then, as he leant back, the board seemed to leap forward, skimming over the waves. Within minutes he was a speck on the horizon.

'No, you're right. Men like Andrew have never appealed to me. If I marry, it will be to someone who likes the same things I do. Someone solid and steady.'

'Someone boring, you mean. Like David. That didn't work very well either.' Brianna laughed.

Brianna had met David on the one occasion she and her family had come back to Ireland for a visit to show off the children to their mother when Ciaran had been two. Caitlin realised that they had never discussed David. She'd assumed Brianna had liked him. Everyone did.

'Hey, you never said you didn't like David. I thought you two hit it off.'

'I didn't say I didn't like him, Cat. I just never thought he was right for you. If you ask me, he squeezed the fun right out of everything. You two were like a couple who had been married for years. You never really struck me as two people in love.'

Caitlin was taken aback. She'd had no idea that Brianna had thought that. But she was right. She had never felt anything more than a deep fondness for David.

'Ah, excitement and passion. Surely that fizzles out in time anyway? Isn't that why marriages fail? Once it's gone, couples are left with nothing to say to each other,' she said. But a tiny bit of her, a side she didn't care to acknowledge too often, wondered what it would be like to experience an all-consuming passion. She pushed the thought away. She was a scientist, and scientists were ruled by their heads—not their hearts.

Brianna looked at her sharply. 'Maybe you and Andrew have more in common than I thought. But, love Andrew as I do, I would advise any sane woman to keep her distance, particularly someone like you, who would have no idea how to handle a man like him.'

'Don't worry, Bri. By the sound of it, he is not my type either.' Caitlin felt a momentary stab of regret. Dismayed at her reaction, she shook her head. Good looking he may be, but her sister was right. Even if she were interested in a relationship so soon after David, the last man on earth she would be interested in would be Andrew Bedi. She didn't think men like him still existed in this day and age. She picked up a tube of sun block, keen to change the subject. 'Fancy putting some on my shoulders?'

Brianna smiled. 'Oh, Cat, I'm so glad you're here. I know I told you not to come, but now that you're here, I'm so happy.' Her voice shook slightly.

'You know I would have been here sooner if I could.' Caitlin took Brianna's cool hand in hers. 'If you hadn't convinced me not to come. Shouldn't I have believed you?'

'But I *was* fine. After all, I had Niall—and Mammy.' The two sisters shared a smile. Although they loved their mother dearly, they both agreed she could be a bit much after a while. Mrs O'Neill insisted on treating her daughters as if they were still about twelve years old and incapable of managing without her. 'I have to admit, Cat, that I was glad when she told me she had to go back home to Dad. She fussed so much, it drove me mad. She would never have agreed to go back to Ireland if you hadn't been coming out.'

Caitlin could only imagine how much her mother had

fussed over Bri. Since her elder daughter had been diagnosed with breast cancer, their mother had been determined that Brianna wouldn't face her illness alone. If it weren't for the fact that her three sons were needed back home to help on the horse farm their parents owned, Caitlin was sure that their mother would have ordered her whole brood to Australia. Strapping young men though her brothers were, they were no match for Mrs O'Neill when she made up her mind about something.

'I should have come sooner, Bri,' Caitlin said softly. 'I can't believe it's been three years since we saw each other! Why on earth did we leave it so long?'

The sisters shared a look. Why *had* they left it so long? They had always been close, and when Brianna and Niall had decided to emigrate to Australia, they had promised each other that they would visit at least every couple of years. But it hadn't worked out like that. Apart from that one visit to Ireland three years ago, Brianna hadn't made it back. And Caitlin had never managed to come to Australia. Work had always got in the way.

But then, three months ago, Brianna had phoned with the devastating news that she had discovered a lump in her breast. A biopsy had confirmed their worst fears. It was cancer. Caitlin wanted to fly to her sister's side immediately, but her mother and Brianna had persuaded her to wait and apply for a sabbatical. That way her career wouldn't suffer while she was away. Indeed, having secured a post at the prestigious Brisbane hospital, there was every chance her career would be helped by her time in Australia.

Despite being pleased at the way it had worked out and delighted to be in Australia with her sister at last, Caitlin wished the circumstances had been different. She couldn't bear to think about what would happen if Brianna didn't get better. Caitlin shook her head to get rid of the negative thoughts. They all had to remain positive and believe that Brianna would make a full recovery.

'If it hadn't taken so long to arrange the work visa, I would have come as soon as I heard. Or at least been here to help you through more of the chemo.'

Brianna reached over and squeezed her hand. 'You're here now and that's what matters.' Caitlin saw the tears in her sister's eyes before she could blink them away. 'You know we have Andrew to thank for getting you the job,' Brianna continued.

'It seems that I'm in his debt quite a bit,' Caitlin said reluctantly. She hated being beholden to people.

Both women turned their gaze seaward. Niall and the children were finishing off the sandcastle. Out at sea, Caitlin caught her breath as Andrew and his board somersaulted into the air, turning over before landing and shooting along the water.

'What is he doing?' Caitlin asked, impressed. 'I've never seen anyone windsurf like that before.'

'It's called kite boarding,' Brianna replied. 'It's a bit like windsurfing, but with tricks. Andrew's very good. He's been trying to teach Niall, but it's not as easy as it looks.'

'It doesn't look easy at all,' Caitlin said as Andrew did another series of flips. 'What happens if he crashes?'

'He crashes fairly often.' Her sister laughed. 'But it doesn't put him off. He just climbs back on, and away he goes again.'

The two women watched in silence for a while.

'He says the Queensland Royal is delighted to have

someone of your calibre there even for six months. It was good luck that one of the specialists wanted to spend time in the UK. I guess you'll see a fair bit of Andrew at the hospital.'

Caitlin knew she would. As a specialist obstetrician she would be working a lot with the paediatricians, of whom Andrew was one. She wondered what kind of doctor he was. An image of him lounging around flirting with the nurses and female doctors flashed across her mind. She felt unreasonably disappointed. She had no time for doctors who didn't take their work seriously. However, it was none of her business.

The sun had dried her damp skin and she slipped on her sundress. She stood, wincing slightly at the stab of pain in her calf.

'It's getting late, and everyone's bound to be getting hungry. Shall we go back to the house and make the salads?' When Caitlin had seen where her sister and her family lived she had been gobsmacked. Their house, an enormous low-slung affair, was perched on a hill just a few metres from the beach they were sitting on. It had several rooms, a hot tub and an infinity pool and views out over the sea. She had known her brother-in-law was doing well but had had no idea his fledgling business had been so successful.

'Good idea,' Brianna said, unwinding her long legs. 'I'll call Niall to start the steaks.'

'No need to disturb him,' Caitlin countered. 'We can put them on when we get back.'

'A word of warning, sis,' Brianna said, laughing. 'Men out here take their barbies seriously. Women are allowed to make the side dishes, but that's it. The cooking of the meat is a man's job.'

Caitlin laughed, then, seeing Brianna was perfectly serious, stopped. 'Fine by me. You know I hate cooking anyway. Salads are about my limit. If the men want to cook, more power to them.'

By the time the two women returned with salads and rolls, Niall and Andrew were by the fire, flipping burgers and steaks. As the smell tickled her nostrils, Caitlin realised she was starving. She had taken a couple of minutes back at the house to have a shower to rinse the sand out of her hair and off her body, and a little longer to blow-dry her hair, returning it to its smooth waves. She had tied it back in a ponytail to prevent the breeze that had whipped up from blowing it into her eyes and finally had changed into a pair of lightweight trousers and T-shirt. Impulsively, without examining her motives too closely, she applied some lip gloss in the lightest shade of pink. Putting her glasses back on, she looked at her reflection and wrinkled her nose in dissatisfaction. Not normally concerned with make-up, for the first time ever Caitlin wished she took more time and care with her appearance. *To impress Dr Bedi?* a small voice niggled at the back of her mind. Caitlin dismissed the thought immediately. Definitely not! she told herself. The important thing was that she felt and looked in control once more. Back to Dr O'Neill, obstetrician and consummate professional.

When she returned to the beach, the scent of cooking meat was drifting tantalisingly on the slight afternoon breeze. The two men seemed to be taking their cooking duties very seriously, Caitlin thought, amused as she heard them discuss whether a steak needed more marinade. Andrew had turned his wetsuit down to his hips, revealing his muscular chest. Despite herself, Caitlin felt her eyes travel over his torso, admiring the tautness of his abdomen and the defined muscles of his chest. Andrew turned, as if sensing her approving look, and caught Caitlin's eye before she could look away. He winked and she felt herself grow flustered again. Damn the man, she thought crossly.

'How's the leg?' he asked innocently.

'As you predicted, it feels a bit bruised, but otherwise fine. Thanks again. I feel such an idiot.'

'Australia can take a bit of getting used to. I'm sure once you've been here a bit longer you'll know what's safe and what isn't. The coast here has some fantastic beaches, as you will see, but you have to be very careful about where you swim.'

Niall heaped food onto plates and everyone helped themselves to salads and buttered rolls. Niall had set up a table and chairs under the shade of an orange bougainvillea and as Caitlin ate she breathed in the tang of sea air. For the first time in months she felt energised. There was something about being here that made her realise how boring her well ordered life back in Ireland had become. As if he'd read her thoughts, Andrew turned to Caitlin.

'I understand you've been working at the Women and Children's Hospital in Dublin for the last few years. Your colleagues must think highly of you. From what I hear, it's very difficult to get accepted onto the permanent staff there. And you couldn't be more than, what—thirty?'

Caitlin flushed under his frank scrutiny. Did he think after what had happened that she was some airhead who had managed to secure her position because of who she knew rather than on her own merits? Little did he know what sacrifices she'd had to make to earn her position.

'Caitlin is being considered for a chair in obstetrics there,' Brianna said proudly. 'If she gets it, she'll be one of the youngest professors in the country.'

Catching Andrew's raised eyebrow and look of amusement, Caitlin cringed at her sister's unembarrassed boasting.

'My sister-in-law is a bit of a workaholic,' Niall added through mouthfuls of salad. 'She never stops. We've asked her to come and visit us many times since we moved here, but she's refused to take time off from work.' He smiled to show Caitlin there was no malice behind his words. He of all people knew what getting the chair in obstetrics meant to Caitlin. It seemed as if all the years of hard work were about to pay off. Not that she was there yet, but the position was within her reach. As long as she kept focussed and continued to spend her few spare hours working on publishing papers. As she thought back to her hectic life in Dublin, she appreciated for the first time just how exhausted working the hours she had, had made her. Perhaps her time here would help recharge her batteries, not that she expected an easy time of it at the Queensland Royal. Far from it. She intended to apply herself to the post here with exactly the same dedication she applied to all her jobs. At least she didn't have any research on the go at the moment. Any spare time she had here would be spent with Brianna. Of that, Caitlin was determined.

'Andrew works pretty hard too.' Brianna joined in the conversation, having returned from sorting the children out with food.

'Ah, yes, but he also plays hard,' her husband said mischievously. 'Where you get the energy is beyond me. I am far too exhausted after a day's work to do anything except read the paper and potter.'

'But you have a wife and family to keep you busy,' Andrew replied. Caitlin wasn't sure but she thought she heard a note of envy in his voice. 'Once I've finished work I'm free to do what I want.'

'Lucky devil,' Niall said, but as he smiled at his wife, Caitlin knew that he wouldn't swap what he had for the world.

By the time they had finished eating the sun was beginning to drop, turning the sky red-gold. Niall and Andrew, helped by the children, started packing up the barbecue. Caitlin sneaked a look at her sister. She looked tired. The circles under her eyes had deepened. Caitlin felt a pang of anxiety. 'Are you sure you're up to socializing, Bri?' she said. 'Shouldn't you be taking it easy? I could have waited and met Andrew when I started work. Probably would have been better anyway. God knows what impression he has of me. Not that I care,' she added hastily, catching her sister's amused look.

'I wouldn't call having Andrew over as socialising,' Brianna protested. 'He's part of the family—he's Ciaran's godfather after all.' She smiled briefly then grew serious. 'Brianna, you must listen to me. As soon as I was diagnosed, I made up my mind. I'm going to carry on as normal whenever I can. For the children's sake, if nothing else. I'm a bit tired, but as long as I rest whenever I can, I cope.' Caitlin could see the determination in the green eyes which were so like her own. 'I wouldn't have let you come at all if it hadn't been for the job. Love you as I do, the last thing I need is you fussing over me all the time like Mammy. Caitlin, I need you to support me on this and not fuss. Okay?'

'Okay,' Caitlin agreed reluctantly. 'Whatever you say. But I'm here to help whenever you need me. You just have to let me know. Promise?'

Back at the house a little later, Caitlin insisted on clearing up while Brianna went to organise the children for bed.

'I could put the children to bed if you like after I finish clearing away. You have an early night.' Catching the warning look her sister threw her, Caitlin raised her hands. 'I'm not fussing, honestly, Bri. It's just that I'm still on Irish time and suddenly wide awake. No doubt it'll hit me for six soon, but in the meantime, let me help.'

'I'm putting my children to bed,' Brianna said firmly, 'but if you want to clean the kitchen, be my guest.'

As she was stacking the dishwasher in her sister's enormous American-style kitchen, Andrew appeared, carrying some plates. Caitlin had assumed he'd left.

'Has Brianna gone to bed?' he asked, laying the dirty dishes on the granite worktop.

'She's seeing to the children,' Caitlin replied. 'Is Niall still outside?'

Andrew shook his head. 'He must be helping to put the children to bed. I should be going too.'

'How does Bri seem to you?' Caitlin asked anxiously. 'You know her well, I understand.'

Andrew looked at her sympathetically. 'She was—is—the best paediatric nurse I ever worked with. We really missed her when she stopped working to look after the kids, and then this…' He shook his head. 'But you know your sister better than I do. If anyone can beat it, she can. And I know how pleased both of them are to have you here.'

It must have been tiredness, but suddenly Caitlin felt a

lump in her throat. In many ways she wished it had been her, not Brianna, who had been diagnosed. After all, it wasn't as if she had a young family depending on her. She swallowed furiously. Caitlin O'Neill did not show her emotions. Not publicly and certainly not in front of a man she barely knew and who was to be a colleague.

Andrew must have noticed. He patted her shoulder awkwardly. 'They found it early enough, you know. She's really very lucky. Everything is going to be fine.'

Caitlin wasn't convinced. But she was here and would ensure that her sister got through the next few months as painlessly as possible.

'Brianna tells me you're a paediatrician,' Caitlin said, keen to get the conversation onto neutral ground.

'Yep, for my sins,' he replied.

She flicked the kettle on. 'Would you like some coffee before you go?'

'Sure,' he said.

Caitlin looked around for where Brianna kept the mugs. Behind her Andrew reached over her to the top cupboard. For a moment she was imprisoned between him and the worktop. Acutely conscious of the heat of his body, she felt her heart begin to thud. She would have given anything to move away from him, but that would have only drawn attention to the awkwardness she felt. Thankfully, as soon as he had grabbed two mugs, he stepped away. He spooned coffee into the mugs, and then held out the jug of milk and raised one eyebrow in question.

Once their coffee was poured, Andrew sat at the kitchen table and stretched his long legs in front of him. 'Tell me about you,' he said, looking at her intently. At that moment Caitlin felt as if her world had shrunk to the kitchen and him and her. Every nerve in her body seemed to be tingling in response to him. She couldn't remember when she'd last had such an immediate reaction to a man. No, strike that. She couldn't remember *ever* having had a reaction like this to a man. It wasn't just his dark good looks, although he was pretty hot, it was the aura that surrounded him. As if he was pulling her into his magnetic field and she was powerless to resist.

'There's not much to tell,' Caitlin said, desperate for him not to see how he was affecting her. 'I am Irish—but you know that,' she said as his mouth quirked. 'I've always wanted to be a doctor, well, since about twelve anyway. I have three older brothers, whom I love but drive me mad. My mum and dad breed horses. That's about it. What about you?'

'I'm an only child.' For a moment a shadow darkened his eyes. 'My parents are from India, they're retired and live in Sydney. They came here years ago. I was born here but they're still pretty traditional. I didn't know what I wanted to do until my final year at school, but I know I made the right decision to become a doctor. I like all watersports, but am useless on a horse. Anything else you'd like to know?' He grinned at her. Caitlin wondered if he too felt the electricity that was fizzing around them.

'Hey, you started this,' Caitlin rejoined. 'The question-and-answer session, that is...' Oh, dear, what if he thought she meant something else?

Suddenly he frowned, then got to his feet. Caitlin looked up to find him towering above her. What had she said to cause the change? One minute he'd seemed relaxed, the next...as if he wanted nothing more than to get away from her as quickly as possible. A thought struck her. Did he think she was flirting with him? Did he think she had misread friendly interest for something else? She felt her toes curl with embarrassment. She stood too, feeling dwarfed by his size.

'I'll pick you up on Monday morning and take you in to the hospital if you like,' Andrew offered. 'I can give you the lowdown on the way in.'

Caitlin smiled at him gratefully. 'I'd appreciate that,' she said. 'Niall has said I'm welcome to use one of their cars whenever I need to, but I'm not sure I can find my way on the first day. I've a hopeless sense of direction. Oh, and thanks again for arranging the job for me.'

Andrew looked down at her and smiled. 'As I said, no sweat. It'll be great to have you. We're all looking forward to seeing the renowned Dr O'Neill in action. I'll see you on Monday.'

'No pressure, then,' Caitlin mouthed at his retreating back.

As Andrew pulled away from the house and headed towards the freeway that would take him home, he let out a low whistle. Dr Caitlin O'Neill was nothing like he'd imagined. He didn't know what he had expected when he'd offered to help by organising a job out for Brianna's sister. He was thinking about another doctor—a colleague—that was all. But when he had literally fished her out of the sea, he had been immediately struck by her stunning good looks. That incredible hair and those eyes! Although similar in colour to Brianna's, Caitlin's eyes had an intensity that reminded him of a cat pinning its prey. He laughed out loud at the image. Recalling the feeling of the silky-smooth skin under his fingertips, he almost groaned. This was a woman he would like in his bed. Not marriage—no, never that—but an affair. And why not? She looked like the kind of woman whose heart would be difficult to break.

CHAPTER TWO

CAITLIN dressed carefully for work on Monday. She knew that Australian hospitals were less formal than Irish ones, especially given the heat, but she wanted to create the right impression. She chose a floaty skirt that, while cool, still looked smart and teamed it with a short-sleeved white blouse. She twisted her hair into a chignon and then she was ready.

Breakfast was a far rowdier affair than Caitlin was used to. Living alone, she was used to a quiet breakfast with the paper, not this hive of activity. How could such small children make such a racket and how could Brianna think straight with all the noise?

Niall collected his briefcase and slung an overnight bag over his shoulder. He kissed his wife and sister-in-law goodbye. 'I'll be back on Friday,' he told Brianna. 'Are you sure you'll be all right?'

'Go on, you big softy.' His wife pushed him towards the door. 'I've Caitlin here if I need anything—which I won't.' As husband and wife smiled at each other Caitlin felt a pang. What would it feel like to be loved like that? she wondered. Not that she really wanted to find out, she reminded herself. She liked her uncomplicated life back in Dublin exactly the way it was. She had work, loads of friends and plenty of hobbies to keep her busy. The last thing she needed in her life were complications, and if ever she wondered whether she was leading the right life, she just thought about her mother. Although she loved her mother fiercely, her whole life had been taken up with bringing up her large family of three boys and two girls. Caitlin had never seen her mother do anything just for herself. That wasn't the life Caitlin had mapped out for herself.

She had just finished breakfast when she heard a toot from the driveway. Looking out, she saw Andrew had arrived in a sports car. He jumped over the door and came to meet her. Unlike on Saturday, he was dressed more formally, in a white shirt and light-coloured chinos. He looked fresh cool and very handsome. He opened the door for her with a flourish.

'Your carriage awaits,' he said.

'Why, thank you, sir,' Caitlin quipped back. 'You are too kind.'

Soon they were leaving the leafy suburbs behind and were on the freeway. As he drove, Andrew pointed out various landmarks so that Caitlin would find her way the next day. They crossed a bridge, passing modern skyscrapers. Everything seemed as different from Ireland, with its green rolling countryside and the Georgian architecture of Dublin, as it could be.

'What do you think so far?' he asked.

'Apart from the heat? I think it's wonderful,' Caitlin answered.

'It's not just the beaches, although you have to admit

they are the best in the world. The Sunshine Coast is an hour to the north and the Gold Coast about the same distance south. We do some outreach work in both areas, so you'll get a chance to see them.'

'I'm looking forward to it,' Caitlin replied, gripping onto her seat as Andrew passed a car. Catching her nervous look, he laughed. 'Hey, don't worry. You're in safe hands.'

Caitlin smiled weakly in response. 'Tell me about the hospital,' she said.

By the time they had pulled up in front of the Queensland Royal, Andrew had given her a brief overview of how the medical system in Australia worked. He was a specialist paediatrician, which Caitlin already knew, and had a special interest in heart problems in neonates. The hospital was a gleaming, modern affair, all glass and stainless steel. Andrew told Caitlin that it had some of the best facilities in Australia.

As they got out of the car, an ambulance pulled up, its lights flashing. A trio of nurses was waiting at the entrance, ready to receive the casualties. Caitlin and Andrew were about to leave them to it when a nurse noticed his arrival.

'Could you hold on a minute, Dr Bedi?' she said. 'We might need you.'

Unsure where to go, Caitlin watched as the patient was unloaded. Immediately she could see that it was a woman in advanced pregnancy. From the look of distress on her face, it appeared she was in labour. Suddenly she felt her reflexes kick in. She moved towards the group, making a rapid judgement.

'Mrs Roland is in the end stage of labour,' the paramedic intoned. 'She was due to have her baby at home, but the midwife felt that labour wasn't progressing quickly enough and decided to call us. The baby's heartbeat has dropped.'

'I'm Dr O'Neill,' Caitlin introduced herself. 'One of the obstetricians. Let's get her inside so we can assess her.'

Once inside Caitlin carried out a rapid examination of the woman. It only took her a few seconds to realise that the placenta was lying in front of the baby. It was something that every obstetrician came across on a regular basis. Nevertheless, if they didn't get the baby delivered there was a chance the woman would bleed to death. In every country there were several maternal deaths every year due to the condition. There was no time to lose. Every second counted if they were to save the woman and her unborn child. 'Placenta praevia,' she said. 'She needs to go to Theatre immediately.'

'I'll tell Theatre to expect us,' one of the nurses said, turning towards the phone.

'I'll scrub in too,' Andrew said. Even if they managed to get the baby delivered safely there was every chance it might need resuscitating. 'C'mon, Caitlin, let's go.'

Caitlin struggled to keep up with his long strides as they rushed towards Theatre. A nurse handed her some scrubs and clogs and she scrubbed up beside Andrew, mentally counting off the minutes.

'Right in at the deep end,' Andrew said sympathetically. 'We didn't even manage to get you up to the ward.'

By the time they were scrubbed and gowned, Mrs Roland had been anesthetised and was lying prepped on the theatre table.

Caitlin cut into the abdomen from left to right just above the pubic bone. As the skin separated, she made another incision into the uterus, careful not to damage the precious contents. As she pulled the baby out, she glanced at the clock. Ten minutes had passed since the patient had arrived at the hospital. She was pleased to see none of her speed had deserted her.

The baby, a little boy, was slightly floppy and blue. Caitlin handed him to the midwife, who rushed the baby across to the resuscitator.

'He's a bit flat,' the midwife called out. As Caitlin started to close she was aware of the tension in the room. Andrew needed to get oxygen into the baby, and soon. Across the woman's abdomen she watched as he tipped the baby's head back gently before slipping in a paediatric endotracheal tube, feeling his way through the larynx and into the lungs. Then he attached an ambu-bag and started feeding oxygen into the tiny lungs. Every movement he made was calm and assured, and this fed into the atmosphere of the theatre. There was no panic. Everyone was simply going about their jobs quietly and efficiently. Caitlin was impressed. She guessed the team had worked together many times before.'

'Heart rate 140 and he's a good colour now,' Andrew announced to the room to a collective sigh of relief. 'I think baby is going to be fine. We'll get them up to Special Care, but I think we should be able to reunite mother and baby quite soon.'

'Maybe not tonight,' Caitlin said. 'I'll want to keep an eye on her in the labour ward overnight, in case of post-partum haemorrhage.'

While the baby was being taken away to the special care nursery, accompanied by the paediatric nurse and Andrew, Caitlin finished closing the wound. She felt a trickle of perspiration run down her forehead and was grateful when one of the nurses wiped it away. Once Mrs Roland had woken from the anaesthetic, she would see her and let her know what was happening. She was pleased that her first case had gone well—not that she doubted her ability, but Caitlin knew that sometimes even straightforward cases could suddenly go wrong.

After she had finished in Theatre, she asked one of the nurses to take her to Special Care. She wanted to check on the baby before she spoke to the mother.

She found Andrew bending over the infant, listening to its chest. He looked up at her, his deep brown eyes warm. 'He's going to be fine, I think,' he said. 'We'll know better in a few days. You did a good job back there.'

Caitlin looked around the small high-tech unit. It reminded her of the one back in Dublin, but she guessed that there was a uniformity with all hospitals in the Western world. There were five babies in at the moment, with anxious parents sitting by their incubators. Her heart went out to them. It must be so hard to feel so helpless, to know that the life of your child depended on the doctors and nurses.

Having finished examining the baby she had recently delivered, and announcing himself satisfied for the time being, Andrew suggested he show her around.

'We have around four thousand deliveries a year here,' he said. 'We get difficult cases from quite far away. The air ambulance brings mothers and kids in on a regular basis. You might like to go out with the team some time.'

'I'd love to,' Caitlin said enthusiastically. 'I've never been on anything like it before. I guess in a country of this size, it happens a lot.'

'Often enough,' Andrew said. 'We take turns being on

call for the air ambulance. I'll rota you in for the same time as me. Okay?'

At Caitlin's nod he went on. 'I'll take you up to Personnel. I know you sent all your paperwork in advance, but there may be one or two pieces they need from you. After that I'll give you the tour.'

After she'd completed the necessary paperwork, Andrew introduced her to the midwives and doctors she'd be working with. There were too many faces for her to remember everyone's names straight away, that would take time, but all the staff seemed very welcoming.

Her first afternoon was to be spent in Theatre. One of the senior midwives, a cheerful woman called Linda, took her on a round of the antenatal ward. Andrew left them to it while he went to do his own rounds. After the ward round Linda took Caitlin to the general gynaecology ward and introduced her to the patients she had scheduled for Theatre.

After seeing all the patients on her afternoon's list, Linda stopped in front of a woman who was perched on the end of the bed and looked as if she was ready to run a mile.

'This is Mrs Mary Oliphant,' Linda introduced the woman. 'She's in to have her tubes examined. She and her husband have been trying for a baby for a year, and their family doctor thinks she should have her tubes checked before they think about IVF.'

'Good idea,' Caitlin said. Mrs Oliphant seemed to relax a little. 'It's a very quick procedure,' Caitlin said. 'We'll take you down to the scanning room and pass a catheter through your cervix, squirt some dye and have a look. We don't even need to anaesthetise you, but we'll give you a couple of painkillers as it can be uncomfortable. The good news is that you'll have the results straight away.'

'And if my tubes are blocked? What then? Does that mean we won't be able to have children?' Mary's lip trembled. 'We really want a baby.' A tear slipped down her cheek. 'I blame myself. I was determined to wait until my career was established before we started a family. But what if I've left it too late?'

'Hey, let's not get ahead of ourselves,' Caitlin said soothingly. 'Let's do the echovist first and we can talk again then.' She took her hand. 'Anyway, you're not that old.' She smiled. 'Although a woman's fertility does decline markedly after the age of thirty-five, you're still on the right side of forty. And there is a test we can do which will tell us just how well your ovaries are responding. I'll take a blood sample today, and I should have the results for you soon. I also suggest that we test your husband. That way, if you need to think about IVF you'll be ready to go. How does that sound?'

As she spoke a thought slipped into her head. Time was passing for her too. It was quite possible that if she changed her mind about wanting children, she too would find she'd left it too late. It was one thing not to want children, quite another to have the choice taken away. She squeezed the thought to the back of her mind. Why was she suddenly thinking children might be an option in the future, when until now she had been sure children weren't for her? She forced her attention back to her patient. It was Mary who she had to think about. She deserved her full attention.

Mary smiled, seeming reassured. 'That sounds great,' she said. 'I just want to know so we can decide our next step. Thank you for taking the trouble to talk to me.'

'Hey, that's what we're here for.' Caitlin smiled. 'I'll see you down in the scanning room shortly. First let's take that blood sample.'

Quickly, Caitlin took a sample of blood from Mrs Oliphant's arm and passed it to Linda.

As they moved away Linda said, 'There's one more lady I'd like you to see. I've already spoken to Dr Bedi about her, and he's interested to know what you think.' Curious, Caitlin let herself be led across into one of the single rooms. Sitting up in bed, reading a magazine listlessly, was the patient Linda had asked her to see.

'This is Mrs Levy,' Linda said, passing her chart to Caitlin. 'As you can see, she's twenty-nine weeks pregnant. She was admitted earlier today with an elevated blood pressure of 160 over 100, plus protein in her urine. In her first pregnancy she had to be delivered prematurely because of high blood pressure.'

Caitlin had seen the condition often. It was always a difficult judgement call. On the one hand, there was no treatment and the only sure way of preventing the condition from getting worse was to deliver the baby. However, Mrs Levy was only twenty-eight weeks pregnant and although Caitlin knew that the hospital had the necessary equipment to look after a pre-term baby, there was always a chance that the baby would suffer brain damage or even worse if it was delivered so early.

'What does Dr Bedi think?' she asked Linda as they moved away from the patient.

'He'd prefer us to wait and monitor her closely over the next few days.'

It wasn't an unreasonable decision, Caitlin knew. Every day the baby stayed safely in the mother's womb increased its chances of survival.

'Could we arrange to have Mrs Levy scanned?' Caitlin asked, making up her mind. 'I'll do it myself before Theatre.' She went back to her patient.

'You're probably well aware of our concerns, Mrs Levy. I'm sure they have been discussed with you.'

'Please call me Patricia. Mrs Levy always makes me think of my mother-in-law.' She smiled, before the anxious look returned to her eyes. 'That nice Dr Bedi came to see me and explained everything.'

Did he, now? Caitlin thought, wishing that he had spoken to her before discussing options with the patient. She decided to wait until she had spoken to him and had the scan results before speaking to Patricia again. 'I'd like to scan you as soon as we can get a scanner up here,' she told the patient. 'I'll see you in a little while, okay? Then we can decide on the best way forward.'

Patricia clutched Caitlin's hand. 'I really want this baby,' she said. 'They told me it's a girl and as I have two boys, it will make my family complete.'

Caitlin patted her hand reassuringly. 'We'll do our best for you, I promise. In the meantime, the best thing you can do for your baby is try and relax.'

After rounds Linda took Caitlin into the staffroom for a cup of coffee. 'What do you think so far?' she asked as she poured them mugs from the pot that had been made earlier.

'I'm impressed,' Caitlin admitted. 'The facilities, at least what I've seen so far, are impressive.'

'I hear from the others that you know Dr Bedi. He's lovely, don't you think?'

Caitlin wasn't quite sure how to answer. What was she supposed to say to that? That, yes, he was gorgeous and that she fancied the pants off him? 'He seems very nice,' she said noncommittally.

'Half the nurses and doctors here are in love with him. The other half are married.' Linda laughed. 'Thank goodness I'm in the second half. Otherwise I'd be doomed to have my heart broken, like the rest.'

Caitlin wasn't used to such frankness and wasn't sure how to respond. Thankfully, as she was searching frantically for a more neutral subject, Andrew himself appeared.

'They told me I'd find you here,' he said, pouring himself a glass of water from the cooler and gulping it greedily. 'I wondered if you wanted to see the paeds wards before we have lunch. Your theatre list starts at 1.30. Right?' She eyed him, mentally readjusting her opinion of him in light of what Linda had told her.

Caitlin stood. 'I'd love to see the children's ward,' she said. 'And meet the staff.' She finished her coffee and rinsed her cup. 'Thanks, Linda,' she said as she followed Andrew out of the staffroom. 'I'll see you after Theatre.'

She followed Andrew out of the staffroom.

'I don't think we should leave Mrs Levy any longer,' she said. 'She's showing all the signs of pre-eclampsia—raised blood pressure and protein in her urine. If we don't deliver her and her condition gets worse then there is a chance she'll start fitting and we'll lose her. I'm sure neither of us want to be faced with a maternal death.'

Andrew turned and looked at her. 'The last two scans place her at twenty-eight weeks,' he said. 'There's not been much growth since then.' He frowned. Caitlin wondered if he was unused to having his opinion challenged. Underneath his easygoing exterior she thought there was a man who, once he had made up his mind, was loath to change it. It was clear in the way the staff acquiesced to him that he was used to being deferred to. On the other hand, so was she. She trusted her instinct, and if she were back in Ireland nobody would have questioned her decision.

'If we deliver her now, then there is a chance the baby won't survive,' he continued. 'Even another couple of days would give it a better chance.'

Caitlin held her ground. 'If we wait another couple of days and the mother develops full-blown eclampsia then there's a good chance that we'll lose the baby as well as the mother. Is that a risk you're prepared to take? Because I'm not sure I am.'

They stared at each other, neither willing to give an inch.

'We should go and speak to the patient at least,' Caitlin said eventually. 'We should give her all the facts and let her decide.'

'Do you think that's fair?' Andrew countered. 'If she decides to go ahead and let us deliver the baby, and the baby dies, she'll carry that burden always. She'll always wonder if she made the right decision.'

'And if she takes your advice and waits, and she and the baby both die, then what about the rest of her family? She has two children under the age of five. Do you think it's fair to leave them without a mother?' Caitlin felt her voice catch on the last words as an image of her niece and nephew growing up without their mother flashed across her mind.

Andrew looked at her sharply. 'Are you sure this isn't becoming personal, Caitlin?' he asked softly.

Caitlin gritted her teeth in frustration. She never let her

personal feelings or emotions interfere with her professional judgement. But that didn't mean that she looked on her patients just as obstetric dilemmas—she prided herself on taking all aspects of their lives into account when making a clinical decision. How dared he suggest otherwise? Even if he already thought of her as some sort of pathetic female that needed rescuing. Now he was accusing her of being over-emotional and letting her worry about her sister cloud her judgement. Well, she would soon put him right.

'Let me make one thing absolutely clear, Dr Bedi. It's important we understand one another if we are going to be making joint decisions about patients.' Her voice was cold and clipped, even to her own ears, but she made no attempt to soften her tone. 'The decisions I make are *always*—' she emphasised the last word '—made on the basis of what is good for my patient. I never let personal feelings cloud my judgement.' Aware that she had curled her hands into fists, she made herself relax. What was it about this man which caused her to have such strong reactions?

'I'm glad to hear it, Dr O'Neill,' he said calmly. 'Because if I ever had reason to think you weren't up to the job, believe you me, regardless of the friendship I have with your family. I wouldn't hesitate to have you removed from the case. Now, do *I* make myself clear?'

CHAPTER THREE

STUNNED, Caitlin could only stare open-mouthed at Andrew.

'Well, now that we understand each other,' she said stiffly, 'shall we continue?' She marched off in what she hoped was the general direction of Paediatrics, not caring whether Andrew was following or not. Of all the insufferable, conceited, big-headed... She was fuming to herself when Andrew caught her arm and stopped her in her tracks.

She glared at him, before seeing the look of apology in his deep brown eyes.

'I'm sorry,' he said, 'that was unforgivable of me.'

'Yes, it was,' Caitlin said. Then she softened at his look of genuine remorse. 'Do you really have doubts about my clinical judgement?' she asked, puzzled. 'I know you had me checked out thoroughly before you arranged the job for me.'

'I did,' Andrew said. 'And I don't have doubts. It's just...' He hesitated. 'Let's just say that I have my reasons.'

'Shouldn't you tell me what they are?' Caitlin said.

'There's no need. I agree we should wait for the scan results before we decide what to do. Okay?'

Caitlin was tempted to press further, but she could tell from the set of his chin that she was unlikely to get anything more from Andrew. But she was a patient woman. Whatever it was, she would find out soon enough.

'Okay,' Caitlin said. 'Now, let's go and see this paediatric ward of yours.'

After a quick tour of the children's ward, Caitlin left Andrew checking his patients and made her way to the scanning room where Mrs Oliphant was waiting for her.

'Hey, how are you doing?' Caitlin said. Mary just smiled weakly.

Caitlin passed the catheter then turned the monitor towards her patient and pointed to the screen.

'Look,' she told the anxious woman. 'You can see both the ovaries. That's the left one and there's the right. And see that little blob there? That's a follicle with an egg developing inside. So far so good. Everything is normal.' She withdrew the catheter. 'You can get dressed now.'

Once Mrs Oliphant was dressed and sitting down, Caitlin turned to her. 'I've also had the blood results back. And they're consistent with the scan we've just done. Your ovaries are looking good. And the embryologists have told me that Richard's results are also normal. So I'm going to suggest that you go home and keep trying for another six months. If you're still not pregnant by then, we'll talk about IVF. But I've got a feeling that you won't need it.'

Mary relaxed and smiled broadly. 'It's such a relief to know,' she said. 'I can't tell you how worried I've been.'

'Sometimes,' Caitlin said gently, 'I find that once couples relax, nature just takes it course. And if it doesn't, well, you can come and see me again. But for now I want you and Richard to go home and have plenty of sex.'

She saw a happy and relieved Mary out, and then asked whether the scanner could be taken to the antenatal ward for Mrs Levy's scan.

Once back on the antenatal ward, Caitlin prepped Patricia's abdomen with gel, apologising for the cold sensation. Then she placed the wand over her abdomen and turned the screen towards the patient so that she was able to see what Caitlin was seeing.

'See that over there.' She pointed to the heart. 'That's the baby's heart. As you can see, it's beating strongly.' Patricia looked entranced as Caitlin proceeded to point out arms and legs. The image was so good that she was even able to show Mrs Levy her baby sucking her thumb. 'And as you've been told already, she is a healthy little girl. I put her at about twenty-eight weeks and three days.'

Mrs Levy lay back on the bed, looking thoughtful. 'It makes it seem more real, seeing her there on the screen.' She closed her eyes and Caitlin watched as tears slid out from underneath her eyelids. 'I just don't know what to do for the best. If only my Jack was here to help me decide.' Caitlin knew from the notes that Mrs Levy's husband had been killed in a traffic accident early on in the pregnancy. Her heart went out to the distraught woman. 'My other two, my boys, they are my first husband's,' she went on. 'We divorced when my youngest was two. I thought that was me. That it would just be me and the boys. And then Jack came along, and that was that. We fell in love and married a few months later.' She opened her eyes and Caitlin could see the memories brighten her eyes.

Caitlin perched beside her patient on the bed. 'Go on,' she said softly.

'As I say, we got married, once the children had got to

know him, and then started trying for a baby. It took a couple of years for me to get pregnant, you know. I was getting close to forty by this time.' She paused, her eyes misting over. 'He was so excited, he didn't have children of his own, never having married before. He was just like a little kid himself. He even went out and bought a crib the day after I took the pregnancy test.'

Caitlin was aware of somebody coming to stand behind her. She glanced over her shoulder to see Andrew. Patricia went on.

'Then just a couple of months later he was dead.' She started to cry in earnest. Wordlessly, Andrew passed her some tissues and they waited in silence while she fought for control. Eventually, she blew her nose.

'So, you see,' she said once her sobs had subsided, 'I can't risk losing this baby. It's all I have left of Jack.' She looked from Andrew to Caitlin, her eyes begging them to understand. 'Dr Bedi knows all this,' she said quietly. 'That's why he said we might be able to risk waiting a day or two.'

'But,' Caitlin said gently, 'you do realise if we wait too long there's a risk you could develop full-blown eclampsia and might die. What about your other children? They'd be left without a mother.'

'I don't want to die,' Patricia said fiercely. 'I don't want to leave my kids, but Dr Bedi says you'll watch me carefully.'

'Okay,' Caitlin agreed reluctantly. 'We'll watch and wait. But I'm warning you, if there is the slightest sign of your condition worsening, I'm getting you delivered. Agreed?' She looked at Andrew for confirmation and was relieved when he nodded.

'I'll ask them to call me at home if there's any change,' he said.

'As will I,' Caitlin added. 'I'll do the section myself.'

'I'd feel so much better if you'll both be there,' Mrs Levy said, hope brightening her eyes.

'But they might have to go ahead and deliver you if I can't get here in time,' Caitlin warned.

'I understand,' Patricia said. 'Thank you both for taking care of me and listening.'

Andrew and Caitlin left Patricia to get some rest. A glance at her watch told Caitlin that she was due in Theatre.

'Did you know all that?' she asked. 'Is that the reason you wanted to wait?'

'Partly,' Andrew said. 'At the end of the day I want the same thing you do. A healthy baby and a mother who survives to look after it. But,' he said, 'I don't think we should ever look at patients as if they were simply their medical problems. We need to see them as people, all with different needs requiring different solutions.' Caitlin bristled. Was he suggesting that she didn't see her patients as individuals? He had no right to make that assessment of her. But, she admitted to herself, was there just the tiniest bit of truth in it? Was that why she was so drawn to the academic side of her chosen speciality? Because it was easier than dealing with real people and real emotions? He grinned down at her, and Caitlin's heart gave a curious flip. 'You and I are on the same side after all.'

Caitlin's surgeries were straightforward and she didn't see Andrew again until it was time to leave for the day. She felt wrung out, the perspiration trickling down her shoulder blades. Before she left she checked on Mrs Levy. There was no change in her condition. Caitlin asked that the staff be asked to call her should her condition change during the night. When she checked her watch it was after six. It had been a long first day. Suddenly anxious to get home to check on Brianna, she paged Andrew and told him she'd meet him by the hospital entrance. When he finally arrived he was whistling cheerfully.

'Hey,' he said. 'Ready to go?'

As they set off home, the sun was sinking in the sky. Caitlin welcomed the breeze as they made their way through the traffic. She was uncomfortably aware of Andrew in the small space of his sports car. She could smell the faint tang of his aftershave and was conscious of his long fingers as he steered the car through the traffic. What would it be like to feel those fingers on her skin? she wondered. Immediately she was horrified at the direction her thoughts were taking. What was wrong with her? Thinking like this was so unlike her. Maybe the strangeness of a new country was affecting her? It wasn't as if she had the time or inclination for romance. Not with so much on her plate and certainly not with this man.

'I gather you looked in on Mrs Levy,' he said as they reached the edge of the suburb where Brianna lived.

'Yes, before I paged you,' she said. 'All her results are exactly the same as before. So perhaps we made the right decision to wait. I hope so.'

'Mmm. I went to see her too. If her condition changes, they'll call me. Believe me, I'm as determined as you that both will pull through,' he said, his mouth set in a grim line.

They turned into the drive of Brianna's house, sending a flock of rainbow lorikeets into the air. 'They are so beautiful,' Caitlin said, admiring the vividly coloured birds with their bright red beaks and green wings. 'Just like something I'd expect to find in the Amazon rainforest.'

'They're all over Brisbane,' Andrew replied. He looked at her thoughtfully. 'If you're interested in seeing more of the same, as well as experiencing a rainforest, you don't have to go as far as the Amazon. There's a place not far out of Brisbane in the Green Mountains called O'Reilly's.' He grinned at her. 'No relation, I presume?' Not waiting for a reply, he continued, 'I go up there on a regular basis. It's a great way to escape the heat of the city and there are amazing walks in the rainforest. They even have one that takes you right across the treetops.'

'It sounds wonderful,' Caitlin agreed. 'But I'm not really here to amuse myself. When I'm not working, I'd rather spend the time with Brianna.'

'You could go together,' Andrew suggested. 'I believe there's plenty to keep the kids busy. And if you're interested, there's also my house up the coast. Niall and the family often stay there. You're welcome to use it too while you're here.'

'That's very generous of you,' Caitlin said. 'Are you coming in?' she asked, levering herself out of the car.

'No, thanks,' he said. 'You'll want to spend time alone with Brianna, after being away all day. I'll leave you to it.' And with a spurt of gravel he had gone. Caitlin stared after his departing car. He was a mass of contradictions. One minute a flirtatious playboy, the next a kind and sensitive friend. She didn't quite know what to make of him. All she knew was that Dr Andrew Bedi was having a very unsettling effect on her and that was the last thing she wanted or needed right now.

'How did your first day go?' Brianna asked. Caitlin had helped organise the children for bed and the two women were relaxing in the kitchen with some iced tea.

'It was interesting,' Caitlin said slowly. 'But nothing very different from back home. How was your day?' She searched her sister's face for signs of tiredness. Although the tumour had been large enough to be classed as Stage II, the positioning of it meant that Brianna had been able to have a lumpectomy rather than a mastectomy. While the surgery had been straightforward, Caitlin could see that the follow-up chemotherapy was taking its toll on her sister. Thankfully she only had one more session to complete. Then the doctors would wait a month, giving her body some time to recover, before starting Brianna on a course of radiotherapy.

'I feel good, you know,' Brianna said softly. 'The effects of the chemo weren't nearly as bad as I was expecting. Except perhaps for the loss of my hair.' She ruefully touched the scarf she was using to cover her scalp. 'Losing my eyelashes, believe it or not, was almost the worst part of this whole business.'

Caitlin reached over and hugged her sister. 'Were you frightened? Silly question—you must have been.'

'I never once believed that I wouldn't get better. When you have two small children, you have to believe that.'

Brianna swivelled round in her seat and looked at Caitlin. 'What about you, Cat? Have you thought about what this might mean for you?'

Caitlin frowned. 'I'm not sure I know what you mean.'

'C'mon, sis, you're a doctor. Aunty Molly died of breast cancer when she was thirty-six. And now I have it at thirty-two. It's likely there is a genetic component. Don't tell me it hasn't crossed your mind.'

It hadn't. When Caitlin had first heard about Brianna she had been too caught up worrying about her to even consider what it might mean for her. Then there had been the arrangements for her job to think about. But now she thought about it, she realised Brianna was right. There was a strong possibility she might develop breast cancer herself.

'I'll go see someone,' she said. 'Perhaps arrange for a mammogram. But I do check myself regularly, and so far I don't think there's anything to worry about.'

'I think about Siobhan,' Brianna admitted. 'Her chances of getting breast cancer are also increased.' She took a sip of her drink, looking more worried than Caitlin had seen her before. 'You hear about girls having a double mastectomy because they're so worried. How on earth will I advise her when she's older?'

Caitlin's thoughts were whirling around inside her head. This was something she just hadn't thought about. Although she had tried to reassure Brianna, she knew that what she was saying was true. Both she and Siobhan did have an increased chance of getting the disease. And if she ever had a daughter, she too would be at risk. Would she be prepared to take that chance? But she and Brianna were getting way ahead of themselves.

'You know, by the time Siobhan is older, they might well have found a cure. Detection is getting so much better now, as are survival rates. They've come a long way since Aunt Molly's time.'

'I heard somewhere that there is a test that can tell you whether you have the gene,' Brianna said thoughtfully. 'Do you think we can find out about it?'

'Of course,' Caitlin said. 'Leave it to me.' She squeezed her sister's hand, trying to inject all the reassurance she could into the touch.

'I know you are going to be just fine. You'll get through this and I'll be here to make sure you do.'

'Is that the sister or the doctor speaking?' Brianna asked with a small smile.

'Both,' said Caitlin firmly. 'Now, don't you think it's time for bed?'

It felt to Caitlin as if she had only been asleep for a couple of minutes when she was woken by her mobile phone. Switching on the bedside light, she squinted at the unfamiliar number on her phone.

'Hello. Dr O'Neill?' said the voice. 'It's the hospital here. We spoke to Dr Bedi and he said to call you. I hope you don't mind.'

Instantly Caitlin was wide awake. 'What is it?' she asked. 'Is it Mrs Levy?'

'Yes,' the voice replied. 'Her blood pressure has risen, causing some concern. Dr Bedi is on his way in, in case we have to section her. He said that you might want to perform the procedure.'

'I'll be there as soon as I can.'

Twenty minutes later Caitlin was at the hospital. At four in the morning the roads were clear of traffic, and she was relieved that she remembered the way, only taking one wrong turn.

She rushed up to the antenatal ward and found Andrew

already there in discussion with the midwives. Mrs Levy was looking anxiously from one to the other. She seemed even more worried when she spotted Caitlin.

'I guess that means you've made up your minds to deliver me,' she said despondently, sinking back in her pillows.

'Not necessarily,' Caitlin said softly. 'I need to have a chat with Dr Bedi before we decide.' She looked at the chart, which Andrew had passed over. She could see from the notes the night staff had made that Patricia's platelets had dropped and that she was showing the first signs of renal failure.

'I don't think we can wait any longer,' she said. Andrew nodded his agreement. 'I'll let Theatre know,' he said, turning away.

Caitlin returned to Patricia's bedside. 'I'm sorry, Patricia, but we can't wait any longer. We have to get you delivered, and Dr Bedi agrees.'

Patricia squeezed her eyes shut, but not before Caitlin could see that they were awash with tears. 'Please,' she whispered. 'Can't we wait? Just a little longer. It's too soon.'

Caitlin shook her head. 'It's too dangerous,' she said. 'But Dr Bedi will do everything he can to save your baby. You just have to trust us now.'

Suddenly Patricia sat up in bed, panic-stricken. 'I can't see!' she cried out. 'What's happening? Please, someone, help me!'

Caitlin whirled round, her heart sinking. Loss of eyesight was a clear symptom that Patricia's condition had worsened. Now they really needed to get her delivered. Time was against them.

'It's okay, Patricia,' she said. 'It's probably only temporary. As soon as we get you delivered, everything will be okay.' But even as she said the words she wondered if they were true. There was every chance they could lose her and the baby. She glanced across at Andrew and could see that the same thoughts had crossed his mind.

'Let's get her down to Theatre—now! Page the anaesthetist to tell whoever it is to meet us in Theatre,' Andrew said, unlocking the wheels of the bed. Helped by Caitlin and the midwives, they pushed the bed towards Theatre.

Caitlin's heart was pounding as they ran with Patricia. Once there, she still had to scrub up. That would take five minutes, but would give the anaesthetist time to put Patricia under. How quickly they would get the baby out would depend on how quickly she could carry out the procedure. At this point, every second counted.

Leaving Patricia in the care of the theatre staff, Caitlin scrubbed up alongside Andrew.

'It seems you were right after all,' Andrew said grimly. 'I really hoped we had some more time.'

'It was the right decision to wait,' Caitlin said. 'I'll get the baby out, and then it's up to you.'

By the time they had finished scrubbing up, Patricia had been anesthetised and Caitlin wasted no time in cutting open her abdomen. Instead of the transverse incision, which left a neater scar, she went for a longitudinal cut which would allow her to get the baby out quicker. Now was not the time to think about cosmetics. It only took her three minutes from the first incision to removing the baby from its protective sac. A record even for her. She passed the tiny baby, not much bigger than her hand, across to

Andrew, who was standing by with a nurse from the special care unit ready to resuscitate the baby. The tiny girl was so small Caitlin could see every vein through its translucent skin.

'C'mon, darling,' Caitlin whispered as she passed the baby across. 'Fight. Your mummy needs you.'

Caitlin could have heard a pin drop as everyone held their breath, hardly daring to hope. She forced her attention away from what was happening behind her to her patient. Although the baby was out, the mother wasn't out of danger yet. She needed to deliver the placenta and close the wound. Only after that could she be sure Patricia would make it. Behind her she was aware of voices and movement. Eventually, just as she had finished closing, Andrew called out.

'We're taking her up to Intensive Care.' And then with a last flutter of activity they were gone.

Thankfully, Patricia's blood pressure dropped dramatically now that the baby had been delivered. Caitlin waited with her until she came round from the anaesthetic, desperately worried that the loss of eyesight might be permanent. It was so unfair. Patricia already had had more than her fair share of tragedy. What if she were left blind and her baby died or was left brain damaged? It would be too cruel.

But eventually Patricia's eyes flickered open. Caitlin held her breath as Patricia slowly focussed on her face.

'Dr O'Neill,' Patricia said. 'How's my baby?'

Caitlin sighed with relief. Patricia's blindness had been temporary. Thank God they had got her to Theatre in time. Now all they needed to do was to ensure her baby survived.

'She's holding her own,' Caitlin said softly. 'Now that you're awake, I'll go and see her myself and report back.'

Patricia struggled to sit up, her face twisted in pain. 'I want to see my baby,' she cried. 'I need to see her and she needs me!' Gently, Caitlin eased her back down. 'I will take you to see her as soon as it's possible. I promise. And I'll come straight back down and tell you everything once I've seen her. In the meantime, promise me you'll take it easy?'

Patricia closed her eyes, defeated, sinking back into the peace of sleep. 'Be as quick as you can,' she whispered. 'Tell them I need my little girl.'

After she'd left Patricia, Caitlin went to the special care unit. Andrew and the team were still working on the baby. Caitlin stood to the side and watched, not wanting to get in the way. Eventually Andrew stood back from the incubator and peeled off his gloves.

'Right, keep a close eye on her. But well done, everyone. The next twenty-four hours are crucial.' Then he noticed Caitlin and walked across to her. She could see the fatigue in his eyes, but he was smiling. Caitlin's heart leapt. It was a good sign.

'Baby's breathing,' he said softly. 'It's still touch and go and will be for the next few days, even weeks, but she has a chance. How's Mum?'

'She's going to be fine,' Caitlin answered. 'Her eyesight has returned.' She saw the look of relief in Andrew's eyes. 'She'll want to see her baby once she's fully recovered from the anaesthesia. In the meantime, I've promised to report back on how her baby is doing.' She walked across to the incubator and looked at the tiny form that was almost obscured by tubes and lines. Although she had seen babies in such a condition before, she never found it any easier.

She knew Patricia would have to be prepared for seeing her baby like this.

'Does she have a chance?' she asked.

'I think so,' Andrew said. 'We will do everything we possibly can.' He straightened his shoulders. 'But, there's nothing more I can do for the time being—the nurses have everything under control. I'll check up on her once I've spoken to Patricia.'

'The nurses will page me as soon as she comes round properly,' Caitlin said. 'We can both speak to her then.'

'Coffee?' Andrew asked.

'I'd love some.'

Caitlin followed him into the staffroom just off the main ward. As always after an emergency, Caitlin felt the adrenaline drain away, leaving her feeling emotionally as well as physically exhausted. She accepted a coffee gratefully.

'Are you okay?' Andrew asked. Despite her best intentions, it seemed as if he were able to see through the exterior she tried so hard to present to the outside world. His dark brown eyes seemed to drill right through her. But as she returned his gaze, she could tell he was equally affected by the drama.

'She looks so small and defenceless,' she said. 'It's hard to imagine that someone that tiny can survive.'

'Every day more and more babies survive, you know that,' Andrew said gently. 'Her chances were helped by you getting her out so quickly.'

'But even if she survives, we both know she might have brain damage.'

'Yes,' Andrew agreed. 'On the other hand, she could be perfectly all right. That's what we have to hope for. We have to stay positive.'

'How can you do it, day after day?' Caitlin asked. 'You must lose so many children. At least in my specialty, the outcome is usually positive.'

'And increasingly so in mine,' Andrew said. 'The trick, I find, is not to get too emotionally involved.'

'Like me, you mean?' Caitlin said, her temper rising. 'Well, I'm sorry, Mr Cool, that we can't all be machines.'

Andrew placed his mug on the counter and stepped towards her until he was towering over her. His dark eyes glinted dangerously. 'Is that how you see me?' he asked. 'As a machine?' He raised his hand and traced a finger across her cheekbone. Caitlin felt herself tingle. 'I can assure you, Dr O'Neill, that I am no machine.'

Caitlin was rooted to the spot. She felt her breath catch in her throat. She could feel the heat of his body radiating into hers. Then he dropped his hand and turned away from her. Caitlin felt her knees wobble and had to hold on to the worktop to hold herself upright. What was this man doing to her? Why was he having this effect on her? He might be good looking, but he was not her type. Far too masculine and assured of his own sexuality. Caitlin had an image of him flinging her across his shoulder before marching off to some cave. The image made her smile. Just then one of the midwives popped her head in. She stood for a moment, glancing from Andrew to Caitlin, looking puzzled, and Caitlin wondered if she could sense the sexual tension in the room.

'The ward called, Dr O'Neill. They thought you'd be here. Mrs Levy has come round. They said you wanted to know.'

'Thank you,' Caitlin replied. She rinsed her cup in the sink. 'Shall we go, Dr Bedi?'

CHAPTER FOUR

CAITLIN didn't see much of Andrew over the next few days. She went up to SCBU a couple of times a day to check on baby Levy's progress and would sometimes catch sight of Andrew examining a patient or in discussion with the nursing staff. Every time she caught a glimpse of his dark head, she was uncomfortably aware of the effect on her heart rate.

Patricia was always by her baby's cot, willing her on. 'I'm so desperate to hold her,' she told Caitlin. 'I just feel that if I could hold her in my arms, if she could feel me, know that I'm here…' Her voice broke. 'That her mummy is right here beside her…I would feel so much better. All I've been able to do is touch her finger.'

'Just hang in there,' Caitlin said. 'She's getting stronger every day. And she'll recognise your voice. The nurses tell me you talk to her all the time.'

'And sing,' Patricia said. 'Although my voice isn't up to much.' She managed a wry smile. Caitlin glanced around the room. All the incubators had mothers and in some cases fathers by the cots. All wore the same anxious expressions.

'How are your other children?' Caitlin asked.

'My mother has come to stay with them. Thank goodness she was prepared to move out of her house and into mine. But I miss them so much. They come to see me, but it's not the same as being with them all the time. I've never been away from them before. Not even overnight.' Then she started crying again. 'I wish Jack was here. It's not fair. He should be here with me.'

Caitlin felt helpless to comfort the distraught woman. It was so unfair the way life dealt the cards sometimes. She became aware that Andrew was standing behind her. He crouched down beside the stricken woman.

'Hey,' he said softly. 'What's this? Your baby is making progress. She's a fighter. Just like her mother, I suspect.'

'Patricia needs to hold her baby,' Caitlin said.

'I think we can arrange that.' Very gently he reached inside the incubator and lifted the infant out, careful not to disturb any of the lines. In his large hands the baby looked even smaller, more defenceless, if that were possible. Seeing what he was doing, one of the nursing staff came rushing over.

'Dr Bedi, what do you think you're doing? The baby needs to stay in the incubator.'

'What this baby needs, more than any medicine we can provide, is to feel her mother's arms,' he said firmly, before placing his delicate bundle in Patricia's arms. 'Only for a few moments,' he said, smiling down at her.

Caitlin felt a lump in her throat as she watched Patricia gaze down at her baby.

'Hello there,' Patricia said softly, her voice little more than a whisper. 'Hello, my darling girl. This is Mummy speaking.' Caitlin had to turn away as tears pricked her eyes. Impatiently she blinked them away. She was damned if she was going to let anyone see the ultra-cool Dr O'Neill with her defences down. But catching Andrew's look of surprise, she knew it was too late.

On Friday after work, Caitlin lay by the side of the pool, enjoying the cool breeze that rustled the trees. She watched, entranced, as the multicoloured birds danced from tree to tree, calling to each other. She was beginning to see what Brianna loved about living here, although she found the heat difficult to cope with. Even though it was early evening it was still hot and Caitlin felt a trickle of perspiration trickle between her breasts. For a moment she thought of Ireland, the green fields and rolling hills—and the rain. She'd never thought she'd miss that, but after a week of endless sunshine she realised she did.

Brianna had gone to collect the children at a play date, refusing Caitlin's offer to accompany her, saying that she wanted to catch up with one of the mothers. As Niall's plane wasn't due for a couple of hours, Caitlin had the place to herself.

Although she loved her sister and her family dearly, Caitlin revelled in the peace and quiet. The first since she had arrived.

She glanced across at the pool. The water looked so cool and inviting. Making up her mind, she slipped off her shorts and T-shirt, followed quickly by her underwear—there was no one about to see her after all—and jumped into the pool, gasping with delight as she felt the cool water on her skin. She swam a few lengths underwater and then stopped to catch her breath. Good grief, she was out of shape. She must remember to ask Brianna if there was a gym she could join.

As a shadow fell across the pool she looked up to find Andrew standing by the edge of the pool, looking down at her. He had the sun at his back so she was unable to read his expression, but realising she was naked she wrapped her arms around her body. Did no one knock in this country?

He must have read her mind as he said, 'The front door was open so I thought I'd find you round the back.' He grinned down at her. 'I had no idea I'd find you skinny dipping,' he drawled, his Australian accent stronger than ever. 'Do you mind if I join you?' He was wearing a T-shirt and the same Bermuda shorts he had worn the previous weekend. Caitlin felt warmth deep in her belly.

'No,' she said sharply. 'I mean, yes, I do mind!'

'Too bad,' he said, grinning broadly, and with one sweep he had removed his T-shirt, revealing his muscular chest. Caitlin struggled to keep her eyes off his abdomen. She had seen six packs before, but never outside a magazine. He wasn't over-muscular, just perfect. Before she had a chance to protest further, he had dived in. At least he'd kept his Bermudas on, Caitlin thought. The image of them in the water together both naked was too much.

'Excuse me,' she said as he surfaced, water steaming from his black hair. 'I thought I said I didn't want you to come in. Now, either you get out or I will.'

'You're welcome to get out any time,' he said, his eyes creasing at the corners. 'Don't let me stop you.'

'You know I can't,' she protested.

'I won't look,' he said, and Caitlin heard the laughter in his voice.

'I don't care what you say,' Caitlin said fiercely. 'I'm not getting out until I'm sure you're nowhere in sight.'

'Okay,' he said lazily. 'Then you'll just have to stay there until I've finished my swim.' He turned on his stomach and started swimming. Caitlin didn't know what to do. It was ridiculous, being caught here in the pool, completely naked, while he swam up and down without a care in the world. What if Brianna returned with the children and found her in this intolerable situation? It just didn't bear thinking about. Then, to her alarm, she heard the sound of a car pulling up in front of the house.

'Andrew,' she snarled. 'Brianna and the children are back. Will you please get out and pass me a towel?'

Andrew looked at her and for a second Caitlin thought he was going to refuse, in which case there would be nothing for it except for her to take her chances and run for her clothes. But he seemed to take pity on her. He heaved himself out of the pool in one swift movement. As he did so, Caitlin was acutely conscious of his muscles bunching and the crease low on his back. He strode across to her lounger, grabbed a towel and passed it to her, turning his back as she got out of the pool. Wrapping herself in the towel, she had just enough time to snatch her clothes and make it to the downstairs cloakroom before she heard the sound of the children's laughter as they came into the kitchen. As she closed the door she heard a splash as Andrew dived back in to the water. She would make him pay for this, she promised herself.

By the time she had made herself presentable, Brianna was in the kitchen, fixing supper. Andrew was nowhere in sight.

'Niall's plane arrived early,' Brianna told her. 'Andrew offered to go and collect him. He's so sweet.' Sweet was the last thing Caitlin would have called him, but she resisted the impulse to tell her sister exactly what she thought of the man they were so friendly with. 'Don't you think he's lovely?' Brianna went on, oblivious to Caitlin's scowl.

Caitlin started chopping some chicken for the Caesar salad. 'Mmm,' she said. 'He's a little…' She struggled to find the right word. 'Too male for my liking.' It wasn't exactly what she meant, but it was the nearest she could think of without actually swearing.

'Too male?' Brianna said, looking amused. 'Yes, I can see why you would say that, but he's a real softy inside.'

Caitlin looked at her sister, perplexed. 'Are all Australian men like him?' she asked.

'You'll find Australian men are a breed unto themselves, but under that macho image, as you call it, they are real gents. And Andrew is no exception.' Brianna looked at her sister, narrowing her eyes. 'Hey, don't tell me you're falling for him.'

'Of course I'm not falling for him.' Caitlin laughed but even to her own ears the sound was hollow.

'Good, because, as I told you, he is strictly out of bounds. And, Caitlin, although I would love to see you and Andrew together, I also know that he could break your heart. For all your medical competency, I don't think you've ever had experience of a man like him.' She arched her eyebrow at her sister. 'He's as unlike David as it is possible for him to be.'

Before Caitlin had a chance to reply, the children came running in wet from the pool. Siobhan wrapped her wet arms around Caitlin's legs. 'I'm so glad you're here, Aunty Cat. Come and swim with me.'

Happily Caitlin was saved from having to disappoint

her niece—having just washed her hair, she wasn't ready for another dip—by the sounds of Andrew and Niall returning from the airport. Siobhan abandoned her aunt and flung herself into her father's arms, competing with Ciaran for attention. Niall picked up both his children and leaned across and kissed his wife. Once again, Caitlin could almost feel the love that passed between them. Andrew stood to the side, watching closely. Caitlin thought she saw something move behind his eyes. What was it—sadness, envy?

Brianna insisted Andrew stay for supper and afterwards as the children watched TV, the adults moved out to the veranda with their coffee. Although the sun had long set, the air was still humid. Caitlin fanned herself with a newspaper she found on the table. 'When does it get cooler?' she asked.

'I'm afraid it only gets hotter from now until after Christmas,' Niall said, 'but you'll adapt to the heat eventually. Everyone does.'

'What if we all go to the Green Mountains tomorrow and stay the night? I was telling Caitlin about O'Reilly's the other day,' Andrew suggested. 'It's much cooler up there, and Caitlin will get a chance to see a rainforest. It's only just over an hour away from here.' He sat back, looking pleased with his suggestion. Niall and Brianna exchanged glances.

'Why don't just the two of you go?' Brianna suggested. Caitlin was horrified at the proposition. The last thing she wanted was to find herself alone with Andrew.

'Oh, I don't want to leave you on your own the first weekend,' Caitlin protested.

'Uh, Caitlin,' Andrew said quietly. 'I think Niall and Brianna might want a night on their own. After all, Niall has been away several days.'

Caitlin was mortified. She slid a look at her sister, who was blushing. 'I'm sorry, Bri,' she said. 'I wasn't thinking.' She thought for a moment. 'What if we take the children with us? If Andrew's okay with that? It would give you and Niall a night on your own. A chance to sleep late. It will also give me some time with the children.' It was a good idea, she thought. Brianna and Niall probably hadn't many opportunities to spend time alone together. And taking the children along meant she wouldn't be alone with Andrew, as well as giving her the opportunity to get to know them again. Besides, she was keen to see more of this fascinating country. She glanced at Andrew, but in the dim light she was unable to read his expression.

'Sure, we can take the kids. You know I'm happy to help. If I remember, there's a lot for children to do up there.'

Brianna smiled broadly, the tiredness that seemed to haunt her disappearing from her face. 'Are you sure?' she said. 'That would be wonderful. I love my children, but they can be exhausting. Are you sure you two know what you're letting yourselves in for?'

'I think Caitlin and I can cope with most things,' Andrew drawled. He stood to leave. 'Well, that's settled. If they have room for us, the four of us will go up tomorrow. We can stay the night and come back on Sunday. Much as I love your children, I think one night would be enough.' He pulled out his mobile and searched for a number. After a few moments he was put through, and spoke for a few minutes. 'Yep. They can take us,' he said. 'I'll collect everyone about ten. Is that okay?'

'I think you've forgotten something,' Niall said, grinning. He looked pleased at the thought of having his wife to himself even for a short time. 'There is no way you're going to fit four people into your soft-top.'

'I hadn't thought that far,' Andrew admitted.

'You'll take our car, naturally,' Brianna said. 'You'll need it to cart the kids and all their gear.'

As they waved Andrew away, Caitlin found that the thought of a night away in Andrew's company was having a very disturbing effect on her pulse.

True to his word, Andrew arrived at ten to pick up Caitlin and the two children. It had taken the whole of the morning to organise the children. They had rushed around the house in a frenzy of excitement, refusing to stop long enough to have their faces washed or their hair brushed. However, after finally being threatened with having the whole trip called off, they had allowed themselves to be made ready. Caitlin felt exhausted already. If this was what having children meant, she was more sure than ever that it wasn't for her. Much better to have nieces and nephews who she could enjoy in small doses.

Seeing to the children had left Caitlin little time to get herself ready. In the end she had flung some walking boots, a bikini and a change of clothes into an overnight bag, adding a sweater at the last minute when Brianna had insisted.

'It gets cool in the mountains at night. You'll be surprised.' And so she would be. She was already beginning to feel like a washed-out rag in the heat. She couldn't imagine any part of Australia being cool enough for her to need extra clothing.

Andrew, on the other hand, looked fresh and cool in light-coloured trousers and a short-sleeved white shirt. He was wearing sunglasses, but that didn't stop Caitlin from noting his look of horror when he saw how much Brianna had packed for the night.

'You and Niall aren't planning to abscond while we are away?' he said, and Caitlin could tell he was only half joking. 'Because let me tell you, guys, as much as I am fond of your children there is no way I could survive more than one night with them.'

'Hey,' said Brianna, pretending to be affronted. 'Would I ever want to be without my children?' She smiled, but not before Caitlin saw a shadow flit across her eyes. Despite the brave way she was confronting her illness, she must inevitably think that there was always the possibility she wouldn't be around to see her children grow up.

But she brightened up again as she and Niall, their arms around each other, watched their children pile into the car. Several trips back to the house for forgotten toys and must-have books later and they were heading out of Brisbane.

'Only an hour late,' Andrew said, glancing at his watch. 'Not bad.'

'Do you have nieces and nephews?' Caitlin asked. 'Coming from a large family, I have several.'

'I'm an only child,' Andrew replied. For a moment, Caitlin thought he was going to say something else but he seemed to change his mind.

'I can't imagine what that is like. With there being five of us, there was always so much activity in the house. It meant having to share, and often do without, as my parents weren't very well off, but the bonus was we always had someone to play with. And now that we're all older, we're still close.'

'Tell me about Ireland,' Andrew said. 'I've never been there.'

As they drove, Caitlin told Andrew about her life on the farm, how, when farming had become too difficult, her parents had changed direction and started breeding horses, which had turned out to be surprisingly successful. She told him about her three brothers and their families. Then, before she knew it, they were climbing the steep road into the mountains.

'I'm sorry,' she said. 'I must have bored you silly, going on like that.'

Andrew grinned at her.

The children, who had been listening to stories on a tape, perked up as they drove through the trees and emerged at the top of a mountain. Caitlin wound down the window and let the smell of eucalyptus waft in through the window. Flocks of vividly coloured parrots perched on every tree. Caitlin had never seen anything quite like it. As they got out of the air-conditioned car, Caitlin noticed that the air was noticeably cooler, and she sighed with pleasure. Within minutes they were surrounded by a gaggle of bush turkeys with their incongruous red and yellow necks. Gingerly Caitlin edged away from their pecking beaks as they scavenged for scraps.

Andrew laughed at her obvious discomfort as the children scampered away, shrieking with excitement.

'Hey, kids, come back,' Caitlin shouted. What if they fell down the steep slope in front of them? What if they hurt themselves? What if they got lost? She was beginning to regret that she had agreed to this trip. What did she know about looking after children? Although she loved her five nieces and nephews at home, their parents were always around to help. In fact, Caitlin realised with a pang of guilt, she had never taken time to do something with them. Tried to get to know them. She had always been too busy. It had taken something as serious as her sister's illness for her to spend time with these two. But feeling guilty didn't stop Caitlin feeling totally out of her depth.

As she started to run after them, Andrew caught her arm. 'Relax,' he said. 'Let them blow some steam off after the journey. They'll be fine.'

Feeling ridiculously out of her depth, she followed the children over to where the ground fell away. Beneath them she could see the canopy of the rainforest and in the distance the suspended walkway that Andrew had told her about. The one that would take them right across the top of the rainforest. Andrew unloaded their bags and joined her. The children, having lost interest in the rainforest, had discovered an adventure playground and had rushed off to join the children already there.

'It's beautiful,' Caitlin breathed, taking in the view of the mountains in the distance. 'We could be on our own small island here. It's like nothing I have ever seen before.'

'Come on,' Andrew said, appearing delighted with her reaction. 'Let's check in and have some lunch.'

After checking in, they were shown to their rooms. Caitlin was to share the larger of the two with the children, while Andrew had a smaller double to himself. Both had decks overlooking the rainforest and fireplaces. Andrew's even had a hot tub on his deck. Caitlin was glad she'd remembered to pack her bikini.

'We'll round up the children and then go for a walk,' Andrew suggested. But the children were against that plan. They had made friends who were going to the children's club and begged to be allowed to go too.

Caitlin hesitated. Would it be safe to leave them? After all, she was here to watch them and spend time with them. 'I think you should come with Uncle Andrew and me,' she said.

'Do we have to?' Siobhan moaned.

'I want to stay here,' Ciaran added, his mouth set in a mutinous line.

Once again Andrew intervened. He pulled Caitlin out of earshot. 'Let them stay. The playground is supervised. The children need some time to have fun. I know they're both too small to understand what's going on with Brianna, but they are bound to have picked up that something isn't quite right. Let them just have fun for a little while.'

'Okay,' Caitlin conceded. But she was thinking that it was unfair that this man, for all his machismo, seemed to have a better understanding of her niece and nephew's needs than she did. Maybe it was something to do with being a paediatrician. He would have to be good with children to do his job well. In her speciality it was different. Once the babies were safely delivered, she had little to do with them. Hers was an adult speciality. Maybe she should trust his judgement. It was obvious to her he was far more relaxed around them than she was.

So after a very quick lunch, when the children hardly stayed still long enough to eat more than a couple of mouthfuls, she changed out of her shorts and into long trousers and hiking boots. Andrew had warned her about the insects on the forest floor. As soon as they had waved goodbye to Siobhan and Ciaran they set off down a steep track. As they descended the forest became denser, obscuring the sun. 'That's why they call it a canopy,' Andrew informed Caitlin. They followed the stream, the sound of water becoming louder with every step. Soon they came into a clearing where a waterfall tumbled down moss-covered rocks into the stream. A sudden movement startled Caitlin and she grabbed Andrew's arm. She found herself staring into the amber eyes of a brightly coloured toad, or frog—she didn't know the difference.

'You can let go now, if you like,' Andrew suggested. 'I don't think we're in any danger.'

Caitlin was mortified to find she was still clutching his arm. She could feel the heat of his skin under her fingers and the hard muscle of his forearm. She dropped her hand to her side.

'I thought it was a snake or some other beastie,' she apologised. 'I don't do those.'

'They will be more scared of you then you of them, I promise,' Andrew said.

'It seems that whenever I'm around you, I act like some sort of pathetic female out of the nineteenth century.' She laughed to cover her embarrassment.

'I don't think you're pathetic at all,' Andrew said. 'In fact, I can imagine you more of a suffragette. Determined and tough, and not frightened of much, I would say.' Something in the tone of his voice sent a shiver of electricity down Caitlin's spine. The air crackled between them and she felt herself sway towards him. But then, just as quickly, the atmosphere changed. Andrew dropped his hand and moved away from her. Caitlin knew he was feeling whatever it was that lay between them. He was as attracted to her as she was to him. But she realised it was too complicated for them to start a relationship. They worked together, he was a family friend, godfather to her nephew, and then there was that strange comment from

Brianna. The one about her not being Andrew's type. All in all, whatever it was that lay between them was best left unexplored.

They walked for a couple of hours before turning round and strolling back the way they'd come. They chatted easily about work, and Andrew told her about his holiday cottage on the Sunshine Coast, just over an hour's drive from Brisbane. 'I try to go up at least twice a month,' he said. 'About the same number of times I do a clinic up there. You are welcome to use it whenever you like,' he offered.

'Thank you,' Caitlin replied. 'I might just take you up on the offer, if Brianna and the family would come too. You said I'll be doing a clinic or two up there as well?'

'We'll probably do it at the same time. In many ways it's sensible to have a paediatrician and obstetrician there together. It can save time and unnecessary trips for patients. In fact, I'm scheduled to do one next Friday. I can find out whether they've rostered an obstetrician in and ask if you can take their place. You can stay at the cottage as my guest. I could show you around on Saturday.'

Caitlin wasn't at all sure whether a night in Andrew's company on her own was a good idea. But she told herself not to be absurd. He was behaving just as she would expect a colleague who knew the family would. There was no reason to read anything more into it.

'We'll see,' she said. 'It depends on Brianna and Niall and their plans for the weekend. I don't want them to feel abandoned. But whatever, I'd love to do the clinic if that's a possibility.'

After dinner Caitlin put the children to bed. Happily they were exhausted after their afternoon's excitement and soon drifted off. Andrew had suggested Caitlin might like to use the hot tub on his deck. His room was right next door to hers so they would hear the children if they woke up.

Caitlin slipped on her bikini and popped on the bathrobe that had been thoughtfully provided. The sun was turning the mountains purple and she stood on her balcony and watched as the sun slipped below the horizon. Despite all her worries about her sister she felt more at peace than she had been since she had heard the news. David had been dismayed when she had insisted on coming out here for six months, and when he'd refused to support her decision, Caitlin had realised that he wasn't the man she thought he was. Their break-up had brought surprising relief and Caitlin knew, if she was honest with herself, that she had been using her work to avoid him for a while. The break-up had been amicable, but Caitlin had wondered if she would ever meet that special someone who would make her heart race. Much in the same way Andrew did. But that was ridiculous, she told herself. She hardly knew the man. He wasn't her type, he lived thousands of miles away from her home, and—this was the biggie—she, according to her sister, had no chance with him.

The air was much cooler now that the sun had set, and Caitlin shivered. She knew that if Andrew had tried to kiss her back there in the forest she would have kissed him back. She had wanted him to kiss her. She had wanted to feel his lips on hers, his chest against hers. She was in lust. There was no denying the horrible truth. For the first time ever she had allowed a man to get under her skin and she didn't know how she felt about that. Not good, came the immediate reply from that part of her brain that was still capable of rational thought. Not good at all.

She knocked on Andrew's door. He had changed into jeans and a long-sleeved T-shirt. He also seemed oblivious to the fact he had a smear of soot on his forehead. He looked as sexy as hell, Caitlin thought.

'I'm putting on a fire,' he said. 'It's pretty cool now the sun has set.'

'I can see that. You men just like making fires.' Caitlin laughed. 'Hang on just a moment.' She licked her finger and, standing on tiptoe, reached up to wipe away the soot. As she leant towards him her bathrobe fell open. His hands reached down and encircled her waist, but only for a second. She saw surprise in his eyes, followed closely by something else—could it be desire?

'I'll just have a quick soak while you sort the fire out.' She was dismayed to find she was almost breathless. She walked over to the tub and shed her bathrobe, placing her glasses by the side. But just before she stepped into the bubbling water, she noticed something fat and wriggly attached to her ankle. She peered at it in disgust. It seemed to be a worm of some description. She smothered a shriek of disgust and tugged, planning to fling the disgusting thing as far as she could. But the creature, it seemed, had other ideas. Now it was attached to her it seemed it had no intention of letting go. She couldn't bear it any longer. Andrew must have caught the edge of her surprised squeak as he left the fire and came over to her.

'Everything all right?' he asked.

The last thing Caitlin wanted was for him to have to come to her rescue again, but the thought of spending the rest of the evening with an insect attached to her foot was equally unbearable.

'There's a worm or something stuck on my foot! I can't get it off!'

'Here, let me see,' he said quietly. 'Sit down on the chair over there.'

Caitlin hopped over to the chair.

Andrew took her foot in his lap. With one swift yank he had removed the offending visitor from Caitlin's foot. Immediately blood began to ooze. He examined the insect with interest.

'It's a leech, but it's gone now,' he said. 'Remember I suggested that you tuck your trousers into your socks on our walk? This is the reason why.'

'Ugh,' Caitlin said forcefully. All of a sudden she became aware that her foot was still in his lap and she was wearing nothing but her tiny bikini. She felt Andrew's eyes flicker over her body. Slowly they took her in, from the tip of her toes, before coming to rest on her face. Every nerve in her body seemed to be tingling under his look. Abruptly he lifted her foot from his lap and stood.

'We can stick a plaster on it. Reception's bound to have one. I'll just nip across and get one,' he said.

'It's okay,' Caitlin said, scrambling to her feet. 'It'll stop bleeding soon enough.' But it looked as if Andrew couldn't wait to get away from her. Grief, did he think this was some half-baked attempt to seduce him? How mortifying.

'It won't stop bleeding for a while,' he said. 'These guys have anticoagulant in their bites. It's hardly life-threatening, but we don't want you to bleed all over the place, do we?' And with that he left the room.

Giving up on the hot tub, Caitlin retreated to her room, showered quickly and slipped on a pair of jeans and a thin cashmere sweater. While she showered she felt herself flush at the memory of her foot in his hand and his eyes on her body. Whatever this thing between them was, she knew he felt it too. She had thought he was going to kiss her and then he had pulled away. Clearly he was reluctant to start anything between them. Was it because they worked together? In that case, she could understand. But could she? They were both adults. Surely, at the grand age of twenty-nine, she could be expected to behave like one. Maybe it was more to do with him being friends with Brianna and Niall? That she could understand. It would be intensely awkward if anything did happen and then one of them broke it off. And, besides, Caitlin told herself firmly, she didn't want a relationship with a man who lived on the other side of the world from her. There was no future in it. And then there was Brianna. She was here to be with her sister, not be distracted by some man, no matter how gorgeous. She would put any feelings she might have aside and behave towards him as she would towards any other colleague. Why, then, did a little voice tell her that it wasn't going to be that easy?

While Andrew waited for the receptionist to fetch him a plaster, he too was thinking about Caitlin. Why did Brianna's sister have to be so sexy and warm and funny? She was doing things to his libido that he couldn't remember happening before. Sure, he'd had lovers. Sure he'd been fond of them, but they all knew the score and were happy to be lovers until the relationship came to a natural end. Which it always did. And he had to admit usually because he lost interest. But Caitlin was different. He knew deep in his heart that if he allowed her to get under his skin—more under his skin than she already was—she would be a difficult woman not to fall in love with. And falling in love wasn't part of his plans. It wouldn't be fair to her, it wouldn't be fair to him. They could never be anything more than lovers. Deep in his soul he knew that that wouldn't be enough for her. And to complicate matters further, she was Brianna's sister. He couldn't do anything but play fair with her.

Accepting the plaster from the receptionist, he made his way back to his room. Whatever this attraction was between him and Caitlin, he had to put an end to it. He would tell her the truth. It would be her call. If she wanted to take things further, knowing there was no future in it, who was he to stop her? Satisfied that he was doing the right thing, he felt his spirits rise. He would tell her, then leave it up to her.

But when he got to his room, Caitlin was nowhere to be seen. He felt an inordinate sense of disappointment and realised that he'd been hoping that she'd be there waiting for him, happy to pick up where they'd left off. But it seemed that for whatever reason she had decided against it. But she would still need the plaster. Tentatively, so as not to wake the children, he tapped on her door. She opened it, looking wary.

'I have the plaster,' he said. 'I thought you'd still be in my room.'

'I didn't think it was a good idea,' she said, her green eyes glinting. 'I'm tired, I guess I didn't realise how tired till just now. It was an early start, so if you'll excuse me, I think I'll just go to bed.' She held out her hand and took the plaster. Andrew felt crazily disappointed. He knew then he'd been hoping against hope that Caitlin would listen to what he had to say, and that it wouldn't make a difference. But it seemed she had different ideas. Had he read the situation all wrong? He was still thinking of what to say when she quietly but firmly closed the door on him.

CHAPTER FIVE

THE next morning Caitlin was woken by two small faces staring down at her. As she focused, Siobhan and Ciaran giggled.

'We've been waiting ages for you to wake up,' Siobhan said. 'Mummy said we weren't to wake you up, but we've been up for ages.'

Caitlin scrambled for her watch and squinted at the face. Five-thirty. She groaned. It was still the middle of the night! However, realising that the children would never allow her to go back to sleep, she eased herself out of bed. The children had tried to dress themselves, but had made rather a poor attempt at it. Siobhan was wearing a pair of shorts and a dress *and* Ciaran had his T-shirt on the wrong way round.

'Okay, guys, let me just make myself some coffee and then I'll sort you out. After that we'll go for breakfast—okay?'

While Caitlin waited for the kettle to boil she fixed the children's clothes. Then, still in her dressing gown, she opened the curtains and let herself out onto the deck, coffee in hand. Dawn was just beginning to light the sky and a heavy mist hung over the trees. The birds had woken and she listened to the strange chirping and whirling cries as she sipped her coffee. It was like being in another world, on another planet even, she thought.

When she'd finished her coffee, she realised that it had gone unnaturally quiet in the room. She looked around feverishly but the children were nowhere to be seen. An open door suggested that they had got tired of waiting for her and had decided to go exploring. Caitlin flung on her jeans and T-shirt and not stopping long enough to pull a comb through her hair went off in pursuit. How could she have turned her back on them, even for a moment? Visions of them being lost in the rainforest or slipping down the side of a mountain, or, even worse, falling over the edge of the canopy walk made her blood run cold. God, couldn't her sister rely on her for even twenty-four hours? If having children meant having eyes in the back of your head and being on alert twenty-four seven then Caitlin knew she had been right not to go down that route. Clearly she'd be a hopeless parent. Nieces and nephews, preferably at a distance, suited her just fine.

But she had only got as far as the room next to hers when she saw that the door was open. Hearing the sound of giggles, she followed the sound into Andrew's room to find him sitting up in bed looking bemused, a child on either side.

'They got you too, huh?' Caitlin said. The sight of him, all bleary-eyed and looking so aghast, made Caitlin laugh out loud.

'The last time I was awake this early I was on call,' Andrew admitted. 'Hey, I don't suppose you could make some coffee while I get dressed?' He flung aside the sheet, and Caitlin turned away, but not before she caught a glimpse of his torso. Her heart thudding, she busied herself with the coffee while, behind her, she heard him pad towards the shower. 'Give me five minutes,' he said.

His coffee was cooling by the time he emerged from the shower, a towel slung low on his hips. Caitlin couldn't help but look at his muscular chest, golden in colour and perfectly smooth. She was aware of his arms and the muscles that made it seem as if he worked out. Probably all that kite surfing, she thought. For a second she let herself imagine her head against his chest and his strong arms around her. She shook her head to chase away the image. That way lay madness.

By the time they made their way to the dining room, breakfast was being served and Caitlin saw to the children before helping herself to a plate of fruit, some of which she hadn't seen before. Nevertheless it was all delicious. Andrew tucked into a plate of bacon and pancakes. Catching Caitlin's look of amazement at how much he seemed able to pack away, he raised an eyebrow. 'I need to keep my strength up,' he said between mouthfuls. 'I have a feeling I'm going to need it today.'

'What's the plan?' Caitlin asked, rescuing Ciaran's tumbler just in time to stop it tipping over.

'I thought we should take the children on the canopy walk,' he said. 'It's an easy one, so they'll manage fine. After that, lunch and home, I guess. I told Brianna we'd have them back around three.'

'Sounds good to me,' Caitlin said.

'Me too,' said Siobhan. She looked just like Brianna had as a little girl, Caitlin thought. All red curls and freckles. Thinking about her sister, she remembered why she was here. Please, God, she sent a silent prayer heavenwards. Don't let anything bad happen to this family.

'How's your foot, by the way?' Andrew asked, helping himself to another slice of toast. Then he peered at her. 'Are you all right? You looked so sad there.'

'My foot's fine,' she said. 'And so am I.' She glanced pointedly in the direction of the children. Andrew was quick to pick up the signal. He must have guessed she was thinking about Brianna. He leaned over and touched her hand. It was only the lightest of touches but it sent an electric shock up Caitlin's arm. Before she could help herself she jerked it away.

The children, having finished their breakfasts, were growing restive. 'Let's go. Now!' Ciaran demanded. Andrew and Caitlin shared a look of resignation before gathering up the children.

'Surely among the treetops there are no jellyfish or leeches,' she said. 'I think I've had my share of troublesome Australian wildlife for the time being.'

'Don't worry,' Andrew said, grinning at her. 'You'll be perfectly safe.'

The canopy walkway snaked across the top of the trees. They had to cross a series of suspension bridges and there were viewing platforms along the way. The children kept shrieking with delight every time they spotted a different bird. Every now and again there would be sounds like a whip cracking or a rifle shot that made them all, but especially Caitlin, jump. Amused, Andrew explained the sounds were made by birds and that Caitlin shouldn't worry as there were no hunters in the forest waiting to take a potshot at her.

Although it was still early, the sun was already warming Caitlin's skin. At least up here the sun wasn't so unbearable. In fact, the heat was just perfect. As the children ran ahead Andrew said, 'You were thinking of Brianna back there—at breakfast—weren't you?'

Caitlin nodded. 'You could tell?' she asked, smiling wryly.

'You show everything in your face,' he said. 'Every emotion is written there for the world to see.'

Caitlin cringed inwardly. She certainly hoped not every emotion was visible—the last thing she wanted was for him to see how much he was affecting her.

'I guess I'm not as good at hiding my emotions as I thought I was,' she replied. 'Just as well I always tell my patients the truth. Otherwise they'd know immediately when I was lying and lose faith in me. But sometimes I wish I could switch off, not be so involved. I don't think I could be a paediatrician for that reason,' she said. 'Perhaps that's why my career is following the path of academia,' she added thoughtfully.

'I find I have to keep my distance. I worry I'd let personal feelings cloud my judgement otherwise,' Andrew answered.

Caitlin felt herself bristling. 'I don't think I have ever let my feelings cloud my judgement,' she said, more sharply than she'd intended.

'Hey,' Andrew said. 'I wasn't implying that you did. We all have to cope in different ways. I think you're an excellent doctor. Certainly if I had a wife I'd want her looked after by you.'

'And have you? Ever had a wife, I mean?' Maybe that was what Brianna had meant. Of course he was probably involved. After all, it was unlikely that someone as gorgeous as him wouldn't have someone. Maybe he was divorced and that's what Brianna had meant about her not being his type? But what was she thinking, letting her imagination run away with her? She could just ask him.

'A wife?' He shook his head. 'Good God, woman, I'm too young for one of those.'

'How old are you, then?' she asked.

'I'll be thirty on Christmas Day.'

'Most people would say that's not too young to settle down.'

He looked at her sharply. 'What about you? You're twenty-eight or twenty-nine? You don't look it,' he added hastily, 'but you must be at least that to be where you are professionally.'

'I'm almost thirty,' Caitlin said. 'And, no, I've never met someone I wanted to marry. I don't expect to either.'

'What, never? Don't you want kids?' He sounded astonished, Caitlin realised. 'I want several!' he continued, laughing, but she noticed a flicker in his eyes. Probably thinks all women should be barefoot and pregnant in the kitchen, Caitlin thought to herself. But she didn't have to justify her decision—not to him or anybody else for that matter.

She looked across to where Siobhan and Ciaran were playing. 'I have five nieces and nephews. And I have my work. That's enough for me.' By this time Ciaran had moved to the side and was beginning to climb the barrier for a better view. For a moment she thought Andrew was going to say something else, but instead he simply nodded and turned his attention back to the children. He scooped Ciaran up and swung him onto his shoulders. 'Come on, little fella, let's go have some fun.'

It was past three by the time they pulled up outside the house. Brianna and Niall came rushing out to meet them and the children flung themselves into their parents' arms as if they'd been away for weeks instead of a single night. 'Honestly, sis,' Caitlin said. 'We didn't beat them or starve them. Although,' she muttered under her breath, 'I was tempted this morning when they woke me at half-five.'

'Siobhan, Ciaran. What did I tell you about not disturbing Aunty Caitlin too early?' Brianna scolded mildly. 'Sorry, Cat, children have no respect for the adult's need to sleep.'

Caitlin laughed. 'It was no problem. I enjoyed our trip very much.'

'Thanks so much to both of you,' Brianna said. She looked so much better for her night with Niall, Caitlin thought. Brianna's cheeks were pink and her eyes sparkling. She knew how much she loved her children, but guessed the strain of keeping up appearances in front of them took its toll. She'd have to try and give Brianna more breaks.

'Are you coming in, Andrew?' Niall asked.

'No, thanks,' Andrew replied. 'I thought I might get some kite boarding in while there's a bit of a breeze. I was thinking Caitlin might fancy coming too and give windsurfing a go,' he said. 'In fact, we could all go.'

'I think I'll pass,' Brianna said. 'If you don't mind. But you go on. Niall could go with you too, if he likes.'

'I spend enough time away from my kids as it is,' Niall said firmly. 'And although it was a pleasure to be alone with you, my darling wife, I'd really like to spend this afternoon with my family. Or had you forgotten I'm away again tomorrow?'

'No, I hadn't,' Brianna said softly. 'Do you have to?' Then she shook her head. 'Oh, don't mind me,' she said. 'Of course you have to. I'm just being silly.'

Caitlin and Niall exchanged concerned glances. Brianna had been so resolutely cheerful up to this point. The touch of anxiety in her voice was unsettling. Andrew must have noticed it too. He walked over to her and felt her forehead and then her pulse. 'Are you feeling okay?' he asked.

'I've just got a bit of a headache. Nothing a bit of a lie-down won't sort out. Niall can look after the children while I do that, so go on, Cat, take Andrew up on his offer.'

But Caitlin felt strangely reluctant to leave Brianna.

'I'm sure Andrew has had enough of my company for the time being,' she said lightly. 'And, besides, I'm not sure if I'm ready to risk being stung again. Besides,' she went on, 'I was almost eaten alive by this enormous leech after walking in the rainforest. Perhaps I should stay indoors for a while.'

'Wuss,' said Andrew challengely. 'Well, they do say women from the northern hemisphere are more timid. But I know Brianna has a wetsuit you can borrow. That'll keep you warm and safe.'

'You can say what you like,' Caitlin said, unmoved. 'But I quite fancy lying by the pool with a good book for a couple of hours. Maybe another time?'

'Fine by me,' Andrew said. 'I'll see you tomorrow, then?' And he kissed Brianna and the children before leaping into his car and heading off.

Brianna went to lie down while Niall took the children to the park. Caitlin took her book out to the pool and read before having a dip. After an hour's nap Brianna appeared, carrying two tall glasses of cold orange juice. Caitlin sipped hers greedily, then pressed the ice-cold glass to her forehead.

'How are you feeling?' Caitlin asked her sister.

'Much better, thanks. It was only a headache.' She sat next to Caitlin and stretched out. 'Tell me about O'Reilly's,' she said. 'Did you love it?'

'Mmm,' Caitlin said. 'I thought it was wonderful. Maybe you and Niall could come the next time?'

'We'll see,' Brianna said. 'Anyway, although I promised not to pester you, did you get a chance to think about what I said? About getting yourself checked? I need to know you're all right.'

'Once the big sister, always the big sister.' Caitlin smiled. 'I did think about it, Bri, and I'll go for a mammogram—soon, I promise. Just to put your mind at ease if nothing else. But as for the genetic screening, I'm not sure there is any point. If I do have the gene, what then? I don't think I want to live my life knowing that the sword of Damocles was about to fall.'

Brianna took a deep breath. 'I've been thinking too,' she said. 'I spoke to Andrew about it. He knows someone who will carry out the test on me. I need to know if I carry the gene. I need to know because of Siobhan. Do you understand?'

Caitlin hugged her sister. 'You know I'll support you, whatever you decide,' she said. Then a thought struck her. 'But what if you do turn out to have the gene? What then?'

'I'll consider a mastectomy. Above all else I want to be alive for my children, whatever the cost.'

'It's a big decision,' Caitlin said slowly. 'Not one I think I could make. But if you are going to be tested, then I suppose I should think about it too. If you come back positive, there's a good chance I'll also carry the gene. Whew! I hadn't really thought through all the ramifications before.'

'That's why I wanted to speak to you first. Because, whatever I do, it will affect you,' Brianna replied.

'Well, let's hope for all our sakes, not least Siobhan's, that it will all turn out fine.' She felt her voice shake and fought to keep her emotions under control. Then the two sisters were in each other's arms, crying as if their hearts would break.

Later, having cried themselves out, they broke apart, blew their noses and smiled at each other.

'I needed that,' Brianna said. 'I have been holding it together for Niall and the children, but I feel so much better for letting it all out.'

'Me too,' Caitlin said. 'I know you're scared, Bri. I would be too in your shoes, even though I know you're going to be fine. I hate to think of you going through all this. I feel so helpless. But we have to stay positive. Agreed?'

'Agreed. Enough emotional stuff for the time being. Tell me, how did you get on with Andrew while you were away?'

'Fine. He's very…nice,' Caitlin said evasively, but as Andrew had pointed out she found it difficult to hide her feelings, especially from her sister.

'I was right,' Brianna, said. 'You fancy him!'

'He's good looking, I admit,' Caitlin said reluctantly, then catching her sister's eye, laughed. 'Okay, he's the sexiest man with the hottest body I have seen in a long time, but that doesn't mean I fancy him.'

Brianna sighed. 'I'm not sure I believe you, sis, but as I warned you before, don't get your hopes up in that direction.'

'I'm not!' Caitlin protested, crossing her fingers behind her back. 'I've told you many times before, I don't think

I'm the kind of woman who is destined for a long-term relationship. I'm not sure I want kids so what's the point? Besides, if I want to get the chair of obstetrics then I need to concentrate on my career.'

'Are you sure that's still what you want? Didn't coming out here kind of spoil that for you? Besides, Cat, there's more to life than just work.'

'I know that! I have my family, my friends as well. I'm not a recluse, you know. As for the job, they very graciously agreed to this six-month sabbatical. The Queensland Royal is a pretty prestigious hospital and the Dublin Women and Children's likes their consultants to have international connections. Anyway,' she said, returning to the subject she had been thinking about, 'why shouldn't I get my hopes up? Am I so ugly that you think a hunk like him wouldn't be interested?'

Brianna laughed. 'You know as well as I do that you are beautiful—it runs in the family after all.'

'What, then? Has he been married? In a relationship? There's no sign of a woman on the scene.'

'There have been plenty on the scene, as you say, but not at the moment. Look, I don't know how much he told you about himself.'

'Not a lot,' Caitlin admitted. 'We mainly spoke about you guys—and work.'

'You know his parents are from India originally, although Andrew and his sister were born here.'

'I didn't know he had a sister,' Caitlin said surprised. 'He never mentioned her. Is she here too?'

'She was. Sadly she died after a difficult labour. She suffered an unexpected and catastrophic bleed after a stillbirth.' Brianna shuddered. 'I was on that day, in

Theatre. It was awful. It broke everyone's heart. His in particular.' Brianna stopped and looked into the distance as if remembering.

'How tragic. Poor Andrew. Poor family. It's terrible that these things can happen even in this day and age.' She thought back to his words about not being too involved with patients, but it was bound to be there in his mind every time there was an obstetric emergency.

'He was very close to her. They were a close-knit family. Andrew was always the dearly loved only son, but when his sister died, his parents really started focussing on him. He became the centre of their universe. I'm surprised they haven't moved to Brisbane to be closer but I guess the family business makes it difficult for them to leave Sydney.' Caitlin waited for Brianna to continue. This was all very interesting and she felt a shock of sympathy for Andrew.

'Although we've known Andrew for ages he never talks about his sister's death. Or the rest of his family for that matter, although I know he visits his parents often. If his sister hadn't died at the Queensland Royal, I doubt I would even have known about her.' Brianna went on after a pause. 'I tried to raise the subject once, thinking he might need to talk about it, and nearly got my head in my hands.'

'Some men find it difficult to talk about the stuff that really hurts them,' Caitlin said.

'Sometimes I think it's the reason Andrew won't commit. Maybe he's frightened the same thing could happen again.'

'He's a doctor,' Caitlin argued. 'He must know the chances of lightning striking twice are slim, to say the least.'

'Ah, there you go, my dear sister. Assuming everyone

thinks about things as rationally as you do. Where's your heart, woman?'

But Caitlin was beginning to wonder if she could think rationally any more. Not least when it came to Dr Andrew Bedi. And as for her heart? She ignored the warning voice in her head. No, her heart was still safe. Being in lust wasn't the same as being in love. Everyone knew that.

CHAPTER SIX

AFTER a fitful night tossing and turning, Caitlin gave up trying to sleep and instead got up early. It was so unlike her not to drop off as soon as her head hit the pillow. Perhaps it was concern for Brianna that had kept her from drifting off—because it certainly wasn't because Dr Andrew Bedi kept drifting into her dreams. She was attracted to him, she acknowledged that much, but that was as far as it went!

He was beginning to occupy far too much of her thoughts, Caitlin told herself crossly. Normally totally focussed on her work, she shouldn't be allowing that man to distract her—no matter how delicious he was to look at. As she let herself quietly out of the house, her thoughts once more turned to her duties. At least she could get a head start doing rounds of the labour suite and the antenatal ward before tracking down Patricia Levy, she reasoned. She had heard from one of the juniors that she was still in hospital, but due to be discharged later that day. Her baby was still in Special Care, making progress although still being ventilated.

Caitlin had been reluctant to leave Brianna, who still

appeared under the weather, especially as Niall was off on another business trip, but her sister had insisted. 'It's only a touch of flu or something.' She had dismissed both her sister's and her husband's concern the night before. 'Away you go, both of you. You'll just drive me mad if you hang about hovering over me. I'm fine, trust me.'

Caitlin found her patient on the antenatal ward listlessly packing her few belongings. When she looked up and saw Caitlin she gave her a wan smile.

'How are you feeling?' Caitlin asked.

'Oh, I feel perfectly chucker,' she replied. 'I'm being discharged.'

'How's the little one?' Caitlin asked.

Immediately tears sprang to Patricia's eyes. 'They say she's holding her own.' She sniffed. 'But she's so small and defenceless. I can't bear to leave her here all by herself, but I need to go home and see my other kids. If Jack were here, he could stay with her while I'm away.'

Impulsively Caitlin hugged the distraught woman. 'Don't worry, we'll keep a very good eye on her for you,' she said. 'And if there's any change at all, we'll call you.'

'It's only for a few hours,' Patricia sniffed. 'They've given me a room to stay in when I get back. But what if something happens while I'm away?'

'Come on. Let's go and see how she is,' Caitlin said, trying not to look at her watch. She was due in Theatre, but she could see Patricia needed her right now. They took the lift up to the special care nursery. As before, it was a hive of activity with all the cots taken up. And, once again, there were anxious parents keeping vigil. Caitlin recognised one couple from a few days before. However, by the smiles on their faces, it appeared that their baby at least was making good progress. She followed Patricia over to her baby's cot and wasn't surprised to find Andrew's dark head bending over the infant. He looked up at their approach and instantly Caitlin could make out the concern in his eyes. She felt her heart sink. She couldn't bear it if anything happened to Patricia's baby.

Gently Andrew sat Patricia down. 'I'm afraid your baby took a turn for the worse a few minutes ago and we've had to put her back on the ventilator and sedate her again.'

Patricia looked up at him, stricken. 'Is she going to be all right?' she asked, her voice barely audible.

'We're doing everything we can,' he said.

Caitlin caught his eye again. She read pity in his deep brown eyes. It didn't bode well.

'I can't leave her now,' Patricia said. 'I'll need to phone my mum and let her know.'

'Give me the number,' Caitlin offered. 'That way you can stay here. I'll phone from the duty room.'

Patricia nodded gratefully. 'Tell Mum I'll phone her as soon as I have news,' she said, taking a deep breath. Her tears had dried up and there was new resolution in the squaring of her shoulders. 'I need to be strong—for my baby,' she said.

'I'll come back up and see you after my theatre list,' Caitlin said, blinking away the tears. Then she turned and headed towards the duty room. She had just finished relaying the news to Patricia's mother when Andrew came in.

'Are you all right?' he asked.

'Yes,' Caitlin said, struggling to keep her voice under control. 'How is Patricia's baby?'

'We've managed to stabilise her for the time being. She's a little fighter. We're doing everything we can. But all we can do at the moment is take each day at a time.'

'I know we shouldn't get emotionally involved, but Patricia has lost so much already. I don't think she could bear it if her baby doesn't make it.'

Andrew pulled Caitlin round to face him and looked directly into her eyes. 'I promise you that if there is any way on this earth that I can pull this baby through, I'll do it.' Caitlin returned his look. His nutmeg eyes burned with determination. She believed him.

'I know you will,' she said quietly. 'C'mon, let's get back in there.'

Later, after leaving an anxious Patricia by the side of her baby's cot, Caitlin made her way to the antenatal ward for rounds. Out of the ten women in the antenatal ward, most were doing well, although two needed to be taken to Theatre later that afternoon for elective sections. Neither woman was causing Caitlin much concern. The sections would be straightforward, and she was able to reassure both that they would be holding their babies in their arms later that day.

Glancing at her watch, Caitlin saw that she had just enough time for a quick bite before Theatre and made her way to the hospital canteen. Selecting a salad, she realised that wherever in the world you were, canteens stayed the same. She had just finished the last mouthful when Andrew plonked himself down beside her.

'Hey,' he said. 'Busy morning?'

'You could say that,' Caitlin answered. 'I've a list starting in a few minutes.'

'Anything likely to cause problems?'

Caitlin shook her head and gave him a brief run-through of her cases. 'How's baby Levy?' she asked when she had finished.

'She's doing okay,' Andrew said. 'I'll go and see her again before I leave today. By the way,' he said as Caitlin picked up her tray, 'I'm scheduled to visit the clinic up on the Sunshine Coast on Friday. I thought you'd like to come along as the visiting obstetrician. Like I told you, we take turns to go up once a week to see any referrals the GPs have. We find that having a paediatrician and obstetrician there at the same time works well. The paediatricians see any of the kids that they want a specialist opinion on, and you guys see the pregnant ladies as well as the gynae stuff. If there's any problems with your pregnant ladies, one of us is about for a consult. The other specialties offer the same kind of service.'

'I'd love to go,' Caitlin said. 'I'll just need to make sure the labour ward is covered.'

'Done,' Andrew said. 'I saw Dr Menzies earlier. He was scheduled to go with me, but he's more than happy to cover for you to go in his place.'

Caitlin raised an eyebrow. 'Don't you think it would have been better for me to have asked him? Really, Andrew, I'd much prefer to speak to my colleagues myself.'

'Hey,' Andrew said. 'I didn't mean to step on your toes. I just thought you'd like to come, and as I bumped into him I took the opportunity to check it out.'

Caitlin sighed, knowing that she was being unreasonable. Nevertheless, Andrew had to realise that she wanted to be seen as an equal part of the team. Not just some foreign doctor who swanned about the place, picking and choosing her cases.

'I won't do it again,' Andrew apologized, but Caitlin

could tell from the glint in his eye that he wasn't perturbed in the slightest. It seemed as if Andrew Bedi was used to doing exactly as he pleased. 'Remember I told you that I have a house up there I use at weekends. I often stay over for the weekend when I'm up there. It isn't much, more like a cabin, but you'd be welcome to stay too.'

Caitlin's pulse began to race. The thought of spending a night alone with Andrew seemed tantalisingly tempting but dangerous.

'I don't know about staying,' she said slowly. 'I'd really like to spend the time with Brianna. It feels like I've hardly seen her.'

Andrew shrugged. 'No worries. It's up to you, of course. It was just a suggestion. But I can understand you might not want to be alone with me overnight.' This time there was a definite challenge in his dark eyes.

'Don't be ridiculous,' Caitlin retorted. 'That's got nothing to do with it.' She returned his stare. 'Anyway, I'm sure you'd prefer to have your house to yourself?'

She couldn't help but ask the question. Despite herself, she was desperately curious about Andrew's love life. She found it almost inconceivable that he wouldn't have a woman somewhere.

But it seemed that Andrew wasn't fooled by the forced casualness in her voice. He grinned, his teeth a flash of brilliant white against his dark skin.

'Are you asking?' he drawled. 'What is it you'd like to know about my love life, Dr O'Neill?'

'Of course I'm not the slightest bit interested,' Caitlin said, flustered. 'It was just a friendly question from one colleague to another. I'm assuming that we *can* be friends?'

He leaned forward. 'I don't know Caitlin. What do you think?' he said softly. Then he smiled and stood up. 'Let me know what you decide,' he said. 'If you decide to stay we can go in my car, if not, we'll need to take two.'

He left Caitlin sitting, her heart thudding in the most disconcerting manner. She felt she had been thrown a challenge, but what exactly it was she had no idea. Somehow the only thing she felt sure of was that no man had ever made her feel like this before. Perhaps the safest course was to keep as far away from Dr Andrew Bedi as possible. And the safe course was always what Caitlin preferred.

'Of course you should stay over,' Brianna insisted when she and Caitlin were on the veranda, enjoying the evening breeze. The children were in bed, dinner had been cleared away, and it was the first opportunity the sisters had had to catch up. 'Why shouldn't you?'

'Well, first off, the whole point of me being here is to spend time with you,' Caitlin said, smiling at her sister. 'We've missed so much time already. Secondly, it feels a bit strange, spending the night at Andrew's place. A bit too familiar, if you see what I mean.'

Brianna smiled wickedly. 'Putting the first reason aside for the moment, and remembering I don't want people behaving differently around me, it's the second that intrigues me. Don't you feel safe around Andrew? C'mon, 'fess up. What's going on?'

'Absolutely nothing is going on!' Caitlin protested. Then catching her sister grinning even more disbelievingly, she laughed. 'I can't help it, Bri. There's just something about him I find unsettling.'

'Nothing to do with the fact that he's gorgeous, has a body to die for, and is actually a really nice guy?'

'And, as you keep reminding me, unavailable.'

'Hey,' Brianna said, growing serious, 'I thought you weren't looking for a serious romance.'

'And I meant it. And somehow I don't think that's what Andrew wants either. Anyway, all of this is nonsense. I'm only here for a few months, and then it's back to Ireland. I really want the professorship and nothing and no one is going to stand in my way.'

'Hey, I'm not the one who's stressing. If there's nothing between you and Andrew, I don't see why you don't take him up on his offer.'

'I'll sleep on it,' Caitlin conceded. 'But you're right, we've spent enough time discussing Andrew Bedi.'

For the next few days, Caitlin was kept busy. She loved the ambiance of the hospital. The staff all went out of their way to make her feel welcome and she was impressed by the standard of care the hospital offered. She saw Andrew several times during the day. Often he'd be in Theatre with her for the more complex cases, and she found that they had an easy understanding when they worked together. Patricia's baby was improving every day. Caitlin was delighted when one day she found Patricia in the special care nursery, holding her baby in her lap. All the tubes had been removed and the blue tinge which had worried everyone so much had disappeared and had been replaced by a healthy pink.

Caitlin bent over the sleeping baby.

'She looks great,' she whispered.

'I can't believe how much she's improved in the last few days,' Patricia whispered back. 'I'll never be able to thank everyone. Especially Dr Bedi. He's been in to see her every day, at least twice, and as for the nurses—nothing has been too much trouble.'

'Have you decided on a name yet?'

'Do you have a middle name?' Patricia asked.

'Yes, I do. It's Colleen.'

'Colleen,' Patricia said, savouring the name. 'Then that's what I'm going to call her. Colleen—after you. It's a beautiful name and I think it suits her perfectly.'

Caitlin was touched by the gesture. 'I suppose you couldn't call her Andrew.' She laughed. 'When do they think you'll get her home?'

'Colleen's to stay in for another week or two. At least until she puts on some weight. I've taken a room close by and the my boys are coming to stay with me. I've missed them so much. This way, I'll be able to see Colleen every day, as well as the other kids.'

By Thursday, Colleen had put on another two ounces, and Andrew told Caitlin he was confident enough about her progress to leave her in the safe hands of his colleagues while they were up north. On Friday morning they met as agreed at the hospital entrance. Caitlin was still undecided whether to stay the night at Andrew's place, but had packed a small bag, just in case.

'If you decide against staying,' Andrew said, 'I'll drive you back. But you should make the most of the opportunity while you can.' He grinned at her. 'Don't worry, you'll be perfectly safe.'

Caitlin chose to ignore him, throwing her bag into the small boot and climbing into the car beside Andrew. Although it was still early, the morning sun was already scorching. Before long, they had left the city behind. As they drove, Caitlin couldn't stop herself exclaiming in awe and admiration. With the ocean on one side and mountains on the other, the scenery left her breathless. Andrew had let down the hood and Caitlin revelled in the cool breeze as they drove.

'To think that back home it's pouring with rain,' she said. 'When I spoke to Mum this morning she said it hadn't stopped for the last few days.'

'Sometimes it gets so hot,' Andrew replied, 'that we'd do anything to have your weather for a day or two.' Then he looked at her and grinned. 'But only for a day or two.'

The clinic was in one of the health centres on the outskirts of town. By the time they arrived it was almost nine, and Andrew just had enough time to show Caitlin around before he disappeared to see his first patient.

The clinic nurse explained to Caitlin that they only scheduled the higher risk pregnancies and the first-time mothers for the specialist clinics. All other patients saw the midwives and were admitted to the hospital in Brisbane only when they were near their delivery dates.

Her first couple of patients were straightforward. Excited new mums booking in with their first pregnancies. But neither of them were quite as excited as Caitlin's third patient. Amy Jordan was a pretty blonde with anxious blue eyes and a tentative smile. Her husband, Richard, looked slightly dazed.

Caitlin looked at her chart. Amy had had three rounds of IVF. The first two had been unsuccessful, but today after a third round, they were attending the clinic for a pregnancy test. The nurse had slipped the result to Caitlin along with the notes.

'Congratulations.' Caitlin smiled at her. 'Your test is positive.'

The couple in front of her just stared, looking as if they hardly dared believe what Caitlin was saying.

'Excuse me,' Amy said. 'But did you say the test was positive?'

'Yes, but remember it's very early days.'

But nothing was going to wipe the smile off Amy's face. She turned to her husband. 'Did you hear what the doctor said? We're pregnant!' Her voice was low, hushed with barely contained excitement, as if she couldn't quite believe the news.

Then her husband jumped to his feet and, pulling his wife into his arms, swung her in a circle. The happy couple laughed, then as soon as Richard deposited Amy back on the floor she burst into tears. She sobbed for several minutes while her bewildered husband looked on helplessly.

'I don't know why I'm crying,' Amy sobbed. 'I'm so happy. I'm going to have a baby. After all this time!'

Caitlin smiled and passed Amy a box of tissues, giving her time to let the news sink in. As she watched the couple crying and laughing while they hugged, Caitlin wondered for the first time what it would feel like to want a child so much. She had never felt the need for children before, but what if, like the couple in front of her, that decision was taken out of her hands and she couldn't have children? How would that feel? She shook her head. What had prompted the thought? In all the years that she had been working as an obstetrician, she had never really considered a future where she might want kids. Why was the thought entering her mind now? She shook her head to clear it as Richard spoke.

'We've been trying for a baby for so long,' he told Caitlin. 'When it didn't happen at first we weren't too bothered. We just concentrated on having fun and setting up home together. But then after three years and it still hadn't happened we began to get worried, so we went to see our gynaecologist. He suggested IVF. This was to be our last go. If it failed we'd agreed to give up and get on with our lives.' His voice dropped. 'I'm going to be a dad. I can't believe it!' Caitlin could see he was struggling to stop his voice from breaking.

'As I said, it's very early days. We'll only truly know if the pregnancy is continuing at the first scan.' She made a note on the chart. 'I want you to come and see me in Brisbane in a few weeks for your scan. Will you do that?'

Eventually Amy and Richard left the consulting room. Even through the closed door, Caitlin could hear the cries of delight from the nursing staff mingling with those of the ecstatic couple. The next few weeks would be anxious ones she knew. Getting pregnant was only one stage in the difficult IVF journey. She desperately hoped that this couple at least would have the outcome they so badly wanted.

The rest of the day passed quickly. Most of the other patients were straightforward, except for the last woman, a patient who was thirty-six weeks pregnant and who the nurses wanted Caitlin to scan. They told Caitlin that they were a bit concerned that the baby wasn't the right size for its dates. Sure enough, when Caitlin scanned the baby she thought that the baby's heart looked abnormal. Unsure and concerned, she asked Andrew for a second opinion, thinking that it was lucky that he was the visiting paediatrician as she had remembered his special interest was in cardiac problems.

After examining the scan for a few minutes, he took Caitlin to one side. 'I think you're right,' he said. 'It looks as if there is a heart defect. But we need a better quality of scan before we can be sure. Although this machine is adequate for most stuff, we really need to scan her again with the one back at the hospital before I can check all the heart chambers properly.'

Not for the first time, Caitlin wondered about her chosen specialty. One minute you'd be giving patients the best news they had in years, the next you could be giving parents the worst possible news.

'I'll arrange for her to be seen at the Queensland Royal on Monday,' Caitlin said. 'We can scan her again then. But it doesn't look good, does it?'

Andrew shook his head. 'But there is no point in worrying them before we know exactly what we are dealing with here. And, if there is damage to the heart, at least we can make sure that we have the paediatric cardiac team available at delivery. Good call. If it hadn't been picked up and she had gone into labour up here, it could have been a different story.'

'I'll speak to them,' she said.

'We'll speak to them together,' Andrew said.

They returned to the patient, who was waiting anxiously, holding tightly to her husband's hand.

'Dr Bedi and I think it's possible that your baby has something wrong with its heart.' The patient, a young woman in her early twenties, went pale.

'Try not to worry too much at this stage,' Andrew said quickly. 'The abnormality could be something fairly minor. Like a hole in the heart, for instance.'

Seeing that this alarmed the patients even further, Caitlin added hastily, 'I know that sounds as if it's serious, but often it doesn't need treatment and the children go on to live normal productive lives.'

'And even if it turns out to be something that requires surgery, the fact that we know about it in advance means that we will have the full paediatric cardiac team standing by,' Andrew added. 'On the whole, it is very lucky that Dr O'Neill picked it up at this stage. It means that we can monitor your baby for the rest of the pregnancy and ensure that it gets the attention it needs at the right time.' Andrew hunkered down and held the woman's hand. 'I know it sounds scary right now, but you'll have to trust us. The first step is to arrange for you to be seen at the Queensland Royal and have a detailed scan on Monday. Dr O'Neill will arrange that for you, and we'll both see you then. Okay?'

The worried couple looked a little reassured but Caitlin knew that they would have an anxious wait over the weekend. She was very glad that Andrew had been there to check the scan with her. His experience and knowledge meant that he was able to reassure the patients much better than she would have been able to, had she been on her own. But it wasn't just his medical experience that she valued. Seeing the way he spoke to the patients, his obvious sympathy and understanding of their anxiety, at odds with the macho image he presented so much of the time, was revealing another side to a man that she was finding herself increasingly drawn to. More and more she was beginning to realise that she wasn't just attracted to Andrew because of his dark good looks and sex appeal, she was increasingly finding herself warming to Andrew the man. And, as her heart tripped, she knew that spelled danger.

* * *

Later, once Caitlin and Andrew had finished writing up notes and making arrangements for the patients who needed to be seen back at the Queensland Royal, Andrew turned to Caitlin.

'Hungry?' he asked.

'A bit,' Caitlin replied, realising that these days, whenever she was around Andrew, food was the last thing on her mind. 'I don't know about you, but I didn't have time for anything at lunchtime except a quick coffee and an apple.'

'I managed a sandwich,' Andrew replied, 'but that's not enough for a busy man. I need something more substantial.'

'What do you have in mind?' Caitlin asked.

'There's a great seafood restaurant a few minutes' walk from my house. If you would agree to stay the night, we could stop at my place and grab a shower first. What do you think?'

'Dinner sounds good, but I don't think I could be seen anywhere without a shower,' Caitlin said. 'Or a change of clothes. So, okay, I'll stay. Why not? I might not get another opportunity to explore the Sunshine Coast.' *Or another chance to see where Andrew lives, to learn more about the man who you can't seem to get out of your mind.* The voice in her head was back. Caitlin chose to ignore it.

Andrew's house was a wooden affair built on stilts. As Caitlin followed him up the steps to the main door she stopped and looked behind her. His house overlooked a stretch of beach that seemed to go on for miles. Apart from a solitary figure walking a dog, the white sands were deserted. Andrew's house was only one of about five as far as Caitlin could see.

'How on earth did you manage to find this place?' Caitlin said.

'My parents gave it to me,' Andrew said, turning to stand by Caitlin as she admired the view. 'It was their first home when they came to Australia over thirty years ago. Land out here was cheap back then, nobody wanted to live so far away from the city. And then before it became popular the government declared it a national park. No one else can build here.'

'I see why you come here as often as you can,' Caitlin said. 'I can't imagine a more beautiful place to live.'

Although he tried to hide it, Caitlin could tell that Andrew was pleased by her genuine admiration.

'I love it here,' he said. 'It's where I learnt to kite board and waterski and windsurf.' He pointed to a small cove to the right of the house. 'I keep my speedboat over there.' He turned to Caitlin. 'I don't suppose you fancy having a go?'

'What, right now?' He couldn't be serious surely? It wouldn't be long before it would be dark.

He grinned. 'You should try kite boarding in the moonlight,' he said. 'There's nothing to beat it. Just you, the sea and the moon.' He looked directly into her eyes. 'Don't you ever want to stop holding back and just let yourself go? Just have fun? Try new things? Don't you get just a little bit tired of being so, well, serious all the time?'

Caitlin took a sharp intake of breath. There was no mistaking the challenge in his deep brown eyes. Well, she would show him.

'Of course I know how to have fun,' she said defensively. 'I have fun all the time.' But as she frantically searched her mind for the last time she'd had fun, she realised that apart from the trip to the Green Mountains with Andrew she couldn't remember. She had been working so hard for so long, she had forgotten how to take time for frivolous activities. 'Right, then,' she said decisively. 'You're on.'

Andrew looked at his watch. 'I'll book dinner for eight—that will give us an hour or so on the water and time to change.'

'What?' Caitlin yelped. 'You mean go out now? I was thinking some time in the future.'

'No time like the present,' Andrew replied. 'Of course, if you're scared…?'

Caitlin had had about enough. Leeches and jellyfish aside, there was very little she was scared of. Well, very little she was going to admit to in front of this Neanderthal.

'I haven't brought a costume,' she managed, thinking that she had a genuine reason to turn down the challenge. But it seemed as if there was no way out.

'No worries. I have a wetsuit one of my…' He hesitated. 'My friends left behind.' His eyes raked her body. 'You look a similar size—a bit taller and more curvy perhaps, but I'm sure it will fit.'

Curvy? Who was he calling curvy? Okay, perhaps without the benefit of her daily swim she had put on a few pounds, but still—curvy? Caitlin was in no doubt what sort of friend had left a wetsuit behind. However, she reminded herself it was none of her business. She searched frantically for another excuse but, failing to find one, realised that there was nothing for it but to go through with whatever Andrew had in mind.

'Okay,' she said brightly, determined not to let her apprehension show. 'What do you have in mind?'

'You could try windsurfing. I have the board somewhere I used to use as a kid. It's perfect for a beginner. Or you could have a go waterskiing if you prefer. Actually, no, we really need a third person to act as a spotter, so we'll leave that for another day. Windsurfing it is, then. C'mon, let's get you suited up.'

Before she knew it, Caitlin was squeezing herself into a rubber suit. When at first it seemed as if there was no way it would go over her hips she was both mortified and then relieved. But then, with a final tug, the suit slipped past her hips and with a final sigh of resignation she slid her arms into the sleeves. Looking around for a mirror, she glanced around Andrew's bedroom. Simple pieces of wooden furniture lined two of the walls, but even with her limited knowledge of antiques Caitlin knew they were of exquisite quality. The beautiful oak floorboards were partially covered by a Persian carpet of rich jewel colours. Caitlin was slightly taken aback—she had somehow expected it to be masculine and Spartan. Instead it was warm and…she searched for a suitable description…comforting. Her eyes were drawn to the large double bed that dominated the room. No doubt he needed one of those, she thought waspishly. But no mirror. Perhaps it was just as well. Caitlin wasn't sure she wanted to see how she looked. Tentatively she peered into the small sitting room, looking for Andrew. Much like the bedroom, it was thoughtfully furnished, with two large, comfortable sofas arranged in an L facing the expanse of windows overlooking the sea. Plants and knick-knacks adorned the room. This wasn't a bachelor pad, Caitlin thought, it was a home. It seemed just as she was beginning to think she had him pegged, she found out something about him that made her revise her opinion. But not entirely. She wasn't surprised to see there was no television. As she suspected, Andrew didn't seem to be the sort of man who sat still long enough to watch a whole programme. He was just replacing the telephone receiver when he caught sight of her and grinned.

'Table booked,' he said. Then he crossed the room. 'Turn around while I do you up,' he said.

Caitlin felt goose-bumps all over her body as his fingers brushed the back of her neck.

'That's you,' he said, and whirled her around to face him. 'I don't think these are a good idea,' he added, removing her glasses. For a moment he looked into her eyes and her heart started thumping wildly. 'You have beautiful eyes,' he said. 'Why do you hide them behind these?'

Caitlin grabbed her glasses back, desperate for him not to see her reaction.

'I need those. I can't see very well without them.'

'What's there to see?' Andrew laughed and took them again, hiding them behind his back. 'All you need to see is your board and the shore.'

Caitlin gave in, knowing it was ridiculous to be getting into a tug of war over her glasses. But why was this man determined to treat her as if she were a gauche teenager? She was a grown woman, for God's sake, a respected professional.

'Okay, then,' she said, only too aware that she sounded like a sulky teenager. 'But you might have to lead the way.'

Down on the beach the sun was sinking, turning the clouds candy-floss pink. A small breeze had picked up, forming small caps of white on the previously still water. Again Caitlin wondered what she had let herself in for.

'Stay near the shore,' Andrew ordered while he rigged the child-sized windsurfer. 'If by any chance, and I think it's unlikely, you manage to get on your feet and stay upright, don't panic. If you feel you're been carried out to sea, just let the sail go, sit on the board and I'll come and get you in the rescue boat.'

His words made Caitlin determined. Come hell or high water, she'd get upright and stay upright. She would show him in the same way she had shown her brothers every time they had told her she couldn't do something because she was a girl. Finally once the board was rigged and Andrew had given her instructions about how to hold the sail, he retrieved a lifejacket from the speedboat, slipped it over her arms and fastened the straps around her waist. Once more she was uncomfortably aware of him as he bent his head. Her knees began to tremble. Whether it was from fear or his proximity she didn't want to know.

Andrew rolled up his jeans and pushed the board into the water, signalling Caitlin to follow. She splashed after him, pleasantly surprised that even when the water leaked into her suit it was agreeably warm. Her first attempt to pull up the sail ended with her back in the water. Seeing that Andrew was enjoying himself at her expense, she gritted her teeth and jumped back on the board. After another three failed attempts suddenly the board was up and she was off, heading out to sea. She placed her feet on either side of the sail, and put her arms in the bow and arrow position, just as he had shown her. Hey, this isn't so difficult, she thought, not too much different from balancing on a horse, but then, having lost her concentration for a moment, she was back in the water. Looking back to the shore, she was dismayed to find she had only managed a couple of metres. Andrew was watching from the beach, but without her glasses she couldn't read his expression.

Determined to show him, she hauled herself back on the board, pulled the sail out of the water, noting that it was taking all her strength, and set off once more. This time she stayed up and she felt a thrill of exhilaration as she felt the sea race underneath. After a minute or two she began to enjoy herself and played around, moving the sail backwards and forwards, beginning to understand what made the board speed up and what movement slowed it down. But after another few minutes she looked back over her shoulder and was shocked to find that she could no longer see Andrew. If she carried on at this rate, she would be in Timbuctoo before she knew it.

Now, what had he said about turning around and going back? But she couldn't remember. The board continued towards the horizon with Caitlin feeling more horrified with every passing minute. Then she remembered what he had said about letting the sail drop. So she did. And then she was back in the water. She rose to the surface gasping and spluttering, and grabbed hold of the board. Had Andrew said anything about sharks being this far out? She wasn't going to wait to find out. She turned the board around and faced it in the other direction. She discovered it was a lot easier going out than in as she slowly tacked back to shore. She couldn't help but feel a surge of satisfaction as she returned safely towards the beach. Andrew waded in and helped her pull the board up onto the sand.

'Hey, I'm impressed,' he said. 'I was just about to come and get you when you turned around. Next time I'll show you how to do it without having to fall in the water.'

Caitlin scooped some water in her hands and threw it at him. 'Just a girl, huh?'

Working together, they unfastened the sail from the board. The sun had sunk below the horizon, turning the sky cobalt blue. 'How are we doing for time?' Caitlin asked.

'We've another hour or so,' Andrew replied. 'I didn't expect you to get the hang of it so quickly. You grab a shower, if you like, while I put this away. If you could leave the suit by the door, I'll give it a rinse when I get back.'

Caitlin trudged back to the house, the heavy sand making her legs feel wobbly. For the first time in months, even years, she felt exhilarated by something apart from her work. She was glad that she had allowed Andrew to persuade her to have a go. Maybe it was about time she started taking some time off to learn new skills.

She hesitated outside the door. Andrew had suggested she leave the wetsuit here and she didn't want to trail sand into the house. But she was naked underneath. How would she negotiate the distance to the shower from the door? Looking around, she could see no sign of Andrew. She hopped from foot to foot, but then she noticed a towel had been placed over the rails on the veranda. Peeling off the suit, she dropped it by the door, grabbed the towel and wrapped it around herself. She was just in time to cover her nakedness before Andrew appeared.

'You found it, then?' he said. He leaned against the balcony and watched her from hooded eyes. Caught in his stare like a rabbit in headlights, Caitlin willed her legs to move but she couldn't. It was as if she was frozen. The humid air settled around her as she took a deep breath. Then, before she knew what was happening, she was in

Andrew's arms and he was kissing her. She could feel the warmth of his naked chest against her body, the tiny drops of water cooling her overheated skin. Still holding on to the towel with one hand, she melted into his body. His arms curled around her, dropping to her waist as he kissed her with an intensity she had never experienced before. A small voice in her head was telling her to stop, but she pushed it away. The feel of his lips on hers, the pressure of his hands on her lower back as he pressed her hips into his, was too good to resist.

Then suddenly she felt herself lifted as he kicked open the door of the house and carried her towards the bedroom. She snaked her arms around his neck as his kisses grew ever deeper. Everything disappeared around her as she gave in to the delightful sensations that were coursing through her body. All she could think was that she wanted him. Wanted him more than she'd thought it was possible for a woman to want a man.

He laid her on the bed and raised his head. She could read the same urgent need in his eyes, in the curve of his lips, that she felt. He looked at her in a silent question. Her answer was to pull him closer.

Later as she lay in his arms she felt nothing of the embarrassment or awkwardness that—had she given it any thought at all—she would have imagined. Instead, as she ran a finger along the contours of his chest, she felt amazed. Never before had making love felt so right. Although she barely knew this man, she realised she knew everything she needed to.

'Are you hungry?' Andrew asked, tracing the line of her lips with a finger.

'I don't know why, but my appetite seems to have deserted me,' she whispered back.

Andrew jumped out of bed. 'Stay right there,' he ordered. 'Don't you move a muscle.' He returned a little while later with a tray laden with fruit, biscuits and cheese and a bottle of wine. 'I've cancelled the table,' he said. 'But I thought I should feed you up a little. You're going to need your energy later.' He grinned wolfishly as he cut off a piece of Brie and, adding a grape, popped it into Caitlin's mouth. They lay in bed, feeding each other and laughing. Caitlin didn't want to talk about the future, if indeed there was a future. All she wanted right now was to be here in this space that had become her whole world. She didn't want to talk about how she felt. Any admission of love on her part would demand some sort of response from him, and that wasn't the way she wanted it to be.

But deep down in a place she wasn't ready to explore, Caitlin knew that for the first time in her life she had fallen deeply and irrevocably in love and she didn't like it. Not one bit.

CHAPTER SEVEN

WHEN Caitlin woke, the sun was streaming through the window. For a moment she couldn't remember where she was, then it all came flooding back. The night before, Andrew's arms around her, making love. Stretching luxuriously, she turned, only to find the space beside her was empty. From the kitchen the sound of pots and pans clattering assaulted her ears and the smell of freshly brewed coffee filtered tantalisingly up her nostrils.

How had that happened? she wondered. When had she gone from admiring Andrew as a colleague and friend to knowing that she was in love with him? And what was she going to do about it? It was a complication she didn't need in her life right now. His life was here, in Australia, while her future lay in Ireland. She was so close to the position she had worked so hard for all her life, there was no way she was going to give it up now. But, she told herself, it was early days. She still had another few months in Australia, plenty of time to take everything slowly, cautiously—the way she liked her life to happen.

Andrew strode into the room, wearing his jeans and nothing else. Immediately Caitlin felt another surge of desire that left her breathless. This taking things slowly wasn't going to be easy, she thought, not when all she wanted right now was a repeat of last night. In fact, she admitted ruefully, all she wanted was to stay here, in this room with Andrew, and shut the rest of the world out.

'G'day,' Andrew said, smiling down at her. 'I brought you some breakfast.' Caitlin eyed the soggy toast warily and shook her head. 'Coffee is fine for now,' she said.

At Andrew's look of disappointment she almost laughed out loud. 'All right,' she relented. 'Just a bite or two.' She bit into the toast, which tasted as bad as she expected. Clearly, whatever talents Andrew had, cooking wasn't one of them.

'You've got a crumb,' Andrew said, touching the corner of her mouth. 'Just there.' His fingers traced the corner of her mouth then dropped to her jaw. Caitlin felt heat low in her belly as his finger continued over her neck and down to her breasts. He lifted the tray away and dropped his lips to follow the path of his fingers. Caitlin took a sharp intake of breath as he dropped kisses as tender as raindrops ever downwards. She arched her back and raked her nails across his back, pulling him closer. As he lay alongside her she felt his responding desire. She tugged at the button of his jeans, dipping her hands below the waistband. Andrew raised himself on one elbow and looked deep into her eyes. 'Say it,' he demanded, his eyes black with desire.

'I want you,' she whispered. 'Now. Please.'

Much later they lay naked and hot in each other's arms, the sheet entangled in their limbs. Outside Caitlin could hear the crash of the waves on the shore and a gentle breeze cooled her skin. She laid her head on his chest, listening to the steady beat of his heart. Andrew stroked her hair.

'Lunch?' he questioned softly. Whatever was happening between them lay unspoken, almost as if neither of them wanted to break the spell. Did Andrew feel the same way she did? Caitlin wondered. If so, what next? But the never-far-away sensible voice was hovering on the edges of her mind. *Don't think about it, just do what everyone has been telling you to do. Live for the moment and let the future take care of itself.*

She lifted her head and looked into serious brown eyes. It was a different side to Andrew she was seeing. He too looked as if he had been taken by surprise.

'Can we stay here?' Caitlin asked. She wasn't sure she was ready to return to the everyday world. Not now, maybe tomorrow or the next day. At some point she'd have to think about the future but for now it could wait.

'We have all weekend,' Andrew said. 'We don't need to go back until tomorrow evening. I'm happy to stay in bed until then, although I have to warn you, I need to eat some time. In the meantime phone Brianna and let her know that you won't be back until tomorrow.'

Caitlin phoned a distinctly curious Brianna and mumbled some excuse about Andrew wanting to show her something or another. It was clear that Brianna wasn't fooled for a moment.

'What's going on? You and Andrew haven't… God, you have, haven't you? Cat, please be careful. You're not used to men like him.'

'Hey, Bri, I'm old enough to look after myself. Anyway, you told me to get a life and have some fun, and that's what I'm doing.' But even as she was saying the words, Caitlin knew it was far more than that. 'He's teaching me to windsurf and then…' inspiration hit her '…I'm taking him horse riding after lunch.'

'Horse riding? But I don't think Andrew rides. In fact, I'm pretty sure he won't go near them. I suggested it once and he was horrified. Refused point blank.'

'If I can have a go at windsurfing then he'll have to do what I want,' Caitlin said. She had promised to pay him back and this would be a perfect way to do it. 'I'm going to find somewhere.' Her sister coughed. Instantly Caitlin was on the alert. 'Are you feeling okay, Bri?'

'What did I tell you about not fussing?' her sister said. 'I'm fine, Niall's fine and the kids are great. We're going down to the beach later, and to the botanic gardens tomorrow. Niall has to go away again on business on Monday morning, so we want to make the most of the weekend with the kids. Hold on a minute, Niall's saying something.' Caitlin hung on, listening to the mumble of voices. Out of the corner of her eye she saw Andrew gesticulating that he was going for a shower. Then Brianna came back on the phone. 'Niall says could you tell Andrew that he'll be seeing his parents while he's in Sydney. Does he have a message?'

'Hang on a minute until I ask him,' Caitlin said. She passed the message on to Andrew.

'Ask Niall to tell them I'm looking forward to seeing them in a couple of weeks' time,' Andrew replied. 'And say hi to everyone.'

Caitlin did as he requested. By the time she replaced the receiver she could hear the sound of water running. Andrew was going to Sydney soon, then. Caitlin felt her heart dip. How long for? she wondered. She knew however long he would be away she would miss him. It seemed that taking this—whatever it was—casually wasn't going to be quite as easy as she had hoped. She didn't know the rules of a love affair any more. She had met David soon after finishing medical school and their romance had been a slow, considered one. It was only after being together for four years that they had agreed to live together and had spent the next few years in what Caitlin now recognised as palid domesticity. They had talked about marriage, but neither had ever quite taken up the gauntlet. She had loved David, but now she realised it had been the love of one friend for another. She had never felt an iota of the pulse-racing roller-coaster feelings she was experiencing even just thinking about Andrew. She didn't know the rules, she realised. She was already in much deeper than she had ever imagined possible.

Andrew took her down to the restaurant where they had planned to eat the night before. While he was in the shower, Caitlin had arranged a horse-riding trip to a waterhole, assuring the owner of the stables that she had been brought up with horses and they wouldn't need a guide.

She studied Andrew surreptitiously while he perused the menu. Dressed in clean jeans and a T-shirt that showed off his muscular arms, he looked calm and relaxed. She, on the other hand, felt anything but. She desperately wanted him to say something, anything, that might tell her how he felt. She was damned if she was going to be the first to say anything. If the weekend was a one-off, she would have to deal with it when the time came.

'You have to try the Moreton Bay bugs,' Andrew said. 'I never have anything else when I come here.'

'It sounds revolting,' Caitlin said, screwing up her nose. 'Who on earth would want to eat bugs?'

'I thought you were going to try being more adventurous?' he teased. 'Anyway, they're not bugs. They're more like lobster. Trust me?' As she looked into his warm brown eyes, Caitlin wondered if there was a hidden meaning to his words. Did she trust him? As a doctor, yes. As a friend, yes. With her heart? Not really, she admitted sadly.

'Okay,' she said. 'But I have a surprise, well, more like a challenge for you.' She waited until Andrew had given the order to the waiter, before continuing. 'I've arranged for us to go horseback riding this afternoon.' Seeing that Andrew was about to protest, she held up a restraining hand. 'So far, I have done everything you have asked. I think it's only fair that you do something you're not quite comfortable with.'

He smiled wryly. 'Okay. Can't have you going back to Ireland and saying Aussie men chicken out. I hate the brutes, but if that's what you want, I'll give it a go.'

The lunch when it arrived was every bit as delicious as Andrew had promised. So far, she had gone against her instincts to stay safe, and had been rewarded. She only hoped that taking a risk with Andrew wasn't going to be the one that undid her. As they ate they chatted about work.

'Brianna tells me you're some big shot in Ireland,' Andrew said.

'I suppose that's one way of putting it.' Caitlin laughed. 'I have done a lot of research into infertility, which seems to have caught the imagination internationally. It's also gone a long way to raising funds for the university we're affiliated to, and there's talk about offering me a chair on my return.' Although she tried, Caitlin couldn't help the note of pride creeping into her voice. But why not? She had worked hard for her success.

'Good for you,' Andrew said. Although his tone seemed genuinely warm, something shifted in his eyes. 'Seems to me you have your life all mapped out. Career-wise anyway. What about the rest of it. Marriage at least, if not kids?'

Caitlin felt cold fingers of dread wrap around her heart. 'I haven't really thought about it. I was with someone for a few years, someone who works in the same department as me. Neither marriage nor children was really on the agenda back then. We were—are—both too focussed on our careers.' Andrew eyebrows puckered.

'As far as marriage is concerned, if the right man came along, that would be great, as long as he understood how important my career was. And as for kids…' She chewed on her lip. 'Like I said to you before, I don't know if they figure in my plans. Besides, if I get the chair, I'll need to commit myself to the job for a few years before I could even consider maternity leave.'

'What, you'd go back to work after having children? Do you think that's right?'

'Look, it's unlikely I'll have children but *if* I ever do,' Caitlin stressed, 'then, sure, I'd go back to work. I haven't worked this hard and this long to throw it all away.' Andrew narrowed his eyes at her.

'You think that's fair? To have someone else raise your children? Why have them?'

Caitlin was aghast at the turn the conversation was taking. How had they got into this? 'Andrew, loads of women have children and work. It's more the norm than not.'

'I don't accept that,' he said. 'As soon as my parents

married my mother stayed at home to look after the house and the family. She never regretted it. It's the right thing to do.'

Caitlin wasn't sure she was hearing correctly. This was a different, totally unexpected side to Andrew. One she couldn't quite reconcile with the man she thought she was beginning to know. Andrew had never struck her as anything except a modern Australian man.

'My mother was a stay-at-home wife and mother until we left home,' Caitlin said slowly. 'And with five children to bring up, I don't blame her. But I was always aware of how hard she worked. She trained to be a nurse, you know, but she never used her training. I know she always regretted not following her dream, although I also know she loves us and Dad more than anything. It was her who brought me up to believe I should have a career, make something of my life.'

'And you don't think bringing up children is making something of your life?' Andrew argued. 'The most important job of all.'

'I can see we're not going to agree,' Caitlin said quietly. 'Maybe we should change the subject?' But the day had lost its sparkle. Caitlin was only too aware of how different she and Andrew were. Miles apart, in fact. She could never be the type of woman he wanted, and it seemed that he wasn't the sort of man she could ever imagine herself sharing her life with.

After lunch, Andrew called for the bill and insisted on paying. 'Let me pay half,' Caitlin suggested, but one look at the set of his jaw made her back down. It had simply not occurred to her, as masculine as Andrew was, that he was so conventional when it came to gender roles.

'Do you want to forget about the horse riding?' she asked. 'Go back to Brisbane instead?' How could she have been so stupid? This was exactly what happened when you threw caution to the wind. Now she had gone and fallen for a man from whom it seemed she was miles apart.

'Hell, no,' Andrew said, the stormclouds clearing from his face. 'And having you tell everyone I chickened out? Not on your life.'

Caitlin couldn't help a small shiver of satisfaction when she saw Andrew blanch at the size of his horse. Staying resolutely in role, he said nothing, but whistled nonchalantly. But Caitlin wasn't deceived. For the first time since she had met him she was seeing an Andrew Bedi well out of his comfort zone. That would teach him to be so macho all the time.

'You can still change your mind,' she said as he climbed into the saddle. His horse, sensing his discomfort, reared and Caitlin had to lean forward to catch the reins before he bolted with Andrew.

'Let's just get on with it,' Andrew replied through gritted teeth. Caitlin gave him a quick lesson on how to hold the reins and what to do with the stirrups, relishing the opportunity to turn the tables on him. Thankfully for Andrew, the stables had supplied them with American-style saddles that, given their depth, would offer Andrew a little more security. He shifted around in the saddle before leaning towards Caitlin and asking in a whisper, 'What am I supposed to do about…you know?' Caitlin followed his glance downwards and grinned.

'Not a lot you can do, I'm afraid. Just one of those things men have to put up with.' They headed off at a walk, the owner having explained where to go to find the waterhole. As soon as they were out of sight, Caitlin suggested they try a canter. 'You'll probably find it easier than a trot,' she explained. 'Especially on the you-know-whats.'

'Let's get this over with,' Andrew replied through gritted teeth.

Caitlin kicked her horse into a canter, turning around in the saddle to see how Andrew was doing. Unfortunately he was bouncing around like a sack of potatoes, holding on to the reins as if his life depended on it. Trying not to laugh, Caitlin yelled, 'Relax, Andrew. Just go with the movement,' before kicking her horse on.

When she next risked a backward glance she was surprised to see that Andrew was beginning to get the hang of it. He was moving more comfortably with the horse and had loosened his grip on the reins.

Half an hour later they found the watering hole and Caitlin dismounted and waited for Andrew to catch up. The sun was still high in the sky and that, combined with the exercise, had left Caitlin with a sheen of sweat covering her body.

As Andrew came to an undignified stop, she gathered the reins of his horse and tied them to a tree close to hers.

'I don't think I'm going to be able to walk for days,' he groaned. 'Or do anything else for that matter.' He slid her a devilish grin.

'Is there anything likely to be lurking in there?' Caitlin pointed to the pool of aquamarine water.

'No, I think it's pretty safe,' Andrew said, slipping off his T-shirt. 'But even crocs won't keep me out.' His jeans and boxers followed the T-shirt and then he was in the water. 'Come on in,' he called. 'It's great.' And then he disappeared from view as he submerged his head in the murky water.

Caitlin stood confused. Since their discussion over lunch, she had resolutely refused to think about the significance of Andrew's words. But could she really act as if they had meant nothing? Perhaps now was the time to speak to him, before she got in any deeper. But before she had the time to formulate her words, Andrew strode out of the water and picked her up in his arms. Ignoring her squeals of protest, he removed her glasses and baseball cap, placing them a safe distance from the horses, and carried her, fully dressed, into the cool water. Caitlin gasped as the water seeped over her skin, soaking her shorts and T-shirt. But he was right. It was a delicious relief.

As she gasped from the shock of the water on her overheated skin, he brought his mouth down on hers. Despite her reservations of only moments before, she responded hungrily, drawing him closer and kissing him back with all the pent-up passion of the last few years. *Just let me have this time. I'll be sensible later*, was her last coherent thought as Andrew carried her out of the pool and placed her on a bed of leaves. Then they were both pulling at her clothes, urgent in their need. As Andrew's face swam before her, Caitlin once more was powerless to prevent herself giving in to him.

Later, they unpacked the provisions the owner of the stables had provided and Andrew showed her how to brew tea in a billy can while they munched on fruit and fresh bread. Caitlin watched as he worked, relishing the look of his bronze skin and the way his muscles rippled as he moved. As she picked leaves out of her hair that lay in a mass of tangles around her shoulders, she wondered where the cool, calm, collected Dr O'Neill of only a couple of weeks ago had disappeared to. She knew that that woman was gone for ever, but who had replaced her? Certainly not the woman Andrew had described earlier.

As they sipped their tea, Caitlin made up her mind. Regardless of the change in her, she was still a woman who needed to know what lay ahead. She couldn't pretend to herself, no matter how much she wanted to, that she was able to continue with a relationship, no matter how heady, under false pretences. But still she hesitated, knowing somewhere deep in her soul that once she spoke, things would never be the same between them again.

'Tell me about your family,' she said, trying to ease her way into the conversation.

'Not much to tell,' he said. 'Parents are first-generation Australians, came over here just after they got married and have worked incredibly hard to build a successful business.'

'I thought your mother didn't work.'

'She worked to support my father by looking after the home and the children.'

'Children?' Caitlin queried, feeling slightly guilty as she already knew the answer from what Brianna had told her. But she wanted to hear Andrew's story from his own lips. Perhaps it would offer another glimpse of the real Dr Bedi. 'I thought you were an only child?'

Andrew rose to his feet and, keeping his back to her, spoke softly. 'I had a sister, an older sister.'

'Had?' Caitlin prompted.

'She died following a post-partum haemorrhage. The baby died too,' Andrew said curtly.

'I am so sorry.' Caitlin came to stand behind him, wrapping her arms around his waist and leaning her head against his back.

'It was ten years ago,' Andrew said. 'I still miss her.'

'Did she leave any other children?'

'No. It's only me left.' He laughed shortly. 'I'm my parents' whole world now. They depend on me for their future—to carry on the family line.'

'What do you mean?' Caitlin asked, prompted at the strange emphasis he gave the words.

'They hope I'll meet someone—someone from the same background—who will have the same values as we do.'

'Are you telling me that you are considering an arranged marriage? That your parents want you to marry an Indian girl?' Caitlin asked, feeling a cool breeze run through her soul.

'It would make them very happy,' he said. 'But it wouldn't be an arranged marriage as such. I couldn't ever marry someone I didn't like and admire. Not even to keep my parents happy. But you should know, Caitlin, that this isn't something my parents are forcing on me. While I do have a duty to them, I happen to truly believe that Western marriages are more likely to fail than Indian ones, precisely because they aren't built on mutual respect and common values.'

Caitlin was reeling from Andrew's revelations. But hadn't she, until recently, thought the same thing? That the best marriages were based on respect and affection rather than passion, which would inevitably pass with time? And why was she now so certain that she had been wrong? She knew now, with absolute certainty, that she could never marry anyone she wasn't totally, desperately, head over heels in love with. The way she loved Andrew.

'What does that mean for us?' she said softly, willing her voice to remain steady.

Andrew turned and looked at Caitlin, holding her away so he could look directly into her eyes.

'Us?' he echoed. 'I'm sorry, Caitlin, I hadn't really thought about an us. You are a beautiful, exceptional woman, a woman who I want to spend time with, but…'

'But…' Caitlin repeated, feeling chilled to the bone.

'We have different ambitions, goals in life. You want your career—you've made that very clear, and you should be proud of yourself that you are so successful. But as for me, I want my career and eventually, not for years yet, to find someone my parents approve of, who will want the same things in life that I do. We both want different things from our futures. In the meantime, can't we just enjoy what we have? Make the most of our time together?'

She turned away from him, lest he see the disappointment in her eyes. 'I'm sorry, Andrew. I know it's late in the day, and I suppose you could say I came into this with my eyes wide open, but I'm not the sort of woman who can take a relationship casually. Just for sex. That, I suppose, is the main difference between you and me.'

He grabbed her arm and turned her back to face him. 'What are you saying, Caitlin?'

'I'm saying, Andrew, that as much as I've enjoyed this time with you, it's over.' The words sounded formal and stiff, but Caitlin was finding it difficult to speak through the tightness in her throat. If this weekend had meant anything to him, and from the way he had held her, made love to her, she couldn't believe it hadn't, then he'd be willing to try and meet her halfway. But, then, she reminded herself, she really didn't know how men thought.

He gave her one last searching look and then dropped his arms in defeat. 'You're right,' he said. 'I have been a selfish idiot.'

Unspeakably disappointed at how easily he was giving her up, Caitlin tried a smile. If he felt so little for her, she was damned if she was going to let him see how much he had hurt her.

'I think we should go now,' she said quietly. 'I'd like to get back to Brisbane tonight, preferably before it's dark.'

'Caitlin.' He reached out towards her and touched her hair. For a second Caitlin thought he was going to say something that would make this whole horrible mess all right. But instead he stepped away from her. 'We'd better get going,' he said.

The journey back to Brisbane was a quiet affair, both of them preoccupied with their thoughts. They had stopped at Andrew's beach house to collect their belongings and freshen up, but the light had gone out of the day. Caitlin was relieved when they pulled up outside her sister's house. In the fading light, Caitlin could see that no one was home and she was glad that she wouldn't have to face her sister's questions about her early return until later. Her stomach was churning and she felt mildly nauseous.

'Thank you,' she said stiffly as Andrew handed her her bag. 'I'll see you on Monday.'

'Sure. And, Caitlin, I'm not sorry we had this time together.' He looked at her for a long moment.

'Don't worry, Andrew, I won't let it affect our professional relationship. I'm as much to…' She searched for the right word. 'Blame for what happened as you,' Caitlin said. Then, before she lost all self-control, she bolted inside. She only just made it to the bathroom before she was sick.

* * *

'Hey, we didn't expect you until tomorrow,' Brianna said predictably when she found Caitlin wrapped in her dressing gown on the front veranda. She looked at her sister quizzically. 'You don't look great. Are you all right?'

'I think I've picked up a tummy bug,' Caitlin said. And if it was only part of the truth, Caitlin wasn't lying. She had felt dreadfully ill and had been sick twice since her return home.

'Up to bed with you,' Brianna said firmly. 'I'll bring you some peppermint tea. You can tell me all about it tomorrow when you feel better.' Reluctantly, Caitlin let her sister propel her upstairs, dismally aware that it was she who should be looking after Brianna, not the other way round.

When she brought up the tea, she sat on the edge of the bed looking concerned. 'Should I ring someone? Andrew perhaps?'

Caitlin was horrified at the thought. 'It's probably only a twenty-four-hour thing. Plenty of fluids and bed rest is what any doctor would recommend. Honestly, Bri, I'm fine. But how are you?'

'We had a lovely day,' Brianna said. 'It's funny how being ill can make you appreciate all the little things. Every day is special.'

'You're not worried, Bri? You're feeling okay?' Caitlin sat up, almost knocking over her tea in the process. 'You've not felt any new lumps, have you? You're looking a little flushed to me. And I can hear you still have that cough.'

'Caitlin,' Bri said warningly, 'you're fussing again. I'm probably a bit flushed because I caught the sun. And as for the cough, it's hardly more than a tickle. It's just that I have my check-up this week and I guess I'm just feeling a bit ansty, wondering if they'll be recommending more treatment. I wish Niall wasn't going to be in Sydney so he could come with me for moral support.'

'I didn't know your check-up was this week. I'll come with you.'

'What about the hospital? I'm sure they won't be keen on you having time off so soon after you've started. Really, Cat, I'm just being silly, I'll be fine on my own. I know how much you hate missing work.'

Caitlin was shocked that her sister would think, even for a moment, that she'd put work ahead of her. But, then, Caitlin admitted ruefully, all Brianna had ever known of her sister was this work-obsessed dervish, who rarely had time for anything else. Was that how everyone saw her? Someone who couldn't imagine a life without work?

'I'm coming with you and that's that,' Caitlin said firmly.

Brianna leaned across and gave her a hug. Again Caitlin was dismayed at how fragile her sister felt. She was so strong willed, so determined and upbeat, it was easy to forget how much her illness had taken out of her. 'Thank you, love. It means a lot to me.' She lifted the empty teacup from the side of the bed. 'You get some sleep now, if you want to be fit for work on Monday.'

'Bri,' Caitlin whispered just before her sister left the room, 'I'm sorry, if I haven't been a very good sister to you. You know I love you.'

Brianna's smile lit up the room. 'Of course, you idiot, and I love you too. Now, go to sleep.' And she turned out the light, leaving Caitlin to her dismal thoughts.

Andrew let himself into his flat and threw the car keys down on the sideboard. Feeling restless, he contemplated going for a walk, then discarded the idea and switched on the television to watch the news. But it was no use. He couldn't concentrate on the flickering images in front of him. Instead the image of green eyes and red hair kept intruding on his thoughts. He hadn't meant to make love to Caitlin—it had just happened and when it had it had felt so natural. The memory of holding her in his arms, the feel of her satin skin against his, made him groan aloud. He had been attracted to Caitlin from the moment he had pulled her from the water. He smiled as he remembered the set of her mouth as she had tried to hold on to her dignity, the way that she had slowly melted in his arms and the flash of temper whenever she thought herself thwarted. He had loved watching her change from the almost uptight woman with every hair in place to the passionate, fiery, laughing woman whom he had held in his arms. But what had he been thinking? If he had been thinking at all.

He stood and went over to the window, looking out over the lights of the city. Caitlin O'Neill wasn't the sort of woman a man treated lightly. But neither was she the woman he could see himself spending the rest of his life with. He could never be satisfied with a woman who didn't put him and their children first. He admired her as a doctor, of course he did. What was there not to admire in her clinical skills and her obvious empathy for her patients? But…and this was the part he couldn't accept…Caitlin was the sort of woman who would want life on her terms. And it was beginning to dawn on Andrew that perhaps he had met his match in Dr Caitlin O'Neill. She wasn't the kind of woman a man could forget easily. In fact, he realised, as he thought of never holding her again, she was the sort of woman a man couldn't forget at all.

CHAPTER EIGHT

'COME in and have a seat,' the oncologist, a tired-looking woman in her late forties, welcomed Brianna and Caitlin.

'This is my sister, Dr Caitlin O'Neill, Antonia. Caitlin, Dr Antonia Sommerville.'

'I've heard of you,' Antonia said, looking over her bifocals. 'You're the whiz kid obstetrician from Ireland. I hadn't made the connection, I'm afraid.'

'Hardly a kid.' Caitlin laughed.

'But very young to have got where you are all the same,' Antonia said. Then she turned intelligent brown eyes on Brianna.

'My secretary is just rustling up your results. I gather the nurses took some blood from you earlier. We'll just wait until they arrive, but how have you been?' All at once the severe expression was replaced by a look of genuine concern. 'Kids letting you rest?'

'You know kids.' Brianna shrugged. 'But Cat's been a great help.'

Antonia turned her gaze on Caitlin. 'And have you been checked out?' she asked.

'Er, no, not yet,' Caitlin admitted. 'I haven't really had the time.'

'In that case…' Antonia picked up the phone '…I shall arrange for you to be seen at my clinic as soon as they can fit you in.'

Caitlin could only watch open-mouthed as a few minutes later Antonia passed her a slip with an appointment for the following week.

'I know doctors,' she said, smiling grimly, 'being one myself. Unless they are bullied they never quite find the time to look after their own health. Don't you miss it now,' she added, wagging a finger at Caitlin, who suddenly felt six years old. 'These appointments are like gold dust.'

'Okay, Brianna, while we're waiting, why don't you pop up on the table while I examine your breasts?' Just then Caitlin's pager bleeped. She had arranged for one of the other obstetricians to cover her for an hour or two, so was a little surprised.

'You can use the phone on my desk.' Antonia indicated with a nod, before drawing the screen around Brianna.

When the number Caitlin dialled was answered, she was surprised to find Andrew on the other end.

'Oh, hello, Caitlin,' he said, sounding distracted. 'A call has just come through from one of the outlying towns. There's a mother who is in late labour and looks like she'll be needing a section. I'm going to attend, but obviously we need an obstetrician. Would you like to come?'

Caitlin would have loved to go, but it only took her a second to make up her mind. She had promised Brianna she would be with her and unless there was no one else to take the call, here she'd stay.

'Could one of the others go?' she asked. 'Just this once?

I'd love to go, but I have something else I really need to do.' With a pang Caitlin realised this was the first time she had ever put something else before her work. She was beginning to realise how much she had missed.

'Sure. Dr Forest is happy to go. He's the obstetrician on call this week so he'd usually be the first choice anyway. There will be other opportunities. Possibly the week you're on call.' He dropped his voice. 'Is everything okay, Cat?'

It was the first time he had used her sister's pet name for her and she felt an irrational tingle of pleasure. 'It's just I'm in Oncology with Brianna for her check-up. I promised I would stay. So if you're sure Dr Forest is happy to go, then please go ahead.'

'Okay,' Andrew replied. 'I've got to go. The air ambulance is taking off in a few minutes. But, Cat, you will let me know that Brianna's okay, won't you?'

'Yes, of course,' Caitlin said, replacing the receiver.

By this time the secretary had put a set of results on the desk. Caitlin was tempted to lean over and check them out while Antonia was occupied with Brianna behind the screens. But she stopped herself. It would be a breach of medical etiquette as well as a betrayal of her sister's privacy.

Instead she waited patiently until Antonia and Brianna returned to their places at the desk. She watched closely as Antonia read the results and when her expression altered Caitlin knew instantly something was wrong. Cold fingers of dread caressed her spine.

Eventually she put the papers down and leaned across to Brianna. 'The good news is that your breasts seem fine. No recurring lumps or bumps as far as I can tell. But I'm afraid your bloods do give me cause for concern. Your white-cell count is very low. I'm not sure exactly why, but I'd like to admit you to hospital for a few days so we can find out.'

Brianna reached for Caitlin's hand, and Caitlin grasped the cold fingers in hers, trying to pass her strength on to her sister.

'Has the cancer come back?' Brianna breathed.

'As I said, I won't know what this means until we run further tests. But with a blood count that low, you run the risk of infection, or already have an infection. You'll be safer in hospital. I know it's difficult, and easy for me to say, but try not to worry until we know more.'

Brianna turned green eyes on Caitlin. 'Cat?' she said, with only the tiniest tremor evident.

Caitlin knew there could be all sorts of reasons for the white blood count being low. Some fairly innocuous, others less so. But she remembered the cough and the flushed look her sister had had the last few days. If she did have an infection it could be very dangerous. She pushed away the fear and strove to keep her voice calm and steady.

'Dr Sommerville is correct. There could be lots of reasons for the count being low. That's what we need to find out. In the meantime, the safest place for you is in hospital.'

'But what about the children?' Brianna asked. Caitlin could see it was taking all her effort not to break down. 'Niall's not due back until the weekend.'

'Don't you think you should phone him and let him know what's happening?' Caitlin said gently. 'I'm sure he'd take the next plane back.'

'I told you before, Caitlin, I want to keep my life as normal as possible for as long as possible. If I called Niall back every time there was the slightest reason, he'd never get any work done. And he's missed too much time on this important project as it is.' She bit her lip. 'Can't you take some time off and look after the children? Just until Friday? They're at school until after two anyway.' She squeezed Caitlin's hand. 'I know it's a lot to ask. Especially when you haven't been here that long.'

Caitlin knew she couldn't refuse her sister. It would take a bit of arranging, but somehow she would have to manage. For the first time in her life, work was going to have to take second place.

'I'll need to have a chat with my colleagues and see what we can work out. But if they can do without me for a few days then, yes, I'll look after the children for you.'

Caitlin sought out her senior colleague as soon as Brianna had left to return home to pack a bag. Antonia had wanted to admit her straight to the ward, but Brianna had been adamant that she didn't want the children coming home from school to find their mother in hospital. From the set of her mouth, Caitlin could see that she was determined. Although most of the time her sister was easygoing, when she had made up her mind about something, there was no dissuading her. Dr Hargreaves was sympathetic and told Caitlin that he and his other colleagues would cover for her for the remainder of the week. The following week would be difficult, though, he warned, as Dr Foster was taking annual leave. 'But if it's at all possible, could you cover the labour ward until Dr Foster gets back with the air ambulance? I have Theatre in a few minutes, and Susan has an outpatient clinic about to start,' he said, naming the fourth colleague to make up their team.

'Of course I'll stay until he returns. I've patients to pass over anyway. Hopefully Brianna will be out before the end of the week, possibly even tomorrow, in which case I'll be back immediately she's fit,' Caitlin told him. 'At the very least her husband will be back from his business trip and able to step in.'

'I won't expect you until next Monday,' Dr Hargreaves insisted. 'Do what you have to do. We all have lives outside of medicine.'

By the time Caitlin had seen all her patients and passed on their treatment plans, it was after two. She had phoned Brianna and suggested that she bring the children to the hospital with her. To her surprise, Brianna agreed.

'I don't want them thinking that hospitals are big scary places that they have to be kept away from. They know I used to work here and that you and Andrew still do. I think they'll be fine.'

As soon as Dr Foster returned with the air ambulance, he relieved Caitlin. 'We managed to slow down labour long enough to get the patient here,' he told Caitlin. 'Dr Hargreaves is going to do the section now, before the remainder of his list. He explained to me about your sister, so off you go.'

Caitlin smiled gratefully before giving him a rapid summary of the patients who might need his attention. 'The nurse in charge knows exactly what's going on, if I've left anything out,' she said, before leaving the maternity wing and heading for Oncology.

Caitlin found Brianna in bed in the ward. A nurse was taking blood.

'Where are the children?' Caitlin asked.

'Andrew's taken them to the canteen for a drink,' Brianna replied. 'He came to see me as soon as he heard I had been admitted.'

'I'd better go and relieve him, then,' Caitlin said, trying to look unconcerned. She would much rather have hung about with Brianna until the test results came back, but she knew that Andrew would need to get on with his own day, and that the children wouldn't be allowed on the ward. 'I'll phone later and see how you're getting on.' Before she left she leaned over and kissed her sister. 'Are you all right?'

'I'm scared,' Brianna admitted. 'What if the cancer's back? What will happen to Niall and the kids?'

It was the first time Caitlin had heard her sister admit her fears and it worried her. Maybe she should phone Niall after all? But she had promised Brianna. No, she would wait for the test results to come back. It would be time enough to make a decision once they knew what they were dealing with.

'But whatever happens, I've decided to have myself tested for the gene. I don't want Siobhan to go through life wondering if and when she is going to be hit with breast cancer.'

'You must do whatever you think is right,' Caitlin said. 'You know I'll support you.'

'Even if it means facing up to the fact you too might have the gene?'

'Yes,' Caitlin said. 'But we'll cross that bridge if and when we have to.' She leaned over and gave her sister a hug.

'I hate to leave you here on your own,' she said.

'At least you're in the same country this time.' Brianna managed a shaky smile. 'And able to be with the children.

Besides, Andrew said he'd look in later. Speaking of which, hadn't you better rescue him?'

Caitlin found Siobhan and Ciaran in the canteen. Andrew was saying something to them that made them laugh. As she looked at the three familiar heads, she felt her heart constrict. She wouldn't let herself think of the possibility of the children being left without a mother. That wasn't going to happen. She wouldn't allow it.

Andrew looked up and saw her standing there. With a quiet word to the children he strode across to Caitlin. He put his hand on her shoulder and gave it a gentle squeeze.

'I'll go and check up on Bri later, and I'll call round on my way home and bring you up to speed.'

Caitlin was grateful he didn't offer any of the usual platitudes. There was no point in him telling her not to worry. He seemed to know instinctively what she needed from him.

Caitlin spent the rest of the afternoon in the pool with the children. Then it was time for their homework while she made supper. After that it was bathtime. The children were playing up a little, the change of routine obviously unsettling them. But Caitlin eventually persuaded them out of the bath and into their pyjamas. Somehow she had managed to get herself soaked to the skin, and was beginning to wonder how she'd manage the next few days. Just as she'd tucked them into bed and reached for the storybook they wanted, she heard Andrew's car pull up at the door. Although she desperately wanted to find out about Bri, she decided it would be better to wait until the children had gone to sleep.

'Hey,' Andrew said from the door of the children's bedroom. Before Caitlin could stop them the children had leapt out of bed and straight into Andrew's arms. He picked one under each arm and strode back to their beds.

'It's bedtime, guys,' he said firmly. He looked over at Caitlin. She must look a sight, she thought, dismally aware of her wet clothes and that her hair was all over the place. 'Why don't I read you the story while Aunty Cat puts her feet up?'

Caitlin opened her mouth to protest. Despite appearances, she was coping just fine. How dared he suggest that she was less than capable? On the other hand, it had been an exhausting afternoon and, she conceded reluctantly, Andrew seemed to have a natural calming effect on the children. Instead, she smiled her gratitude at him. A change of clothes before she heard about Bri wouldn't be a bad idea. At the bedroom door, she glanced back at the children but already they were cuddled up to Andrew, one on each side, as he read them a story. Her heart twisted. He'd make such a good father one day, she thought. Caitlin sighed inwardly. Another reason why they weren't right for each other, she reminded herself.

Having changed into dry jeans and a T-shirt, Caitlin telephoned the hospital. But the news had been inconclusive—Brianna was to stay in for a few more days yet until the doctors had got all the results back. Which Caitlin knew was perfectly reasonable—from a professional point of view. So why was she feeling so unsettled and fretful about Brianna? She was the cool-headed one—wasn't she? Sighing, Caitlin made her way out to the veranda. The sun had set and the sky was dotted with a thousand stars.

In the distance, she could hear the gentle sound of the waves crashing softly onto the beach. But instead of feeling relaxed, her stomach was taut with nerves.

She sensed Andrew's presence and turned around.

'Fast asleep, both of them,' he said softly. As he eased himself into the chair opposite, his eyes held hers. 'And how are you doing?'

Caitlin swallowed hard to hide the swirl of emotions inside her, caused not only by her concern for her sister but also his presence, if the truth were known.

'I'm fine! Really.' She forced herself to keep her tone even. 'Just worried about Brianna. I phoned the hospital but there's no news. Just that she's settled and sleeping.'

'I know you must be worried about Brianna. It's only natural.'

'Brianna's going to be fine,' she replied firmly, but without warning her throat tightened up and tears that she had been unaware of suddenly threatened to spill. Horrified, Caitlin wiped them away with the back of her hand, not wanting Andrew to see. But it was too late. In one movement he was up and had crossed over to her. He took her in his arms, as she leant into him. She felt safe and secure, and the tears flowed in earnest. 'I'm sorry,' she choked into his chest. 'I'm overtired.'

'Shh,' he said. 'Just let go. For once. You're entitled to be upset. She's your sister, for God's sake.' Caitlin allowed herself a moment, but then pulled away.

Caitlin shook her head in frustration. 'The professional side of me knows that it's probably nothing more sinister than an infection. Horrible as that is, it's treatable. Besides, Brianna needs me to be strong for the kids—and for her.' She blew her nose, mortified that he had seen her blubbing like a baby. Instead, to her surprise, Andrew leaned across and took her hand and wrapped it in his.

'And who is strong for you? Who do you turn to? Because we all need someone to lean on from time to time—even you, Caitlin.' He said the words softly and she could feel the tears threaten to fall again.

Caitlin tried to pull her hand away, but he held on firmly. 'I don't need someone to lean on—I'm not the one going through what Brianna's going through. I can't imagine the fear and uncertainty she must be feeling—especially when it comes to Siobhan and Ciaran, not to mention Niall. And even though I'm a doctor, I can't do one damn thing to help my sister medically.' She breathed deeply, trying to get her emotions back in check. 'So the very least I can do is keep myself together for her and her family. It's what my sister expects of me.'

'You're doing your sister an injustice if you think that. You know as well as I do how a serious illness affects not only the patient but all their loved ones too. The patient has the symptoms, but everyone around them is fighting and coping with the disease too. And just because you're a doctor, it doesn't mean that you have to be in control all the time.'

'I know. I *know* that.' Caitlin wished he would stop being so sympathetic and understanding and so…near. But, she realised suddenly, it felt so good to be able to talk about Brianna's illness with someone. Her mother had been here and her dad had refused to talk about it—as if by not mentioning the word 'cancer', it didn't exist. As for her brothers and sisters, they all looked to her for support and reassurance, even though she was the youngest. She was always the sensible, together sibling of the family. She looked up at Andrew, her eyes large in her face. 'Sometimes I'm so…' Caitlin hesitated, almost unable to bring herself to say the word.

'Scared?' Andrew finished for her.

Caitlin nodded. 'Terrified.' She sucked in her breath. 'Not only for myself if anything happened to my sister, but for her children and her husband. How would they cope? Never mind my parents and the rest of the family. It just doesn't bear thinking about, but sometimes I can't help it. Ridiculous, I know, because so far her treatment has gone well and we owe it to her to be as positive as she is.'

Andrew traced his thumb gently down her cheek, wiping the tears away. 'It's going to be all right, I promise you.'

Although Caitlin knew that he was only trying to reassure her, she was grateful for the words of comfort. For the first time in her life she wished she could draw on the comfort of someone else. Someone like Andrew. Whatever life had to throw at her, she could face it with him at her side. But there was no use thinking like that. He had made it perfectly clear she wasn't the woman he wanted. Whatever she thought she saw in his eyes, she was mistaken. She and Andrew could only ever be friends. She would have to make do with that. Not for the first time, she envied Brianna. However terrible and frightening her life was right now, she had Niall to share her fears with. She would never experience the loneliness that had become a permanent feature in her own life almost without her realising.

The crunch of car tyres on gravel interrupted her thoughts. Caitlin jumped up and looked out of the window. Against the dark she could make out the contours of Niall's car. He must have finished his business early and hoped to surprise Brianna. 'Oh my God, Niall's come home early—he can't see me in such a state. He'll think something really terrible has happened. What am I going to tell him?'

'I called him,' Andrew said calmly. 'I know Brianna didn't want me to, but Niall's a good mate and I know he would never forgive me if I didn't let him know his wife needed him. Sometimes we have to go against the decisions of our friends.'

For a second, Caitlin was furious. How dared he think he knew better than her what was right for Brianna? But just as quickly she knew he was right. Brianna was trying to protect Niall, but Caitlin knew her brother-in-law well enough to know that he'd never forgive himself if something happened to his beloved wife and he wasn't there. How was it that Andrew's intuition as far as her family was concerned was better than hers? She had spent so long cocooned away from real life it seemed as if she had forgotten how to behave.

'Would you mind meeting him and bringing him up to speed while I go to the bathroom to freshen up?' she said. 'Seeing me like this will only scare him half to death.'

CHAPTER NINE

BY THE time Caitlin joined the men in the kitchen, she had got herself back under control again. She kissed her brother-in-law on the cheek and the three of them sat round the kitchen table, discussing Brianna's condition. Niall had gone straight to the hospital from the airport and had little to add to what the nurses had told Caitlin except that Brianna, after her initial annoyance with Andrew, had been delighted that Niall had come.

'She says to tell you she's going to chew your ear off when she next sees you,' Niall told Andrew. Then he turned to Caitlin. 'She was relieved it wasn't you who had told me. She says to tell you she needs someone she can trust not to betray her.'

They discussed Brianna for the next half hour, but there was little either of them could say to really reassure Niall. He looked haggard, Caitlin thought. She could only imagine the toll the last few months had taken on him. What would it be like to be loved the way Niall loved Brianna? she wondered. It seemed to Caitlin as if Niall was doing his best to pretend he believed their optimistic forecast, but she wondered if Niall was doing much the same as she was, hiding his emotions and fears behind a mask of normality. She glanced over at Andrew—perhaps he had comforted his friend in private, the way he had done with her this evening? Despite herself, she felt a rush of affection and gratitude towards Andrew. He had so many layers to him—it was a pity that she would never get to know them all. Because what an intriguing journey that would make!

Eventually Niall changed the subject. 'Had a lovely visit with your folks in Sydney, Andrew. Guess who was there at the same time? Raffia—the beautiful daughter of your dad's business partner. You didn't tell me she's got brains to boot—a mathematician no less!' Niall winked. 'No wonder you've been keeping her a closely guarded secret, you sly devil.'

Andrew laughed shortly, holding up his hands. 'I've been doing nothing of the sort, mate. It's nothing to do with me. It's our parents who want us to meet.' He glanced over at Caitlin, looking uncomfortable. 'We'll see what happens from there. Maybe she won't like what she sees.'

'As if she wouldn't—a fine specimen of a man like yourself?' Niall nudged Caitlin. 'What do you think? Don't you agree, Caitlin? She'll be swooning at his feet.'

Caitlin fought the urge to stalk out the room, horrified that the thought of Andrew holding another woman in his arms filled her with bleak despair. She forced herself to smile. 'What woman wouldn't?' she replied lightly, hoping the two men couldn't hear the irony in her voice. But their words had brought her to her senses. Once her time in Australia was up, and Brianna was well again, she would be going back to Ireland. And to her old life, where she belonged.

* * *

Thankfully, Caitlin's initial instincts and diagnosis had been right and with a short dose of IV antibiotics Brianna was discharged home from hospital after a couple of days. Once again, life returned to its normal routine, although Brianna was still weak. Caitlin worked a full day, then rushed home to help with the children. After they were in bed, Brianna usually went too, leaving an exhausted Caitlin to drag herself off to bed.

At the end of the week, reassured that he was no longer needed, Andrew left on his two-week holiday to see his folks in Sydney. Caitlin missed seeing him around the hospital and couldn't stop herself from thinking about him down in Sydney with the gorgeous mathematician. No doubt he'd be wining and dining her and checking out her credentials as a possible mother of his children, she thought bitterly, before reminding herself for the umpteenth time that that was exactly why he was wrong for her. However, as the days passed, she couldn't stop her heart skipping a beat at the thought that in a day or two she'd be seeing Andrew again.

Between the hospital and Bri, Caitlin was kept busy and was surprised to be paged one day by Dr Sommerville. Her initial flutter of anxiety that the oncologist was phoning with bad news about Brianna was soon dispelled.

'Dr O'Neill,' Antonia said sternly. 'Have you forgotten you have an appointment to see me?'

Caitlin had completely forgotten. Everything that had happened over the last week or so had pushed it out of her mind.

'Would you mind if we reschedule?' she said.

'Are you in the middle of something?'

Caitlin glanced down at the cup of coffee she was

holding in her hand. She had seen all her patients and her theatre list wasn't due to start for another hour. The nurse she had been chatting to was within earshot, so Caitlin could hardly lie.

'I'm on my way down right now,' she said, resigned. Her appointment would only take a few minutes and at least it would keep Brianna happy.

But it seemed as she lay on the examination couch, having her breasts examined, that she had misjudged Antonia. The doctor was obviously determined to be thorough. As Caitlin lifted her arms and answered the older woman's questions about her medical history, she let her mind drift to the patients she had scheduled for later.

Her thoughts were interrupted by Antonia frowning down at her. 'There's a lump here,' she said. 'It's probably nothing but, given your history, I think we should investigate it to be on the safe side. I'd like to do a fine-needle biopsy and send you for a mammogram. Is there any chance you might be pregnant?'

Caitlin's mind was whirling. A lump? She hadn't been aware of anything. Her breasts were usually a little lumpy. Especially around the time of her period. And then just as quickly the thought hit her like a bolt of lightning. But she had missed her period. She was at least five days late. Was it possible that she could be pregnant?

Aware that Antonia was waiting for a reply while she unwrapped the needle she would be using to draw fluid from the lump, Caitlin thought frantically. She'd been on the Pill when she had slept with Andrew. But she had been sick the night she'd returned, and she more than most knew that it could mean she had no longer been protected. And she was never late! She was as regular as clockwork.

Perhaps the anxiety over Bri had made her late? But she was beginning to develop a hollow feeling. She had been feeling nauseous the last couple of mornings. It was entirely possible she was pregnant, regardless of how much she wanted to believe otherwise.

'There's a small chance I might be pregnant,' she admitted. 'So until I know for sure, I think we should leave the mammogram.'

Antonio looked at her sharply, but otherwise said nothing. She inserted the needle into the lump and Caitlin grimaced as she withdrew some fluid.

'You can get dressed now,' Antonio said. 'We should have the results for you quite quickly—hopefully by Monday, Tuesday at the latest. I know it's not great to have to wait even a couple of days, but I'll phone you as soon as I have them.' She looked at Caitlin and must have recognised the stunned expression. 'Why don't I leave you here for a while?' she said sympathetically. 'It will give you a bit of time and privacy before you go back to work.' Caitlin nodded mutely and Antonia left her to her thoughts.

Dazed, all Caitlin could think about was the chance she might be pregnant or could have cancer. Either prospect was almost too much to contemplate but together? What if she was pregnant *and* had breast cancer? She knew that treatment for breast cancer was incompatible with pregnancy. And if she did require treatment there was every chance it would make the chances of her ever falling pregnant again remote.

Now that the chances of having children seemed about to be snatched away, Caitlin felt bereft. It was one thing not planning to have children, it was quite another having that decision taken out of her hands.

And if she was pregnant with Andrew's child, how did

she feel about that? How would *he* feel about that? Should she even tell him?

Slow down, she told herself. Think it through calmly one step at a time.

Firstly, she told herself, she needed to take a pregnancy test. She would find one down in the clinic. But the last thing she wanted was to draw attention to herself. No, she would stop at the pharmacy on the way home. She would have to wait until that evening before she could take the test. And as for the possibility that the lump Antonia had found was more than a benign cyst? Well, she would just have to wait for the results of that test too. There was no point in worrying about something that might never happen. She would just need to keep herself busy, which shouldn't be difficult, bearing in mind her busy schedule over the next few days. Then the scientist part of her brain told her that once she had all the facts, then she could decide what to do. Right now she had a job to do, and her patients needed her to be focussed. There would be time later to make decisions.

Caitlin looked at the blue line on the stick and knew her instincts had been correct. She was pregnant. Good going, she thought wryly, for a consultant obstetrician to find herself with an unplanned pregnancy. Surely she of all people could have avoided this? But she hadn't been thinking straight lately. First her concern for Brianna and then her feelings for Andrew had sent her usually ordered mind spinning in all directions. And now that she was faced with the consequences, what was she going to do?

In her head she worked out the dates and how far along her pregnancy was. Although she wasn't far advanced at all she could imagine exactly how the foetus would look at this stage, and she felt the first stirring of protectiveness deep inside her. But she wasn't ready to be a mother. She had her future to think of, her career. Life as a single mother didn't fit into those plans. She shook her head. If the result of the needle biopsy was positive and she needed chemotherapy, she would have to consider terminating the pregnancy anyway. Either that, or not have the treatment and allow the cancer to progress, which it would do more rapidly feeding on the hormones that would be surging around her blood. But although the rational part of her said a termination was a straightforward procedure, something inside of her balked at the idea. How on earth had she, of all people, managed to get herself into this mess?

Brianna tapped on the bathroom door. 'Dinner's ready, Cat.'

Caitlin knew she couldn't stay in the bathroom much longer. Brianna would guess that something was up, and she didn't want to worry her sister. Not when she already had so much on her plate. She wrapped the test in a piece of screwed-up paper and hid it in her pocket. She'd dispose of it later in one of the outside bins. Somehow she'd have to get through the weekend, pretending everything was okay.

But Caitlin had underestimated her sister's perceptiveness. All through Saturday she could feel Brianna's speculative eyes on her and, sure enough, in the evening, while Niall was putting the children to bed, Caitlin found herself cornered.

'Let's take our tea onto the veranda,' Brianna suggested. They sat on the swing seat in companionable silence for a few moments, enjoying the cool evening breeze after the heat of the day. Caitlin was even getting used to the flying ants.

'I have some good news.' Brianna smiled. 'The results of the gene screen came back negative. I know it doesn't mean Siobhan will never get breast cancer, but the odds are more in her favour.'

'I'm so happy for you, Bri. It must be a load off your mind.' Caitlin hugged her sister. It meant that she herself was less likely to have the gene. However, not having the gene didn't mean she didn't have cancer. But she couldn't tell Brianna now, when she looked as if a weight had been lifted from her shoulders. It just wouldn't be fair.

'What is it, Caitlin?' Brianna eventually ventured. 'You're not taking my news with your usual "I told you so." I get the feeling something's up. Is it work? Are you needed back in Ireland? Do you want to go home? Is it Andrew? Something's bothering you for sure. So give.'

'I'm pregnant.' The words slipped out before Caitlin could stop herself. Now she had said them it all seemed so much more real.

'Oh,' Brianna said. Then a few seconds later, 'How do you feel about that?'

'I don't know. That's just it. You know it's not in my plans. At least not right now.'

'Is it David's?'

Caitlin stood and walked across to the edge of the veranda. She laughed shortly. 'No, it's not David's. We hadn't…you know, towards the end, not for a long time. It had all really fizzled out, even before I told him I was coming over here. But I had carried on taking the Pill. Just habit, I guess.'

'Then who…?' Caitlin could hear the sudden realisation in Brianna's voice. 'You don't mean that it's Andrew's? Oh my God, Cat. You do! There's been no one else. I've seen the way you look at him, but I never thought it had got this serious.' She came across and stood next to Caitlin. 'But that's wonderful, isn't it?'

'Wonderful? To be pregnant by a man who doesn't love you? With whom there is no kind of future? Who thinks that women should stay at home, look after the children and be grateful to bring him his slippers at the end of the day? No,' Caitlin said heavily, 'even if he cared for me—which he doesn't, he's made that much clear—Andrew Bedi and I have no future. It's all been a ghastly mistake.'

'Are you going to tell him?' Brianna said quietly. 'Don't you think he has a right to know?'

Caitlin sighed from a place deep in her soul. 'I haven't really decided what to do yet,' she said. 'I don't know if I'm up to bringing up a child on my own. Is it fair, do you think? Me, working all hours, leaving the baby with a childminder. I don't think that's the kind of life I envisaged for myself.'

She wasn't going to tell Brianna about the lump. There wasn't any point, at least not until Monday when she would get the results. Her sister had been through so much already, it would be unfair to worry her further. She should have kept the pregnancy to herself too, she thought, furious with herself. Why involve Brianna when she didn't have all the facts herself?

Brianna had slumped back in the swing seat, looking dazed. 'You don't mean you'll consider not having it? Oh, Caitlin, think very carefully before you go down that road.'

'I need time to take it all in,' Caitlin said. 'It's all come as a shock. You know me—up until now, up until I came to Australia, my life had been organised, planned down to the last detail. There has never been any room in my life for the unexpected.'

'From that point Australia's been good for you.' Brianna touched Caitlin on the arm. 'You know I hate to say this, Cat, but when you first arrived, I couldn't believe how serious you'd become. You already looked the part of the stereotypical professor. I couldn't see the mischievous Caitlin I remembered anywhere. It's as if you'd had the life sucked out of you.'

Caitlin slid her sister a look. She was horrified but deep down knew her sister was correct. She had been working so hard for so long she had forgotten how to live. Even her relationship with David had been almost, well, convenient. They were two people who shared the same *academic* interests, but that was all. She couldn't remember laughing with David the way she had laughed with Andrew. In fact, she couldn't even remember having fun with David. Not once. The more she thought about it, the more she knew Bri was right. The last few years back in Dublin hadn't really been living. But since she had arrived in Australia, although the circumstances were not what she would have wished, she had never felt so alive. And that's what Andrew made her feel. Alive from the tips of her toes to the top of her head. What on earth was she going to do?

CHAPTER TEN

ANDREW took a sip of his drink and studied the woman opposite him. She was beautiful, with her olive skin and luxuriant mane of hair, as well as being bright and amusing. In short she was everything he thought he wanted in a woman. Why, then, did the image of glittering green eyes and auburn hair keep transposing itself on his thoughts? Why had he been unable to stop thinking of Caitlin and the feel of her silky skin under his fingertips for even a moment?

'I'd love to have children,' Raffia was saying. 'At least half a dozen.'

'What about your degree?' Andrew asked. 'I thought you planned to be a teacher?'

'Only until I have a family,' Raffia replied. 'I do think women should stay at home—if they are lucky enough to be able to afford to. Don't you?'

He did. Or at least he had. Suddenly like a bolt from the blue he realised that something fundamental had changed. He couldn't imagine any sort of life without Caitlin in it. Whatever that life was. What was the point in having children if it wasn't with the woman who made you feel as if your life was complete? Without Caitlin he would only ever be half-alive. Despite his best intentions he had done the very thing he had thought impossible. He had fallen irrevocably in love with the most unsuitable woman. The realisation took his breath away. What a fool he had been. He became aware that Raffia was looking at him curiously.

'You haven't heard a word I've been saying, have you?' she said softly.

'I'm sorry,' he said. 'Please forgive me. But I have to go.' He stood, suddenly desperate to see Caitlin again. He needed to tell her how he felt. Needed to convince her that they should be together. Regardless. If she didn't want children, well, that would be a blow, but maybe he could convince her in time. She could continue working. Women did these days and their children didn't always suffer for it. He might have to do his bit. He pictured himself changing a nappy, his tiny son laughing up at him, and the thought didn't seem quite as ridiculous as it once had. Millions of men, even men he knew like Niall, managed so why shouldn't he?

Raffia was smiling at him. 'You're already in love with someone, aren't you?' she said softly.

Andrew brought himself back to the present. Was it that obvious?

'Yes,' he said. 'How did you know?'

'Oh, we women have a sixth sense as far as these things are concerned. She's a lucky woman.' She smiled ruefully. 'Does she know?'

'No,' Andrew admitted. Then he smiled, knowing that his life was mapped out for better or for worse. That if he had anything to do with it, he had the rest of his life to spend with Caitlin. 'But she will soon.'

'Then don't you think you should find her and tell her?' Raffia suggested.

Andrew bent and kissed her on the cheek. 'I'm sorry… about all this,' he said.

'Hey, don't worry about it.' She giggled. 'The truth is, I'm sort of seeing someone too. I only agreed to tonight to keep the folks happy, but this way I'll be able to tell them truthfully we weren't right for each other. Now scoot. Before I change my mind.'

On Monday, Caitlin had work as usual. She knew Andrew was back from Sydney and she both dreaded and longed to see him. Arriving early at the hospital, she made her way up to the special care nursery, to check on baby Colin, who had been delivered safely after her initial diagnosis that he might have a heart problem when they had been at the Sunshine Coast clinic. After that, she would go and see Patricia's baby. As it was still early, she hoped to avoid bumping into Andrew. She wasn't ready to see him yet. She was on call for emergencies today, so wouldn't have Outpatients or Theatre.

But as she stepped into the ward she was dismayed to find Andrew lounging against the nurses' station, coffee in hand, laughing at something with one of the nursing staff. At the sight of the familiar features and tall frame, which had haunted her dreams over the last couple of weeks, she felt her heart somersault. Was it possible that he was even more good looking than she remembered? He looked up and caught her eye. A broad grin spread across his face.

'Caitlin,' he said. 'It's good to see you. Have you come to make sure we're looking after your babies?'

He meant baby Colin, but for one horrific second Caitlin thought he knew about the pregnancy. If she decided to tell him, and she wasn't about to, at least not until she knew that she was going to keep the baby, and she was a way off making any decision at all.

'I've been up to see him most days,' she admitted. 'Is he still doing well?'

'Come and see for yourself,' Andrew said. 'We've finished rounds, but I'm sure his parents won't mind another visit from you.'

Baby Colin was indeed continuing to make progress. As Caitlin looked down at the tiny form, still attached to a ventilator but gaining weight and getting stronger every day, she felt her heart shift. She slipped a hand inside the incubator and into a tiny hand. Colin's mouth was like a rosebud. Long lashes lay against delicate cheeks.

'We can't thank you and Dr Bedi enough,' his mother whispered. 'We know without you both our baby could have died.'

'That's what we're here for,' Caitlin said softly. 'It's our job to bring healthy babies into the world and to help those who aren't so healthy survive. It is an honour and a privilege for us to play our part.' She laughed, suddenly self-conscious. She wasn't usually so philosophical. 'But you have the hard part. Eighteen years or more looking after him. Our part was easy in comparison.' She was uncomfortably aware of Andrew's speculative look.

'We'll never forget either of you. Or the nurses. Everyone has been so fantastic,' the husband added. 'You've all made a very stressful time bearable.'

'I'll come in to see you again tomorrow,' Caitlin said. 'In the meantime, Colin's in the best possible hands.'

'Hey,' Andrew said as they walked away, 'is this the *uber*-cool Dr O'Neill showing a softer side? I thought you didn't like to get too involved with your patients? You've been here every day. And to see the Levy baby too, the nurses tell me.'

'I just like to make sure my patients are doing well,' she said defensively. 'That's not the same as being involved.'

Andrew wiggled his eyebrows at her. 'Sure, if that's what you want other people to believe. But you don't fool me. I can see right through that tough exterior.'

Caitlin drew a sharp breath. There was something in the way he was looking at her, as if… She banished the thought. Her hormones were playing up, that was all. She was reading things into situations that didn't exist.

'I was going to look in on baby Levy—little Colleen—on the paeds ward since I'm up this way. Have you seen her since you got back? She's doing fantastically well.'

'Yes,' Andrew said. 'It won't be long before we can discharge her.' He looked at his watch. 'I need to be somewhere,' he said. 'But before I go, how's Brianna? I spoke to Niall on the phone yesterday and he said she's fine. Should I believe him?'

'Why don't you come round this evening and see for yourself?' The words slipped out before Caitlin could stop herself. Once again there was that speculative look in Andrew's eyes.

'Do *you* want me to come?' he asked, his eyes drilling into hers. Caitlin's heart began to gallop in the most uncomfortable way.

'How was the gorgeous mathematician?' she queried instead. Once again the words slipped out before she could stop them.

Andrew's eyes crinkled. 'You're interested? In my love life? I thought you couldn't care less.'

'Of course I don't,' Caitlin retorted. 'Whatever you get up to is up to you. I was only making polite conversation. As one friend to another.'

'Caitlin, I need to speak to you, but in private,' he said. He reached towards her, but before he could say anything more, Caitlin's pager bleeped.

'I need to answer this,' Caitlin said, moving towards the phone. Whatever it was he needed to talk to her about, Caitlin wasn't sure she wanted to hear it. She suspected it had something to do with the woman his mother had lined up for him.

The call was about the woman Caitlin had seen up in Noosa. The one who'd had the positive pregnancy test after IVF. Caitlin's heart sank when the nurse told her that she had presented at the hospital in pain. It sounded ominous to Caitlin.

'I'll be right there,' she said. She turned to Andrew, but he had already gone.

'I'm sorry,' Caitlin told the frightened couple. 'It seems from the scan that you have a twin pregnancy. The trouble is, although one is developing in its proper place, the other is in your Fallopian tube.'

'Can you do anything?' Amy asked shakily.

'I'm sorry,' Caitlin said again, taking Amy's hand in hers. 'I'll have to remove the pregnancy from the tube and possibly the tube itself. The other baby will be fine.'

'But I want them both,' Amy cried. 'I don't want to lose either of my babies.'

Caitlin's heart went out to the young couple. They

wanted these babies so badly. Without thinking, her hand dropped to her own belly. It was early days yet, but the irony wasn't lost on Caitlin. In front of her was a young couple who had fought very hard to have children they desperately wanted. And here she was pregnant without meaning to be, and unsure how she felt about it. For the first time she really thought about the baby growing inside her. What if someone told her she was going to lose it and she might never get pregnant again? How would she feel about that? Then suddenly, sitting in front of the distraught couple, she knew the answer. She wanted this baby. Regardless of how difficult it would make her life, and she was under no illusions as to how difficult her life as a single working mum was going to be, the baby was here now, and for better or worse, if it was at all possible, she was going to keep it. As she made the decision she felt a huge weight lift from her shoulders.

'I know this is difficult for you both, and I know you'll need time later to grieve for the lost baby, but believe me if there was any way to save it I would. And I wish I could give you time to come to terms with it, but I need to operate today. There's a real chance that if we don't, and soon, your tube could rupture, putting your own life in danger. At least, and I know right now it's little compensation, your other baby should be just fine.'

Shaken, Caitlin left the couple in the care of the nursing staff. If she was going to get so involved with every patient, she thought grimly, she'd have nothing left. She realised now why the academic route had seemed so enticing. It had just been another way for her to hide from the harsher realities of life. Being an academic would be so much easier than having to face the difficult emotional issues of her patients every day. But at the same time, Caitlin thought about the babies she had helped save. There was the reward of knowing that she had really made a difference. Although caring brought sadness and pain, it also brought an enormous feeling of satisfaction.

Caitlin kept looking at her watch, wondering when Antonia would call her with the results. Every hour she had to wait was agonising. Now she knew exactly how her patients felt. Even an hour when you were waiting for important results could seem like an eternity. But when Antonia did page her, it was to tell her that her results wouldn't be back for another couple of days due to a backlog at the lab. She apologised profusely but Caitlin knew that it wasn't her fault. Somehow she would have to get through the next couple of days as best she could.

As she was on call for the labour ward, Caitlin would be staying at the hospital overnight. Brianna's house was simply too far away for her to get back to the hospital quickly enough should an emergency occur and, sure enough, just as she was finishing writing up her notes for the day, her pager bleeped. Caitlin was almost grateful. Anything that would keep her mind occupied was welcome.

It was Dr Hargreaves. 'Ah, Dr O'Neill,' he boomed down the phone. 'I hope I didn't disturb you, but I wondered if you'd like to go with the air ambulance to attend a patient with an unstable lie. If you would, I'll cover the labour suite until you get back.'

'Sure,' Caitlin said. 'I'd like to go.'

'The air ambulance leaves in about ten minutes. There's not much time. The pilot will want to get back before dark if possible. Dr Bedi is going too.'

At the last bit of information Caitlin's heart jumped. On

the one hand she didn't want to spend time with him, not until she knew for certain what she was going to do, but on the other hand she was glad it would be Andrew that would be the paediatrician on this, her first callout.

'What about equipment?' she asked.

'Everything you might need will be on the plane,' Dr Hargreaves said. 'Good luck.' And then he hung up.

Caitlin thought quickly. Then she grabbed her stethoscope and white coat. On her way to the pick-up point, she'd collect some scrubs as well.

Andrew was already waiting for her next to the small Cesna. There was no way to talk over the roar of the engines, but Andrew flashed her a smile, before taking her by the elbow and ushering her on board. Inside there was only room enough for the two of them plus an incubator and a stretcher should they need to transport the patient back to hospital. The two seats up front were taken by the pilot, an efficient-looking woman somewhere in her early thirties, and the copilot, an older man with a face like a bloodhound. Andrew introduced them simply as Fran and Steve, and it was obvious that he knew them both well from the easy banter.

Minutes later and they were taking off. Caitlin stared out of the window as they left Brisbane behind. She could see the river snaking like a major artery through the city, crossed by the numerous bridges.

'How far?' she shouted to Andrew, struggling to make herself heard above the noise of the engines.

'About forty minutes,' he replied. 'Just try and relax while you can.'

The noise of the engines made conversation difficult and Caitlin was left alone with her thoughts. She sneaked a look at Andrew, who was sitting with his eyes closed. Once more she felt a mix of emotions. Attraction, there was no denying that, she thought ruefully. She had known she was attracted to him since the first time she had clapped eyes on him, but what she felt was more than physical. She loved being in his company. Life seemed to glitter when he was around. Life just felt more…exciting somehow. But it was no use. If it wasn't for Brianna, Caitlin would be tempted to go back to Ireland and try and get her life under control. But she couldn't. She had promised her sister that she'd be here for six months, only just over a month had passed and she would keep her promise, however difficult she found it. But, she thought, what would happen if she continued with the pregnancy? It would be impossible to keep it from Andrew. What then? She shook her head. Stop it! she told herself. Remember you were going to take one step at a time?

It only seemed like minutes before they were landing. Andrew had passed Caitlin a copy of the woman's notes as they were flying. Just before the plane had started to descend he had brought her up to speed with what he knew about the patient, which he had to admit was very little.

'All we really know is that the nurse is concerned enough to want a doctor on hand,' he had told Caitlin. 'As is often the case, we really don't know exactly what we are dealing with until we get there.'

They jumped out of the plane as soon as Fran said they were free to go. 'There's only an hour before sunset,' she told them, 'and I'd really like to be in the air by then. So I'd appreciate it if you could be as quick as possible.'

The nurse rushed over to meet them. 'Hi, guys. Am I

glad to see you,' she said. 'My lady really needs to be in hospital, I think. C'mon, let's take you over. I'm Tanni, by the way.' Then she stopped and looked thoughtful. 'Which one of you is the paediatrician?' she asked.

'That would be me,' Andrew said, as he followed her into the clinic.

'I hoped there would be someone on this flight. I have a two-year-old I'd like you to have a look at when you're finished with Mrs Crouse. It's not an emergency as such. It's just that there is something about him that worries me. And since you're here anyway, it would save him and his parents a long and perhaps unnecessary trip to Brisbane.'

'No probs,' Andrew agreed. 'I'll be happy to have a look just as soon as I'm finished with the woman you called us to see.'

The nurse's fears turned out to be justified. Mrs Crouse's third pregnancy was almost at full term, but the baby was lying bottom first instead of head down. As Caitlin examined her she could tell that the patient was already in advanced labour.

'It's a breech lie,' she told Andrew. 'And her contractions are less than three minutes apart. It's too late to transport her and too late to do a section. We're just going to have to deliver her here.'

Caitlin could tell from Andrew's expression that he recognised the difficult situation their patient was in. If the baby got stuck during labour, and that was a real possibility, they could be dealing with a dead baby. The thought filled Caitlin with dread. She was used to dealing with similar scenarios, but always in fully equipped hospitals. Not in a clinic that was only set up with basic equipment for routine emergencies. But at least, thank God, Andrew was there to help.

But for the time being there was little either of them could do, except wait. While they waited Andrew rummaged through the bag they had brought with them to see what was available.

'I need a paediatric endotracheal tube and a laryngoscope,' Andrew said. 'If the baby's in poor nick, I'll need both.'

Thankfully their search produced both items. At least, if the worst came to the worst and the baby needed resuscitating after delivery, they had the right equipment. Caitlin also found a pair of forceps. Now at least they were as prepared as they could be.

Caitlin felt the women's abdomen. 'Contractions are still around three minutes apart,' she said. 'The baby could come any time. In the next half-hour or not for hours yet. I'm afraid this is just a waiting game now.'

Tanni popped her head back in. 'Could you come and see the child now, Dr Bedi? I'm becoming increasingly concerned about him.'

'Will you be okay here?' Andrew asked Caitlin. 'I'll be as quick as I can.'

Caitlin nodded. 'I'll yell if I need you,' she said, sitting down next to Mrs Crouse. 'We'll be fine.' She smiled at her patient, who was concentrating on coping with her contractions.

When Andrew returned, Caitlin could see that he was frowning.

'What is it?' she asked. 'Is everything all right?'

'Not really,' he said. 'I'm pretty sure he has meningitis—we need to get him to hospital stat so he can have a lumbar puncture.'

'But Mrs Crouse—Magda—shouldn't be moved,'

Caitlin said. 'Why don't you go back with the child while I stay here with Magda? The plane can come back for us.'

'I don't want to leave you on your own. If something goes wrong…' He stared into the distance. 'I think I should send Tanni back with the child. Nothing is going to happen on the flight. I'm confident of that. I'll start him on IV antibiotics just in case. Then once she has seen him admitted she can come back on the flight that picks us up. Dr Hargreaves will just have to stay on until we get back.' He stood, and stretched. 'That's what we'll do,' he said decisively. 'It's not a perfect arrangement, but we'll just have to make the best of it.'

Caitlin nodded. 'You're right. We don't have any other choice.'

Twenty minutes later, they heard the plane take off. Caitlin settled herself by her patient, prepared to wait out the next couple of hours or however long it took for the plane to return. Magda was comfortable enough to close her eyes and fall asleep.

The room they were in was sparsely furnished with a bed and basic monitoring equipment. Apart from one armchair there was only one other uncomfortable-looking plastic orange chair.

Andrew must have noticed her looking indecisive. 'You take the comfy chair if you like. It could be a few hours yet, so get some rest.' But Caitlin was having none of it.

'No. You have it,' she insisted. 'I don't mind.'

Andrew glowered at her. 'Do you have to argue with me about everything, woman?' he said. 'I told you Aussie men don't let their women suffer. Not if they can do anything about it!'

Caitlin felt a frisson run down her spine. Their women?

But she wasn't Andrew's woman. He had made that perfectly clear and, besides, she wasn't anybody's woman. She was her own person. She suppressed a smile. Andrew made her feel as if she was in the Wild West. For a moment an image of him tossing her over his shoulder as he walked into the bush, brushing away crocodiles with a disdainful flick of his boot, flashed through her mind, and she felt heat rise from low in her abdomen. God, now he had her thinking the same way. What on earth was happening to her?

'Speaking of which,' she said, 'how was your trip to Sydney?'

'Ah, Sydney,' he said slowly. 'I want to talk to you about that.' He looked down at the sleeping patient. 'But it will have to wait. I don't want an audience. She might wake up at any time.' He looked her in the eye. Could she be mistaken? Or was he looking at her as if, well, as if he cared?

'I'm starving,' he said suddenly. 'It's well past my dinnertime. Why don't I go and see whether I can rustle up something to eat?'

Caitlin didn't really feel like eating. The feeling of nausea that had started on the plane journey was coming back now that she wasn't concentrating her whole attention on her patient.

'I'm not hungry,' she said. 'But why don't you go and get something? I'll shout if I need you.'

But Andrew hadn't been gone long before he was back, holding a couple of plates loaded with food. 'I thought you might be tempted when you smelled it,' he said. But the smell of cooked meat was having the opposite effect on Caitlin. Without warning, her stomach heaved. Covering her mouth with her hand, she rushed over to the basin and was violently sick. Right there. Next to her sleeping patient and in full view of Andrew. Had she not felt as if she were about to die she would have been mortified. Nothing like this had ever happened to her in all the years she had been a doctor. Losing control had never been part of Caitlin's make-up. Until now. She felt a cool hand on her forehead.

'Take it easy,' Andrew said. He waited beside her as she took deep breaths. Eventually the cold sweaty feeling disappeared along with the nausea and she was able to speak. Impatiently she moved away from him.

'I'm sorry you had to witness that,' she said, and slumped down in the armchair.

Andrew moved across the room and knelt by her side. He felt her forehead and then her pulse. 'You should lie down,' he said. 'Perhaps you've picked up the same bug Brianna had.'

'I'm perfectly all right,' Caitlin almost snapped. She would have given anything to be far away from Andrew's searching gaze. 'I'll just splash my face and rinse out my mouth,' she added, starting to rise.

But Andrew was still looking at her, concern deepening his brown eyes. 'If you have some sort of virus, you shouldn't be looking after patients. What if you pass it on?'

'It's not a virus,' Caitlin said before she could stop herself.

Andrew's eyebrows snapped together. 'How can you be so sure?' he asked.

Caitlin was thinking rapidly, unsure of what to do. He was quite right. If she was unwell she shouldn't be around a baby as fragile as this would be. The last thing a premature baby needed was to be exposed to viruses. But she didn't have a virus. She knew exactly what had caused her to be ill. But the last thing she wanted to do was tell him.

On the other hand, if she didn't, she would have to excuse herself from the care of the woman and her baby. Could she in all honesty do that?

'I am fine. Please, just trust me on this.'

Andrew narrowed his eyes at her. 'It's all very well to play the martyr,' he said. 'I know we doctors don't like to admit when we are ill, but if it's for the good of our patients, sometimes we have to. So I'm sorry, Cat, you're off the case.'

'Oh, for God's sake, Andrew, I'm pregnant. I've been sick and I'm perfectly all right now.'

He looked at her, stunned. 'Pregnant!' The room was suddenly deathly silent except for the sound of the sleeping woman's breathing. Caitlin watched as emotions chased across Andrew's face. Disappointment, then puzzlement, then slowly a dawning realisation. 'How far on are you?' he asked abruptly.

Caitlin chewed her lip. It was the moment of truth. What should she do? If she led him to believe her pregnancy was more advanced than it was, he'd believe it was David's. That way he would leave her alone. But was that fair? Could she bring herself to tell him an outright lie? On the one hand it would mean that she was free to make her own decision about the pregnancy and he wouldn't have to be involved should she need to make the choice between continuing the pregnancy or, if she had cancer, terminating it. Was it even fair to tell him? Especially when she was certain that should the lump turn out to be malignant she wouldn't want him to know. One thing she knew about Andrew with absolute certainty was that he would feel an obligation towards her if she was pregnant. And an even greater one should she be ill with a possible life-threatening illness. But before she could decide what to say, he stood up and pulled her to her feet. Holding her roughly by her upper arms, he looked her directly in the eye.

'Is it mine?' he demanded. 'For God's sake, Caitlin, tell me. Are you having my baby?'

CHAPTER ELEVEN

IN THE end she couldn't lie and Andrew must have seen the truth in her eyes. They stared at each other in silence.

'I don't think this is the time to talk about this,' Andrew said, indicating their patient with a nod of his head. Caitlin realised that Mrs Crouse was beginning to surface from her sleep, and suddenly she cried out in pain, clutching her stomach.

Quickly, Caitlin bent over to examine Magda. 'I can see a foot,' she called out. 'And a loop of cord.' Then she listened for the baby's heartbeat. 'Foetal heartbeat is dropping. We need to get this baby delivered. Right now!'

She turned to Magda, who was screwing up her eyes in pain.

'Magda, I need you to push. As hard as you can. Do you understand?'

Magda nodded, her eyes wide with fear and pain. Caitlin carefully wrapped her hand around the tiny protruding foot, aware that Andrew was standing by, ready to help. Carefully but firmly she tugged on the foot, acutely conscious that she needed to apply slow but steady pressure. As the baby began to appear she called out. 'Pass me the forceps, Andrew.'

Silently he passed her the forceps and then with a final tug the baby was out. Quickly Caitlin removed the cord from around the baby's neck.

'Two minutes,' Andrew called, holding his arms out to receive the baby, a girl, from Caitlin. It was up to him now. She had done everything she could. Her heart in her mouth, she watched as he placed the still blue form down on the trolley he had prepared earlier and slipped the laryngoscope down the tiny throat. Caitlin sighed with relief as the tube slipped in and Andrew followed it with an endotracheal tube.

'Andrew,' she said as the baby began to pink up, 'don't you think she's a little small for her dates?' The baby should have been a good bit bigger if Mrs Crouse's dates were correct, and then, as Mrs Crouse let out another cry of pain, she locked eyes with Andrew. She knew they were both thinking the same thing.

She whirled around and was just in time to deliver another baby, this time a boy, as Magda gave one final push.

'Did you know you were expecting twins?' she asked the exhausted woman.

'No.' Magda looked astonished. 'I had no idea.'

Caitlin wrapped up the tiny boy and then slipped it in next to Magda. The heat from the mother's skin was the best way to keep the premature infant warm. But at least this one was healthy.

Just as she placed the infant next to his mother, a cry came from where Andrew was working with the baby girl. Caitlin smiled. Somehow she and Andrew had pulled it off and Mrs Crouse had two healthy babies.

Magda was still groggy so Caitlin went over to the cot

and picked up the crying infant. As she felt Andrew's eyes on her, the irony of the situation wasn't wasted. Here she was holding a completely helpless baby while inside her was another even more helpless child totally dependent on her as to whether it would live or die. But she couldn't bear to think about it as a baby. She had to think of it as no more than a collection of cells less than a centimetre in diameter. The moment she started to think of it as anything more she'd be lost. It would be too cruel to have to decide whether her life or that of the baby was more important. She felt her eyes fill with tears as she realised it was too late. Whatever she wanted to believe, she knew in her heart of hearts that she had already fallen in love with the tiny life growing inside her. It was hers and Andrew's baby and whatever the future held, she couldn't imagine not having his child.

A short time later, as they finished making Magda and her two babies comfortable, they heard the drone of the plane returning from Brisbane. Looking out of the window, she could see dark clouds had formed overhead, adding to the darkness of the late afternoon, and without warning heavy rain began to lash down. Caitlin jumped as suddenly, without warning, a crack of thunder split the air followed by torrential rain.

'It's a thunderstorm,' Andrew said. 'It'll be over soon, but it might mean a delay getting back to the hospital.'

More than anything else Caitlin wanted to get away from Andrew. The last thing she wanted was a conversation about the pregnancy. Not yet.

'How long will it last, do you think?' she said, anxiously scanning the dark sky.

'I have no idea,' Andrew said shortly. 'At least Tanni will be back, and as soon as she relieves us we are going to find somewhere quiet so we can finish this conversation. In the meantime, why don't you go and find us some coffee?'

Glad to remove herself from his glowering eyes and formidable expression, Caitlin needed no second bidding. Outside the room she leant against the wall and took deep breaths. There was no doubt in her mind that Andrew intended to finish the discussion they had started. What on earth was going on in his mind? Was he shocked? Don't be stupid, woman, she told herself. Of course he was. Or angry? Probably both. But he had been an equal partner in this mess, she reminded herself. She would make him understand that this was *her* problem. She didn't expect him to play any part.

A flash of sheet lightning was followed closely by a crash of thunder that reverberated around the building. The lights flickered and then moments later went out, plunging Caitlin into darkness. She stood horrified. What if the plane couldn't land? While Magda and her babies were in no immediate danger, the best place for them was in the hospital. And the last thing she needed this evening was a third-degree grilling from Andrew about her pregnancy. But to her relief the power cut only lasted a few seconds, before the electricity supply sprang back into life. Caitlin stood still and watched the progress of the plane as its lights circled over the dusty landing strip.

The next half-hour was spent loading Magda and her babies onto the plane. Caitlin felt immensely thankful there was no opportunity for Andrew to get her on her own. While the pilot carried out last-minute checks, Caitlin took the opportunity to slip back outside and let the now cooling night air wash over her.

She hadn't heard Andrew approach, only becoming aware of him when his hand grasped her arm firmly. He pulled her round to face him, his dark eyes unfathomable in the dim light. She could feel his energy, his intensity surround her like a cloak. Her skin prickled with the tension of being so close to him. She would have given anything to lean into him and let him wash away her fears.

'It is mine, isn't it?' he asked.

She nodded.

She heard him take a deep breath and then he was reaching for her, pulling her into his arms. She could feel his lips on her hair, the softness of his breath in her ear. Too drained to fight him any longer, she leant her body into his, revelling in the feeling of being in his arms. She snuggled into his chest, breathing in the familiar scent of him. If she could have asked for anything right then it would be to stay there for the rest of her life.

'We'll get married,' he said. 'As soon as we can.'

She pulled away from him, feeling the cool wind of their separation. She looked up at him. His dear, puzzled face.

'That's very honourable of you,' she said stiffly, 'but I haven't decided what to do yet.'

He narrowed his eyes. 'What do you mean?' Then he cursed. 'You can't be thinking of getting rid of it? My God, Caitlin, does the thought of having a child, my child, revolt you so much?'

She shook her head at him. 'The timing—' she managed, before he interrupted her.

'You mean that the timing is all wrong? That it will interfere with your career plans? God, Cat.' He tried to pull her back into his arms but she resisted. 'There will be plenty of time for your career when the baby, our baby, is old enough.'

She tried a laugh, but it wasn't very successful. 'You've changed your mind. I thought you disapproved of women who combined motherhood with careers.'

He looked sheepish. Raising his hand, he drew a finger down the contours of her cheek, following the trail to the base of her neck. Caitlin shivered, feeling desire throughout her body. 'I was wrong, okay? I hadn't met you when I thought all that. Now I have…' he laughed, as if astonished '…I realise that being with the right woman, supporting her, is what matters. I couldn't help falling in love with you, and I guess I wouldn't have if you hadn't been you.' He laughed again. 'I'm making a mess of this, aren't I? I guess it's because I have never been in love before.'

In love? Caitlin's mind was reeling. He was in love with her? For a brief moment her heart soared. He loved her and wanted to marry her. She could be with him, grow old with him, share her life with a man who made her world come alive. But then she remembered. She might not have a future. And could she really believe him? What if he was just telling her he loved her to convince her to have his child? And if she told him the truth and she turned out to have cancer, what then? Would he pity her? Stay with her because of a sense of duty? Persuade her to terminate the pregnancy to save her own life and then spend the rest of their lives together, however long that was, resenting her? Even coming to hate her? She could never, ever allow that to happen. She loved him too much. But perhaps, she thought, hope springing, the results would be negative. If that was the case, then they could be together, if she could bring herself to believe he was telling the truth that he loved her. That he didn't want to marry her because of the baby.

He was looking at her expectantly, a small smile playing on his lips. Caitlin took a deep breath, knowing she was about to hurt him deeply.

'I haven't decided what to do about the pregnancy,' she said. 'There's a good chance I may not keep it.' As she said the words she knew it was as if she was stabbing him in the heart. The smile froze on his lips and he drew his brows together. He had never looked so handsome or so frightening to Caitlin before.

'You are a piece of work,' he said at last. 'I have never met a woman like you before.' He laughed bitterly. 'I know you told me your career is important, but I thought you had changed. God, woman, I thought you felt something for me. It just goes to show you how wrong a man could be. I was prepared to go against everything I'd been brought up to believe just to be with you.' He shook his head. 'What a fool.'

Caitlin reached out for him, wanting to tell him the truth. But she let her hand drop to her side. She still thought she might be right. If he couldn't have the baby, then he didn't want her.

'Then I've just prevented you from making the biggest mistake of your life,' she said gently, before turning on her heel and leaving him standing in the darkness.

Later, when Mrs Crouse and her baby had been taken to the ward and Dr Hargreaves relieved, Caitlin made her way tiredly to the on-call room. She had no idea where Andrew had disappeared to, she was simply relieved that they were no longer confined in the small aircraft together.

Wearily she decided against a shower and lay down on the single bed, still in her crumpled theatre greens. It had been a long and emotional night. Her thoughts jumbled around her head. It was all such a mess. If she had known that coming to Australia would throw her life into such turmoil, would she have come? But then she wouldn't have met and fallen in love with Andrew. And while that might have been easier in many, many ways, she would never have known what it was like to be in love. She would have continued through her life, shutting out the world, only half-alive. Whatever happened, she knew that something inside her had changed irrevocably. At the very least she knew she'd be turning down the chair of obstetrics. She would never again seek to hide from life behind papers and research. She would stay with clinical medicine. Her first love. And if she had breast cancer? Well, she would cope with that too. If Bri could get through it, so could she. *And the baby?* the thought whispered in her mind. *What about your baby? Can you really terminate it, even if it means saving your own life?* The thought brought tears to her eyes. How ironic. She had never wanted children and now here she was, possibly having to decide between her own life and that of her unborn child. It was an impossible decision.

She thumped the pillow, rolling over on her side. Please, let her sleep. Let her have a little peace. Just for a while. Perhaps by tomorrow she would know the worst. But she couldn't help the tears from falling when she thought about living the rest of her life without Andrew.

A soft knock on the door woke her from an uneasy sleep. It was still dark and a glance at her watch showed it was just after six in the morning. Caitlin assumed it was someone from the labour ward come to fetch her, but instead when she opened the door it was to find Andrew. He looked dishevelled and haunted. Without waiting for her to invite him in, he strode into the room.

'I've been walking for hours,' he said, keeping his back to her, 'thinking about everything, and it just doesn't make sense.' He turned around and Caitlin could see the lines of anguish around his mouth. 'I *know* you, Caitlin. I've come to know you almost as well as I know myself.' He raked his hand through his hair as he paced the tiny room. Suddenly he looked over at her and Caitlin felt the intensity of his eyes burn into her soul. 'I've watched you with your patients—how dedicated and emotionally involved you are with them, despite yourself. And I know you're not the type of person to have a termination just because a baby is inconvenient.' Caitlin's heart thumped painfully in her chest as she noticed a wave of despair flit across Andrew's face. 'Please, darling,' he whispered hoarsely. 'Tell me. Tell me what's wrong.'

Caitlin couldn't trust herself to speak as she threw herself into his arms. How could she have ever doubted his love? she wondered, feeling Andrew's powerful arms wrapping round her body and holding her tightly, as if he was afraid she would vanish into thin air.

She felt his lips against her hair. 'Please, Caitlin. Tell me what's really troubling you.' He cupped his hand round the back of her neck, letting out a wry laugh. 'I never believed those soppy love songs—but, my God, I'd move heaven and earth for you.'

Caitlin twisted her hands into his shirt. She wanted this moment to last for ever. But she was gaining strength from the love emanating from him, she realised. He had a right to know. And somehow they would face the difficult decisions together.

'I know now why I always told myself I didn't want children,' she mumbled into his chest. 'It was because I saw so much fear and longing with my own patients. It was easier to pretend that that wasn't for me, rather than imagine going through all that heartache. And I thought my career would be enough. But that was before I met you.' She pulled her head back, her eyes searching his. He had the right to know the truth. She took a deep breath. 'Andrew, I might have breast cancer too. That's why I wasn't sure if I could carry on with the pregnancy.' The thought of losing the life inside her welled up again, and Caitlin choked back the tears that were threatening to overwhelm her.

'I love you,' she added, feeling a weight lift from her shoulders. 'I love you more than life itself. I know that now. But this has to be my decision and despite what I said earlier, I don't know if I could go through with a termination.' Caitlin shuddered at the thought.

Before she knew it, Andrew was across the room and lifting the telephone. 'Who is doing the tests for you?' he asked tersely.

'Dr Sommerville,' Caitlin replied. 'But, Andrew, it's only 6.30! You can't get her up…'

'Can't I? Watch me!' His eyes held hers as he waited for the operator to pick up. 'You're not going through another second of this agony, waiting to hear whether you've got cancer or not.' He turned his attention back to the receiver. 'This is Dr Bedi—can you page Dr Sommerville straight away? Yes, yes, I know what time it is, but tell her it's an emergency.' Dropping the phone back in its cradle, Andrew pulled her back into his arms. 'If the test is positive, I'll respect your decision—no matter what it is. All I know is that I want you in my life. Strong and healthy. That's what matters.'

Caitlin attempted a smile. 'Whatever happens, I'm not going to take the post in Ireland. I'm going to live here with you and near Bri. She can help with the baby.' She smiled at the image.

'You'd do all that? For me? Risk your life? Not that there's a chance in hell I'm going to allow you. And give up your career?' He pulled her closer. 'I love you more than I thought it was possible to love a woman.'

'I don't mean give up my career entirely,' she said warningly. 'I have to work, but there's no reason, if you help, that I can't have both.' She snuggled into his arms. And if she had cancer, well, life sometimes dealt a blow. She would just have to take her chances. She knew that even short a life with Andrew was better than a long life without him.

'I suppose I can learn how to change a nappy,' he said. 'Better men than me have managed. Just don't expect me to make a very good job of it.'

Caitlin giggled, imagining his large hands struggling with the fiddly ties of a small nappy. Just then the phone rang. Andrew and Caitlin stared at one another, the air suddenly thick with tension. They both knew it was Dr Sommerville returning Andrew's page. The next few seconds would determine their future—and that of their baby.

Caitlin picked up the phone. She was right. It was Dr Sommerville.

'Oh, Dr O'Neill, I thought it was Dr Bedi who was

paging me. It sounded pretty urgent. Switchboard must have put me through to you by mistake.' Before Antonia could end the call, Caitlin interrupted.

'Please, don't go. He was phoning on my behalf. We were wondering whether you had my results. I know it's pretty early to be calling but…' She was aware of Andrew hovering directly behind her. She knew he was perfectly capable of wrestling the phone from her hand.

'Of course. I know you must be anxious. As it happens, I have your results right here. I did try to catch you at home earlier, but Brianna said you were out on a call.'

Suddenly Caitlin couldn't bear to know. If it was bad news, she didn't know if she could hold it together. But for once she had someone to share the burden with. She didn't have to be the strong one all the time. Not any more.

'Antonia,' she said softly, 'I'm going to pass you to Andrew. Could you tell him the results please?'

As she held out the phone to Andrew their eyes locked. As he took the receiver he tipped her face to him.

'I love you,' he said. 'Whatever happens, it's you I want. You will always be enough for me.' As she returned his steady gaze, she felt his strength flow through her. With him by her side, she could face any thing.

It was only when Andrew replaced the receiver that Caitlin realised she had been holding her breath.

Fear clenched her throat as she noticed tears glistening in Andrew's eyes. Her heart sank. She had cancer. Instinctively, her hand fluttered protectively over her stomach, until she realised Andrew was smiling.

'What…what did she say?' she whispered.

'The tests have come back negative. It's a benign cyst. You're all right. Thank God!'

And then there was no more need for words. Wrapping her arms around him, Caitlin knew she would never live in fear again. With Andrew by her side, and their baby to look forward to, life was going to be a real roller-coaster. And she couldn't wait for it to begin.

0909/03a

Coming next month

ITALIAN DOCTOR, DREAM PROPOSAL

by Margaret McDonagh

Gorgeous but shy Dr Ruth Baxter doesn't do relationships – until a seductive encounter with her handsome new boss, Dr Rico Linardi! An encounter that convinces Rico that he wants Ruth not only as his lover...but his wife!

WANTED: A FATHER FOR HER TWINS

by Emily Forbes

Dr Rosie Jefferson's priority is caring for her orphaned twin niece and nephew, not her appearance! But deliciously attractive Dr Nick Masters makes her feel beautiful again and this single mum finds herself wishing for the impossible...

BRIDE ON THE CHILDREN'S WARD

by Lucy Clark

Years ago, Dr David Montgomery and Eden Caplan shared a soul-searing kiss. Now, gorgeous doctor David realises that one kiss wasn't enough – he wants a lifetime, with Eden as his bride!

MARRIAGE REUNITED: BABY ON THE WAY

by Sharon Archer

The Campbells' marriage fell apart when doctor Liz's gorgeous firefighter husband Jack thought he couldn't give her the family she wanted. Now one miraculous night leaves Liz pregnant, and Jack's determined to be the perfect husband and father.

On sale 2nd October 2009

Available at WHSmith, Tesco, ASDA, Eason and all good bookshops.
For full Mills & Boon range including eBooks visit
www.millsandboon.co.uk

M9ZEN

2 FREE BOOKS
AND A SURPRISE GIFT

We would like to take this opportunity to thank you for reading this Mills & Boon® book by offering you the chance to take TWO more specially selected books from the Medical™ series absolutely FREE! We're also making this offer to introduce you to the benefits of the Mills & Boon® Book Club™—

- **FREE home delivery**
- **FREE gifts and competitions**
- **FREE monthly Newsletter**
- **Exclusive Mills & Boon Book Club offers**
- **Books available before they're in the shops**

Accepting these FREE books and gift places you under no obligation to buy, you may cancel at any time, even after receiving your free books. Simply complete your details below and return the entire page to the address below. You don't even need a stamp!

YES Please send me 2 free Medical books and a surprise gift. I understand that unless you hear from me, I will receive 5 superb new stories every month including two 2-in-1 books priced at £4.99 each and a single book priced at £3.19, postage and packing free. I am under no obligation to purchase any books and may cancel my subscription at any time. The free books and gift will be mine to keep in any case.

Ms/Mrs/Miss/Mr ______________ Initials ______________

____

Surname ______________________________________

Address _______________________________________

____

______________________________ Postcode ___________

Send this whole page to: Mills & Boon Book Club, Free Book Offer, FREEPOST NAT 10298, Richmond, TW9 1BR

Offer valid in UK only and is not available to current Mills & Boon Book Club subscribers to this series. Overseas and Eire please write for details.. We reserve the right to refuse an application and applicants must be aged 18 years or over. Only one application per household. Terms and prices subject to change without notice. Offer expires 30th November 2009. As a result of this application, you may receive offers from Harlequin Mills & Boon and other carefully selected companies. If you would prefer not to share in this opportunity please write to The Data Manager, PO Box 676, Richmond, TW9 1WU.